I0564561

Battle For Earth

Battlefleet Series: Book 4

Theo Mann

Invisible Publishing Company

Contents

Chapter 1

A bone-breaking explosion hurled Captain Ellis "Sailor" English out of his seat.

He flew across the bridge and smashed into the opposite wall before the *Lightning Rod* righted herself.

Explosions blasted from one of the bridge stations and hurled Master Chief Julia Avila backward.

Avila slammed into the XO's station and hit the floor, but English didn't have time to check him. English staggered to his feet and fought against the G force to fight his way to the XO's station.

"How bad is the damage?!" he bellowed to his son, Captain Andrew Carter English, who manned the station as the *Lightning Rod's* acting XO.

"They clipped us!" Andy yelled back. "The *Lone Ranger* and the *Aileron* are down along with three rebel destroyers! The rebel fleet is......"

Another boom cut him off and nearly hurled English off his feet again. He held onto the console and dragged himself around the station to Andy's side.

Even then, it took English a few minutes before he could read enough of the controls to understand the state of battle outside.

The alien ships that appeared in Earth's atmosphere had spread out even farther than they had been when English first spotted them. They'd taken up positions all around the planet.

United Space Force destroyers from both the rebel and loyalist side lay smoking on the ground. The rest realized the danger and launched a counterassault against the invaders, but nothing in the Force could stand up to the alien's firepower.

The aliens smacked down destroyers with each well-aimed shot. The destroyers that had just been fighting amongst themselves couldn't coordinate with each other or even communicate with each other. They couldn't mount an effective defense or even avoid the aliens' assault.

The rebel destroyers that had just been about to finish off the *Lightning Rod* did the same thing. Four alien warships that first attacked the *Lone Ranger* and the *Aileron* hung in midair over Point Hope, Alaska. The others moved off, but those four stayed where they were.

Six rebel destroyers remained of the original twelve. They bombarded the aliens and flew around the warships in combined flight patterns trying in every way to distract and disorient the aliens.

Nothing worked. The warships stayed firmly planted in position and spat one precise blow after another at the destroyers. The aliens took down two more.

English didn't see anything else before another explosion sent the *Lightning Rod* cartwheeling out of the way. He couldn't even see what caused these explosions.

The ship turned a complete somersault and threw English, Andy, and Lieutenant Brock Eismann off their feet. The three men tumbled in all directions, hit the ceiling, and then slammed down hard on the floor.

English hauled himself to his feet. Andy and Eismann weren't moving. English didn't have time to check on them, either.

He dragged himself to the XO's station and grabbed the helm. The *Lightning Rod* still had enough engine power to stay in the air, but barely.

He struggled to hold the ship steady. He couldn't let the ship crash, but he couldn't see any way to avoid the aliens' shots.

His only hope was to get the ship on the ground without crashing. The engines kept belching and coughing. They alternately shut down, flared to life, and stuttered in all directions.

He descended a little lower and then a stray shot from one of the alien vessels smashed into the ground right below him.

The blast hurled chunks of soil and vegetation into the air that pummeled the *Lightning Rod's* underside.

The shockwave smacked the ship upward straight into the aliens' path and one of the warships delivered the killing blow to the *Lightning Rod's* aft section.

The ship rolled backward, toppled over her tail, and then an almighty crash threw English off his feet again.

He hit the floor with a punishing slam. He felt through his chest and stomach that the ship wasn't moving anymore.

She was on the ground and the engine noise had died, but he still felt endless concussions and explosions going off all over the place.

He pried himself up, but before he could even get onto his hands and knees, another explosion detonated the port side of the bridge near the captain's ready room. He had to get out of here before the whole ship went up in flames.

He crawled over to Andy and English rolled his son over. Andy jolted back to consciousness the minute he got onto his back. "Huh!" he yelled and flailed around trying to orient himself.

"The ship crashed, son!" English yelled to him. "We gotta get off the bridge and get everyone out if we can! Can you stand up!"

Andy jerked the other way and looked around. English couldn't waste any more time on him.

English scrambled over to Avila and then to Eismann. Avila was already dead. Eismann was out cold.

English looked around. He would have to go all the way through the ship to get to the cargo hold to get off the *Lightning Rod*. He didn't even know how much of the ship was still intact.

Just then, another explosion went off near where the ready room had been. This one blasted into the bridge and a flaming ball of fire consumed that side of the bridge.

English couldn't wait around anymore. He grabbed Eismann by the wrist, hauled the man into a sitting position, and English used all his remaining strength to hoist Eismann onto his shoulder.

"Come on, son!" English grabbed Andy's arm and pulled him up.

English guided Andy off the bridge, but Andy could walk perfectly well. He veered from side to side a few times, but he straightened up and his vision cleared the longer he remained upright.

They got as far as the outer corridor before another boom took out the whole righthand bulkhead. The impact threw all three men into a side compartment and then the ship rolled in that direction.

The blast crushed the compartment walls all around English, but the ship kept pitching from one side to the other so he couldn't even stand, much less find a way out of here.

Without warning, a catastrophic blast struck the *Lightning Rod* from somewhere. The ship twirled into the air and came down even harder with a devastating crunch.

English floundered to sit up and realized that most of the other side of the compartment had been torn off. Ten feet of the compartment's interior remained attached to what was left of the ship.

The rest of the compartment yawned open to the chilling weather outside. English looked out over the empty tundra and hundreds upon hundreds of miles of nothing.

Someone touched his back. "Dad...." Andy croaked. "Are you all right?"

English pulled himself together with an effort. "I'm okay." English looked up. "Are you?"

Andy nodded and glanced toward the back of the compartment. Fire consumed the other side of the corridor. "We gotta get out of here before the whole ship goes up."

English nodded and forced himself to his feet. He went over to Eismann and knelt down next to the man. English didn't expect to find Eismann alive, but he was and he had his eyes open.

He blinked through the breach at the bleak scenery outside.

"Lieutenant...." English began.

Eismann didn't react. English waved his hand in front of Eismann's eyes. "Lieutenant! Look at me!"

Eismann frowned at the landscape, but he still didn't respond. English grabbed Eismann by the jaw and forced him to turn around and look at his captain.

As soon as they made eye contact, Eismann's expression started to clear. "Captain? Captain English?"

"Come on, Brock," English choked. "We gotta get off the ship."

English helped him up. Eismann did everything slowly and held his arms out at his sides like he might fall over.

The three men stepped outside and English saw more *Lightning Rod* crewmen stumbling around in ones and twos. A few had gathered into groups.

English helped Eismann over to a group that was gathering around Lieutenant Charlie Frasier. Dr. Eva Cassidy went through the assembled crewmen treating people's injuries.

English did a quick head count and spotted Lieutenant Hammil from Engineering in the crowd. At least English had someone here who knew how to work on the ship—if she wasn't already beyond repair.

He glanced at the ship and immediately regretted it. The center section between the tail and the main fuselage had been squashed and blackened by the fire and explosions.

English would be very surprised to find out that the ship's plasma core was still intact. If it wasn't, he could forget about propulsion—or life support.

English handed Eismann off to Dr. Cassidy and made another assessment of who in this crowd he could possibly count on to help him salvage this disaster. He turned to Andy and then to Frasier.

"Who do we have left?" English asked. "None of the wing pilots made it."

"They were still in the air when it happened, Sir," Frasier replied. "None of them went down with the ship. They're smart kids. They would have hit the high road when the shooting started."

"I didn't see the aliens targeting fighter craft anyway," Andy added. "They're too small."

English looked up at the sky, but the aliens weren't here anymore. Andy must be right. The aliens no longer considered the *Lightning Rod* a threat.

English waved at the two men. "Let's take a walk and assess how bad the damage is. We're gonna need some shelter tonight and the ship is all we have. We'll need to put out any fires and use what's left of the ship to house these people."

Andy and Frasier only nodded. English headed aft and circled the ship's tail.

The aft hull had been crumpled by gunfire, but the hatch was still closed. Enough of the tail remained that the survivors could shelter in the cargo hold if they had to—or even on the flight deck.

English cast a flinty gaze across the tundra. The *Lightning Rod* had gone down far away from any human habitation. A stretch of rocky beach separated the ship from the choppy, frigid Bering Sea.

A few swells in the landscape gave him enough of a view of the surroundings to see that the *Lightning Rod* and her few remaining crewmen were the only people for miles around.

He circled to the other side of the ship. He wasn't expecting to find much left. This was the side of the ship where most of the explosions came from.

Sure enough, most of the hull on that side had been blasted out and charred to a crisp. He could look straight through multiple breaches to torched bodies, components, and sections inside.

He walked around what was left of the port side, but he stopped when he saw a bunch of people in USF dress uniforms climbing through one of the breaches.

General Caleb Halstead helped Admiral Everette Chambers, Admiral Grace Schroder, Colonel Landon Roderick, Colonel Mackenzie Levitt, and Captain Nathan Thorburn crawl through a piece of torn bulkhead.

English's hackles rose when they dusted themselves off and straightened up in front of him. Their expressions went through a few different changes from defiance to terror when they saw the look on his face.

Halstead glanced up and his expression changed, too, but he didn't stop helping these people get out of the ship.

They'd all been locked up in the brig before the battle started. The damage to the ship must have torn the brig open. Now all these prisoners were free.

Halstead bent his head back to what he was doing. He pulled Admiral Christopher Simpson and Major General Charles McClure out last. McClure's face was still swollen and purple from Andy punching McClure.

Simpson went through a matching turmoil of reactions and emotions that he was confronting English again. McClure did his best to grin, but the swelling in his face only made the grin look ghastly and disgusting.

A dangerous silence fell over the group once Halstead finished getting everyone out—everyone there was to get out. A few of these people shifted their weight and averted their eyes so they wouldn't have to look at English. Them being his superior officers didn't mean squat right now.

McClure actually had the nerve to chuckle in English's face. "Well, Sailor? We're out of the brig, so what are you going to do about it? You can't keep us locked up."

"Don't listen to him, Sailor," Colonel Levitt cut in from the back. "None of us had anything to do with kidnapping your daughter."

"We would tell you where she is if we knew," Halstead added. "Don't do anything to us...I mean....You know what I mean. We're stranded here along with you. We won't cause you or your crew any trouble. I swear it."

English's eyes danced from one face to the next. His hatred for these people didn't abate at all and he put no faith in their promises.

He wasn't about to cut them any deals or go easy on them, but Halstead was right. These people were as defenseless and stranded as the rest of the *Lightning Rod* crew.

That was the real bitch of the situation. He'd taken responsibility for his prisoners' safety when he locked them in the brig. Now he was responsible for getting them out of this so they could go back to the USF and stand trial for treason.

His gaze flicked back to McClure. Simpson stared at the ground and refused to look at English at all.

McClure kept grinning like a crazed lunatic. He focused all his attention on English. McClure didn't even seem to realize where he was, how he'd gotten here, or what it all meant.

"What are you going to do, Sailor?" he sneered again. "Are you gonna lock us up again? That won't bring back your daughter."

Andy surged forward, but English stopped him and pushed Andy behind him. English didn't have to wonder what Andy would do to Simpson and McClure if Andy got his hands on them.

English would have liked to do the same thing, but he still had to look himself in the eye tomorrow morning.

He held McClure's gaze while English snapped over his shoulder, "Charlie, go back to the group, round up as many security guards as you can, and go inside the ship to see if you can find any other survivors. Take Lieutenant Hammil with you and see if the plasma core is still functioning."

Frasier said, "Yes, Sir," and walked away. English waited for Frasier to come back with his party. They crawled through the breach the officers had just used to escape.

English waited for the noise to die down before he confronted the rebel officers—the traitors.

English waved at the surrounding countryside. "All right. You're free. Go on. You're free to go. I won't stop you."

English propped his hands on his hips to show that he wouldn't stop McClure from leaving if he really wanted to.

McClure glanced out at the tundra and his maniacal grin evaporated when he realized what English meant.

"Don't throw us out, Sailor," Colonel Levitt pleaded again. "We'll cooperate with everything you want us to do. We'll consider ourselves your prisoners even though we're out of the brig.....just don't throw us out. Don't make us go out there. We'll all die out there. You know we will."

"Are you people happy now?" English spat. "Do you realize now what the hell you did to the Force?"

"What.....what do you mean?" Halstead stammered.

English opened his mouth to tear them a new one....and then he stopped. They didn't know. They'd been in the brig when the aliens showed up.

He heaved a sigh and turned aside to regain his composure. "Aliens invaded. There's an overwhelming alien force surrounding Earth right now and steamrolling its way through the USF as we speak. That's who shot us down. It wasn't rebel destroyers. We were in the middle of the battle against the rebels and the aliens came in and squashed us all. That's how we wound up here."

He waited for that to sink in. It took a while. Some of the officers frowned. Some opened their mouths to argue back and then changed their minds.

One by one, their eyes widened and they gaped at him in horror. "Www.....What are we gonna do?" Levitt stammered.

"There's nothing we can do because we don't have a ship," English snapped. "All the other loyalist destroyers that were in the area got shot down, too. Do you get it now? While you geniuses were mounting your great and glorious rebellion to reform the USF, you left us defenseless against an alien invasion and now we have no way to stop these invaders from conquering Earth. I hope you're satisfied. This is what I've been trying to tell you from the beginning, but you wouldn't listen."

"Well.....what do you want us to do about it now?" Halstead asked. "There's nothing we *can* do about it from here."

English looked away. He already knew that.

He hated to give these people a pass, but he had bigger fish to fry right now. He strode away from them, but that only brought him face to face with the wrecked *Lightning Rod*. She'd been in the air for less than three hours. Now she was down again, possibly for good.

He finally forced himself to face the rebel traitors. He had to take a deep breath to summon the courage to say what he knew he had to say.

"This is what I've been telling you all along. We have to work together. We can't have any divisions or conflicts or fighting amongst ourselves. We need to drop this whole rebellion right now and join forces to fight this new enemy. That's the only way any of us are going to survive. This rebellion of yours is over. If you can't put that aside and help me fight the aliens, then you really do belong out there and may God have mercy on your souls. That's all I have to say to you."

Chapter 2

Andy followed English back to the other side of the ship where Dr. Cassidy was treating more wounded.

English gritted his teeth on the way back there. He couldn't stand the sight of the rebel officers. Just being in their presence took all his patience. He didn't trust himself to even stand on the same side of the ship with them, much less look at them.

"You were too nice to them, Dad," Andy murmured under his breath as soon as they got out of earshot.

"What choice do I have?" English muttered back. "I would be no better than they are if I just killed them outright when they're defenseless and stranded just like we are. Anyway, maybe now they'll pull their heads out of their asses and actually get on board with running the Force the way it should be run."

He turned back to what was left of the crew when Frasier showed up with a few more people. Half of them were wounded, but there were still only forty people here counting the rebel officers.

"What's the situation with the engines?" English asked Lieutenant Hammil.

"The core is still intact. Everything else is completely shot to hell."

"Can you get her in the air again?" English asked. "I'm not asking if she could fight anyone or even fly anywhere very fast or even clean up her hull. I'm just asking if you could get her off the ground to take us somewhere we could get some help."

Hammil shrugged. "It would take a while and I don't even know if I can."

"You have nothing else to do," Andy pointed out.

Hammil only shrugged again. "True."

"How safe is it in there?" English asked. "Is the ship in any danger of experiencing any more explosions or any other safety hazards?"

"Not that I could tell, Sir," Hammil replied.

English turned back to Dr. Cassidy. "You can take your wounded back to Sick Bay...or wherever you *can* take them. Get them out of the weather and under cover. Do what you can for them and then come back and report to me."

She started gathering up her patients and steering them toward one of the larger breaches on this side of the ship.

English turned to Charlie Frasier, but before English could say anything, the rebel officers came over—or rather, Halstead, Levitt, Thorburn, Roderick, Schroder, and Chambers came over.

Simpson and McClure lingered in the rear at a distance from the other. Simpson still wore the same hangdog expression like English was supposed to believe Simpson regretted his actions or some bullshit like that.

Halstead pulled himself up in front of English. "Sailor....I mean Captain.....we'd like to dedicate our service to helping you defeat the aliens....if you'll have us. We understand if you don't want to.....and we understand if you feel the need to keep us confined.....but we.....we realize you're right. We all need to pull together to defeat this threat. Whatever beef we had with the Force will have to wait until we repel the invasion."

"Whatever beef you had with the Force will *not* wait until we repel the invasion, General," English fired back. "Whatever beef you had with the Force is dead and buried as far as I'm concerned. We're all facing extermination from an alien foe thanks to whatever beef you had with the Force. Either you lay it to rest and put it completely out of your minds—and I mean forever—or you aren't in the same Force with me. If you don't see that this beef is the reason we're in this peril, then you're a bigger problem to the rest of us than the invasion itself. Now, I'm busy. If that's the best you can do, it isn't good enough, so go back over there and talk amongst yourselves until you see reason."

He was just beginning to turn his back on them when Colonel Roderick stepped forward. He was a big, sturdy man of forty with all his faculties and military expertise still in hand.

"We agree with you, Sailor," he announced in his deep, chesty voice. "That's what we're saying. That's why we're all willing to put ourselves under your command. Whatever you think is the best way to tackle this invasion, we'll go along with you. You won't have any reason to question our motives or our loyalty. You have our word on that."

English turned around extra slowly and raised his eyebrows. "You .....you're putting yourselves under my command.....all of you?"

His gaze traveled from person to person. Everyone here outranked him. Some outranked him by miles.

They all nodded—at least, Chambers, Schroder, Roderick, Levitt, Thorburn, and Halstead did. Simpson and McClure stayed in the back and didn't get involved in the conversation.

In that moment, English realized the true magnitude of what Roderick was saying. If these people really did put themselves under his command—under the command of someone so far below them in rank—then they must truly regret their mistake. They were serious about changing their ways and making up for it.

He didn't want to soften toward them, but he had to. He had to let them at least try. He needed people too much to turn them away.

He puffed out his cheeks and waved toward the ship. "Fine. You can go on board. Sergeant Grimes will find quarters for you to stay in."

"Thank you, Sailor!" Halstead quavered. "Thank you so much! We won't let you down. I swear it!"

He only muttered, "We'll see about that," over his shoulder.

Grimes stepped forward to lead the officers back on board, but English stopped him. "Put them somewhere away from the rest of the crew—somewhere they won't be able to interact with any of our people."

"Should I post a guard to keep an eye on them?" Grimes glared at the rebel officers. "I don't like letting them wander freely about the ship."

"I don't like it, either," English replied, "but we don't have the manpower to guard them twenty-four-seven. If they're serious about helping us, then we won't need to guard them."

Grimes glared at them. "What about *those* two?"

English couldn't even look at Simpson and McClure. "I'll deal with them. Just take the others inside and do your best to keep them away from those two. Keep them away from everybody."

Grimes left and took the officers inside. Hardly anyone remained standing outside the ship.

English couldn't decide if he wanted to go inside or not. Anything would be better than standing out here in this freezing wind, but he didn't want to take his eyes off the landscape. He didn't want to take the chance that he might not see another enemy coming up on him unawares.

He realized how ridiculous that sounded. No one could come up on him unawares out here. He would be able to see them coming from miles away. Not a single tree interrupted the barren landscape.

He wouldn't be able to see them coming from miles away if he was inside the ship. That was the problem. He would only be able to see them coming if he stayed standing out here.

Someone had to stand guard. It shouldn't be the captain, but he didn't feel right about leaving or assigning the job to anyone else.

He would have kept scanning the horizon for the rest of eternity. Then he noticed Andy glaring at Simpson and McClure.

English wanted to deal with them least of all, but he had to. He couldn't keep letting them stand there spoiling the scenery.

He forced himself to turn around, and since the sight of McClure made him sick, English chose to approach Simpson first.

"Look at me, Chris," English snapped. He would never give these jackasses any military courtesy again as long as he lived.

Simpson raised his eyes. The pathetic, hopeless misery in those eyes got even worse when he faced English.

"Make your move, Chris," English told him. "Stay or go. I don't care. Just do whatever you're gonna do and stop dragging the rest of us down with you."

Simpson opened his mouth and choked on the words. "You won't let me stay."

"Give me one reason why I should," English snapped. "You don't really expect me to believe you would turn over a new leaf and join forces with us to defeat these aliens, do you?"

Simpson floundered for a while before he summoned the nerve to speak again. "You wouldn't let me! You would never believe I want to."

"*Do* you want to?" English demanded. "Do you even *want* to put this rebellion behind us so we can all be one Force again?"

"Of course!" Simpson rasped. "Of course I do!"

English had to compress his lips and fight himself under control before he dared to speak again. "If you really expect me to believe that you want to change, then tell me where my daughter is."

"I don't know!" Simpson exclaimed and then shut his mouth in a hurry when he shot a terrified glance at McClure. Then Simpson bowed his head and looked the other way. "I don't know where she is. I would tell you if I did."

English followed that glance and found McClure grinning at him again. No way in hell would McClure ever change. He would never put the rebellion behind him.

Now English understood that the rebellion had never been about reforming the USF—not for McClure.

Maybe it just gave him a vehicle to wreak as much mayhem as he wanted to. Maybe it was a way for him to finally let his destructive tendencies have some fun in the wartime playground.

English didn't know why McClure participated in the rebellion. English really didn't give a shit about that anymore.

He barely glanced at Simpson. "You can go inside, Chris."

Simpson made himself scarce and left the field clear for English to finally confront McClure. English could feel the murderous rage pulsating off Andy behind him. English didn't blame him.

English's hatred for McClure turned to ice-cold clarity when English stepped over to the man. English lowered his voice to a barely audible snarl.

"You have a choice, Charles. You can start walking with my best wishes for your success or you can tell me where my daughter is. If you don't tell me truthfully right now, you'll never set foot on board the *Lightning Rod* or any other USF ship ever again. If I find out later that you lied to me, I'll turn you over to Andy here and I'll make sure no one ever finds out what happened to you. Do I make myself clear? Whatever the next words are that come out of your mouth, make sure they're truthful. Otherwise, I'll make sure you never get off this beach."

McClure's eyes darted behind English. English didn't have to wonder what McClure saw back there.

McClure forced another maniacal smirk. English really would have liked to pound the guy's face to a bloody pulp. When the time came, English was going to savor the sight of Andy doing it.

"Oh, have it your way, Sailor," McClure finally lilted. "She's at the Oaxaca Repair Yard....in an underground bunker under the control tower. She's been there ever since she left Vancouver. We tracked her movements after she escaped from Antwerp and we decided to put her on ice so we could show her to you if we ever wanted to rein you in."

English made a snap decision not to argue with McClure any further, threaten him, or even talk to him again. Whatever else came out of McClure's mouth would either be a taunt, a lie, or just some stupid gibberish English didn't have time for.

He walked back over to Andy, who stood seething with barely suppressed fury. He never took his narrowed eyes off McClure.

English would have to keep an eye on Andy, too, which could turn out to be a nightmare considering that Andy was supposed to be English's XO right now.

Fortunately, Grimes and Frasier both came back outside just then. "The officers are all in their quarters, Sir," Grimes reported. "They're all extremely grateful."

He sneered these last words with such contempt that English almost smiled—almost.

"Take General McClure inside, find any cabin anywhere on the ship that you can still lock from the outside, and confine him there."

"But you said…." McClure interrupted.

English rounded on him and gave him a vicious glare. That shut McClure's mouth right away.

"I don't care if you have to put him in my cabin," English finished. "Make sure he's locked down and can't get out." English allowed himself to turn back to McClure. "If I see you outside your cabin even once, Charles, I'll kill you myself. You stay confined to your cabin and stay out of my sight if you want to live." English nodded at Grimes. "Get him out of here."

Grimes grabbed McClure hard by the arm and marched him on board the *Lightning Rod*.

English didn't even care that Grimes was treating McClure much more roughly than any prisoner should have been treated.

English half-hoped Grimes would rough the bastard up on their way to wherever Grimes was going to lock up McClure.

"You should have let me have him, Dad," Andy growled as soon as they went inside.

"I really wish I could, son," English muttered. "I'd like to take him apart one body part at a time, but we have a planet to defend here and no ship to defend it with." English turned to Frasier. "What's the situation inside?"

"Hammil is working on the engines. That's about all I can tell you. Dr. Cassidy has a Sick Bay full of patients. That's about the size of it, Sir."

English snorted. "So we're stuck here while an alien invasion force is marauding the planet."

"Yes, Sir," Frasier replied. "We don't have any fighter craft, any pilots, or any way to get off this beach. We're lucky we even have power."

Chapter 3

C aptain Matt Radcliffe opened his eyes and blinked up at the sky. It wasn't a clear sky. A few clouds scuttered across it, but it was still beautiful.

Then he felt the wind. It bit through his clothes and chilled him. He sat up.....and that's when he realized where he was. He was still wearing his uniform.

The memory came rushing back. He'd been on the bridge of the *Infinity* engaged in a massive air battle against rebel destroyers. He'd spotted the alien invaders practically materialize directly on top of him. They fired on the *Infinity*....and then he woke up here.

He frowned at the surroundings. He sat on a rocky beach dotted with driftwood. The freezing wind kicked up white caps out on a restless sea.

A vast wasteland of flat, barren tundra stretched away in the other direction. He didn't see a thing out there.

He had been fighting those rebel destroyers in the skies over Point Hope, Alaska. Something must have happened when the aliens attacked his ship. He must have gotten thrown out and he landed here.

Now he was all alone and hundreds of miles from anything.

He dragged himself to his feet, but everywhere he looked, he came to the same conclusion.

He was alone in the middle of nowhere in an inhospitable environment with nothing but the shirt on his back.

He forced himself to think and decided to get a better view of the landscape.

Then, if he still didn't see anywhere to take shelter, he would have to build something out of all this driftwood. He couldn't spend even one night out in this cold wind.

He set off down the beach, but he still didn't see anything or anyone. No trace remained of the *Infinity*—no wreckage, no debris, no bodies—nothing. Did she survive the attack? Was he the only one left alive of the whole crew?

He discovered after walking a hundred yards that the landscape wasn't perfectly flat. Rises and hollows dotted the tundra.

He climbed up one of the rises to get a better look around. His heart leapt when he saw a bunch of people walking down the beach.

They were walking away from him heading north, which was the same direction he'd been walking just now. He couldn't recognize them from this distance, so he took off at a brisk walk to catch up with them.

He was really hoping they'd be locals. They would be able to take him somewhere he could contact the USF and find his way back to some military installation.

He got a big surprise when he got near enough to recognize them. They saw him coming, turned around, and their eyes and mouths fell open when they recognized him, too.

"Commander....." Racer exclaimed. "I mean...Captain....."

Radcliffe had to smile at them. "I'm glad I found you." He checked each face.

Besides Racer, Gunnery Sergeant Sam Hughes, Airman Rich Hoskins, Ben Ritchie, Henry Janacek, August Stoval, and both Duran brothers were also here.

There were also four other people from the *Lightning Rod* crew. None of them had been pilots before, but Ash Walker from maintenance, Rosa Smythe from the enlisted mess kitchens, Vinnie Waterman from the flight mechanical crew, and the medic Bobby Laughlin were all here.

Racer frowned at Radcliffe. "Are you all by yourself, Sir? Where's the *Infinity?*"

"I don't know, Airman....I mean, Gunny."

She burst into a huge grin at his mistake.

"The ship got hit and then I woke up down the beach over there," he told her. "I must have gotten thrown out. What about you? How did you get here?" He glanced around. "Do any of you have your birds?"

"We wouldn't be here if we did," Walker replied. "We all got shot down."

"Not shot down, exactly," Ritchie explained. "The aliens did something to our engines and shut us down. Our birds are all over there, but they're grounded. We can't power up."

"Really?" Radcliffe rubbed his chin. "That's weird."

"We were just going over there, Sir." Racer pointed to the north. "The *Lightning Rod* went down over there. We were gonna go over there and see if anyone is still alive."

Radcliffe brightened up. "She did? Oh. Good idea. I'll go with you."

She smiled at him again and they all turned to head up the beach. The pilots talked on the way there.

"Did you see the way those aliens flattened the rebel destroyers?" Ritchie began. "Man, we should have had weapons like that on the loyalist force."

"We wouldn't have the *Buckingham Palace* and all the new fleet ships with us now if we did," Sean Duran pointed out.

"We need those ships for after the rebellion is over anyway," Ezra added. "Once this war ends, we're gonna need all the ships we can get."

"I think the war *is* over, Gunny," Walker cut in. "The war against the rebels is, anyway. Everyone is gonna have to knuckle down, put their differences aside, and start fighting a brand new war against the aliens now."

"You're dead right, Airman," Radcliffe replied. "I just hope we still have enough ships and firepower left to defend Earth."

"What are we gonna do if we *don't* have the ships and firepower to defend Earth?" Racer asked.

"Then the aliens win and they get to decide what happens to us—which is why we aren't going to let that happen."

"How are we gonna stop them when we can't even get off this beach?" Waterman pointed out. "No one knows where we are, and even if they did, they'd be too busy fighting the aliens to come and get us. It looks an awful lot to me like *our* war is over either way."

"You might be right," Radcliffe told him. "We can only keep doing what's right in front of us."

"Did you see where any of the other destroyers went down, Sir?" Janacek asked. "We might be able to connect up with all kinds of people out here."

"I told you, Airman. I didn't see a thing," Radcliffe replied. "I was on the bridge fighting the rebels one minute. The next thing I knew, I was opening my eyes on the beach over there. I have no idea how I even got there."

Racer turned white. "So....the *Infinity* is just...gone?"

"I don't know, Gunny," Radcliffe repeated. "She could be just fine and flying around out there somewhere."

"Without a captain," Laughlin finished.

Radcliffe had to smile again, but he didn't say anything. He'd been captain of the *Infinity* for only a few days and today was the very first time he'd ever flown her.

The group passed around another swell and Racer's hand shot out. "Look! There's the *Lightning Rod!*"

The group charged forward. Radcliffe picked up the pace when he spotted Captain English, his son Andy, and Charlie Frasier standing outside the smashed, blackened hull.

"Captain!!" Racer and the other pilots jumped up and down, waved their arms, and then took off running for the ship. "Captain English!!"

English turned around, and at that moment, a deafening smash sent a shockwave across the landscape. Two ships materialized over the *Lightning Rod*.

They seemed to appear out of nowhere, but a slight blur around their hulls at the last possible second indicated that they'd just traveled here at impossible speed.

One was an alien warship with all those strange spikes and weapons sticking out of its outer hull. The other ship was a USF destroyer and the warship plastered the destroyer with one brutal smash after another.

Radcliffe couldn't see from here which destroyer it was. It didn't matter anymore because USF destroyers didn't stand a chance against these aliens.

USF destroyers couldn't travel that fast, either. The alien warship must have transported the destroyer here along with itself.

They both appeared directly above the *Lightning Rod*, but as soon as they got into that position, the warship pounded the destroyer backward across the landscape.

The alien warship spat some kind of strange glowing white energy weapon. It didn't crack or fork like lightning. It flowed and streamed like plasma, but it wasn't plasma. It looked more like liquid light pouring from all the warship's weapons.

One ear-splitting boom after another ricocheted to the horizon and beyond as the weapon pulverized the destroyer. The energy didn't look strong enough to do that kind of damage, but it did.

The warship delivered one crushing strike after another. Each blast slapped the destroyer backward and the ship reeled under every blow.

The ship skidded backward and struggled to correct and stand her ground before another vicious strike knocked her even farther backward.

Radcliffe stood rooted to the spot. Every nerve commanded him to go out there and do something to protect the destroyer from this enemy.

He couldn't do that, though. He was stuck on the ground without any weapons besides his bare hands.

Brock Eismann and a few other people came out of the *Lightning Rod's* crumpled hull to watch. All eyes turned eastward as the warship drove the destroyer away from the beach.

The destroyer fired at the alien ship, but the destroyer's plasma shots just bounced off the warship and did no damage. Nothing penetrated the warship's tough exterior.

The destroyer stayed in the air all the way to the eastern horizon. English, Radcliffe, Andy, Racer, and the other pilots stepped forward as the battle got farther away. Radcliffe wanted to see the end even if it went the way he suspected it would go.

The warship hammered the destroyer over a few more low hills and then delivered a brutal takedown by firing straight into the ship's nose.

The bridge exploded and then the warship unleashed an even more sadistic bombardment that tore the ship apart.

Radcliffe picked up his pace. He wanted to be there when the ship went down. He wanted to help anyone who made it out alive.

The ship tilted to one side and he burst into a run. He had to cover the landscape as quickly as possible so he would get there in time to save anyone he could.

More explosions went off all over the ship. Radcliffe became aware of people running on both sides of him. He wasn't alone.

He sprinted into a hollow and raced up the other side. He made it to the top just as the destroyer detonated in midair and plummeted tail downward into the ground. The whole vessel erupted in a blistering fireball. No one could survive that.

He stared at it and then realized in another moment of world-changing clarity that the destroyer had crashed right next to the *Buckingham Palace*. The *Buckingham Palace* sat crumpled and partially torched only a few miles from where the other vessel went down.

Radcliffe spotted people huddled behind the *Buckingham Palace*. They hid behind the wrecked fuselage for protection from the crash, from the fire, and from the aliens.

The aliens didn't pay any attention to anyone on the ground. The warship hovered in the same place for a second and then zipped away as quickly and as suddenly as it appeared.

Chapter 4

Racer, her fellow pilots, and a bunch of people from the *Lightning Rod* charged over to the *Buckingham Palace,* but Commander Radcliffe got there first.

Racer had to remind herself that he was a captain now. He was Captain Radcliffe even if he didn't have a ship.

He sprinted around the *Buckingham Palace* and everyone stopped in front of what was left of the *Buckingham Palace* crew.

Her new captain, Ted Church, crouched behind the hull with Sergeant Morrison, Lieutenant Rickenbach, Corporal Towne, the younger Dr. Cassidy, and Corporal Norris. They were all alone.

"Ted!" English blurted out. "Are you all right? Where's the rest of your crew? Did they survive the battle?"

Church stood up slowly, but he barely glanced at English or the others standing around. Church's eyes wandered out toward the horizon.

He waved the *Buckingham Palace* and covered his face with his hand to hide his mouth wrenching the wrong way. "The core overloaded and breached when we crashed. If anyone is still in there, they're dead by now. We're the only ones who made it out. I tried...." His voice choked and he broke off.

English laid a hand on Church's shoulder and squeezed. "All right, Ted. It's over now. Come back to the *Lightning Rod* with us—all of you."

He had to pull Church away from the ship. Church cast backward glances toward the *Buckingham Palace*.

He kept trying to turn around so he could go back there, but if the core breached, it would have contaminated the whole ship with toxic plasma. The *Buckingham Palace* would never fly again.

The group finally got far enough away that he stopped looking. The fallen destroyer kept poofing in flames not far away, but none of the group looked at it again. The group wouldn't be able to save anyone from that.

Racer fell in behind the four captains: Church, Radcliffe, and both captains English. English and Radcliffe talked on their way back to the *Lightning Rod*. Radcliffe related how he'd woken up on the beach after the battle.

"The *Lightning Rod* still has power and my engineer is trying to carry out repairs," English told him. "If it works, we might be able to limp to the nearest base or else contact someone about where we are."

"How did you survive the alien assault?" Radcliffe asked. "They knocked down the *Aileron* and the *Lone Ranger* in one hit each."

English cocked his head. "You remember that? You said you didn't remember anything after the *Infinity* getting hit. The *Aileron* and the *Lone Ranger* went down after the *Infinity* went down."

Radcliffe frowned and scratched his scalp. "Oh, yeah. You're right. I can't remember how I knew about that."

"Anyway, the aliens only clipped us—at first, I mean," English replied. "We were still airborne for a few minutes afterward. Then they hit us with everything after that to make sure we stayed down."

Radcliffe faced front. "We could be in trouble with these people—whoever they are."

"You can say that again," Andy chimed in.

The conversation died when the group made it back to the *Lightning Rod*. Everyone split up. English ordered Sergeant Grimes to assign quarters to the *Buckingham Palace* personnel. Racer and her fellow pilots went to the enlisted mess. They were the only people in there.

She probably should have gone to the officer's mess. She wasn't enlisted anymore and hanging out with the other pilots basically constituted fraternization, but she didn't care.

Hughes and the Duran brothers came, too, and the three of them were all gunnery sergeants now, too.

No one else mentioned it. They just sat down in their places and started lounging around the way they used to when they all belonged to the flight squadron.

"The *Lightning Rod* feels like a ghost ship with so few people on board," Janacek pointed out.

"At least you have a ship to go back to," Hoskins grumbled. "We don't even have that anymore."

"It looks like we'll all be flying on the same wing again," Racer pointed out.

"We aren't a wing and we won't be flying if we can't get our birds in the air," Laughlin corrected. "Even if we got them in the air, the enemy would just shut us down again."

Walker grimaced and looked away. "Here I went to all the trouble of becoming a pilot and I don't even get to fly. This is just my luck."

"You're still a pilot," Racer told him. "We might not get our birds in the air again, but you're still a pilot and a damn good one." She cast her eye around the circle at Smythe, Waterman, and Laughlin. "You all are. One of these days, the Force is gonna need us to fly something. Then we'll be the ones to defeat this enemy and we'll be heroes."

She realized in that moment that everyone in the room was looking at her, including the other three gunnery sergeants and all her old crewmates from Wing 8. They all listened to her.

She looked back down at her plate and forced herself to keep eating. She wasn't sure she believed her own words, but she sure hoped the others did.

She didn't want Walker, Waterman, Laughlin, and Smythe to lose hope—not when they'd come so far in such a short time.

They really impressed her in the training arena. They'd all handled themselves well during the battle to retake Earth.

They'd flown in combat and fought the enemy on their very first day in the air. They'd endured a trial by fire and come through it with flying colors. She couldn't ask for better than that.

Now the four of them slouched around the enlisted mess shooting the bull with their fellow pilots. The four of them belonged here if anyone did.

She was just wondering when someone would bail her out by breaking the oppressive silence when the door opened and Captain English walked in.

Racer and her fellow pilots fell over themselves trying to stand up. Laughlin accidentally kicked over his chair, tripped on it, and hit the floor.

"Take it easy, Airman," the captain told him. "As you were, all of you. You don't have to get up on my account."

It was too late. The pilots were all already standing up. "Sir......" Racer stammered. "Is there something we can do for you, Sir?"

"I want to talk to you." He glanced up and down the table at them all. "Captain Radcliffe was just telling me that your birds are grounded down the beach. He says you told him the enemy shut down your birds in mid-flight. Is that true?"

"Yes, Sir," Hughes replied. "We were all flying together when it happened. Our engines just powered down in midair."

"But they did it gradually," Sean corrected. "They didn't just die cold turkey. They powered down slowly enough for us to land safely ....Sir."

English raised his eyebrows. "Really? So none of you sustained any damage when you landed?"

"I sustained damage in the battle before that happened," Hoskins added. "But not during the landing, no, Sir."

"So your birds are all still perfectly intact—all except yours, Hoskins?"

"If by 'intact' you mean their engines don't start, then yeah, they're intact," Walker clipped. "They might as well have crashed and burned for all the good they can do us."

"Not if we can get them running again," English countered and he turned back to Racer. She couldn't for the life of her figure out why he was suddenly treating her as being in charge of this group. "I want you all to show Lieutenant Hammil where your birds are so he can take a look at them. If he can get them running again, you can fly back to some USF base, let the Force know where we are, and maybe arrange a liftoff for the rest of us."

Racer stiffened. "Um....Sir.....maybe Lieutenant Hammil isn't the best person to send on this job."

"Why not?" English asked. "He's the only engineer we have that's qualified to troubleshoot your birds."

"He just......" Racer glanced around at the people nearest her. "You see, Sir....."

"Spit it out, Gunny. If you know some reason Lieutenant Hammil shouldn't work on your birds, I need to hear it."

"It isn't that he shouldn't work on our birds, Sir. I'm sure he would do fine with that. It's just....he applied to be a pilot on our new wing. He was on Wing 10...."

"For about half an hour," Walker interrupted.

English frowned at him and then at Racer. "I don't understand. What's the problem?"

"We got out to the arena to practice flying against armed targets," Smythe explained. "As soon as Gunny Franz turned on the weapons system and started flying through the course, Lieutenant Hammil got cold feet and beat it back to the *Lightning Rod*. He said he always hated being an engineer, but as soon as the shooting started, he backed out and left."

"Oh, I get it," English replied. "In that case, you can go alone, Racer. All I need is for you to show him where the birds are. You don't all have to go. In fact, none of you needs to interact with Lieutenant Hammil at all. Will that work?"

The other pilots nodded. English told them to carry on and left the mess.

Racer and her fellow pilots collapsed back into their chairs. "Phew!" Laughlin breathed. "I thought he was coming in here to bring the hammer down on one of us."

"No way," Ritchie countered. "Captain English is a rock."

"He's also damn scary when he gets mad or when someone steps out of line," Sean pointed out. "If he did come in here to bust one of us, it wouldn't be pretty."

"At least we don't have to face Hammil," Walker added. "I don't think I could stomach that."

"Who would walk away from a training run?" Janacek asked. "Who would walk away from a chance to fly on the fighter wing? There must be something wrong with the guy."

"I guess not everyone is cut out to be a pilot," Smythe remarked. "I don't understand it because I've always wanted to be a pilot, but I guess not everyone does."

"He said he wanted to be one," Laughlin pointed out. "He said he hated being an engineer, but that's exactly what he went back to instead of growing a pair and doing the run. It wasn't like the rest of us weren't scared, too."

"You weren't scared," Smythe countered. "You were right in there with us on the very first run."

"I was still scared," Laughlin told her. "I just didn't want any of the rest of you to think I was a coward."

"I was scared," Waterman growled. "I was shitting myself."

"But you did it anyway," Racer told him. "You overcame it and you kicked ass. That's something to be proud of."

He smiled at her. "Thanks, Gunny. I couldn't have done it without you."

"That's what I'm here for."

Chapter 5

E nglish stood outside the *Lightning Rod's* cargo hold and watched Racer and Lieutenant Hammil walk away south down the beach.

English really hoped they would get to the grounded fighter craft and come back quickly. He didn't want to wait before he found out if the birds could be salvaged.

He wanted even less to hear that the birds *couldn't* be salvaged, but he would like that better than sitting around waiting.

He didn't worry about Racer being able to put Hammil's cowardice behind her. She wouldn't hold it against him. English couldn't say the same for the other pilots.

He dragged himself away and went up to the bridge. He had to readjust his whole concept of reality when he walked in to find Andy, Church, and Radcliffe all working the controls at different bridge stations.

English didn't even feel qualified to talk to them about the *Lightning Rod*. He wasn't the captain on the bridge anymore and he couldn't call any of these men his XO no matter what rank they might have held before this.

Church and Radcliffe worked at the XO's station together. "The plasma mixture is holding steady," Church reported. "Hammil corrected it after the crash. It would have overloaded and wiped out the ship otherwise."

"It's running fine now," Radcliffe remarked. "It's feeding power to the whole ship—the parts of it that are still operational. Sick Bay is up and running, Sir. Lieutenant Eismann is back on duty and on his way up here now."

English nodded. "Excellent."

He didn't say anything about Radcliffe calling him "Sir", but a second later, Church did the same thing. "Sergeant Morrison just logged in under Sergeant Grimes's command, Sir. Morrison is requesting permission to post a watch on the rebel officers on board."

English looked up and his eyes met Church's. "Is that so?"

Church bit the inside of his cheek to stop himself from smirking. "Yes, Sir. Morrison also requested quarters on the same deck and in the same corridor as the rebel officers."

Now it was English's turn to avert his gaze to hide his grin. Good old Morrison. Nothing got past that guy.

English didn't get a chance to answer before the bridge door opened. General Halstead, Captain Thorburn, Colonel Levitt, and Admiral Chambers strode onto the bridge. "We didn't know where to go, so we just came up here," Colonel Roderick explained. "We're reporting for duty, Sailor. Just tell us what you want us to do."

"You can join the medical crew," Andy called over his shoulder from the logistics station. "They're working overtime to get all the dead bodies off the ship. You could do us all a big favor by helping them. We have everything covered up here." He didn't change his tone at all before he went on. "We have hull breaches on ten decks including engineering. This ship won't be breaking orbit again until we get to some USF repair yard."

"You mean like Oaxaca?" English asked.

Andy shot him a look, but Andy didn't answer. He went back to what he was doing. "I'm rerouting power away from the affected decks. We're venting life support through all the breaches. We don't want to waste the power if we don't have to."

"See if you can patch into any of our grounded birds," English told him. "See if you can remotely power them up or override whatever shut them down."

Admiral Chambers went over to Andy's station and watched him over his shoulder. Colonel Roderick and Colonel Levitt both went to the XO's station. Church glared at them when they observed what he and Radcliffe were doing.

An alarm went off on the logistics station and startled everyone into turning around. "We got something!" Andy called. "Gunny Franz is on board one of the grounded birds and signaling Squadron Command."

"Get Frasier down to the deck on the double!" English ordered. "No, scratch that. Put it through up here."

Andy opened the channel, but before English could make a sound, Admiral Chambers cut him off. "You can't communicate sensitive logistical information over an unsecured channel, Sailor. The enemy could be listening."

"The enemy already knows where we are and they know we're grounded, Everette," English countered. "Racer won't be telling me anything the enemy doesn't already know."

"They would find out that one of our birds is operational. They would find out that we're about to fly one of them....wherever you're gonna fly it to."

"One bird in the air won't make any difference to the enemy," Radcliffe pointed out. "They could just shut her down again if they wanted to. Besides, Racer isn't going to fly anywhere near an enemy combat zone—or any other combat zone. She's going to fly up the beach from there to here. No one could possibly see her as a threat."

"You're putting us all in danger, Sailor," Chambers insisted. "If you're going to be in command of this operation, you have to play it by the book and follow USF protocol."

English opened his mouth to say something, but Andy swiveled around in his seat and interjected first. "You said you were going to put yourself under Captain English's command. You said you were going to subordinate yourselves to his decision on account of you all being too stupid to command a flock of sheep, much less any USF vessel or personnel. What happened to that?"

Church burst out laughing. Chambers jolted, spun around, and glared at him.

English intervened. "Open the channel. Let's hear what she has to say."

Andy turned back to his controls and none of the rebel officers interfered this time. "Go ahead, Gunny," English told her. "You're patched through to the bridge. What's the situation there? Did Hammil get your bird going?"

"He got the power system on, which is a damn sight better than nothing at all if you get what I mean, Sir."

English had to smile. "I get what you mean, Gunny. So what's the status? Can he get them flying again or what?"

"He's working on the engines, but he can't figure out what's stopping them from powering up. He says whatever it is doesn't have anything to do with the electrical system."

"Okay, good to know. You come on back to the *Lightning Rod*. He can work on the birds without you."

"Yes, Sir. Do you want me to run a few scans of the countryside while I'm down here? I wasn't sure if the *Lighting Rod's* systems were working or not."

English glanced toward the XO's station and Radcliffe nodded. "Go ahead, Gunny," English told her. "What do you see?"

"Not a whole hell of a lot, Sir. The aliens are covering most of the planet. I don't see any USF ships in the air fighting them."

"That's because they're all already down," Andy cut in.

"Yes, Sir.....None of the old hotspots are doing anything. Everyone's lying low."

"Can you pick up any other downed USF vessels in the area—like walking distance from the *Lightning Rod?*" English asked.

"No, Sir. Just the *Lightning Rod,* the *Buckingham Palace,* the wreck of the other ship.....and the *Aileron,* Sir. She isn't reading any life signs, Sir."

"Okay, good work, Gunny," English told her. "Come on home and leave Hammil down there."

"Yes, Sir. Wing Leader 10 out......Whoa! Wait a minute, Sir! I'm picking up something. There's another ship down, but she isn't within walking distance. She's about ten miles north and five miles inland. It's the *Apache,* Sir."

English stiffened at the name. "That's a rebel ship."

"Yes, Sir," Church replied. "She was in battle against us over Point Hope when the aliens attacked."

"She's reading thirty life signs, Sir—and she's running at full power," Racer went on. "She just isn't going anywhere. I'm not picking up any engine activity—just main power, life support, medical.....all the other essential systems, but no propulsion."

"What about weapons?" English asked. "Are her weapons systems active?"

"No, Sir. Completely without power."

"Just like us," Andy pointed out. "These aliens cover all the bases."

"You did great work, Gunny," English told her. "You can come back now."

"Yes, Sir. Wing Leader 10 out."

She cut the signal. "Well, that's something," Radcliffe remarked. "At least we know the electrical systems are working. If we can't raise anyone with the *Lightning Rod,* we could use the birds to contact....
.someone."

"Are the *Lightning Rod's* communications working?" English asked.

"Let me check." Andy went back to work on the controls. "We have a few relays down, so we won't be able to transmit until Hammil gets back and reconnects them."

"I really have to protest, Sailor," Chambers piped up again. "Contacting one of your birds is one thing. Transmitting a message to any USF base would definitely attract enemy attention."

"You really aren't as smart as you think you are, are you?" Andy snapped. "Use your brain. We aren't a threat to the enemy and the most we would transmit would be our location and that we're in distress. The enemy wouldn't have to do anything except leave us here and you just heard Racer say that no other USF vessels are moving anyway. They can't with the enemy stationed all around the planet."

"Captain English never said he would transmit," Radcliffe pointed out. "He just asked if we could get the system up and running. You're shooting your mouth off over nothing."

"I think it's time for you to step off the bridge, Admiral," Church added. "You're just getting in the way and distracting us from doing something useful. If you really want to do something useful, go downstairs and help the medical team get rid of those dead bodies."

"You're living on this ship by Captain English's good grace," Andy went on. "He didn't have to let you stay here and he had every reason to turn you out and leave you to your deaths. You might show your appreciation for his generosity by making this ship as livable for all of us as you can possibly make it. You said you'd cooperate. Now go cooperate."

Chambers and the other rebel officers jerked from side to side following the dialogue from person to person. English's heart swelled listening, too. He didn't have to say a word. These three captains did it for him.

The rebel officers exchanged uncomfortable glances, did their best to stand up to the three captains, and then hustled for the door. They collided with Lieutenant Eismann who just happened to be walking onto the bridge at the same moment.

He tried to jump out of their way, but they barged past him and disappeared down the corridor. He looked back and forth between them and everyone standing around on the bridge. "What was that about? Did I miss something?"

"You didn't miss a thing, Brock," English told him. "Welcome back. Take your station. We could really use your help."

Eismann headed for the XO's station and stopped in his tracks. "Um....which station do you want me to take?"

"Take any station you like," Andy replied over his shoulder. "Captain English is the only person with any rank around here. Why don't you take that one over there?" He pointed to the scanner station next to his.

Eismann sat down and started working on the controls. Church and Radcliffe met English's eye for a minute before they went back to work.

"I think I'll assign Sergeant Morrison to take our guests under his wing," Church mused. "They need a strong leader to give them some direction in life."

Now it was Andy and Radcliffe who laughed. "I really wish I could be there to see it," Andy replied and they all went back to work.

Chapter 6

E nglish and Andy left the bridge and stopped in front of the elevator. English glanced back down the corridor toward the bridge, but Church, Radcliffe, and Eismann were too far away to overhear him.

English turned to his son. "Are you doing all right?" English asked.

"Me? I'm fine." Andy glanced at him and then faced front.

"You aren't....you know....frustrated about getting demoted to my command, are you?" English asked.

Now Andy really did spin around. "No! Why would I be? I told you to give me a post. You could have posted me to the flight squadron as a gunnery sergeant the way you did. I don't care what post I take. You know that."

He faced front again, but English didn't want to believe him. "I wouldn't blame you if you did. Demotion stinks."

"It isn't like I can really complain, is it?" Andy countered. "Church and Radcliffe are both doing it and I don't hear you asking them if they're all right."

"They've both been my subordinates before," English pointed out. "Church was my XO and Radcliffe was a lieutenant."

"And that makes a difference how?" Andy asked.

English didn't answer, and right then, the elevator came. The two men stepped inside and English waited for the doors to close, but he wasn't prepared to let this go.

He waited for the elevator to start moving before he said, "You don't seem like yourself. You've had a massive attitude since we crashed here. If you directed it at me the way you're directing it at everyone else, I would have to bump you down to something less than an airman."

Andy didn't even look at him. He kept his eyes focused straight ahead. "I haven't directed it at anyone who didn't deserve it. I won't say I'm myself. I'm mad as hell about Melanie. *You* can give those assholes a second chance. It doesn't mean I have to."

"I appreciate you speaking up for me on the bridge," English told him. "Just remember that we're all fighting the same war now. As long as those guys cooperate and don't interfere with our efforts, they have as much right to defend Earth as we do. They thought they were helping Earth and the USF by starting this thing. I'm not saying they did right. They're idiots, but they mean well."

"McClure doesn't," Andy snarled. "I swear to Christ, Dad, if I ever lay eyes on that guy again, I don't know what I'll do."

"I don't blame you, son," English replied. "I feel the same way."

"I'm not bent out of shape about getting demoted," Andy muttered through clenched teeth. "I'm glad you're the one in command so I don't have to pretend to be polite to those cocksuckers."

English relaxed and faced front. "I understand. I'm glad you aren't bent about serving under me. I know we talked about this before and we agreed that you and Dan would never serve under me....."

"That's all ancient history now," Andy countered. "This is an exceptional circumstance and I would never buck your command, especially not at a time like this. Someone has to be in charge and it wouldn't work for you to become *my* subordinate, would it?"

English shrugged. "No. You're right."

The elevator doors opened just then and both men stepped out into the cargo hold. They met Grimes, Morrison, Towne, Norris, the younger Dr. Cassidy, and all the pilots from the *Lightning Rod's* new reduced squadron. Church and Radcliffe showed up a few minutes later.

Everyone gathered around the weapons locker while Grimes handed out weapons to everyone. "We don't know if the *Apache* crew will be hostile," he told everyone. "We need to be prepared to defend ourselves. They may not have gotten the memo about the alien invasion and the rebels and loyalists needing to work together. We're on a humanitarian mission to help anyone we can, but if the rebels turn against us, don't hesitate to respond in kind and get the hell out. I don't want to see any heroics out there. Understand?"

Everyone nodded and said, "Yes, Sir."

English gave the word to move out, but before they left the ship, Admiral Chambers, Colonel Roderick, and General Halstead stepped out of the stairwell.

The three officers glanced around at the armed crewmen and everyone turned around to glare at them. The officers had to summon their courage to walk through the group to get to English.

They planted themselves in front of English and did their best not to notice the hostility surrounding them on all sides. "Sailor....." Chambers began.

"You might show a little respect," Andy snapped. "You are in the military, after all, and you're addressing a superior officer."

Chambers cleared his throat with difficulty. "Yes, of course." He squared his shoulders a little more. "Captain.....Captain English....S ir.....we'd like to come with you."

"Don't think you're going to step in and negotiate with the *Apache* crew in Captain English's place," Church chimed in. "If you come, you're coming as a subordinate, not as a commanding officer."

"Of anything," Andy finished.

Chambers cleared his throat one last time. "Of course. I mean…Yes, Sir."

English measured the three of them. He really couldn't afford to keep pushing these men out. If they were sincere and planned to pull their weight on this crew, he needed them too badly to refuse them.

He took an extra weapon from Morrison and shoved it into Chambers's hands. "Don't screw up," English snapped.

Chambers stammered, "Yes, Sir," again and English turned away. He was just about to walk outside when the stairwell door opened for the third time and Admiral Simpson came out.

He cast a pleading look around the group, but he didn't approach or say anything. He hovered there by the stairs looking lost and forlorn.

English didn't say anything, either. He walked out of the hold into the cold wind. The group followed him.

English pretended not to notice Simpson hustling over to the weapons locker, taking down three of the remaining plasma rifles, and hurrying to catch up with everybody.

They had to hike a long way to get to the *Apache*. Fortunately, the flat, featureless landscape didn't offer any obstacles to the crew cutting straight overland. They followed a diagonal route straight to the downed ship.

English spotted it long before they got anywhere near it. If the crewmen who survived the *Apache* crash saw the *Lightning Rod* crew coming, no one reacted. No one came out to confront or greet the approaching crew.

English slowed as he got nearer. He tried to see whether anyone on or around the *Apache* was preparing to ambush him and his people.

He didn't see anything. A few people walked around the outside of the ship, but they always went back inside to be replaced by different people a few minutes later.

He tried to remember anything he could about the *Apache* crew, but he'd been out of the service for so long that he didn't know any of her crew. A much younger captain had replaced the man English had known during his former service days.

No one did come out to confront the crew. If Racer was right, the *Apache* still had bridge scanners. The *Apache* crew would be stupid not to monitor the surroundings for anyone to approach, either friend or enemy.

English halted at a distance to observe the ship and crew just to be certain. He didn't want to believe it could be this easy. The *Apache* crew and her senior staff could be inside the ship right now planning to restart the rebellion.

If they were, he would have to neutralize them all. That was the last thing he needed—and the last thing Earth needed.

"Are we going?" Church asked.

English nodded. Why prolong the inevitable?

He took one step before another alien warship zipped into view above his head. It skidded to a halt a mile away, but it didn't open fire—or at least it didn't fire the way it fired at the destroyers.

It stopped on a dime and fired some kind of strange gleaming white energy beam into the ground. It formed a cylinder of light between the enemy ship and the surface. It was the same type of energy the aliens used to fire their weapons.

Dozens upon dozens of masked alien creatures materialized at the point where the beam hit the ground. The aliens themselves walked upright on a pair of legs jointed backward at the knee.

Elongated feet lay flat on the ground at the base of each foot and the creatures walked with a loping, bouncing gait. It made their bodies rise and fall in a slow, fluid movement each time the aliens took a step.

English couldn't see any of their heads behind their masks. They all wore some kind of glossy black armor that encased their bodies.

The creatures had four arms, two to a side, that also jointed in a strange way English couldn't make out from this distance.

He would have had to be blind not to see the weapons they carried in those arms. They were all armed and they set off marching toward the *Apache.*

He instinctively raised his plasma rifle, but he hesitated to fire until he saw what the aliens planned to do. He didn't dare to hope they were here for any peaceful purpose—not armed and suited up like that. Their warships had made their intentions plain enough already.

Church, Morrison, Hughes, Racer, and everyone else in their party raised their weapons, too, but before anyone could move, the alien ground troops opened fire on the *Apache.*

Three people happened to be outside right at that moment. The aliens landed so suddenly that none of the *Apache* crewmen had time to prepare before the aliens bombarded the vessel with gunfire.

The ground troops' weapons spat the same kind of energy as their transport beam and the warships' weapons. The aliens' shots smashed the *Apache's* hull and the three crewmen dove for cover behind the ship.

English opened fire on the aliens and so did the rest of his crew. No alien scumbags were going to invade his planet and shoot at his people—not while he could do something about it.

He hit ten aliens before he realized his mistake. The alien platoon split in half with one group heading for the *Apache* and one group coming after the *Lightning Rod* crew.

English fired a few more times, but one of the alien shots hit Grimes right next to English and the whole crew had to duck behind a swell. They didn't get there in time before another shot hit Simpson in the side.

Church and Morrison hauled Grimes into the hollow and English grabbed Simpson by the hand. English dragged Simpson over the swell where Dr. Cassidy pounced on him.

Everyone flattened themselves behind the rise to unload on the approaching aliens.

English moved down a dozen of them, but the others just kept on coming. They didn't even try to take cover.

They just kept on marching, always marching. They walked straight into the crew's gunfire no matter how many aliens the crew killed.

English gave them what they asked for and carved a path of destruction through their ranks. He saw and heard plasma shots coming from the *Apache* crew, but he couldn't take the time to see what was happening over there.

More aliens seemed to appear out of nowhere. He paused his fire long enough to look around.

The warship still hovered directly overhead and more and more alien ground troops transported to the ground through that beam.

English raised his head a little higher just to make sure. It was true. Troop after troop of aliens marched out of the beam coming from the ship. English didn't see how the ship could be carrying that many aliens, but what did he know about these creatures?

Whoever was managing this campaign didn't give a damn how many soldiers they lost. The aliens marched straight into the crew's gunfire with no regard for their comrades falling by the dozen.

Twenty people had come out of the *Apache* and were using its crumpled hull for protection while they hammered the aliens with gunfire.

One of the *Apache* crew glanced in English's direction and saw him looking their way. English couldn't recognize the person from here except that it was a man with dark brown hair and a beard.

English used his crewmen's covering fire to push himself up on his knees and pointed toward the beam. The man hiding behind the *Apache* used his own people's covering fire to look where English was pointing and then some of the *Apache* crew raised their guns to aim at the beam instead.

English swept his weapon that way and fired into the beam. The *Apache* crew did the same thing and unloaded on the beam where the aliens emerged.

Nothing happened except that the shots took out some more aliens, so English raised his weapon and fired at the top of the beam where it came out of the warship.

The *Apache* crew did the same thing and they all fired upward toward the source of the beam. It shattered and broke contact with the ground.

The beam didn't reappear and no more troops transported to the ground, but that didn't help the *Lightning Rod* crew with so many aliens already spreading out all over the area.

English went back to firing at them instead and so did the *Apache* crew. If the two crews kept working together like this, they would cut down every alien on the field.

English should have considered that a victory, but he didn't like it. Something was wrong. He just couldn't put his finger on what it was.

He got his answer when he sprayed gunfire back the other way across the assembled alien force. Another twenty aliens toppled onto the grass and lay still.

Only fifty aliens remained and they didn't mount an effective defense. They didn't mount any defense at all. They just stood out there and made themselves targets for the two crews shooting at them.

English started to lower his weapon. Maybe he should try to talk to them. He might at least try to find out why they were here and what they wanted.

He didn't get a chance before the warship aimed a brutal shot at the *Apache* and struck the ship right in front of where the crew had been hiding.

The ship bounced off the ground and the crew bolted away, but there was nowhere left to hide. They had to run out onto the tundra.

The warship kept hammering the *Apache* again and again, flipped the ship into the air, hit it a few times, and then swatted it down onto the ground with a vicious assault.

English spun around and grabbed Simpson. "Run for it! Get out of here! Go!"

He pushed everyone away. Morrison had to pause long enough to pick up Grimes who had lost a leg below the knee.

English didn't have time to see how much Dr. Cassidy had done with Simpson. At least Simpson was still alive.

English dragged him to his feet. English didn't dare to look behind him. He already knew what was coming.

He wasn't even surprised when the enemy ship fired at his fleeing crew. The first shot smashed into the lip of the swell where the crew had just been hiding.

The impact flung a pile of dirt into English's back and he staggered under Simpson's weight. English had been in the act of pulling Simpson's arm over his shoulders so he could support the man to get away.

Simpson pulled out of English's grip and ran a few stumbling steps on his own while he scrambled to get his weapon into position.

Simpson almost fell over when he turned around and aimed his weapon behind him toward the aliens still advancing across the open terrain.

"Get out of here, Chris!" English thundered and pushed Simpson away.

The warship opened fire again, dissolved the swell that was the only thing giving the crew any protection, and then the warship turned its attention back to the *Apache*.

English yelled to his crew to run for it. Church, Radcliffe, Andy, and Morrison were all yelling the same thing and the crew took off running south toward the *Lightning Rod*, but they were too far away. They would never make it in time.

English sprinted over two more swells. He lost track of who was near him. A dozen people ran ahead of him. He only took the time to check that no one was behind him.

They weren't. He and Simpson were in the very rear.

English had to slow down to keep pace with Simpson, but at least the man could run on his own. He kept wincing, doubling over, clutching his stomach, and grimacing in pain, but he never stopped running.

English moved closer to him, but at that moment, another crushing blast struck the swell he and Simpson happened to be running over. The swell exploded under their feet and hurled English away.

Chapter 7

E nglish tumbled through the air and heard more explosions going off all around him. He turned a revolution and slammed down hard on the ground. He tried to blink the stars out of his eyes, but before he could move, someone grabbed him and dragged him behind another swell.

He picked up his head and saw Christopher Simpson crouching behind the same swell. Simpson ducked when another shot smashed into the swell from its other side, but Simpson didn't protect himself.

He arched his back and spread his arms over English. Dirt clods rained on both of them, but Simpson's arms, head, and body protected English from most of it.

Simpson clamped his eyes and mouth shut until the bombardment stopped. He stayed like that spread over English until the noise of gunfire moved away. English heard smashes and crashes in the distance.

Simpson took a peek over the edge of the swell. "They're still hitting the *Apache*. We need to make another push to get farther away."

English didn't realize there was anyone else here until General Halstead replied, "We would never make it all the way back to the *Lightning Rod* and we don't want to draw the enemy's fire to the ship anyway. I say we stay here and hold our fire until the warship leaves. The aliens haven't attacked us before. They only did it now because we fired on their ground troops. They'll leave us alone as long as we don't threaten them."

"You're assuming a lot," Admiral Chambers cut in from farther down the swell. "You have no clue what's motivating them to shoot at anyone. The *Apache* wasn't firing at the aliens and now the aliens are out there pounding the ship to scrap metal. We can't make decisions based on assumptions."

"The *Apache* crew fired on the alien ground troops," Halstead pointed out.

"After the ground troops fired on the *Apache* crew," Chambers countered.

"Both of you shut the hell up," Simpson snapped. "Captain English is in command here, not you." Simpson turned back to English. "Are you all right, Sir?" Simpson glanced around. "Dr. Cassidy isn't here. If you're injured, we'll take you back to the *Lightning Rod* for medical treatment." He squinted over the swell again. "We just need to figure out how."

"I'm all right." English pried himself off the ground and forced himself to sit up.

He followed Simpson's gaze toward the *Apache*. The enemy stopped shooting right at that moment, but the warship didn't leave. It towered over the *Apache* which lay squashed and inert a few hundred yards from where it had been before. English didn't see any people over there.

Colonel Roderick huddled behind the swell with English's group, but Roderick didn't get involved in the conversation. He just sat there listening to the other three officers arguing.

"What do you want us to do, Sir?" Simpson asked.

"We can't stay out here," English decided. "Even if the enemy doesn't shoot at us, the sun will go down and we would freeze out here overnight. We'll head back to the *Lightning Rod.*"

"It's already afternoon now. The sun will go down long before we get back to the *Lightning Rod.*"

English turned to the last two people hiding behind this swell. Apart from the four rebel officers, Rosa Smythe and Ash Walker from Wing 10 sat apart and listened to the officer's conversation.

This was the first time English had ever spoken to Rosa Smythe, but he read her in a split second. She was an older woman who'd spent her career as a cook in the enlisted mess kitchens.

There must be more to her if she signed up to be a pilot in Wing 10. Now here she was speaking up in front of admirals and generals.

English rubbed his head. "We have to fall back to the *Lightning Rod.* We don't have a choice about that. We can head westward toward the beach and follow the coastline south. We can't blunder around in the tundra in the dark. If we keep moving, we should stay warm enough to make it."

"What about the others?" Walker glanced over his shoulder at nothing. "Are we just going to leave them out here?"

English scanned the countryside. The remaining aliens who had been on the ground when the beam cut off now approached the *Apache.*

"I don't see any of them and we'd have to risk our lives trying to find them in the dark. The *Lightning Rod's* birds have enough power that we can use their controls to scan the countryside. We'll be able to find any survivors more easily that way."

No one argued. English made sure everyone in his group had weapons.

"Follow me," he ordered. "Stay behind the swells and keep your heads down."

He flipped onto his knees, made one last assessment of the countryside, and crept away. He crouched low behind each swell, stole peeks toward the *Apache,* and then darted across open places to the next protected spot.

He kept working his way west, but a few minutes later, when he looked out to make sure the way was still clear, he froze when he saw the aliens come out of the *Apache* leading a bunch of people at gunpoint.

The aliens only brought ten crewmen out of the *Apache.* None of them was the bearded man English had seen before.

The aliens lined the crewmen up next to their destroyed ship and the aliens moved back. They raised their weapons to shoot the crewmen down.

English reacted without thinking, lunged for the nearest swell, flattened himself on his stomach, and opened fire on the aliens. He popped off ten shots and took down the aliens who had been about to shoot the *Apache* crew.

The crew spun around to see who was shooting, but they couldn't see English from this distance. They responded beyond his wildest dreams by charging the fallen aliens, snatching their weapons, and turning the enemy guns on the remaining alien troops.

English swiveled his gun to take down the rest when Chambers grabbed him. "No! Don't shoot!" Chambers tried to wrench English's gun up to stop him from firing.

English's instincts took over and he retaliated more harshly than he would have if he'd been thinking clearly.

He threw himself on his side, craned up his leg, and kicked Chambers away with all his might. Chambers stumbled and sprawled across his back on the ground.

Smythe and Walker both rushed to English's side, flattened themselves on the ground next to him, and all three opened fire on the aliens.

Chambers started to sit up. Simpson sprang in front of him, turned his back to English, shouldered his weapon, and aimed at Chambers's head. "Don't move, Everette! Stay down!"

English was too busy shooting to pay attention to them. He, Smythe, and Walker unloaded on the remaining aliens. The freed *Apache* crewmen finished off the rest until no alien ground troops remained.

The *Apache* crewmen swept their new weapons back and forth across the dead bodies and then a few people raised their heads to look toward English's swell.

He pushed himself up on his knees to wave at them, but at that moment, the warship fired into their swell again. The shot exploded in the dirt right in front of English and the impact hurled him backward against the next rise.

He sprang up instantly and pulled Smythe and Walker away from the edge. "Come on! We gotta back off! Move it!"

He pushed them away and everyone took off running. He couldn't take as much time or trouble to check if he was leading his people into the open. He just had to keep on running.

He crouched under his arms as another brutal shot detonated against the swell right next to him. Dirt, rock, and debris pelted him in the face and he tumbled down into another hollow.

Hands grabbed him and pulled him to safety before he realized that someone else was hiding behind this swell. They didn't belong to his crew.

English scrambled to plaster his back behind the swell and came face to face with the brown-haired, bearded man he'd seen at the *Apache*.

Neither of them had time to say a word before the rest of the *Lightning Rod* crew tumbled in behind them. They fell all over each other getting to safety in time.

Simpson yanked Chambers down by the collar, shook him, and then shoved the man hard against the dirt slope. Simpson stood over Chambers and aimed his gun barrel straight in Chambers's face.

"Don't you ever interfere with Captain English again, Everett! Do you hear me?!" Simpson barked. "If you EVER lay your hands on Captain English again, I swear to Christ I'll shoot you in the face! Don't move, you traitorous piece of filth!"

No one moved for a second, especially not Chambers. He kept his eyes averted, but Simpson didn't relax.

Smythe broke the deadly silence by looking over the edge of the swell. "They aren't shooting anymore. The aliens aren't shooting at the *Apache* anymore, either. The *Apache* crew is standing guard around the ship, Sir, and the....."

She didn't finish before the warship zoomed away somewhere. It vanished in a heartbeat and left the landscape deserted and empty.

English swiveled onto his stomach and followed her gaze, but he didn't see anything she didn't already tell him.

The ten people the aliens had been about to slaughter now stood guard around the *Apache*. All those crewmen held alien weapons and they paced around their ship in a threatening posture.

English didn't see any other sign of alien activity. None of the aliens had ventured out into the tundra to hunt down survivors. The warship was gone, too, but he hesitated to show his face in the open in case something else went wrong.

He sat back down and pulled Smythe away from the edge. "Stand down, Airman. There's nothing to see out there."

English glanced toward Simpson. He still held Chambers at gunpoint. English didn't intervene.

He finally turned back to the bearded man. He watched all their interactions and his eyes flicked to English. "You're......you're Sailor English.....from the *Siskiyou?*"

English sighed. "That was a long time ago. I'm on the *Lightning Rod* now." English held out his hand. "I don't know you. Who are you?"

The bearded man locked piercing brown eyes on English and then glanced down at English's hand. "The *Lightning Rod* is a loyalist ship."

"That's all finished now, too," English told him. "There are no loyalists or rebels anymore. It's just humans versus aliens. We all need to pull together to drive these cocksuckers off our planet. What do you say?"

The bearded man glanced around the circle of faces. He took in Simpson holding Chambers at gunpoint and the bearded man finally shook English's hand. "Nathan Lowery, XO of the *Apache.*"

English grinned at him. "Good to meet you. Are you in command of the ship?"

"I am now. Our captain got killed when the aliens shot the *Apache* down." Lowery jerked his thumb over his shoulder at five people sitting behind him. "We were the ones outside shooting at the aliens when the warship opened fire. We had to run for it."

English nodded and sat up. "We should head back to the ship and clear out any survivors. You can all come back to the *Lightning Rod* with us. We have power and medical. We got some of our communications and scanner equipment working, too. We're getting ready to transmit to the USF to let our people know where we are."

Chapter 8

Radcliffe ran from swell to swell to take cover from the alien bombardment. A few swells exploded right next to him, but the farther he ran, the more distance he put between himself and the battle.

He realized he was running eastward—away from where he should be going if he wanted to get back to the *Lightning Rod.*

He couldn't turn around, though. He had to keep running away from the gunfire until he found somewhere to hide.

He wasn't looking where he was going before he dove behind another swell and tripped over someone already hiding there.

He went down hard on the ground only for a bunch of people to grab him and pull him under cover.

He rolled over on the ground and looked up at Andy English, Racer, Laughlin, Waterman, Ezra Duran, and Corporal Towne from the *Buckingham Palace.* They all flattened themselves against the swell and hid under their arms every time the aliens fired in their direction.

Andy leaned forward, grabbed Radcliffe by the jacket, and pulled him into a sitting position. "You okay?" Andy yelled in Radcliffe's face. "Are you alone?"

Radcliffe nodded fast, but he couldn't say anything over the noise. He crouched there with the others, but the shooting stopped in a minute.

Andy looked up, but he didn't stick his head up. Towne started to get onto her knees to take a look, but he pulled her down. "Stay hidden, Corporal."

"Did you see anybody else?" Radcliffe asked. "Did you see what happened to Captain English?"

"We didn't see shit," Laughlin replied. "We just ran. The explosions separated everyone."

Radcliffe waited a second longer, and when the shooting didn't restart, he straightened up himself.

He glanced over the edge of the swell toward the *Apache* in the distance. "That ship isn't going anywhere ever again."

"What are they doing?" Andy asked.

"The aliens are going to search the ship." Radcliffe scanned the countryside. "I don't see anybody. They're all hiding the same way we are."

He sat back down and made another assessment of the people in the hollow. They were all armed and he didn't see that any of them were injured.

"What do you want to do?" he asked Andy.

"Me?" Andy snorted. "I'm not in charge here. I don't make decisions. I do what I'm told."

Radcliffe had to grin at him. "Since when?"

"We gotta meet back up with the others," Duran suggested. "Captain English might have a plan for how we can tackle these aliens."

"We ain't tackling nobody," Waterman countered. "No one on the planet can tackle these aliens."

"We don't even know where Captain English is," Towne pointed out. "It will be night soon and we'll freeze to death out here on the tundra. We would throw our lives away looking for him. He wouldn't want that."

"The aliens will be able to see us if we go out into the open to return to the *Lightning Rod,*" Racer pointed out. "We might have to stay here."

"It looks like you're the ranking officer here, Matt," Andy told him. "You can decide our fates."

Now it was Radcliffe's turn to snort. He inched closer to the edge of the swell to take a look at the *Apache.* He froze when he saw the aliens come out of the ship leading a bunch of crewmen at gunpoint.

The aliens lined everyone up to shoot the crewmen down. Radcliffe raised his weapon to intervene when gunfire erupted from another swell farther west. It came from a hundred yards away from Radcliffe's position—on the other side of the *Apache.*

He had a split second to recognize English before all hell broke loose. He opened fire on the aliens, brought them to the ground, and the *Apache* crew sprang forward to attack, too.

The gunfire from English's position cut out for a second and then multiple guns unloaded to decimate the aliens.

The noise attracted Radcliffe's companions' attention and everyone looked up. They pulled their guns into position to help out, but the *Lightning Rod* crew only just started shooting before the warship opened fire on them.

The swells sheltering English exploded. Radcliffe couldn't think of any other way to help English, so Radcliffe raised his weapon and fired on the warship.

He didn't expect it to make any difference, but it did draw the warship away from English's position. Racer, Andy, Towne, and Duran all joined their gunfire with Radcliffe's before the warship turned on them instead.

The crew squashed themselves as far down in the hollow as they could. Dirt and rubble rained all around them.....and then dead silence fell over the landscape.

Radcliffe took a long time to lift his head. Dirt clung to his hair and sprinkled down the back of his collar into his clothes. He blinked dust out of his eyes and dared to look over what was left of the swell.

The aliens were all dead and the *Apache* crew stood guard over their ship, but Radcliffe didn't see English anymore. Radcliffe didn't see anyone behind the swell where English had just been shooting.

Radcliffe sat back on his heels. Everyone else in his group was fine. They were just pinned down.

"What do you want to do about the *Apache* crew?" Andy asked. "They were a rebel ship until this happened."

"What are you asking me for?" Radcliffe asked. "I'm not in charge. I don't make decisions. I do what I'm told."

Andy chuckled. "Good answer."

"Your dad would say that there are no more rebels," Radcliffe pointed out. "He just risked his ass to save those people. If he was here, he'd tell us to help the *Apache* crew and get them fighting on our side."

"Right. Then I guess that's what we have to do."

He looked up and started to climb onto his knees to look over the swell, but right then, the alien warship shot away to the west and vanished.

"I really wish they wouldn't do that," Racer murmured. "Why can't they come and go like normal people?"

Andy and Radcliffe looked out at the *Apache,* but there was nothing else to see. The field was deserted, now that all the alien ground troops were dead.

"Let's skirt around over there." Radcliffe pointed to the right. "We can get closer to the ship without anyone seeing us. That way, if something goes wrong, we'll still be hidden until we're sure something *won't* go wrong."

"You're the boss," Andy replied. "I just do what I'm told."

Radcliffe made a face at him and ducked back down. "Everybody keep low," he told the others. "Don't stick your heads out. The *Apache* crew is armed and they'll be looking for anything coming at them from any direction."

He hunched behind a few more swells, darted across the low places, and made his way around the field. He used the swells to work his way closer to the *Apache* until he squatted less than thirty feet away.

"Ready?" he asked Andy.

"Do I look like I'm in command here?" Andy asked. "You go out there and stick your head in front of a gun. You won't catch me doing it."

"Thanks a lot, pal," Radcliffe countered. "It's nice to know I have your unconditional support."

Andy grinned at him and pulled his weapon forward. "I'll be back here covering your backside. If anyone threatens you or tries to shoot at you, I'll take 'em out first."

He scooted to the top of the nearest swell, propped his gun on the rise, and sighted down the barrel toward the *Apache* personnel pacing around their ship.

Radcliffe wilted in relief when he saw that. At least he wouldn't be going out there with his pants around his ankles—figuratively, of course.

He still had to muster his courage before he showed himself. He took a deep breath, put his own rifle on the ground, raised both hands, and climbed up onto the rise.

The *Apache* crew spun around instantly and aimed their new alien weapons at him.

"Don't shoot, man!" Radcliffe called. "I'm human! I'm USF just like you!"

Three men from the *Apache* crew held him at gunpoint, another four came over as soon as they heard voices.

"What do you want?" one big bruiser demanded. His eyes darted down to Radcliffe's uniform. "You're no captain."

"I'm Captain Matt Radcliffe of the *Infinity*. I just got promoted from XO last week. My ship went down out here and I'm stranded just like you. Don't shoot! I can help you. I swear it."

"Help us—how?" another barked. "You're all alone."

"I'm not alone. I'm with the *Lightning Rod* crew. She's down the coast and we have full power and everything. You can come over and join us. You have my word no one will harm you."

"The *Lightning Rod* is a loyalist ship," another guy pointed out. "How do we know you won't arrest us?"

"The rebellion is over, man," Radcliffe told him. "Those aliens are crawling all over Earth knocking down any destroyer that tries to launch. We all have to put the rebellion behind us and fight together to retake the planet. Come on. Put your guns down." He dared to measure the group. Three of them were lieutenants. One of them was a gunnery sergeant with pilot's wings and the other two were airmen pilots. "Who's your commanding officer?"

The *Apache* crewmen exchanged glances. Then the first guy said, "We don't have one. I'm the most senior officer left. The captain's dead and the XO isn't here anymore. He was in charge of us after we crashed, but he disappeared when the aliens started shooting at us just now."

Radcliffe made an executive decision and put his hands down. "Then you men can come under my command until we find someone more senior. We have way bigger fish to fry dealing with these aliens. We don't have time to go arresting anybody over the rebellion. Come on. I'll take you the *Lightning Rod.* "

He started forward to walk over to them. The first two lieutenants raised their weapons higher to threaten him. Radcliffe hesitated for a second and then decided to ignore the guns.

He crossed the last few yards, stopped in front of them., and read their name tags one after the other. The three lieutenants were Provost, Kilpatrick, and Entwistle. Radcliffe smiled at them and stuck out his hand. "It's good to meet you all."

They scowled at him. None of them shook hands with him. He was just making up his mind on what to say next when they all jolted to high alert and raised their weapons to aim at something behind him.

He glanced over his shoulder and saw Andy, Racer, Waterman, and the others standing up and climbing into the open. None of them held their weapons up where the *Apache* crew could possibly consider them a threat.

"It's all right," Radcliffe told the three lieutenants. "They're with me. They're all from the *Lightning Rod.* This is Captain Andrew English. He was on your side during the rebellion."

"So what's he doing with you?" Kilpatrick demanded. "Did you capture him?"

"He wouldn't be armed right now if we did. I told you. The rebellion is over. Now we all have to pull together so we can fight the....."

He broke off when another group stood up behind some nearby swells. Radcliffe's tension drained away when he saw English, the four rebel officers, and a bunch of people from the *Apache* walk toward the ship.

"Commander!" Provost exclaimed and rushed over to a tall guy with brown hair and a beard. "We thought you were gone."

"I'm all right, Lieutenant." The commander stopped in front of Radcliffe. The guy had piercing brown eyes and an intimidating presence. He didn't seem at all put off by Radcliffe's new rank. "Can I help you with something....Sir?"

"He's with me," English cut in. "Captain Matt Radcliffe of the *Infinity*, meet Commander Nathan Lowery, XO of the *Apache*. I was just telling Lowery to bring his people down to the *Lightning Rod* with us."

"I was just telling these gentlemen the same thing," Radcliffe replied.

"So.....you're all working together?" Lowery's gaze snapped back and forth between Radcliffe, Andy, English, and the rebel officers. Lowery was starting to get the picture.

"That's what I'm telling you," English replied. "We're all in the same boat here. It doesn't look like your ship is going to be able to give you any shelter and it will be dark soon. We need to head back to the *Lightning Rod* before it gets dark."

"It's getting dark now," Smythe pointed out.

Radcliffe glanced at the sky. She was right. The sun was going down.

"We better stay here tonight, then. We'll need to use the ship for shelter." English turned to Lowery. Then he changed his mind and turned to Kilpatrick instead. "What's the situation inside? How bad was the damage after that last attack?"

Kilpatrick shrugged and looked away. "It was pretty bad and there are a lot of dead bodies in there. We don't have power anymore."

"Is the plasma core intact?" Andy asked. "We won't be able to use the ship if it's contaminated."

"The core was fine until just before the aliens came on board and decided to execute us," Provost replied. "The core went offline and our engineers are all dead. None of us is qualified to restart the core."

"Just leave it for now," English replied. "We'll just have to clear out at least one room where we can hunker down and keep warm tonight."

A blast of cold wind struck the group right then. It gave Radcliffe goosebumps.

"Let's go inside," English finished. "Everyone spread out, search every room, and we'll reconvene to find out which is the clearest and the most secure. We can't stay out here any longer."

Chapter 9

Racer squatted on the floor of the conference room down the corridor from the captain's ready room on board the *Apache*.

"The ship is secure, Sir," she told English. "Laughlin just left to hike back to the *Lightning Rod* to tell Lieutenant Eismann where we are and what's going on. Laughlin will go straight west until he gets to the coast and then south to the ship."

"Good work, Gunny. Thank you." English looked up at her for a split second and went back to what he was doing.

He'd broken a piece of wooden furniture into splinters. Now he gathered them into a pile on the floor and used one of the alien weapons to set them alight.

Just then, Commander Lowery entered the room carrying another wooden chair. He sat it next to English. "Captain Corning has a bunch of other wooden furniture in his ready room and more in his quarters. We can burn that to keep warm tonight."

"Excellent." English added a few more sticks to the fire. The rest of the crew came in while he worked. The smoke from the fire drifted up to the ceiling and vanished into the ship's ventilation system.

"The aliens still aren't coming back," the younger Captain English announced. "It's all quiet out there."

"We won't have any warning if they do come back," Lowery pointed out.

"Why us? That's what I don't understand," Kilpatrick added. "Why did they come after the *Apache* of all ships? We were down with no weapons. The aliens could have gone after any destroyer in the fleet, but they had to come after us. The ship wasn't even shooting at them when they fired on us for no reason."

"We might never find out why they're here or what they want," English pointed out. "We don't even know what species they are or where they come from."

"What difference does it make what species they are or where they come from or what they want?" Smythe asked. "They're here to destroy us. That's all we need to know."

"If we knew what they wanted, we might be better able to decide on a strategy to fight them," Radcliffe replied. "If we knew what species they were, we might be able to find some vulnerability of theirs that we could exploit. The more information we have about them, the better."

"There are plenty of dead ones outside," Walker remarked. "We could study one of them."

"I didn't mean now," English replied. "We wouldn't be able to learn anything about them now, but someone from the USF could take one of the dead aliens back to the Command Center and study the body and its weapons and armor. The Command Staff could find out what kind of weapons the aliens are using and how we can counteract them. We won't be able to do any of that here."

"At least we got some of their weapons." Entwistle picked up his and studied it.

"Can you tell us anything about how it works?" English asked.

"Are you kidding me? I didn't even graduate from high school. I don't understand this stuff."

Lowery held out his hand. "Let me see it."

Entwistle handed it over and Lowery bent over to study it. "What do you see, Commander?" Racer asked. "Do you understand weapons systems?"

"I studied mechanical engineering before I joined the Force." Lowery frowned at the weapon in his hands. "That's interesting."

"What's interesting?" Radcliffe asked.

"It seems to be some kind of plasma or energy transfer system, but the weapon doesn't have a magazine, a plasma chamber, or reservoir that would hold the plasma or power source."

"It must have something," the younger Captain English countered. "How does it fire if it doesn't have an ammunition source?"

"That's what I'm telling you." Lowery held up the weapon and pointed to something on the back end. "This seems to be come kind of power coupling where the weapon would be hooked up to something. Maybe they charge it that way."

"But that makes no sense," Ezra Duran argued. "You said it was some kind of plasma or energy transfer system, so it would need some sort of plasma or energy source to run it. If it charged up, it would have to run on electricity or something like that."

"That's why it's strange," Lowery replied. "I don't understand it, but we would have to know what power source it uses before we understood how to neutralize it."

"The warships seemed to work on the same energy system," English pointed out. "The weapons the warships used to knock down our destroyers, the energy in that transport beam, and the energy coming from these weapons were all the same type."

"I noticed that, too," Radcliffe remarked. "It makes sense."

"Whatever it is must be awfully powerful," Waterman pointed out. "Those warships can move so fast."

"None of us will be doing anything against the enemy tonight," English interjected and he turned to Lowery. "How much do you know about the rebel movements around the planet?"

Lowery's head shot up. "You said you were dropping all that."

"I am. I just want to know if the rebels had any more destroyers stashed away anywhere."

"What do you mean—stashed away?" Lowery countered. "We don't have anything stashed away. Everything we had was out there fighting the loyalists."

"The rebel command had a secret fleet of destroyers hidden at Point Hope. They sprang this fleet on us to try to overwhelm us and finish off the loyalist effort. I want to know if the rebels had another force hidden somewhere that we might be able to use against the aliens."

"No USF force would be of any use against the aliens," the younger Captain English pointed out. "You should know that by now."

"Shouldn't you be asking *us* about the rebel's secret fleet?" Simpson asked. "Commander Lowery is only an XO." He glanced at Lowery. "No offense, Commander."

"If you knew about any secret rebel fleet, I think you would have told me by now," English replied. "Besides, General McClure made it sound like you guys don't know everything your rebel friends have been doing behind your backs. Some other people might know something you don't." He turned back to Lowery. "Well? Do you know anything?"

"Sorry," Lowery replied. "I don't know anything and I'm certain Captain Corning didn't know anything, either. He was against the rebellion from the start. He didn't want to fight any other USF ships, but he felt like he had to follow orders."

English snorted and looked away. "Whatever."

"There has to be some way to fight the aliens, Sir," Racer interjected. "I mean....we can't just let them take Earth."

"They already have taken it, Gunny," Corporal Towne pointed out. "They have us on the ropes. They have warships stationed all over the planet and no destroyers can get off the ground without getting smacked down. I don't see how we can stop these aliens from doing what they want."

"Well, we have to do something," Racer countered. "We can't just sit here and do nothing."

"That's exactly what we will do and that's what we have to do," Waterman replied. "We have nothing to fight them with. We don't even have a single operational destroyer between us or even any way to get off the ground. The war is over for us until we get out of here—which could be never."

No one answered. Silence fell over the crew except for the fire crackling. English kept adding wood to it.

Lowery and Kilpatrick kept leaving the room and coming back with bigger and bigger pieces of furniture. The two men broke the furniture into pieces and gave it to English to burn.

Racer stared into the fire. The heat and flame patterns made her sleepy, but that conversation made her think too much to sleep.

A few hours later, Lowery left again and came back with an armload of blankets. He handed them out to everyone. "It's getting cold out there. We should bed down in here. We'll stay warmer."

Racer wrapped her blanket around her shoulders. People started to stretch out on the floor. She turned away to look for somewhere she could lie down, but she stopped herself when she saw Walker, Smythe, and Waterman sitting near her.

"You should all get some sleep, too," she told them. "Tomorrow is likely to be another crazy day."

Smythe opened her mouth to say something and shut it again. She didn't look away from the flames. "I never thought it would be like this. That first day was so awesome.....and then it all went down the drain after that."

"You did great, Rosa," Racer told her. "You've all kicked ass since this started. No one can fault your conduct. You've faced challenges more demanding than most pilots face in their entire careers. You've overcome every obstacle and you're here right now fighting the good fight. I've never been prouder to fly with anybody."

"Do you think we'll make it back, Gunny?" Walker asked. "Do you think we'll make it out of this?"

Racer had never heard him sound so uncertain. He'd always acted determined and hellbent to prove himself before now.

She had to take a deep breath before she answered. "I don't know what will happen to us. I don't know what will happen to Earth, either. I do know that everyone here will give their best to turn this war around and take back Earth. You're all a part of that. Joining the USF means accepting the dangers of war. We all signed up for that and it's never been more important that we stick by that commitment. The whole planet is counting on us. If we're the last of what's left of the USF, then we'll just keep fighting. That's all we can do.....but we aren't the last of the USF. There are plenty of other people out there working toward the same thing. We won't stop as long as even one of us can fight."

"I'm glad we got you as our gunny," Waterman murmured. "I wouldn't want to go with any of the others."

She smiled back at him. "I'm glad I got you, too, Airman. Wing 10 forever."

Smythe burst into a huge grin and Walker muttered, "Hell yeah," under his breath.

"Now lie down and get some sleep," Racer ordered. "We all need to be ready to kick some more ass tomorrow. Move over, Waterman. Make some room for Ash's legs."

The three pilots scooted around on the floor, wrapped their blankets around themselves, and stretched out.

Racer turned the other way looking for somewhere big enough for her to lie down. She rotated away from the fire and noticed almost everyone in the circle watching her and listening to their conversation.

Racer squirmed under their gaze. Captain English, his son, Radcliffe, Church, Towne, Morrison, Rickenbach, the two Durans, Frasier, the rebel officers, and everyone from the *Apache* stared at her with the firelight flickering on their cheeks.

She looked away and went back to curling up on the floor. She pulled the blanket over her shoulders and rested her head on the floor.

Another silence fell over the room. Racer shut her eyes and exhaustion caught up with her immediately.

She felt herself drifting off, but she couldn't help but see all those people watching her. She saw herself reflected in their gaze. They saw how much she'd changed since she first came on board the *Lightning Rod*.

She really hoped she said something just now that made it easier for her pilots to cope with this. They'd been on the job less than a week and they already found themselves in the middle of a war.

That wasn't much different from what happened to her and Wing 17. They'd barely learned to fly before the rebellion broke out.

Now she was a gunnery sergeant in charge of her own wing. She considered it a massive privilege to do her best for them, to encourage them, and to give them all the support they needed to get the job done.

They sure had a daunting job in front of them. They deserved her best. They needed every resource just to face this. Some of them probably wouldn't even survive.

She considered herself extremely lucky that she got to serve on Wing 17 with Captain English before he went back to being a captain. Those few weeks serving under him changed her life.

Maybe she would be able to be that for someone else. She would never be that to anyone if she'd stayed the way she was before. She hadn't been any good to anyone then, especially not to herself.

If she gave her life to help the USF retake Earth from the aliens, maybe her life would mean something.

She couldn't go back to the way she was before and she didn't want to. She wanted to be what all these people needed her to be. That was the best she could hope for out of this life.

Chapter 10

English sat up and frowned when he saw Admiral Simpson sitting by the fire in the *Apache's* conference room. "What are you doing up, Chris? You should be asleep."

"Someone had to stay awake and keep watch." Simpson picked up a fragment of Captain Corning's desk and put it on the fire to keep it going. "Did you get enough sleep, Sir?"

English winced. "You don't have to call me that. You outrank me."

"We're all subordinate to you. Someone has to be in charge and we've all seen what a mess this situation turns into when people don't follow your command."

English clamped his mouth shut to stop himself from arguing. He didn't want a bunch of generals, admirals, colonels, and other senior officers as his subordinates, but it sure looked like he was going to have them anyway.

"Thank you for supporting me the way you did," English murmured. "I really appreciate you having my back out there."

Simpson made a face. "You're the one who had my back. You had it in a much more perilous situation than this. I'll never forget that."

English decided to drop the subject. "So.....do the rebels have another secret stash of destroyers somewhere."

"I didn't know about the stash at Point Hope." Simpson stared down into the flames. "I guess I was never important enough to the rebel cause for the others to tell me their secrets."

"Maybe that's because they understood at a gut level that you're a good person."

Simpson didn't look up. He just stared into the flames. "I'm really sorry about your daughter. I'll never be able to live that down."

English didn't want to talk about Melanie, but Simpson was the one person who could give him some useful information. "Walk me through how it happened. You were with McClure when he recorded that message to send to me. Where were you when it happened? When did he separate you from Melanie? When would he have had time to hide her at Oaxaca?"

"We recorded the message at Point Hope. We had her there for most of the war. I don't know when he snuck her out. He didn't tell me anything." Simpson kept his eyes down. "I guess I was never anything more than his patsy. He must have realized I was gullible enough for him to make use of me. That's all I ever was to the rebel cause."

"There's still time for you to do the right thing. You're doing it now."

Simpson shrugged. "I guess so." He glanced around at the rest of the sleeping crew. "You always had a way of bringing out the best in people, Sailor."

"Or maybe I just got lucky and happened to wind up with the best people."

"No, you were always like this even back in your early days," Simpson replied. "We could have stuck you on any ship in the fleer and you would have accomplished the same things. You just have that effect on people."

English glanced over at Racer. She lay on the side of the room near Waterman, Smythe, and Walker.

That speech she gave them last night was really one for the record books. He couldn't have been prouder of how far she'd come if she'd graduated with honors from the USF Academy.

She'd come from nothing and grown to some of the finest officer material he'd ever met anywhere.

He knew now that nothing could stop her from accomplishing anything she set out to accomplish. She would probably become a captain, especially if this war kept knocking off everyone above her in rank.

He couldn't wait to see what she achieved, but right now, she was still just a young, green pilot with way too much responsibility on her shoulders.

She was too young and too inexperienced to be the gunnery sergeant of a combat fighter wing, but that's what she was.

He was still admiring her from afar when the rest of the crew started to stir. Everyone woke up and scowled into the fire for a long time.

They cheered up when Lowery and his crew raided the *Apache's* kitchens and brought out crateloads of food. They ate around the fire and then English put the fire out before everyone went outside.

The crew loaded up with as many supplies as they could carry to take back to the *Lightning Rod*. The sun shone and the wind didn't bite the way it did yesterday.

English ordered the crew to go from one dead alien to another. Everyone loaded up with as many alien weapons as possible and then the crew set off striking overland heading southeast.

English should have played it safe and headed for the coast, but he didn't want to waste valuable time. He wanted to get back to the

Lightning Rod as soon as possible. If he missed his mark, he would get to the coast and follow that back to the ship.

Everyone else in their party walked well and kept a good attitude. Dr. Cassidy had rigged up a makeshift crutch for Sergeant Grimes to hobble on, but Grimes still managed to keep up with everyone else.

English didn't see any conflicts between the former loyalists and the former rebels. Everyone in the crew acted like they really had put the rebellion behind them.

He only hoped it would stay that way for the rest of forever. He never wanted to hear about the rebellion again as long as he lived.

People handed each other food and water out of their supplies. Goods passed from hand to hand without regard to which crew anyone had been on before this disaster.

No one talked much, though. A cloud hung over the group and everyone faced their destination with grim determination.

Dr. Cassidy stayed near Grimes the whole time. The party had to stop more than once to let Grimes catch his breath, but he refused to sit down, to stop, or to rest for very long before he started hiking again. He wouldn't let his injury slow the party down.

The crew did miss their mark and hit the beach five miles north of the ship. They turned south and made it another two miles before three USF destroyers came pelting out of the east under heavy bombardment from two alien warships.

The destroyers rocketed across the Bering Sea coming from Siberia. Their engines howled at their highest pitch and they unloaded to the rear trying to drive the warships off.

The warships unleashed one crushing barrage after another and brought the three destroyers to a standstill five miles south of the crew's position. Everyone stopped walking to watch.

The destroyers tried to flee, but another volley from the aliens smashed one of their engines off. The ship staggered and her sister ship dodged behind her to defend her against the enemy.

The warships never stopped firing. They could shoot in dozens of directions at once without swiveling or adjusting position at all. They pounded the defending destroyer and held the third ship at bay at the same time.

The stricken ship tried to correct and move into line with her sister ship. They both opened fire on the enemy, but as usual, none of the USF destroyers could even scratch the aliens' hulls.

English couldn't see from here which of the aliens' spikes might be weapons or what purpose the others served. He couldn't really see where on the warships the shots were coming from. They seemed to come from all over the hull at once.

The defending ship took a wicked strike across the nose and the blow smacked her behind the ship she'd just been defending. The first stricken destroyer swerved to the front to guard her sister ship.

The aliens responded with impossible ferocity. Both warships unloaded on that one ship and imploded the whole front half of the fuselage. The ship detonated leaving only the rear tail section to plummet toward the ground.

The second ship dodged forward to take up the fight. One of the warships aimed a strategic blow and carved off the ship's port wing along with the engines on that side.

The ship tilted out of control. Its starboard engine struggled to reestablish the ship's attitude before another brutal smash in the tail brought that ship down, too. Now the third ship stood alone against both warships.

English couldn't watch this anymore. He sprinted forward, but the battle was still too far away.

He yanked his weapon forward and fired at the nearest warship. He hadn't been thinking of doing anything in particular. He just couldn't stand here and do nothing while those destroyers went down.

The instant he fired, he realized he was holding one of the alien weapons he'd taken from the *Apache*.

The gun erupted in his hands and the shot streaked skyward and hit one of the warships. It caused a small explosion on one of the spikes. USF guns couldn't damage the enemy, but the aliens' own weapons could, even if it only made a small difference.

That one shot triggered a matching response from everyone in the group. They all grabbed their weapons and opened fire on the warships. The crew set off at a run for the battle and everyone unloaded on the fly.

English targeted that one warship. He didn't care if he couldn't bring it down. He just wanted to damage it in any way possible no matter how small.

Andy and Radcliffe pulled alongside him and added their fire to his. The crew split into two with one group targeting this warship and the other group concentrating on the other ship.

Their attack worked to draw the warships away from the last destroyer, but everything went to shit when the warships turned their fire on the crew instead.

A single alien blast stuck the ground between the two groups. Grimes hadn't been able to shoot at the aliens because he had to use his hands to hold onto his crutch.

He'd limped and hopped after the crew and Dr. Cassidy stayed with him. They wound up between the two groups and the first alien blast landed right on top of them.

English yelled out and veered away from the explosion. He didn't have time to say anything before a deafening bombardment hammered the countryside all over the place.

He dove away and the whole crew scattered. He lost track of everyone in the confusion. He couldn't shoot anymore, and when he dove behind a swell for some protection, he found himself alone.

He crawled up behind the swell to see what was happening. He lay still watching the two warships finish off the last destroyer.

He brought his weapon forward to shoot again, but the warships delivered two combined concussions to the destroyer on both sides, imploded both her wings along with its engines, and then the two warships vanished off the map before anyone could do anything.

They disappeared before the damaged destroyer even started falling. She creaked and groaned in midair, tipped over onto her tail, and then somersaulted backward falling faster and faster.

She yawned onto her back picking up speed and then smashed into the ground flat on her back. English vaulted to his feet and charged the ship searching for any way to get on board to rescue the survivors.

The top half of the ship lay flattened and buried under the smoking remains of the ship's bottom half. Before he got near the wreckage, the cargo hold slammed open and dozens of people poured from inside.

They helped, supported, herded, and carried each other away from the wreckage just as English and the rest of his friends ran over.

English saw the ship's nameplate when he got nearer. She was the *Champion*. He barely registered that she was another rebel ship. All of that seemed so far in the past now.

"Is anyone else trapped inside?" English panted. "Is anyone still in there?"

A young man with blood running out of his brown hair waved toward the hold. "There's everyone who was in the top section. We don't know if anyone made it off the bridge, either."

"I'll go, Sir," Andy interrupted and he nodded toward the other two wrecked destroyers. "See if you can find anyone over there."

He grabbed Walker and Rickenbach and the three men strode into the hold. English made sure all the *Champion* survivors got clear of the wreck before he turned to the other two ships.

He circled what was left of the tail section first. Not enough of the ship remained even for him to identify which ship she'd been.

He went around to the end that had been attached to the ship, but when he looked inside, he saw the whole interior engulfed in flames. No one could have survived that.

He turned to the last ship. She was the *Cobalt*. She'd been a loyalist ship stationed at Antigua.

She'd lost control in midair and nose-dived face first into the ground before slamming down on her belly.

The whole front of the ship had been smashed in, but the back half was still relatively intact. People started coming out of that ship before he got there, too.

He made sure they made it out and joined up with the rest of the *Champion* crew. Then English took Morrison and Towne on board the *Cobalt* to make sure no one was left injured or trapped inside.

He made it as far as the fourth deck before he came to the damaged part of the ship. The forward ten decks had been compressed into a solid wall of crumpled metal. He couldn't even get through to the bridge or any of the other decks to check for survivors.

He finally turned away and went back outside. "The top half of the *Champion* is completely crushed," Andy reported. "This is everyone that's gonna make it out."

"Same with the *Cobalt*," English replied. "We gotta get everyone back to the *Lightning Rod.*"

He turned to both crews. None of them had any senior staff anymore.

He raised his voice to make himself heard. "I'm Captain English from the *Lightning Rod*. My fellow captains and I and these senior officers are taking command of your crews. We're taking you back to our ship where we can give you medical attention and shelter. Follow us. The ship isn't far away."

He turned away and both crews set off to follow him in one jumbled crowd. There must have been three hundred people here.

He walked back to the crater where the alien warship had fired on his crew. Nothing remained of either Grimes or the younger Dr. Cassidy.

English surveyed the crowd and the countryside just to make sure, but they were both gone. He didn't look forward to the conversation he was going to have with the older Dr. Cassidy when he got back to the ship, but he couldn't avoid it.

There were plenty of wounded in the *Champion* and *Cobalt* crews. He would need her more than ever now and these people wouldn't get medical treatment anywhere else around here.

Chapter 11

Racer stood back and watched the *Champion, Cobalt,* and *Apache* crews file on board the *Lightning Rod.* She and the other pilots stayed outside and kept watch on the countryside, but no aliens came back to bother the crew.

She supposed she better start thinking of all these people as the *Lightning Rod* crew. They were all in the same predicament.

Maybe some of these people would be engineers, mechanics, and maintenance people who could help repair the ship and get the *Lightning Rod* airborne again.

Racer no longer held out any hope of the *Lightning Rod* going back into battle against the aliens. Someone would have to be stupid to fly one single ship against such a powerful enemy.

The crew just might get lucky and end up back at some USF base somewhere. That would be good enough for her.

She waited for the crowd to disperse. Then she and her fellow pilots had to wait again for Sergeant Morrison and Corporal Towne to take all three crews on board the ship and assign them quarters.

By the time the stairs cleared, all the senior officers had left. Captain English and his closest associates went back to the bridge along with Commander Lowery. He was the only senior officer from any of the three crashed destroyers who survived.

Racer, Walker, Smythe, Laughlin, the two Durans, Rickenbach, and Waterman went to the *Lightning Rod's* enlisted mess. A bunch of pilots from the new crews were already in there.

The *Lightning Rod* didn't have a cooking crew in the kitchen anymore, so the new pilots went through the kitchen supply rooms, helped themselves to whatever they wanted, and sat down at the tables to eat it.

"Maybe I should do something to stop them," Smythe remarked. "I don't like this."

"You aren't a cook anymore," Racer told her. "You're a pilot now, and since no one is cooking for these people, they have to eat somehow. We all do."

"Besides, if anyone is going to do anything, it would be Sergeant Morrison," Walker pointed out.

Waterman sighed. "I guess Morrison is our new security chief, now that Grimes is gone."

"At least we can trust Morrison." Laughlin made a face at the people around him. "Some of these people were rebels until yesterday. How do we know they're as keen to put the rebellion behind them as we are?"

"None of these people were rebels," Rickenbach told him. "No one below the rank of captain had anything to do with planning or carrying out the rebellion. These people were just doing their jobs. The orders about who to attack and what to do came down from the top. None of these people probably even realized who they were shooting at."

"I'm leaving this one with the captain," Sean remarked. "I don't understand this shit and I don't want to. He's the one making the decision to take these people on board. If it's good enough for him, it's good enough for me."

"I guess so," Laughlin muttered, but he didn't stop scowling at the *Champion* crewmen.

They certainly made themselves at home. They treated the *Lightning Rod* as if it was their own ship—which Racer supposed it was now.

She saw plenty of the *Champion* crew approaching, socializing, and laughing with *Cobalt* and *Apache* crewmen.

The *Champion* personnel seemed as friendly and down to earth as anyone she'd ever met—not that she'd actually met any of them.

Still, something in the way they just moved right in set her nerves on edge. She wouldn't have moved into someone else's ship and just started helping herself to the food out of their pantry—at least, she hoped she wouldn't. These people didn't even ask permission.

What were they supposed to do—go hungry?

The situation bothered her so much that she wound up leaving the mess. All her fellow pilots stayed behind.

She went down to the flight deck even though there wasn't a single bird, pilot, or mechanic on it. She stepped out of the stairwell and got a surprise when she found Lieutenant Frasier standing at his desk.

"What are you doing down here, Lieutenant?" she asked. "There's no squadron for you to command."

He waved at his computers. "These are working again. I just thought I'd take a look. I need something to do. What are you doing down here, Gunny? There's nothing for you to do down here, either."

"I know. I guess I just need somewhere to be."

"I hear you." He turned to his machines. "We might all wind up doing a whole lot of waiting before something happens."

He went back to work. That left her to.....do whatever she was gonna do. She wandered over to the right side of the deck where Wing

10 had been. The place sure felt lonely without all the birds and pilots around.

She had nothing else to do, so she went through every tool chest in the whole wing and organized them all. She found food wrappers in some of them, dead bugs in others, wads of tangled hair, and plenty of broken tools that didn't even work anymore.

The job took hours, but she didn't care. Frasier left long before she finished.

She opened Rickenbach's old tool chest and found it perfectly clean and immaculately organized. Every tool shone in its proper place. She burst into a grin when she saw it. She should have known.

She pushed it away and pulled forward the chest that Harlow Babbitt had been using before Wing 8 moved to the other side of the deck.

She dreaded what she would find inside it and he didn't disappoint her. She had to dig through mounds of nameless debris and even a few rotten, moldy old crusts of prehistoric sandwiches before she found any actual tools.

She grimaced and turned away in disgust before she buckled down and started cleaning it. She was in the middle of the top tray when the stairwell doors opened.

Two young pilots came out of it. They were both men and they both belonged to the *Champion* crew—the former *Champion* crew.

She pretended not to see them step behind Frasier's desk and fiddle with his computers. Then they went over to Wing 8's side of the deck before they approached her.

The first one was taller than the other with glossy black hair, black eyes, and a wild, crazy, easy grin that reminded her of Laughlin. This guy slouched when he walked and he moved his arms in a swinging way that almost made her think he hesitated to approach her.

He didn't stop grinning, though. She couldn't figure out if he was grinning because he was nervous or because he was just over-the-top delighted to see her—God only knew why.

The other guy was shorter with a heavier build. He had a thick neck, a heavy jawline, and a powerful, almost brutal presence.

He had a very intense way of holding eye contact with her. His gaze would have reminded her of Rickenbach except that this guy had a much more challenging way of doing it.

"Hey, Gunny!" the first guy called out. "Hard at work as usual?"

"Or not as usual." She bent over Babbitt's tool chest. "What are you two doing down here? There aren't any birds for you to work on or to fly. You can go off duty."

"We aren't here to fly or to work on any birds," the second guy replied. "We came down here to talk to you."

He had a much more straightforward way of talking. He didn't strike her as hesitant about anything—certainly not about talking to her.

She stopped what she was doing, straightened up, and gauged both men more closely. "What do you want to talk to me for? You don't even know me."

The first guy stuck out his hand. "I'm Manuel Sandoval and this is Logan McKee.... and you're Gunny Racer Franz. Everyone on board talks about you."

Racer bent over the tool chest so she wouldn't have to shake his hand. "I doubt that."

"You're in charge of the fighter wing," he went on. "You know all the pilots. You were the one Captain English sent down the coast to see about getting the *Lightning Rod's* birds in the air. He must trust you a lot if he did that."

She looked up at both of them. She didn't ask how he found out about that.

She also didn't tell him *why* Captain English sent her and not any other pilot from her wing. Whoever these two guys were, they'd certainly been busy little beavers since they came on board.

"So what do you want to talk to me about?" she asked. She really didn't want to know. She knew now that it wouldn't be anything good.

"Well....." He dragged the word out extra long. "The *Champion* crew is here.....and the *Apache* crew is here.......and a bunch of officers from the rebel command are here.......and the younger Captain English is here......It just seems like we should be the ones in charge, not the loyalists. They were already losing the war before the aliens invaded."

"As soon as Captain English gets the *Lightning Rod* squadron up and running, he'll bring the birds back here," McKee added. "He'll have to fly those birds with pilots. That's us. Then we can steer this war where we want it to go. No one will be able to stop us."

Racer looked up again, but she was so surprised that she didn't know how to react right away. Captain English would have known exactly what to say to these men, but words failed her.

"You.....want to use the *Lightning Rod* squadron to......" She trailed off. Her mind staggered when she finally actually realized what they were suggesting.

"We have the pilots from the *Apache* with us. We just need someone on the inside of the *Lightning Rod* squadron to turn the tide. Everyone on the squadron listens to you. You can convince them that this is the right thing to do."

"And what would I say to them to convince them that this is the right thing to do?" she asked. This conversation was spiraling in directions she didn't want to think about.

"Just what I just said," Sandoval replied. "We can steer the war back the way it was going before the invasion. The loyalists would have been defeated and we could have reformed the USF the way it's supposed to be."

Racer shifted her weight from one foot to the other. "So let me get this straight. You've been on the *Lightning Rod* for a matter of hours and you've already talked the *Apache* pilots into going along with this. Did you talk to Hughes and Hoskins from the *Buckingham Palace*—or Lieutenant Rickenbach? Who else have you talked to the *Lightning Rod* squadron?"

Her mind went into a tailspin thinking about all the possibilities. She could just imagine the reaction Sean, Ezra, Hughes, Walker, and the other pilots would have when they heard about this.

She should have been more outraged by the suggestion that these pilots might actually restart the rebellion at a time like this—when the fate of Earth hung in the balance. If the aliens had their way, there wouldn't be any USF left for anyone to reform.

Then she remembered Rickenbach's comments in the enlisted mess earlier. These two pilots had been in the *Champion* squadron until just a few hours ago.

These pilots hadn't been in any command post. They hadn't been involved in making any decisions or even been party to any strategic discussion with anyone steering the rebellion in any direction whatsoever.

The whole ludicrous idea fascinated her so much that she didn't even have the wherewithal to tell these two men exactly what she thought of them. She became intrigued to find out all the intricate details of their scheme, so she kept them talking.

"Our other people are talking to the rest of the squadron," McKee told her. "Once we get their answers, we'll know better where we stand."

"But we can't do anything until Captain English brings the *Lightning Rod's* birds back," Sandoval went on. "You were there when your engineer was working on them. How close do you think he was? How long do we have before we might need to act?"

She pursed her lips while she decided how to answer. "Hmm. Hard to say. He couldn't figure out what was wrong with them, so I'd say we have at least a week."

Sandoval's and McKee's jaws dropped. "A week!" Sandoval gasped. "That long?!"

Racer nodded. "Lieutenant Hammil is working on them, but he might not even get them done in that time. I don't know. You'd have to ask him."

The two pilots exchanged glances. Sandoval gulped and McKee cleared his throat. "Well....Gunny.....thank you for your help. I hope we can count on you."

"Let me know what the other pilots and gunnies say," she told him. "Once you get them on board, then I'll know whether this plan has any hope of succeeding."

"Oh, it will succeed," Sandoval exclaimed. "We'll make sure of it. We worked too hard to bring the rebellion to a successful conclusion. We can't let this alien invasion stop us from finishing the job. We have these birds. We would be stupid not to use them."

McKee saluted Racer. She just stared at him in stupid shock until he and Sandoval left the flight deck.

Neither of them had saluted her when they first introduced themselves. They didn't call her Ma'am or use any other military courtesy. They treated this conversation like a casual chat between equals.

What in the name of God were they thinking? She seriously wondered who they'd been talking to in the enlisted mess. It couldn't have been anyone from the *Lightning Rod* or *Buckingham Palace* squadrons. She would never believe that.

No one from either squadron would have given these guys reason to think they could talk her over to their side. They must have just asked around to find out who the pilots and gunnies were.

None of these conspirators knew anything about the *Lightning Rod* squadron. They couldn't have if they actually believed anyone from the *Lightning Rod* squadron would ever support the rebellion.

Chapter 12

M att Radcliffe had his back to the bridge door when he heard it open behind him. He looked up from the XO's station, glanced over his shoulder, and froze when Racer Franz walked onto the bridge.

"Gunny?" Radcliffe asked. "Can I help you with something? What are you doing on the bridge?"

"Sir....I was hoping I could speak to Captain English.....if he's available."

"He's in a meeting with Church, Andy, and some of the senior officers." He frowned at her even more deeply. "Is something wrong?"

"Um.....Sir.....would you mind.....?" Her eyes darted to the side. Lieutenant Eismann, Commander Lowery, and Lieutenant Rickenbach sat at different stations around the bridge working on their controls.

She finally summoned the nerve to look Radcliffe in the eye. "Would you mind if I speak to you.....in private, Sir?"

"Um....okay." Radcliffe thought fast. Racer had certainly distinguished herself recently. Radcliffe had started to understand why English thought so highly of her.

He left the XO's station, crossed the bridge to the captain's ready room, and pushed the door open. "Come in here."

She stepped past him and he shut the door behind himself, moved behind the desk, and faced her. "What's this all about, Gunny?"

"I was just working on the flight deck just now and two of the *Champion* pilots came down there to talk to me. They said they've been going through the *Champion* and *Apache* crews getting people on board who want to restart the rebellion. They have the idea that, when Captain English brings the *Lightning Rod's* birds back, these pilots will take control of our birds and use them to steer the war where they want it to go—which I assume means restart the rebellion. They say the loyalists would have lost the war and the rebels could have reformed the USF the way it should have been reformed. They say they won't let the alien invasion stop them from finishing what they started and the *Lightning Rod's* birds are too valuable a resource to waste—seeing as how these birds are their only chance to accomplish their goals....Sir."

She blurted this all out in one breathless rush. Radcliffe stared at her trying to take it all in.

She waited for him to say anything, and when he didn't respond right away, she started up again.

"They say they're canvasing all the pilots on board. They say they're sending people out to talk to Sean, Ezra, Rickenbach, Hughes, Hoskins, the new Wing 10 pilots—everybody. I don't know who these people have on their program already. They made it sound like they had everyone from the *Apache* and the *Champion*. Don't ask me how they're doing all of this so fast—unless they're pulling shit out of their asses.....Sir. They made it sound like a done deal....and they wanted to know what I saw when I went with Lieutenant Hammil to assess the birds. These guys wanted to know how close he was to getting the birds airborne so they knew how much time they had to prepare their.....whatever it is."

Radcliffe gulped to get his throat working. "Thank you, Gunny. I really appreciate you telling me this."

"So.....you'll tell Captain English? How will you stop these guys from taking our birds?"

"I won't tell Captain English," Radcliffe replied. "You will."

Racer froze and all the color drained from her face, but right then, the door burst open and English barged in with Andy, Church, Simpson, Morrison, and Halstead.

English called over his shoulder, "And organize a security team to go down to the....." He stopped in his tracks when he saw Radcliffe and Racer already in his ready room.

English's eyes darted back and forth between them. "Is something going on?"

Radcliffe moved his head to one side. "General Halstead and Admiral Simpson, would you mind giving us a minute?"

Simpson and Halstead left the room. Church shut the door on them. Now only English, Andy, Church, Morrison, and Radcliffe remained to face Racer. She cringed in front of them.

"Go on, Gunny," Radcliffe prompted. "Tell Captain English what you just told me."

She had to open and close her mouth more than once before she got her voice working. Then she launched into the whole sordid tale.

"I wasn't sure what to say, so I told them to let me know what the other pilots said before I committed myself....Sir," she finished.

The four captains stared at her in silence for a minute. Radcliffe saw their attention making her uncomfortable, so he told her. "Take a seat, Gunny."

She glanced over at him, but she was too stunned by her own audacity to respond. She didn't even seem to hear him.

English finally shook himself out of his trance and moved behind the desk. Radcliffe stepped out of the way to make room for him.

English turned around very slowly and finally looked up at Racer. "Thank you for telling us, Gunny. You're dismissed. We'll take it from here."

"What should I do if they come around asking about it again, Sir?" she asked. "Should I go along with it or should I tell them to take a flying leap?"

He cracked a very slight smile and immediately bit it back. "I'll leave that up to you, Gunny. Whatever you tell them I'm sure will be perfect."

She opened her mouth to argue and then changed her mind. She mumbled, "Yes, Sir," saluted everyone in the room, and left.

"Idiots," Andy growled as soon as she left. "These gasheads must not have a clue what the alien invasion is really like if they're planning something like this."

"It doesn't matter because they are never gonna get their hands on our birds," English replied.

"No one is flying our birds because they're non-operational," Radcliffe pointed out. "The whole thing is a non-issue."

"It's an issue if we have rebel crewmen planning on mutinying against us while we're trying to mount some kind of defense against the aliens," Church pointed out. "We can't allow that."

"It's really simple," English replied. "All we have to do is make sure none of these pilots ever get into a position to fly our birds." He turned to Morrison. "Talk to all the *Lightning Rod* pilots—all the pilots we know we can trust—including Frasier and Rickenbach. Find out who's been talking to whom and we'll transfer all the *Champion* and *Apache* pilots to our cannon battery. That will take the pilots out of danger and it will give them an eyeful of what the alien invasion is really like. Maybe that will wake them up. Racer must be right about these guys not knowing what's going on out there."

"But the *Champion* was in battle against the aliens right before she crashed," Morrison pointed out.

"That's exactly why the pilots wouldn't have seen," English replied. "The *Champion* wasn't flying any of her birds against the aliens. The pilots would have been locked down with the rest of the crew. They may have been locked down the entire time—which explains why they think the rebellion is still the most important thing."

"So that's it?" Andy countered. "You aren't going to do anything about these conspirators?"

"I can't do anything right now," English replied. "I need every hand I can get."

"We aren't going anywhere anytime soon, either," Radcliffe pointed out. "If the birds don't fly and we don't fly, it will all come to nothing."

"It will all come to nothing until we do fly," Andy countered. "Then these conspirators will be running loose in the USF with access to all the ships and weaponry they could ask for."

"I have a better idea." English went over to the door, opened it, and called out onto the bridge. "Would you gentlemen step in here, please?"

He held the door open for Simpson and Halstead. Radcliffe, Church, Andy, and Morrison crowded together on the other side of the room so the two senior officers could stand in front of English's desk.

He gave them a quick rundown on Racer's report. "You two plus Chambers, Schroder, Roderick, Levitt, and Thorburn were in command of the rebel campaign," he told them. "Now's your chance to make good on your promises to move past this rebellion. Sergeant

Morrison here is going to identify the conspirators. I want you and your fellow officers to go through the ship person by person and bring them around to our way of seeing things. You can inform them that the rebellion is over and why. These people will be much more valuable to us fighting on our side. We would only weaken our own position if we tried to get rid of them all."

Simpson frowned. "But they're only pilots. How did they find out about anything? How could they get into a position to care so much about the rebellion? It makes no sense."

"Who knows why they're doing anything? Just talk to them and make them see reason. We don't have time to deal with any insurrections or conflicts in our own crew."

Halstead and Simpson left. As soon as the door closed, Church spoke up. "Excuse me for saying so, Sir, but this is a big mistake."

"What is, Ted?" English asked.

"Trusting those guys." Church waved toward the door. "They're rebel commanders. They could stab you in the back and use this opportunity to turn these conspirators against you."

English looked up. "You think so?"

"Of course! These officers are only here because they wouldn't have survived if they went anywhere else. They've been defying your orders ever since. They could see this as their chance to take control of the *Lightning Rod* and rejoin the rebellion. Hell, the senior officers might be the ones who started this conspiracy."

English leaned back in his chair. "I don't see it that way."

"Obviously!" Church countered. "You've given these guys way too much rope."

"And they've used that rope to help us," English pointed out. "Simpson...."

"Have any of the others helped you?" Church interrupted. "I know what you said about Simpson. I'm talking about the others. Of course they haven't helped you. They've interfered and argued and contradicted you at every step."

"Well, I am their subordinate."

"You can't think like that," Church countered. "You're the one who put yourself in command of them. You have to enforce your authority and you can't trust them to handle this conspiracy. They could use it against you if they didn't set it in motion themselves."

English turned to Andy and Radcliffe. "What do you two think? Do you think I'm making a mistake by trusting these officers?"

"Church has a point," Andy replied. "You have to admit that. None of these officers would be going along with your orders if they didn't have to."

"And you don't think any of them has the brains to realize that the rebellion is over and finished?" English asked. "Apart from Simpson?"

"I'm saying you need to take better precautions," Church went on. "I trust Lowery more than I trust these guys."

"Lowery doesn't have the same rank," English pointed out. "These officers would have more pull with the pilots involved."

"Lowery probably has more pull with the *Apache* crew," Andy pointed out. "If you want someone to convince them, he'd be the one—not some general or admiral."

English turned to Radcliffe. "What do you think, Matt? What would you do in my place?"

"I think there's a better way of dealing with this," Radcliffe replied. "It's like you said before. None of these conspirators are going anywhere as long as our birds and the *Lightning Rod* are all grounded. I say you maneuver these guys into a position where they see firsthand what the aliens are capable of—but since we don't have any weapons systems, you'd have to come up with something more direct."

"What did you have in mind?" English asked.

"You put these conspirators on the ground against the aliens. The next time the aliens come around, you use these conspirators to fight the aliens. If one of the conspirators gets hit, we haven't lost anything. If they don't get hit, they'll see what we're up against and all thought of turning our birds against USF targets will vanish out of their minds."

Andy chuckled. "That's cold-blooded. I love it."

"You would actually put these guys in the line of fire—against an enemy you know they can't defeat?" English exclaimed. "That would be illegal. It would be pre-meditated murder."

"Actually," Church cut in, "the USF Uniform Code of Military Conduct states that the penalty for mutiny in wartime is instant execution. Even if you shot them all in the head the way you executed Filmore, you would only be giving them what they deserve."

"Someone is going to have to face the aliens the next time they come around," Radcliffe went on. "We're a lot more likely to meet them on the ground than we are in the air. The *Lightning Rod's* weapons systems aren't even working. Assigning the conspirators to the battery won't accomplish anything. You asked what I would do in your place. This is what I would do. I would get Morrison here to draw up the list of names and assign the conspirators to the front lines. If you really want to be compassionate, you can give the conspirators alien weapons to use against the ground troops. If that doesn't convince them, nothing will."

"If you want to transfer these jackasses to some other department," Morrison interjected, "you can transfer them to mine. That would be the quickest, easiest, most straightforward way to put them on the front line. My teams will be the first to face the enemy anyway. Give the conspirators to me, Sir. I'll clean them up for you. When I get through with them, rebellion will be the last thing on their minds."

Chapter 13

E nglish stepped outside the *Lightning Rod's* cargo hold and watched Morrison running his new security team through their training drills.

They advanced across the field, fell on their stomachs, crawled a hundred yards, pivoted onto their knees, and fired at a bunch of targets Morrison had set up.

Morrison had drawn up a list of fifteen names of people who'd been going around trying to recruit pilots, gunnery sergeants, and a few lieutenants to take control of the *Lightning Rod* and her squadron. Now they were all out there on the course trying to cope with being under Morrison's command.

Church, Andy, and Radcliffe stopped on either side of English and all four men watched. Morrison strode up and down the line yelling at everyone that what they were doing wasn't good enough. Then he told them all to go back to the start and do it again.

"You really are a sadist, Matt." Andy clapped Radcliffe on the shoulder. "I couldn't have come up with a better punishment for these dopes."

"I wasn't trying to punish them," Radcliffe countered. "I just wanted to neutralize them."

"No one besides the four of us knows that our birds are operational," English added, "and no one is gonna find out until we're ready to use them. When we do, we'll send our own squadron down there to fly the birds against the enemy."

"Don't fly our birds against the enemy until you can figure out a way to do it without our birds getting destroyed within the first five seconds," Church told him.

"What do you take me for, Ted?" English asked. "Why do you think I want to keep it a secret?"

"Our weapons system is back online, too," Radcliffe reported. "Hammil just finished it this morning."

"Leave that inactive, too," English replied. "Don't do anything at least until we get the hull repaired."

No spoke for a few minutes while Morrison sent his new goons through their course again. He was hands down the most ruthless drill instructor English had ever seen.

Morrison stood right next to his new team members and bellowed in their ears while they did their best to fire at their targets.

"If you can't hit your target now while you're lying safe and sound on the ground, you won't be able to hit them in battle!" he roared. "Am I distracting you, Airman McKee? Am I talking too loud for you? How do you think you're going to hit your target when you have explosions going off in your ears?"

Andy laughed again. "Man! I'm sure glad he wasn't at the Academy when I went through. I would have packed up and gone home."

"He's laying it on extra thick for these morons," Church explained. "Al is a really nice guy when you get to know him."

English found himself laughing, too. "I can personally attest that he's downright terrifying if he doesn't like you."

The new security recruits made it to the end of their course and Morrison barked at them even more loudly if that was possible. "That was terrible—absolutely terrible! Line up here! I hope you all have life insurance. None of you could hit the broad side of a barn. God only knows how you got through Basic Training. Plan on being back out here at six o'clock tomorrow morning, and if I see even one wrinkle in your uniforms, you'll all be cleaning the toilets on the whole ship for a month."

"Aw, come on, Sarge!" Sandoval groaned.

Morrison pounced on him instantly, stormed up to Sandoval, and bellowed in the guy's face. "Do you have a problem with me, Airman?! Do you have a problem being under my command?! Just for that, you can clean the toilets on the whole ship starting tonight—and you better have them finished by six o'clock tomorrow and be out here with bells on or you'll be dreaming about cleaning toilets as a blissful fantasy compared to the job I'll give you next!"

English and his three companions laughed, but they did it quietly. More of the recruits groaned, but Morrison let it slide. He dismissed them and they nearly collapsed in relief when they turned toward the *Lightning Rod* to go back on board the ship.

They dragged their feet and let their weapons hang from their limp arms. Morrison grinned at English and the others behind the recruits' backs. Then Morrison went through the course picking up all his targets.

English and the other three captains stepped aside to let the recruits come back on board. English did his best not to smile when the recruits approached him, but Andy didn't bother. He smirked at them in outright triumph. He barely stopped short of actually laughing in their faces.

English couldn't tell if any of the new recruits noticed the captains' reactions or, if the recruits did notice, they understood what it meant. He'd gotten reports from a dozen other *Lightning Rod* pilots about the conspirators approaching them and trying to swing them, too.

English turned back toward the cargo hold to go inside, too. He had a ton of work to do before the *Lightning Rod* would be ready to fly against the aliens—if she would ever be ready to fly against the aliens.

He had been becoming more and more convinced that Church's plan was the soundest. What was the point in even lifting the *Lightning Rod* off the ground if the aliens were only going to flatten the ship again the minute she took wing?

He didn't have a clue how to fight this enemy and he hadn't heard back from anyone on the USF Command staff. No one had responded to his attempts to communicate with USF bases.

He really hoped that didn't mean the USF was down for the count. There might be no one left in command from either the rebel or the loyalist side. Racer might be right and the *Lightning Rod* could be the last ship left on the field. He really hoped not.

He was just about to go back inside when an ear-splitting thump distracted him. He glanced up at the sky just as three alien warships zipped into view.

They didn't stop near the *Lightning Rod*. They came to a halt a few miles away—where the *Champion* and the *Cobalt* went down.

The warships floated there for a second and then fired their transport beam to the surface.

"They're landing ground troops!" Morrison spun around, dropped all his targets, and charged his recruits. "Let's go! Get your weapons up! We gotta defend the ship!"

"But Sarge......," McKee began.

"What the hell do you think I've been training you for?!" Morrison thundered. "Get your weapons up and let's go! They could be coming for us next!"

He gestured for them to follow him out onto the field. They hesitated and then raised their weapons.

Radcliffe spun the other way, raced into the cargo hold, and hit the emergency alarm by the elevator. It set off a howling siren all over the ship to call every available hand to defend the *Lightning Rod*.

English, Church, and Andy bolted inside after him and all four attacked the weapons locker. The new alien guns hung inside along with the USF weapons. All four men took the alien weapons first.

The four of them stormed back outside just as every able-bodied crewman on board came pouring out of the stairwell. They all ran to the weapons locker and the alien weapons vanished first.

Morrison had already gotten his recruits fifty yards away from the ship by the time English and the other captains got there.

English advanced to catch up with them. Morrison seemed to take that as a sign to continue. He kept striding out onto the field heading toward the alien ground troops.

English heard lieutenants and gunnery sergeants giving orders to the crew behind his back. He could just imagine everyone who was back there.

The crew crossed half a mile of swells before they got near enough to see the enemy. Hundreds of alien ground troops surrounded the *Champion* and *Cobalt* wrecks.

"What are they looking for?" Church muttered. "There's no one there."

"Maybe they want to study us," English suggested. "Maybe they want to take samples and find out how we work and how we're made. That's what I'd do if I was in their position."

Morrison just kept walking. He didn't look like he planned to stop until he got right up in the enemy's face.

"Hold your position here, Sergeant!" English called out. "Don't go any closer."

Morrison signaled his recruits to stop there, but he kept snapping orders at them the whole time. "Line up here! Keep your weapons up! If they come after us, you'll be the first people they meet! Be ready to take down as many of them as you can! Got that?"

English couldn't see the conspirators' reactions, but they stood up straight and kept their weapons shouldered. He could just imagine what must be going through their heads.

English was quite certain it didn't have anything to do with re-belling against the *Lightning Rod* staff or restarting the civil conflict between rebels and loyalists.

The aliens took a long time to search the three crashed ships. English saw their small black shapes going into and out of both cargo holds. He didn't see anything the aliens might be doing there.

He stiffened when the aliens left the crash site and set off marching overland straight for the *Lightning Rod*.

"Stand fast!" Morrison bellowed. "Stand your ground and don't let them near the ship!"

English brought his weapon to his shoulder, but it didn't feel the same as a USF rifle. It was an alien weapon.

"Fire on the ships!" he ordered. "Target the nearest ship and fire at will!"

He jerked up his weapon and everyone else opened fire at the same time. They all focused their fire on the closest warship.

The same thing happened. Each gun burst created a tiny explosion on the warship's surface—at least, the explosion looked tiny from this distance.

All those shots combined worked wonders. More and more blasts erupted from the ship's side. The plume of fire roiled and expanded until it detonated with a colossal boom.

The ship staggered. The other two warships veered out of position and opened fire on the *Lightning Rod* crew.

The first shot smashed straight into the conspirators the way Radcliffe said it would. The rest of the crew scattered the way they did before. English dove aside and hid behind a swell.

"Keep firing!" he bellowed over the noise. "Target those ships and bring them down!"

He couldn't tell if anyone heard him, but when he flipped onto his back and fired at the next ship in line, a dozen other guns erupted nearby.

They all slammed into the same ship and that one started to disintegrate, too. The first warship groaned, tried to steady itself, and then listed hard to the left as continuous blasts ejected from its sides.

The explosions kept escalating and cascading until they consumed the warship's outer skin. English was still shooting at the second ship when the first one plummeted a thousand feet, but it exploded before it hit the ground.

He cut his fire to stare at the glowing fireball. He did it. *They* did it. The *Lightning Rod* crew destroyed one of the enemy warships.

He had begun to question if anything could destroy these aliens. Now he saw confirmation right in front of his eyes that it was possible. Earth would win this war and get rid of these invaders. It was only a question of how.

That realization flooded him with unstoppable power. He snapped up his weapon and unloaded on the second ship.

More guns went off all over the place. The same energy shots sizzled upward from swells all over the field. English couldn't see from his position who was firing from where.

It didn't matter. All those shots smashed through the enemy's hull and that ship started to go up in flames, too.

The two remaining warships fired into the ground again and again. The *Lightning Rod* crew must have spread out across the whole field.

The warships sprayed their fire all over the countryside, but nothing stopped the crewmen from firing from everywhere at once.

English counted down the seconds before the aliens fired at him next. It was bound to come sooner or later. He just had to keep on firing and firing and firing until the very last second.

A concussion went off on the second ship and part of its hull evaporated in flames. The ship zipped backward and then pitched hard onto its side. It stayed aloft, but it stopped firing.

The third and last ship kept bombarding the countryside in all directions. Crashes and booms echoed in English's ear, but he didn't pay any attention.

He fired at the third ship, but this time, he was the only one who did. Was anyone else left alive out here?

He squashed his finger on the trigger even harder and gritted his teeth to keep on shooting until the bitter end. He barely got the first shot off before the warship turned on him, fired into his swell, and blasted him to pieces with one hit.

Chapter 14

Radcliffe charged away from the battle, dove behind a swell, and rolled over. He pulled his weapon to his shoulder and fired into the second warship.

More energy blasts erupted from all over the field. They combined and carved a breach in the alien warship's hull, but just then, the third ship fired into the swell in front of Radcliffe.

Dirt plastered his face and he sprang to his feet to run for it. He bolted to the next swell, jumped behind it, and landed on top of Ted Church crouching there.

"Watch it!" Church snapped.

"Sorry!" Radcliffe panted and scrambled to duck behind the swell.

Church glared at him and then squinted up at the remaining two ships. The second one was already starting to lose control.

"Where is everybody?" Radcliffe gasped.

"Out there somewhere." Church turned onto his stomach and stole a peek over the swell. "No one is shooting anymore. If we shoot now, the aliens will target us."

"Are you saying no one is alive out there?" Radcliffe hissed.

"Of course not! They're hiding just like we are."

Radcliffe opened his mouth to say something else and stopped himself. He'd been working with Church for a week since the *Light-*

ning Rod and the *Buckingham Palace* had crashed out here on the remote Alaska coastline.

Radcliffe hadn't gotten as close to Church as Radcliffe had gotten to Andy. Radcliffe couldn't exactly call Church a friend. They weren't even on a first-name basis.

Radcliffe vacillated about what to say next—or if he should say anything at all. Church had the kind of commanding personality that Radcliffe associated with USF captains.

Radcliffe didn't have that kind of personality. He liked his people too much. He would never be as stern as Church.

Church kept shooting threatening glances over the top of the swell.

When nothing else happened, he flattened himself against it on his back, clutched his weapon, allowed himself to relax, and looked at Radcliffe for the first time.

"How did you get over here?" Church asked.

"The same way you did. I ran away."

"We should get back to the *Lightning Rod,*" Church muttered under his breath.

"And leave all these people stranded out here?" Radcliffe countered. "You're crazy."

Church gave him a hard look. "Do you have something you want to say to me, Captain?"

Radcliffe's eyes popped. "What?! No! What would I have to say to you?"

"You have some beef with me," Church went on. "It's been eating you up since day one."

"Day....." Radcliffe blinked rapidly trying to understand this. "I don't have a beef with you! Are you kidding? You've been on the *Buckingham Palace* while I've been on my back in...."

"That's what I'm talking about. That right there. You resent me for being English's XO."

"What are you talking about?!" Radcliffe fired back and had to check himself to lower his voice. "I don't have any issue with you being English's XO. It isn't like I could do it while I was wired up in traction. Someone had to be his XO and no one is more qualified than you. You're a hell of a lot more qualified than I am."

Church scowled at him. Radcliffe went through some rapid mental gymnastics to comprehend what was really bothering Church.

Radcliffe took a deep breath. "Look, man. Things are messy right now. You've always been polite to me and even congenial, but we've never been friends. You've always held me at a distance even when we've been working together on the same bridge."

"I!" Church countered. "I held *you* at a distance?! I never held you at a distance. You were the one holding *me* at a distance. I always assumed it was because you wanted to be English's XO and now neither of us outranks the other. You and me and Andy are all basically his XOs."

Radcliffe shut his mouth to steady himself. He had to think. "I was thinking the same thing about you. You always treated me like a subordinate even though we both hold the same rank....."

"I never treated you like a subordinate!" Church insisted. "You were the one treating *me* like a subordinate."

"I thought you were acting so formal toward me out of some competitive hostility over our positions compared to English."

"Hell, no!" Church snapped. "If anyone is gonna be English's XO, it's Andy."

"That's what I'm saying," Radcliffe explained. "I feel the same way, but instead, all three of them are somehow equals and none of us outranks each other. It would be easier if English just told us who he wants as his XO...."

"You know he'll never do that," Church pointed out. "He doesn't want to upset any of us by elevating one of us above the other two."

Radcliffe shrugged. "I just thought the whole subject just kind of got lost in the confusion."

"So....you don't feel competitive toward me?" Church asked.

"Not at all!" Radcliffe insisted. "What is there to feel competitive about? I wouldn't care if I was your subordinate. I wouldn't mind that in the slightest."

Church frowned. "You wouldn't?"

"Of course not. I can't think of anyone I'd rather be subordinate to except for English. You're beyond qualified—way more qualified than I am."

Church frowned some more and then shrugged. "Oh. I didn't realize."

"Dude, I don't give a damn who English's XO is. I never thought it was me. It's like you say. If anyone is going to do it, it will be Andy."

Church nodded at nothing, stole a glance over the swell, and then settled back down again. "Sorry about that."

"Forget it. So what do you want to do about this?"

Church looked over the swell again, but he only did it for a second. He was about to sit down again when he jolted upright. "The aliens are on the move again."

Radcliffe crawled over to lie down next to Church. Radcliffe never dreamed in a million years he would have that conversation with Church, but in the end, Radcliffe supposed it was bound to happen sooner or later.

He didn't have time to think about that because, as Church said, the aliens were on the move. The ground troops had recovered from two of their ships being destroyed. The troops reformed in ranks and started their unstoppable march across the landscape toward the *Lighting Rod.*

The remaining crewmen still on the field did their best to stop the aliens or at least slow them down. Morrison ran with the retreating crewmen and shouted orders at them.

The crew retreated behind swells, fired at the aliens, cut down a dozen or so with each barrage, and then had to retreat even further when the aliens kept advancing.

The aliens didn't return fire. They threw one flank of troops after another at the crew. Bodies toppled in all directions, but the aliens never stopped coming.

The one remaining warship kept pounding the countryside with brutal fire. Swells detonated all over the map. Dirt, grass, and vegetation exploded in the air and left the crew no choice but to keep falling back.

"This is hopeless," Church muttered. "The troops will push the crew all the way back to the *Lightning Rod.* Then it will be all over."

"We have to stop them," Radcliffe insisted. "We can't let this go on."

"How?" Church asked. "If we start shooting, the warship will open fire on us and then we won't be around to do anything."

Radcliffe assessed the situation. "I have an idea. We'll skirt the troops, fire at them from behind and the sides, and as soon as we hit them, we'll run for it to a different location and do it again. That should distract them from the crew. It might even give the crew a chance to advance and drive the aliens back toward the crash site."

Church frowned again. "Will that work?"

"It's worth a shot. You can stay here and watch while I try it. Then, if it doesn't, there won't be any harm done."

Church glared at him. "You're joking, right? You think I'd sit here doing nothing and watch you shoot at the aliens so I can make sure it's safe enough before I stick my neck out? Thanks a lot."

Radcliffe bit back laughter. "All right. Be that way. You stay here while I scoot around to the other side of the troops. Then we can hit them from both sides and they'll have to split off to come after us."

"And then?" Church asked.

"Like I said, as soon as you make your shot, run for it to another location. The warship will fire into the location where you shot from, but you won't be there anymore. Then you can shoot from somewhere else and repeat. See?"

Church pursed his lips. "Now you're just being annoying."

Radcliffe grinned at him. "When you see me in position, make your first shot."

Radcliffe didn't wait for Church to agree. This plan was the best they were likely to come up with.

Radcliffe kept his head low and crouched behind the swells as he made his way behind the troops. They didn't pay any attention to anything behind or on either side of their ranks. They just kept marching straight ahead.

He dashed from swell to swell until he circled the troops from behind. They made it extra easy for him by always advancing westward. They left plenty of room for him to get into position facing Church with the aliens between them.

Radcliffe crept up the nearest swell, but he didn't lie down on his stomach. He had to be ready to run the instant he opened fire.

He pushed up onto his knees, locked his weapon to his shoulder, and then sprang up and fired. He didn't waste time aiming. He just unloaded into the alien troops and cut down twenty of them.

Church fired at the same time from the other side. The plan worked better than Radcliffe ever could have imagined. The aliens spun in all directions trying to confront their new enemy.

Half of them turned toward Radcliffe and came face to face with their own comrades who were turning the other way to confront Church.

Radcliffe had to remind himself to stop shooting. He could have killed a lot more aliens while they had their backs to him facing Church.

Radcliffe tore himself away and sprinted for the rear of the alien column. He barely made it out from behind the swell before the warship fired and smashed the swell to oblivion.

He kept on running, skirted the column from behind, popped up over another swell, fired again, and took off running. He didn't make the mistake of sticking around as long this time.

He repeated the process seven more times, darted to a new position, fired, and ran off somewhere else. More energy eruptions spat from Church's weapon. Church kept swiveling behind and across the other side of the alien position.

The two men fired at the aliens from so many different places that the troops couldn't keep track of both of them. The column came to a halt while the aliens tried to decide what to do and where to go.

Out of Radcliffe's wildest dreams, Morrison bellowed, "Attack!!" and the *Lightning Rod* crew made a massive surge to drive the aliens back.

The aliens faced front to meet the assault and Radcliffe took that moment to fire into the alien's rear ranks again. The column stopped again, but at the same instant, the warship fired straight down at Radcliffe.

He would have been dead if he hadn't already been standing up. The shot hit the swell in front of him and it exploded in his face.

The impact made him stagger and he blinked dirt out of his eyes trying to see where he was going. He wheeled away, plunged behind another swell, and kept on running, but he couldn't go back to shooting at the column.

The warship hunted him down without mercy. It left its position and zipped back and forth across the field pelting him with shots. The warship completely ignored Church who kept bombarding the ground troops from his side and from behind.

Radcliffe had no choice but to run away, but the warship never let up. It hounded him back and forth, behind one swell and then another, and it obliterated them one after the other to rob him of any hiding place.

He felt himself losing steam. He needed to hide somewhere and rest before he fell over. He stumbled and lost his footing. The warship would finish him off with its next shot.

At that moment when he thought he was doomed, another gunshot rocketed out of nowhere and hit the warship. Radcliffe didn't see where the shot came from. It was a blast from an alien energy weapon and it struck the warship from Radcliffe's left.

He didn't see any more before he toppled behind a different swell. He plastered himself against its sides wheezing for breath.

His chest hurt, but the warship didn't come after him again. It moved off in the direction of those shots. Someone saved Radcliffe's bacon.

The shots didn't come from Church. Someone else was out there shooting at the warship.

Radcliffe dragged himself onto his knees. He was nowhere near the ground troops, the *Lightning Rod* crew, or Church.

Radcliffe gasped a few more times and slowly, carefully, crawled back to where he started. He found Church huddled behind another swell.

The alien ground troops had finally mustered the brain power to shoot back at the *Lightning Rod* crew.

The two sides engaged in a brutal firefight, but the *Lightning Rod* crew fired from behind the swells. The aliens stood out there in broad daylight and didn't even try to take a defensive posture.

Radcliffe collapsed behind the swell and waited for Church to finish shooting at the aliens from behind. They were too busy fighting the *Lightning Rod* crew even to look in his direction.

Church sprang down into the hollow, leaned back against the swell, and caught his breath. Concussions kept going off outside.

He finally looked up and cracked in a huge grin that showed all his brilliant white teeth. "Good thinking....Matt."

Radcliffe had to laugh. "Good shooting....Ted."

They both laughed, but just then, the warship came back, parked right on top of the ground troops, and used its energy beam to transport them all on board before the ship flew away.

Church sank back into place with a sigh. "That's the end of that."

"At least we know we can kill these suckers now."

"Yeah, that's something," Church breathed. "We made them run today."

Both men checked outside and saw Morrison sticking his head up not far away. No one moved for a minute.

"I guess they aren't coming back," Church remarked.

"Until they do," Radcliffe finished.

"Let's go." Church stood up. "I want to find the captain."

He didn't explain which captain he meant. There was only one no matter what rank anybody else held.

Chapter 15

C hurch and Radcliffe climbed out of their hiding place just as
Morrison, Andy, Charlie Frasier, Maverick Rickenbach, and a
dozen other *Lightning Rod* crewmen stood up from the other side of
the battlefield.

Church and Radcliffe went over to them and Church's eyes narrowed. "Where's Captain English?"

"We haven't seen him since the shooting started." Andy scanned
the battlefield. "You didn't see him out there?"

"I know where he is." Radcliffe pointed behind him. "He's over
there."

"How can you be sure?" Morrison squinted into the distance.
"There's no one over there. It's directly under where the warship just
was."

"That's why the warship was over there. It followed me and he fired
at it to draw it away from me."

Andy's eyes fell out of their sockets. "Is he dead?"

Radcliffe's blood ran cold. Did English get himself shot saving
Radcliffe's life? English better not have.

Andy hardened his features, clamped his mouth shut, tucked his
chin, and set off at a fast walk toward the spot that Radcliffe indicated.

Radcliffe, Church, Morrison, and Rickenbach followed him, but they'd only gone a dozen yards before English stood up from behind one of the swells.

He was nowhere near where those shots had been coming from. Maybe he got the idea to run around the warship, too.

He hung his weapon strap over his shoulder and sauntered slowly out to meet the crew. Andy hustled up to him. "Are you okay? We thought you got hit."

"I'm okay." English studied him and then the rest of the crew. "Are you all okay?"

"We lost a few...." Morrison waved behind. "A few of the new people."

"Too bad it wasn't all of them," Andy muttered.

"Don't be like that," English chided. "They'll be all right as soon as they wake up and smell the coffee."

"You are way too soft....." Andy began, but they all cut it off when the rest of the crew caught up.

A handful of Morrison's new recruits had survived the battle, including Sandoval and McKee.

They hovered exceptionally close to Morrison now. The two men kept casting fleeting glances around the countryside and tightening their grips on their weapons.

English, Andy, Radcliffe, and Church barely looked at them. Radcliffe had seen enough. Maybe now these chumps would realize who the real enemy was.

"Let's get back to the ship," English ordered. "We know now that we can kill these aliens. We just need to combine all our firepower to get the job done."

The crew turned back to the west. Radcliffe and his friends had to wait for the others to go first, but at least Radcliffe could call Church a friend now. The tension between them evaporated during the battle.

Just before they set off, English paused to look back. Dozens of dead alien bodies covered the ground. Part of one of the warships lay smoking in the distance.

"Are you okay, Sir?" Church asked. "Are we falling back or what?"

"You go ahead," English replied over his shoulder. "There's one more thing I want to do."

"What is it?" Andy asked. "Whatever you're doing, you sure as hell aren't doing it alone."

Morrison heard them and turned back to listen. "Is there a problem, Sir? Do you see something over there?"

"Yeah, I see something." English strode over to one of the dead aliens.

Its armor seemed to be made of multiple interlocking metal plates—or what looked like plates. It might have been made of any substance Radcliffe had never seen or heard of before.

The metal—or whatever—had a blackish color with what looked like colors melted into its substance. The aliens' helmets and weapons had been made up of the same substance.

The armor plates covered each alien's torso and extended down over the thighs. The armor left the legs exposed from just above the knee joint—or hock or whatever it was.

More plates jutted from the creatures' shoulders but didn't cover any of the arms. The armor left the aliens completely mobile while protecting any vital organs.

English bent over, took hold of the creature's mask, and pulled. He tugged at it, and when it didn't come loose, he planted his foot on the creature's neck and heaved with all his strength.

Even then, English couldn't tear the mask off. It wouldn't come off no matter what he did. He finally let it go and straightened up. "Damn it."

"Do you want to study it?" Radcliffe asked. "We would probably have to take the body back to the ship and cut the mask off with a welding torch."

"Is this really what we've come to?" Church asked. "Doing autopsies on aliens?"

"How else can we learn about their vulnerabilities?" English asked. "They're wearing these masks. The aliens obviously aren't compatible with an oxygen atmosphere."

"So what are you going to do—pump oxygen into their warships?" Andy asked.

"Well, what the hell do you suggest?" English countered. "We have to find some way to fight them and we can't do it with birds and destroyers and plasma rifles."

"Maybe Lowery can find a way by studying one of these weapons," Radcliffe suggested.

"That reminds me." English turned away again and headed for the downed warship this time.

The others followed him. He stopped a dozen feet from the ship. It had been constructed of the same metallic substance as the aliens' armor and weapons, but the ships weren't composed of interconnected plates.

Even at this close range, Radcliffe couldn't tell which of the spiky things on its outer hull might be weapons. They all looked the same and the aliens' shots came from all over the ship during the battle.

English circled the vessel and found a breach not engulfed in flames. He approached it and peered inside. Then he stepped across the threshold and the others followed him inside.

They stepped into an oblong, blackened compartment full of dead aliens. They all wore masks and a dozen bodies lay draped over consoles of electronic equipment.

English went over to one, pulled the dead alien off, threw it on the floor, and stepped into place where he could see the controls. Radcliffe, Church, and Andy flanked him and they all looked down at the instruments.

Strange symbols Radcliffe didn't recognize covered the panel from one side to the other. They must have been intended to light up while the ship was in flight. They weren't lighted now because the ship was totally dead.

More panels of these symbols covered every station and even the walls. Radcliffe didn't see any screens or any way the crew could see what was happening outside the ship, but nearly half the room had been blasted to kingdom come. The crew couldn't make a decent assessment from this.

Radcliffe circled the room going one way. Church, Andy, and English searched every corner of the room.

Morrison stood guard outside the breach to make sure no one came. Radcliffe saw Rickenbach, Hughes, Stoval, and a few other pilots from the *Lightning Rod* squadron pacing around out there.

Radcliffe looked everywhere for a door to get out of the room, but he couldn't find anything. He couldn't find a single crack in the walls to show where people might get into and out of this ship.

The warship was way too big to be flown by twelve people. A ship this size should have a crew of thousands—or maybe the thousands of people on board were all ground troops.

If they were, they were all trapped on board right now. Were they alive or dead?

That thought made Radcliffe's skin crawl. He left the ship and stood outside with the pilots.

He expected English to give up and just leave, but when Andy and Church came outside, English stayed inside. He used one of the alien weapons to cut off one of the control panels, hoisted it onto his shoulder, and carried it outside.

"You can NOT be serious," Church growled.

"We need to study it," English chirped. "Hammil can take a look at it."

"How can he take a look at it when we don't have a power source to run it?" Radcliffe asked. "He could take a look at it for the next ten years and never figure it out if we have no way to power it up."

"Well, we won't learn what power source they're using if we don't study some of their equipment." English walked straight past them, past the pilots, and headed back westward toward the *Lightning Rod*.

Radcliffe and his comrades exchanged glances. Even the pilots glanced back and forth between English and the other three captains. The pilots hesitated to follow English like maybe he really had flipped his lid this time.

In the end, everyone had no choice but to follow him. They had nowhere else to go but the *Lightning Rod* and he was going to the *Lightning Rod*.

They made it back to the ship by sunset. Morrison and Rickenbach sent all the pilots off duty. English left to take the control panel to engineering where Hammil could work on it.

"Like he doesn't have enough to do," Church muttered after English left.

Radcliffe and the other two captains went up to the bridge, but Radcliffe couldn't put his heart into his work.

Like English, Radcliffe wanted to hurry up and find a way to defeat these aliens so the crew could go home.

He wound up staring at the bridge controls for way too long, but he couldn't get his brain to engage. He kept replaying the battle.

He'd actually killed some of them. The *Lightning Rod* crew had destroyed two warships. Today had been a telling victory, so why couldn't he enjoy it?

No one else on the bridge said a word. Andy, Church, and Eismann went through the motions, too, but after a while, all four men dispersed and went their own way.

English didn't come back. He must have been up to his eyeballs in studying that panel, now that he knew there had to be a way to defeat this invasion.

Chapter 16

Racer shoved a few extra grenades in her backpack and checked her weapons and ammunition for the thousandth time.

"What are you bringing all that for, Racer?" Janacek asked. "We'll be flying around in our birds. You won't get a chance to use those against the aliens."

"We won't be flying around in our birds before we hike down there and get on board our birds," she countered. "I don't want to get caught unarmed on the open beach. You might want to arm yourselves, too. We don't know what we'll find out there."

She pretended to go back to packing her gear, but she definitely noticed the others putting a few extra grenades and more ammunition in their packs, too.

She, Hughes, Hoskins, Janacek, Ritchie, Stoval, the two Durans, Smythe, Walker, Waterman, and Laughlin stood around in the *Lightning Rod's* cargo hold waiting for the word to leave the ship. They'd been waiting for hours and the order still hadn't come down.

"What's the hold up?" Sean muttered for the hundredth time. "What are we waiting for?"

"Hey, did you hear the one about the foot-long sub that got lost in the ocean?" Janacek asked.

"Not now," Hughes snapped.

"Why not now?" Janacek asked. "We aren't doing anything else."

"You may have noticed that some of us are packing our gear," Hoskins told him.

"Don't give me that!" Janacek countered. "We all finished packing our gear hours ago. You're all just fiddling with it to give yourselves something to do. You aren't really packing your gear."

No one said anything. Racer bent over her gear so no one would see her fiddling with it. He was right. She'd been ready to go for ages. She just couldn't quell her nervous agitation.

She nearly jumped out of her skin when the stairwell door opened and Rickenbach entered the hold. "You can all go now," he told them.

"What the hell has been taking so long?" Sean demanded. "We've been standing around here like idiots for hours."

"I'm not sure," Rickenbach replied. "The captain and the bridge staff have been busy with something or other. I don't know what it is. They don't tell me."

"So that's it?" Racer asked. "We just go—just like that?"

"Yep." Rickenbach surveyed them all. "Unless you aren't ready or something....in which case I'll have to tell the captain that...."

"We're ready." Sean hefted his pack onto his back. "We're more than ready."

"All right. Good luck. I'll be on Squadron Command....."

"What about Frasier?" Janacek asked. "Why isn't he doing it?"

"I don't know," Rickenbach replied. "The captain has Frasier doing something else. They don't tell me shit."

The pilots stared at him, but since he couldn't tell them anything, they had no choice but to exchange glances and leave.

Racer saluted Rickenbach before she left. "See you on the air, Lieutenant."

"Fly safe, Gunny," he told her.

He stayed in the hold and watched them out of sight. Racer would have liked to ask a few more questions, but what was the point if he couldn't tell her anything?

She walked off with the others and they made their way down the beach. Janacek kept trying to joke with the others, but he only wound up annoying them.

"Why do you think the captain is being so cryptic about his plans?" Ritchie asked.

"He isn't being cryptic," Sean fired back. "Since when has he ever shared his plans with us? He barely knows we exist."

"At least he trusts us to go get these birds," Hoskins remarked. "I'd hate to be the *Champion* pilots and be stuck on board the ship while someone else did it."

"They got exactly what they deserved," Hughes snarled. "They got a hell of a lot better than they deserved."

"Another battle like the last one and they *will* get what they deserve," Walker added. "Sergeant Morrison had the right idea putting them in the front line."

"I can't think of a worse punishment than getting transferred to his command," Ezra remarked. "There is no fate worse than that."

The others laughed for the first time—and the last. The mission in front of them demanded all their attention.

Racer didn't know what to expect when she finally launched her bird. Was the alien enemy monitoring all of Earth for any aircraft activity? They might pounce on the crew the minute they fired up their engines.

The crew would be lucky if the aliens just shut down the fighter craft's engines the way they did last time. In the worst-case scenario, the warships could shoot these birds out of the sky with everyone on board. The crew would never know what hit it.

She wasn't the only one to scan the countryside in all directions on their way south, but constantly looking around didn't help anything, either. The warships could move too fast. They could overtake the crew in a split second without warning.

The sun reflected off the pilot's fighter craft long before the crew got near them. The birds sat in the same place where Racer and her friends left them.

Her heart raced as she climbed into the cockpit and powered up. "Here we go, folks!" Sean called. "Ready to roll!"

"Wait for the word from Squadron Command," Hughes told him.

"I know that, chump!" Sean countered.

"How's it gonna work—us flying with four different gunnies?" Ritchie asked. "Which of you are we supposed to listen to?"

"All of us, fool," Sean told him. "Just do what you're told."

"What if you give us conflicting orders?" Janacek asked.

"Why is it always you two?" Sean asked. "I don't hear Hoskins, Stoval, Smythe, and Walker complaining about flying with four gunnies."

"The *Lightning Rod* is running with four captains, so four gunnies only makes sense, right?" Laughlin pointed out.

"This war is throwing everything out of whack," Sean agreed and bent over his controls. "This bird is dialed in exactly the same way it was when I landed it."

"What did you think—that Lieutenant Hammil adjusted it for you while your back was turned?" Racer asked.

"Actually, yes," he replied. "That's exactly what I did think."

Just then, Rickenbach connected to them from the *Lightning Rod*. "Squadron Command to Wing Leader....." He trailed off. "Which wing are you kids flying under?"

Racer glanced to her left just as Sean, Ezra, and Hughes all looked around at each other. "Umm......" Hughes stammered.

Rickenbach laughed. "How about we call it....Wing Zero?"

"Hell no," Walker countered. "We'll be Wing 1 since we're number one."

"Yeah!" Ritchie crowed. "Wing 1!"

"So who's your Wing Leader?" Rickenbach asked. "Don't get into a fistfight about it. Just make a decision."

The four gunnery sergeants exchanged glances and Sean shrugged. "I say Racer should be our Wing Leader."

"Why me?" Racer asked.

"Yeah," Hughes agreed. "It has to be you, Racer."

"Why does it have to be me? You're senior to me, Sam, and Sean is senior to all of us."

"This isn't about who's senior," Sean replied.

"Then what is it about?"

He studied her with his head on the side and then shrugged again. "I don't know. I only know it has to be you."

"He's right, Racer," Ezra insisted. "You should be our Wing Leader."

She opened her mouth to protest, but Rickenbach interrupted. "Squadron Command to Wing Leader 1. Stand by the launch, Wing Leader, 1."

She sighed. "Wing Leader 1 to Squadron Command. Standing by to launch on your command."

That did it. Everyone else got to work. Racer still couldn't figure out why, but it looked like she'd just been elected wing leader.

The others went through their checks, but Rickenbach still didn't give the word. "What's going on, Lieutenant?" Hughes asked.

"I don't know," Rickenbach replied. "I'm just waiting for word to come down from the bridge."

Walker sighed loudly. "Hurry up and wait. That's the story of my life."

"Check out the long-range scans," Racer told them. "The Force is launching an offensive against the aliens."

Everyone looked down at their controls and a hush fell over the crew. Three theaters of battle had opened up in different locations around the planet.

A fleet of twenty destroyers were getting their asses kicked near Harare. Another fourteen were making a stand over Paris. They did their best to stop four warships from reducing the city to ruins.

No matter what the destroyers did, they couldn't budge the warships. The warships just stayed in one place, completely ignored the destroyers, and rained hellfire on most of northern France.

The other theater was rapidly degenerating into a death zone with forty destroyers trapped on the ground. Seven warships hovered in the atmosphere over Singapore. They laid down such a devastating carpet of shots that the destroyers couldn't launch at all.

"I can't watch," Sean groaned and turned off his scanners. "Tell me when the word comes down. I'll turn them back on then, but not before."

Racer kept watching. The aliens' activity fascinated her.

"Why do you think they're working so hard to destroy USF vessels but not take out the ships over Paris?" she asked. "Did the aliens somehow figure out that the USF Command Center was in Paris?"

"That makes no sense," Hughes pointed out. "No one has been using the Paris Command Center since the rebels took out the city. The aliens didn't have to attack Paris to get rid of the USF Command."

"Then that begs the other question—the more crucial question," she countered. "Did the aliens know Earth was engaged in this civil war? Did the aliens choose now to attack because the USF had weakened itself by fighting internally?"

"How could the aliens possibly have found out about that?" Sean asked.

"Maybe they've somehow been monitoring Earth for exactly that reason," Stoval pointed out. "Maybe the aliens had been casing Earth for years just waiting for the right time to strike."

His words cast a chill over the group. Racer didn't like to think about that, but a second later, Walker interrupted. "That made no sense, either. These aliens are powerful enough that they could have walked all over the USF even when it was at its strongest. If the aliens attacked now or if the aliens attacked three years ago wouldn't have made any difference."

"Can we please not talk about this?" Sean cut in. "Don't we have enough problems to worry about without spending our free time dragging out the whole war?"

"I could tell you a joke," Janacek suggested.

Everyone else yelled, "NO!!" That shut him up—for now.

Another silence would have followed this, but Rickenbach's chuckle startled everyone into paying attention. That chuckle seemed to say it all and the conversation died.

The word kept not coming down. The endless waiting was really starting to get on Racer's nerves.

She was just going back to watching the three unfolding disasters when Rickenbach said, "Squadron Command to Wing Leader 1, you are clear to launch."

"Finally!" Sean gasped.

"Wing 1—launch!" Racer ordered and the fighter craft shot off the ground. Racer hit the throttle, vaulted off the ground, and started gaining altitude.

She cast a wary glance around. Could she get lucky enough that the enemy warships would all be too busy fighting other people to come after her crew?

"We're away!" she called to Rickenbach. "Where are we going, Lieutenant?"

"Head south toward Mexico. There's another wing coming out from Fort Lauderdale. They should be meeting up with you."

"I see them! Divert to intercept, Wing 1."

Wing 1 veered to port. The other wing swooped south to fall in with Wing 1. They crossed Mexico on their way toward South America.

Racer opened her mouth to ask Rickenbach what destination the crew should head for. At that moment, an enemy warship materialized right in their path.

"Pull out!!" she hollered. "Double back! Lieutenant—we're cut off! We're making contact with the enemy! Alien warship dead ahead!"

Rickenbach didn't answer. Racer listened and listened and listened. Something must have gone seriously wrong if Rickenbach didn't answer.

"Cut away!" she ordered. "Cut back to North America! We need to regroup!"

No one in the wing answered her, either. She glanced to starboard where Stoval and Ezra had just been flying.

Ezra looked in her direction and she saw his mouth moving. No sound came through their communications systems. They were completely cut off from each other.

At that moment, the enemy fired into their midst and a brutal smash struck Ezra's wing. He banked away with smoke billowing from the impact site.

He plunged off into the sky, but Racer didn't have time to check on him. Enemy gunshots peppered all over the place. Explosions blasted in her face. She couldn't tell if her own pilots were getting slaughtered out there.

She yanked her helm hard to starboard planning to pull away back across North America. She made it as far as Texas before she realized she wasn't alone. Sean, Hughes, Hoskins, and Smythe surrounded her.

The pilots who came out from Florida to join Wing 1 were still pinned down in front of warships. The warships spat cruel shots in all directions. The other wing's birds were the ones blowing up one after the other.

Racer gulped and tried one more time. "Lieutenant? Are you there?"

No one answered. This was bad. This was really bad.

She was all alone. She couldn't even instruct her wing to fall back. No one on board the *Lightning Rod* had told her anything about their destination or their mission.

Captain English and the bridge staff wanted to keep it a secret to stop any hidden rebel elements from finding out what they were up to.

The wing running into a warship—or multiple warships—wasn't part of the plan—not that anyone told Racer the plan.

She wanted to dive in with guns blazing and help the Florida wing, but she already saw that it was hopeless. Wing 1 would get wiped out if she did that—the same way this other wing was getting wiped out.

She waved her hand above her head and pointed behind her to tell the wing to fall back. The *Lightning Rod* squadron's fighter craft were the only birds they had. She couldn't let anything happen to them.

She pulled aside and headed back across North America. As soon as she hit Oklahoma, her communications system switched back on. "Racer!" Rickenbach hollered. "Gunny Franz—respond!"

"I'm here, Lieutenant!" Relief flooded her. "I'm here! We lost you for a second!"

"What's going on up there?" he snapped. "None of you was responding."

"The warship must have jammed us," Hughes replied. "We couldn't communicate with each other, either."

"What do you want us to do, Lieutenant?" Racer asked. "Please tell me you don't want us to engage that warship."

"No, don't engage it. Fall back to the *Lightning Rod*. We need you here."

"What was that about?" Sean asked. "Why were we even going to South America?"

"That's the captain's business," Rickenbach replied. "As soon as you get here, you'll see and then I won't have to explain it to you."

Racer frowned at her fellow pilots, but at least they could communicate now.

She put on speed and burned north over Canada. Sure enough, when she got closer to Point Hope, she realized that Rickenbach was right.

A dozen USF destroyers surrounded the *Lightning Rod* and a bunch of mechanics and engineers swarmed all over the ship. Welding torches flashed on the outer hull while ten ships hovered overhead to guard the *Lightning Rod*.

The destroyers' fighter wings buzzed around, too. "Fall into formation, Wing 1," Rickenbach ordered. "Keep your eyes open for incoming enemy warships."

"Yes, Sir," Racer replied.

Wing 1 headed that way, but Racer had a really bad feeling about this. This many destroyers in one area were bound to attract attention.

Wing 1 didn't even get as far as Alaska before the enemy responded exactly the way she feared. She crammed her throttle down trying to get back to the *Lightning Rod* before the aliens showed up.

When it happened, they rocketed into the field so fast that she almost smashed straight into the warships.

Five of them zoomed between her wing and the *Lightning Rod*. The destroyers blasted out of position, opened fire on the warships, and the fighter wings attacked in fury.

They pounded the warships with brutal fire and buzzed in all directions to stay out of the path of the warships' guns, but nothing made a dent.

The destroyers vaulted aloft and flew at breakneck speed to draw the enemy away from the *Lightning Rod*. The crews on the ground worked their fastest to get the *Lightning Rod* airborne before the warships overcame the USF assault.

Racer unloaded on the enemy from behind. Her wing didn't have time to get into formation with the other squadrons. As soon as the enemy struck, all formation dissolved anyway.

She flew run after run, carved in dangerously close to the warships, and pounded her guns into their sides, but she didn't see her weapons doing any damage. None of the destroyers or fighter craft could do any damage at all.

The warships spat shots in all directions. The destroyers took dozens of hits, but the warships had trouble keeping up with the fighter craft's speed. As long as the squadrons continued to fly evasive maneuvers, the warships couldn't hit them.

That didn't help the destroyers nor did it make the fighter craft's weapons any more effective against this enemy. The alien invasion was turning into a crushing defeat for Earth. No one could stand against this enemy.

Racer didn't see what this whole maneuver was supposed to accomplish except that the destroyers kept moving farther and farther away from the *Lightning Rod*. The warships pivoted to follow the direction of combat.

The crews on the ground went into a frenzy, and as soon as they got the *Lightning Rod's* hull patched up, all the crews vanished on board the ship, her engines fired up, and she took wing.

Chapter 17

"Target all batteries and fire!" English ordered.

"*Nightside* and *Greyhound* are taking damage!" Radcliffe reported from the XO's station. "None of the birds' weapons are doing anything. No one's weapons are doing anything."

"Coordinate with the *Riordan*," English ordered. "Get in close and combine our firepower. There has to be a way to damage these things."

"There is," Church replied from the logistics station. "You have to use alien weaponry."

"We don't have that option," English countered. "Get between the warships and the *Greyhound*. Cut the alien flank apart and lure them away from each other. They're causing too much damage this close together."

Radcliffe steered the *Lightning Rod* into the battle. The starboard cannons erupted and splattered shots across the warship that had been targeting the *Greyhound*.

The destroyer was sinking fast and the *Lightning Rod* didn't get there in time. The warship swiveled to follow the *Lightning Rod's* movements and the *Greyhound* dropped away toward the surface.

The *Lightning Rod* kept on going, but one less warship didn't make any difference to the battle. Radcliffe increased speed to put more distance between the *Lightning Rod* and the enemy.

The warship unleashed a vicious torrent of shots that peppered the *Lightning Rod's* flank. "Starboard batteries are out!" Andy reported. "We're lucky we're still in the air."

"Come about and stand to!" English ordered. "How many destroyers are still in the air?"

"Ten left," Church replied. "The *Greyhound* is down and evacuating. The *Nightside* is barely holding on. The others...."

He didn't finish before another blast of enemy fire slapped the *Lightning Rod* out of position. She wheeled to face the enemy, and at the same moment, the rest of the USF destroyers raced out of the battle to form ranks with the *Lightning Rod*.

They all opened fire. Their previous maneuvers had stretched the enemy line. The warships didn't crowd as closely together.

The destroyers unloaded on the enemy, and at the same time, the destroyers all made a combined rush to push the warships even farther apart.

Cannon fire detonated against every enemy hull. The impact pushed the warships away from each other and the destroyers darted into the gap, turned their guns outward, and hammered the warships with gunfire.

The warships staggered under the onslaught. For a few blissful seconds, it actually looked like it might work. The warships retreated in opposite directions and left the destroyers in possession of the field.

Just as fast, the warships opened up with an answering barrage and the tables turned. The warships fired inward and the destroyers found themselves trapped in a shooting gallery they couldn't escape.

A pounding smash struck the *Lightning Rod's* tail section and then another shot hit the ship on the forward port side.

The impact flung the ship backward and she crashed into the *Outrigger*. The two ships collided and had to adjust their positions to avoid bringing each other down.

The *Lightning Rod's* cannons exploded again, but English couldn't tell anymore if they even hit their targets. Such a dense curtain of enemy shots burst in front of the *Lightning Rod* that he couldn't see a thing.

An even more bone-crunching smash struck the ship, and when the confusion cleared, he saw that she'd staggered out of the circle. The *Riordan*, the *Outrigger*, the crippled *Nightside*, and four other ships remained trapped between the enemy warships.

The *Lightning Rod*, the *King Lear*, the *Catherine the Great*, and the *Afrikaans* had gotten pushed out. The warships stayed where they were. They could shoot in all directions without moving.

Matching barrages erupted from the warships to decimate the destroyers trapped in the ring.

Another fountain of energy blasts plastered the *Lightning Rod* and her sister ships on the outside to hold them at bay and even bring them down. The *Lightning Rod* couldn't help anybody, not even herself.

Enemy shots scattered across the ship's nose that the repair crews had just sealed. Radcliffe bent over the controls working himself into a sweat trying to counteract all the enemy's moves.

The remaining batteries fired at their top speed, but the warships flattened every blast and drove every shot back toward the ship.

A vicious barrage struck the port side again. "We lost the port engine and hull breaches are venting life support!" Andy reported. "If we stay up here much longer...."

He didn't finish before all the warships fired in unison. English didn't see how it happened. The same overwhelming force that took out the *Aileron*, the *Buckingham Palace,* the *Lone Ranger*, and the *Infinity* smacked the *Lightning Rod* down hard.

English didn't see the shot coming until an unstoppable force slammed the ship down on the ground from more than two thousand feet in the air. An instant later, she crashed onto her belly and the power flicked off for a second.

It blinked back on and Andy, Church, and Radcliffe attacked their controls. "The aliens are landing ground troops!" Church reported. "They're all converging!"

"Arm the crew to get out on the ground to defend the ship!" English ordered. "Arm the front line with alien weapons. Are the ship's weapons systems still online?"

"We have forward and starboard batteries," Radcliffe reported.

"What about propulsion?" Andy asked.

"Not enough to get airborne. We have enough to turn the batteries on the ground troops. That's all."

"Do it," English ordered. "Stay on board and use the ship's weapons systems to defend us. Don't let the ground troops take the ship. Ted and Andy, you're with me."

English stormed off the bridge, but the crew was already crowding downstairs so fast that the three captains had to wait in the back.

All the alien weapons were gone by the time they got to the weapons locker. English had to settle for USF plasma rifles.

Everyone on board besides Radcliffe and Eismann assembled outside to face the enemy ground troops.

The air battle had migrated a few miles away. The warships now pulled the same maneuver on the USF fleet ships that English and his fellow captains tried to pull on the warships.

The aliens worked the destroyers away from each other. Multiple warships surrounded each destroyer so the aliens could knock every destroyer out of the sky one after the other.

Five warships positioned themselves around the *Lightning Rod.* Each warship fired its transport beam into the ground and unloaded countless ground troops. The aliens advanced on the *Lightning Rod* from all sides.

Morrison paced back and forth yelling orders to the defenders. "Circle the ship and fire outward! Second rank, fire on the warships! Combine your firepower and take them out the way we did last time. Anyone with a USF weapon, concentrate on the ground troops and take down as many of them as you can!"

English, Church, and Andy took their places in the ranks. The warships kept disgorging more and more troops.

Hundreds of black bodies covered the landscape. If someone didn't start shooting soon, the aliens would overrun everyone no matter what kind of weapon they were using.

English opened his mouth to give the order to open fire. He didn't get the chance before Morrison bellowed, "Fire!"

Everyone opened fire at once. Those with alien weapons on that side of the ship raised their weapons to shoot at the warships.

Plasma rifles and alien weapons erupted to cut down the ground troops. The aliens fell in waves, but the warships unloaded so many aliens that the defenders couldn't stem the tide.

English jerked his weapon from side to side blowing away every alien in sight, but his rifle didn't do as much damage as the aliens' own weapons.

The ranks behind him raised their stolen weapons, took aim at the nearest warship, and fired. Explosions went off on the ship's outer skin, but drawing those weapons away from the ground troops gave the aliens the opening they needed to gain ground.

They spread out to ring the *Lightning Rod* crew. English's instincts took over and he fired faster, but more aliens surrounded him on every side.

At that moment, the *Lightning Rod's* engines howled to life. She lifted a few feet off the ground and her hull creaked when the engines tore it out of the soil.

She wheeled and the whole crew had to hit the bricks when her batteries opened fire on the ground troops. She rotated in circles and sprayed gunfire in all directions.

English rolled onto his stomach and pumped his rifle into any aliens still standing. A dozen of his crewmen flipped onto their backs and fired alien weapons into the warships from below.

The crew brought down another warship, but not even the *Lightning Rod's* cannons could slow the enemy down. They kept advancing in a tidal wave of bodies.

English saw the aliens about to overrun the ship. He sprang to his feet and stalked out to meet them. He fired again and again blowing their heads off and exploding their bodies apart.

He didn't see or care what anyone else was doing. He just had to stop these aliens from getting near the ship.

Another warship exploded over his head and then a brutal crack of enemy weapons fire pounded into the dirt a few feet away from him. The blast slapped him off his feet and he flew twenty yards before he crashed to the ground.

He had just enough strength to look up at the sky and see a squadron of USF fighter craft drop out of the atmosphere.

They ran across the battlefield carpet-bombing the ground troops with devastating fire before the fighters sailed off into the mayhem of destroyers and warships battling in the sky.

English tried to pick himself up, but at that moment, a wave of cold darkness overpowered him and he passed out.

Chapter 18

"Give 'em hell, Wing 1!" Racer called. "We might not be able to do anything against the warships, but we can damn well drive these assholes away from the *Lightning Rod.*"

"Watch out!" Hughes warned. "The crew is firing on the warships again! Clear away from that warship! She's going down!"

Racer whizzed through the battle, dropped low over the field, and rained hellfire on the alien ground troops again.

More USF fighter wings followed her lead, abandoned their hopeless fight against the warships, and concentrated their fire on the ground troops.

The troops got distracted by so many people targeting them from so many directions. Some of the aliens tried to continue their march toward the *Lightning Rod.* Others turned to aim their weapons at the fighter craft.

Racer carved a swatch of destruction through their ranks and blasted back into the atmosphere for another pass.

Her fellow pilots pulled in behind her and they banked downward, but at that moment, the *Lightning Rod* swung around and laid down a curtain of shots to flatten the ground troops.

More alien weapons spat from the ground. Ten of them concentrated on a different warship. The battle was getting so chaotic that Racer hesitated to go back in there.

That was the moment when she spotted one man striding out onto the battlefield. He jerked his rifle from right to left picking off any aliens who survived the rest of the *Lightning Rod* onslaught.

Her vision expanded and she realized he wasn't the only one. A bunch of other *Lightning Rod* officers also advanced onto the field to hunt down any aliens still alive. These officers took the fight right into the heart of the alien ranks.

"Let's go, Wing 1," she ordered. "Our people need us."

She punched the throttle, tilted into a dive, and circled the ground troops from the side so she wouldn't hit any of the *Lightning Rod* personnel.

She veered in hard in front of English, mowed down another platoon of aliens, and headed around to help defend the *Lightning Rod* crew.

She made it as far as the end of the warship line before three of them opened fire on the *Lightning Rod* crew on the ground. A wicked crack smashed into the ground right where the crew had been firing on the warships.

Explosions boomed all over the field and Racer saw one shot struck near English. He flew into the air and landed thirty yards away. "Captain English is hit!" she yelled. "I'm going in!"

She ripped her helm to starboard and rocketed back onto the field. She had to work hard to dodge enemy shots, but she never took her eye off English.

He tried to sit up and collapsed back on the ground. At least the ground troops were nowhere near him. They were all too busy trying to overrun the *Lightning Rod*.

She picked up speed. She had to decide what to do about him.

Should she land and try to take him on board her fighter? Should she just stay airborne and defend him until the battle was over?

That could take hours and she could get shot down in the process. She could get shot down with him on board.

She couldn't think about that. She just had to keep going. She had to get to him before......

She swept over the last swell when, without warning, the warship directly overhead fired its transport beam, but it didn't pick up the ground troops. It fired at English and he vanished off the face of the Earth—literally.

"CAPTAIN!!" Racer bellowed, but it was too late. He wasn't there anymore.

She was flying too fast to stop and plummeted straight into the beam, but it evaporated right in front of her and vanished, too. She kept flying and wound up circling the battlefield from the back.

More shots from the *Lightning Rod* crew bombarded the warships. The crew had taken down four of them so far.

They started on their fifth when the remaining warships fired their transport beams, removed all their surviving ground troops from the field, and disappeared as suddenly as they had arrived.

Racer stayed where she was fighting down a wave of sickness in her stomach. English couldn't be gone. The aliens captured him. How would the crew ever get him back?

There was nothing more to see up here. The destroyers limped away to the south. They flew extra slowly so the *Nightside* could keep up.

Racer tried contacting Squadron Command, but Rickenbach didn't respond again. The ship probably sustained damage to her communications or power systems when she crashed.

"Gunny?" Waterman asked. "What do you want us to do?"

She shook the fog out of her head and looked down at the ship. Most of the crew was still outside standing guard with their guns. She could see a few officers moving around down there.

"Follow me and set down near the *Lightning Rod,*" she ordered. "We need to touch base with....whoever is in charge now."

She set down and the crew unloaded.

Captain Andrew English strode back and forth barking orders at the crew. "Get out onto the field and gather up every alien weapon! Ignore the bodies. Morrison, I want you to organize a rescue party to go out to the *Greyhound* and bring in any survivors. Take the *Cobalt* medical staff with you. We need our own people here. Engineering crew, get on board and start bringing the power and communications systems back online pronto."

Racer stood off to one side watching him. He stepped into his father's place without a word of negotiation with anyone. Neither Captain Church nor Captain Radcliffe said a thing against him taking over.

Church and Radcliffe walked straight out onto the field with the regular crew and started gathering armloads of the aliens' weapons. They brought them back and mounded them up on the cargo hold floor.

Someone came over, stopped in front of the younger Captain English, and saluted. It was Kilpatrick from the *Apache.* "Sir! Permission to speak freely."

"What is it, Lieutenant?" Andy asked.

"Sir....my weapon, Sir....I was using one of the alien weapons in the battle....and in the middle of the fight....it ran out of juice, Sir. It stopped working. It's dead now, Sir."

Andy cocked an eyebrow at him. "Is that so?" He turned to some of the people nearest him. "Did anyone else's weapon cut out in the middle of the battle?"

About ten people said, "Yes, Sir," and "Mine did, Sir."

"I guess we should have expected this," Andy remarked. "Stack all the unusable weapons in a corner of the hold—over there. Keep them separate from the ones we've just taken. Thank you, Lieutenant. Carry on."

Kilpatrick went back to work. Racer didn't see Andy about to say anything to anyone, so she stepped forward. Facing him was nothing like facing his father.

She'd come to see Captain English as a father figure. She always knew she could confide in him in ways she couldn't confide in anyone else. She would never feel that way about his son.

Not even knowing the risks Andy had taken for the loyalist cause softened the tension of facing him alone for the first time.

He narrowed his eyes at her and said, "Gunny," in a cutting, authoritative tone.

"Sir.....the aliens captured Captain English, Sir."

He whipped around fast. "What did you say?"

"The aliens...."

"I heard you, Gunny. Are you certain?"

"I saw it with my own eyes, Sir. He got hit with one of their shots and thrown clear. He was semi-conscious and lying on the ground. I flew over there to get him and one of their transport beams snatched him right in front of me....Sir."

He glared at her so hard she cringed. She really wished she could disappear right now.

He turned back to the battlefield, clenched his teeth, and snarled, "Son of a bitch!"

"Sir?" she choked. "We're going after him, aren't we? We're going to rescue him, aren't we? We can't just leave him up there?"

"Where, Gunny?" Andy snapped. "Where can't we leave him?"

She opened her mouth, glanced out at the field, and the words died on her lips. She really had no clue where Captain English was—or anything else for that matter.

He didn't look at her. He growled under his breath, but she definitely heard his voice shaking. "You're a smart young woman, Gunny," he muttered. "Captain English thinks a lot of you. You think about it and discuss it with your wingmates over there. You and your fellow pilots come up with an idea for how we can rescue Captain English. As soon as you come up with something, you tell me about it and we'll put your plan into action. Does that satisfy you?"

She opened her mouth a second time, but the words wouldn't come. How exactly was she supposed to come up with a plan to rescue Captain English?

"Um......you want me....to come up with a plan....Sir?" she stammered. "But......I don't know anything about the war."

He finally turned around and stared at her. It was only a slightly softer stare than the glare he'd given her just now. "I can promise you, Gunny, that all of us will be thinking the same thing. We'll all be thinking about how to get Captain English back. If one of us comes up with something, we'll let you know and you and your wingmates will be the first people we call to go and get him. Now take your crew off duty while the rest of us clean up this mess."

"Um....Sir....." she went on. "What do you want us to do with our birds? If we keep them here, one of the conspirators might get the idea to steal the birds....but if we keep them here....."

"Take your birds back to the flight deck," he interrupted. "Lieutenant Rickenbach will supervise you making any repairs or adjustments. You're dismissed, Gunny."

He walked away from her and she headed back to where the other pilots waited for her. "What did he say?" Sean asked.

"He said for us to take our birds to the flight deck. Lieutenant Rickenbach is Squadron Commander now. Don't ask me what happened to Frasier."

"Maybe Rickenbach can tell us," Hughes suggested.

"So....." Ezra glanced past Racer toward the *Lightning Rod.* "Is *he* the captain now?'

"He's sure acting like it," Racer replied. "And he is a captain, after all."

"Is he mad at us?" Smythe asked. "Did we do something wrong?"

"Of course he isn't mad at us," Sean countered. "He has no reason to be. We did everything we were supposed to do."

"He's mad because his father got captured by the aliens," Stoval chimed in. "He's mad because he thought his father got killed in the battle and now he found out that Captain English got captured instead—which is a hundred times worse than if he did die."

"Captain English—the younger Captain English—says for us to put our heads together and come up with a plan to rescue Captain English—the older one." Racer shut her eyes and shook her head. "This is getting way too confusing."

"Why don't we just bite the bullet and call them Andy and Sailor from now on?" Janacek suggested.

"That wouldn't be respectful or polite," Ritchie countered. "I could never call Captain English, 'Sailor'. He's our damn captain! Only his closest friends call him Sailor and we aren't that."

"We'd only call them that amongst ourselves," Janacek explained. "So we don't have to keep calling them both, 'Captain English'. It's too confusing like Racer says."

"I agree with Janacek," Sean interjected. "But only between ourselves. You all call me and Ezra, 'Sean and Ezra'. You don't keep saying, 'the older Gunny Duran and the younger Gunny Duran'. That would be stupid."

"All right. I guess we have to," Racer agreed. "But I agree with Ritchie that we shouldn't call Captain English, 'Sailor'. We should just keep calling him, 'Captain English,' and his son, 'Andy'. Now let's get our birds inside. Then we need to get busy coming up with a rescue plan."

She and her fellow pilots mounted up, flew their birds onto the flight deck, and landed on their launch pads. The pilots went through their old routine of making repairs and adjustments, but Racer's mind wouldn't keep still.

How the hell was she or anyone else supposed to rescue Captain English from the aliens?

No one on Earth could even make a dent in their warships, much less get close enough to get on board or steal a prisoner from them.

Chapter 19

Radcliffe crossed the bridge to the logistics station and checked the readings coming from the engine room. "The plasma core is running too high," he told Eismann. "Turn down the reciprocation frequency by ten megahertz."

"This is the frequency Hammil sent up," Eismann pointed out.

"He obviously made a mistake. Look at that." Radcliffe pointed to a feedback wave running through the electrical system. "If you don't turn it down, it will overload the electrical system and we'll all be in trouble."

He stayed where he was and watched Eismann turn it down. The feedback slackened and the system settled back down to normal.

Radcliffe returned to the XO's station and checked the communications system. "Communications are back online," he announced.

"I'm picking up a distress call coming from the *Greyhound,*" Lowery reported from the communications station. "Their systems must be working, too."

"Send them word that our rescue team is on its way to bring them down to the *Lightning Rod.* No, correction. Tell them the *Lightning Rod* is available to them if they need it. Tell them we're here to offer any assistance they need."

"Yes, Sir," Lowery replied and turned back to his station.

Charlie Frasier and Admiral Simpson worked at the other two bridge stations. Radcliff monitored what they were doing and then went back to working on the communications system.

He started going over log data from the fighter squadron for the time Lieutenant Rickenbach said the warship jammed communication between Squadron Command and the fighter wing and between the fighter craft themselves.

He was just checking the data from the Florida wing's battle when Church showed up. He stopped next to the XO's station, watched what Radcliffe was doing, and then went over to the captain's chair.

Church sat down in it and started working the controls. "We have scanner data from the battle. Hammil should study this and see if he can figure out what power source the alien weapons are using."

Radcliffe bent over his controls and didn't look up. "Did you hear what Kilpatrick said about the guns losing power during the battle? It looks like you were right, Lowery. The aliens charge those weapons with power and now they're running out of juice. We can't use those guns anymore."

"All the more reason to figure out what energy source they're using," Church replied.

"I've already studied it," Lowery interjected from his station. "The energy source doesn't match anything we have on Earth. We won't likely be able to replicate the energy, so we'll have to come up with something else."

"Then come up with something else," Church told him. "We need to develop a weapon that can combat those warships. We can't keep relying on those puny stolen rifles to defend the planet."

Lowery bent over his controls and mumbled, "Yes, Sir."

Radcliffe went back to what he was doing. He didn't let himself think about the fact that Church was sitting in Captain English's chair. It was the only station left on the bridge. Where else was Church supposed to sit?

Just then, the doors opened and Andy strode in. "The fighter wing is back on board and logged in for duty," he said to no one in particular.

Radcliffe turned around and snapped to attention. "Attention! Captain on the bridge!"

Church and everyone else present stood up and turned around to present themselves to Andy, too. "We made contact with the *Greyhound*, Sir," Lowery reported. "They're communications systems are up and running just like ours."

"We're undertaking a study of the captured alien weapons, Sir," Church reported. "We're studying ways to modify our weapons to counteract the aliens' defenses."

Andy looked back and forth between everyone present. "What are you doing? I'm not in command here."

"Of course you are!" Radcliffe countered. "You have to be."

"I don't have to be," Andy returned. "I'm nobody. You two are in charge."

"You're better qualified than either of us," Church pointed out. "You've been a captain for longer. You're senior to both of us."

"I'm not in charge here and I'm not going to be. I'm a pilot—nothing else. You two keep doing what you're doing. I'll be your XO if I have to be anything."

Church and Radcliffe exchanged glances. "You couldn't be both of our XOs," Radcliffe pointed out.

"Then decide between the two of you who's gonna be in charge," Andy countered. "I'm not going to be."

Church and Radcliffe looked at each other again. They and Andy all being equally ranked never presented a problem as long as they all served under English. Now he was gone.

It wouldn't work for both Church and Radcliffe to be in command of the *Lightning Rod*. Three XOs or even two XOs made more sense than two captains.

"You do it, Ted," Radcliffe finally told him.

"No, you should," Church countered.

"Oh, will you stop it?!" Andy snapped. "You take command, Church."

Church shrugged. "Fine. So which of you is going to be my XO?"

Now it was Radcliffe and Andy who exchanged glances. "Why not both of us?" Andy asked.

"Whatever." Church turned back to the captain's chair and sat down in it.

"The flight squadron wants to mount a rescue mission to retrieve Captain English," Andy reported.

Church turned around and raised his eyebrows. "How do they plan to do that?"

"I told Racer to come up with a strategy and present it to us," Andy replied. "She and her fellow pilots are thinking about it now."

Church snorted and turned back to his controls. "I'm sure they'll come up with something brilliant."

"She's also concerned about the conspirators stealing our birds," Andy went on.

"Which conspirators do we still have on board?" Church asked.

"Just Sandoval and McKee," Andy replied.

Radcliffe was just about to mention the senior rebel officers when the door opened for the third time. Admiral Chambers, Admiral Schroder, Colonel Levitt, and Captain Thorburn strolled in.

Radcliffe had to marvel at the irony that he was just about to mention them in the same sentence with the rebel conspirators. Now here they were, showing up at the worst possible time.

Andy didn't give them a chance to make fools of themselves by opening their mouths. "Are you here to report for duty? That's excellent. We're probably going to be having a bunch of crewmen come over from the *Greyhound*. You can welcome them, show them to their quarters, and arrange to work them into our crew rotations. We need extra people after the casualties we took just now."

Admiral Schroder looked down her nose at him. "You aren't in command of this ship, Captain. Don't think you can step into your father's place and start barking orders at everyone now that he's gone."

"I don't think that," Andy replied. "Captain Church is in command of the *Lightning Rod* now."

The four senior officers spun around fast and stared at the back of Church's head. He didn't even look up or turn around to confront them. "He's....what?" Admiral Chambers husked.

"You four are members of this crew," Andy went on. "You made yourselves subordinate to Captain English. Now he's gone and Captain Church is taking over in his place. That makes you Captain Church's subordinates."

"We are not subordinate to any captain—especially not you!" Admiral Schroder fired back. "We're senior USF Command Staff...."

"Then, by all means, go command the USF." Andy waved toward the door. "Go on and do it. From what I can tell, there is no USF Command Staff anymore or any USF Command or any USF at all. It's every ship and every crew for themselves. Captain English coordinated those destroyers to come and help us without any intervention from the Command Staff. We can't even raise anyone on the Command Staff through our usual communications system. So if you want to be USF Command Staff, go do it out on the tundra because you sure as hell won't do it here."

Just then, Simpson called over from his station, "The medical staff is reporting that General McClure is dead. He got thrown against a wall during that last alien assault and he broke his neck."

"Good," Andy snapped. "Throw his body out with the aliens."

No one said anything for a minute. Church still kept his back to the room and studiously worked over his controls. He pretended not to notice Andy reading the senior USF Command Staff the riot act right here on the bridge.

Radcliffe didn't dare to speak up. He really wished now that he hadn't just agreed to be Church's joint XO with Andy.

Andy really should just take the job of commanding this ship. He was born for it. He should have been the captain, but he obviously didn't want that.

The four officers gaped at him, opened their mouths a few times, and kept glancing around at everyone and waiting for someone to intervene on their behalf.

Simpson's announcement startled everyone into turning around to gape at him. "Are you really going along with this, Chris?" Admiral Chambers demanded. "Are you really throwing over the chain of command to sign on with these....these outlaws?"

"Don't look at me," Simpson replied over his shoulder. "I have work to do here. The *Lightning Rod* is the only ship in the fleet that's in any position to mount any kind of defense against the aliens. You won't catch me making waves or taking command away from the people who are the most qualified to hold it. If you have a brain cell between you, you'll knuckle down and do the same thing."

He went back to work and erased them out of his awareness. Radcliffe's stomach turned a somersault at those words.

"Well?" Andy demanded. "What are you going to do? If you stay on board, make this the very last time you come to the bridge or question any of us, especially the captain."

"We just got word from the *Greyhound,* Sir," Lowery interrupted. "The rescue party just arrived. They think they can salvage the ship. She just needs extensive hull repairs and a few systems adjustments, but they're down an engineer. The *Greyhound* is requesting some of our staff to help get the ship in the air. Captain Moreland is requesting that he bring the Greyhound to land next to the *Lightning Rod* so we can share resources."

"Tell him he's more than welcome." Church stood up and finally, finally turned around. "Andy, you and Frasier come with me. You have the bridge, Matt."

Radcliffe said, "Yes, Sir."

Church made a show of walking around the senior officers to leave the bridge. Andy glared at them right until the moment when he turned away to leave. Frasier didn't look at them at all.

Radcliffe glanced at them and then went back to his work. Eismann and Simpson pretended not to hear anything.

The four senior officers waited for a minute. Their eyes kept darting from one person to another like they really expected someone to come forward and beg them to take over.

No one said anything. No sound disturbed the silence except the occasional beep from the controls when someone pushed a button.

Radcliffe expected the senior officers to leave, but after way too long, Schroder stepped over to the XO's station and murmured to Radcliffe under her breath. "You don't have to go along with this, Matt. We could make you captain of the *Lightning Rod* if you cooperate and help us reestablish the chain of command. The USF Command Staff is the best qualified to form a strategy to retake Earth from these invaders—not some rogue captains stranded in the middle of nowhere."

Radcliffe stared at her trying to get his brain to comprehend that she was serious. He didn't waste his breath explaining to her that he already could have been captain of the *Lightning Rod*. Both Church and Andy would gladly have stepped aside in Radcliffe's favor if he'd only said he wanted them to.

"Are you finished yet?" he finally asked. "I'm busy here."

She shut her mouth with a click. "I only meant we can't expect these captains to come up with a strategy that works for the whole planet. They might understand the situation on the *Lightning Rod,* but they don't understand the larger picture."

He had to restrain himself from laughing in her face. She seemed completely oblivious that these rogue captains she was referring to included himself.

"Exactly what strategy are you going to come up with to defend Earth against the invaders?" he asked. "Assuming you four, Colonel Levitt, and General Halstead are the Command Staff—the only Command Staff we know exist—what strategy are you going to come up with? If you've been doing your jobs, you should already have been thinking about it while we've been stranded out here. So what have you come up with? What's your plan?"

"Well.....we don't have access to scanner information.....and all that....." Admiral Chambers cut in. "We haven't been able to see anything because Sailor wouldn't let us on the bridge."

"Admiral Simpson is on the bridge." Radcliffe waved at the man who kept his back to the room. "Captain English gave Admiral Simpson free rein of the bridge. All Admiral Simpson had to do was make a commitment to cooperate with English's command. You could all have been doing the same thing. Instead, you've been causing trouble all this time." Radcliffe turned back to the XO's station. "I'll make you a deal. I'll transfer scanner control to your quarters. You can see exactly what the aliens and every USF vessel on the planet are doing. Then you can get to work coming up with a strategy. I'm sure Captain Church will be delighted to hear it just as soon as you share your ideas with him."

Radcliffe turned back to his work and put the senior officers out of his mind. A few minutes later, they really did leave.

Silence descended over the bridge again, but their departure didn't give Radcliffe any relief. He really needed to tell Morrison about this. These people would never stop causing problems as long as they were on board.

Chapter 20

English came to his senses lying on the floor in darkness. He blinked the dust out of his eyes before he realized he wasn't in complete darkness. A reddish-yellow light glowed from somewhere nearby.

He pried his aching head off the ground and had to blink a few more times before he fully believed where he was. He was inside the little oblong flight compartment of an alien warship.

All the symbols, controls, and displays he'd seen on the downed warship now shimmered with light. They flickered on and off in different patterns he didn't understand.

A single alien stood at the control panel in front of English. It was the same control panel he'd cut off with his stolen weapon—or it was in the same position as the one he cut off.

This one was fully operational with all the lights and symbols flickering in front of the alien's eyes. All those symbols and readings reflected on the creature's mask. English still couldn't see what this alien looked like underneath.

The pilot moved from one control to another, tapped different things on the wall, and adjusted everything to fly the ship. The creature kept his back to English the whole time and didn't check once to see if English was awake.

English sat up and studied the room more closely.

The whole front wall displayed an image of space outside. English didn't see that before because the first flight compartment he and his staff had searched had been blown wide open. That part of the wall had been destroyed.

Now it presented a huge, curved surface in front of the pilot. The screen projected more symbols, data, and smaller inset images of different scenes all over Earth.

The main image showed the sky whizzing past while the pilot flew through Earth's atmosphere. The insets showed USF destroyers in battle against more warships in different locations.

Most of the battles were taking place at USF sites where the Force might have been trying to mount some kind of counter-campaign.

English couldn't tell where the pilot was or where he was going. This warship was too high in the atmosphere. From what English could see, the ship was climbing higher to break orbit.

More warships dotted the area of space between Earth and Mars. English didn't see that the warships were doing anything out there except hovering in space.

The ship broke orbit and picked up speed to go after them when, without warning, the pilot veered hard to the left and the warship plunged. English held onto the floor to stop himself from sliding around.

He braced himself into the corner and stared at the screen in horror. The pilot drove the warship on an intercept course for four USF destroyers on their way across the Atlantic.

English didn't notice them before. The destroyers hadn't been involved in any battle against the aliens. The ships had just been flying somewhere minding their own business.

The pilot opened fire on them and slapped one of them down into the ocean with the very first shot.

The screen somehow distorted the warship's speed so the pilot could see and react to everything even with the ship moving at high speed.

The pilot turned on the three remaining destroyers. English couldn't watch this. He had to do something to help those destroyers before the pilot finished them off.

He clambered to his feet against the crushing G force and tackled the alien from behind. English's weight ripped the creature away from the controls and they both hit the floor.

The alien turned out to be incredibly strong—much stronger than English realized.

English jumped up and tried to get on top of the creature. He landed one punch before the alien tossed him off easily and hurled English against the wall.

English smashed into the wall and hit the floor again. The alien got up, walked over to him, and kicked him hard in the head.

English flipped onto his back and lay there with his head reeling while the alien stalked back to his controls. English couldn't see any part of the creature's expression behind the mask.

The alien pilot went back to bombarding the destroyers with punishing shots. English forced himself to get up. He couldn't lie here with his head in the clouds while this bastard destroyed USF vessels.

English measured his next move with care, but every delay risked USF lives.

He charged the alien, slammed his shoulder into the creature's side, and knocked the pilot away from the controls. The alien stumbled to his left and English pounced on the controls trying to find both the helm and the weapons system.

The alien reacted by punching English hard across the side of the head. English buckled onto the panel, but he didn't fall. He kept straining his eyes trying to understand all the symbols in front of him.

The pilot straight-armed him away with one brutal shove and stepped back into place. English jerked away out of position, but he still didn't fall.

The pilot went back to working the controls and ignored English standing right next to him.

English floundered trying to understand what the pilot was doing. The pilot swerved the warship back toward the three remaining destroyers and opened fire.

English grabbed the pilot's wrists and tried to wrench the controls out of the alien's grip. The alien's limbs felt like iron chains of muscle buried under thick, leathery skin.

The creature's hands had four finger appendages sticking out of them. None of them was opposable.

The creature held onto the controls and resisted English's interference. He yanked at the creature's wrists, but nothing English did could tear the alien's hands away from the helm or the weapons system.

The pilot kept firing at the destroyers and another battle broke out right in front of the screen. A few more warships showed up just to finish off the destroyers once and for all.

English lost his head. He couldn't let these destroyers go down. He'd been seeing too many USF vessels getting flattened and too many USF personnel getting killed lately. He had to take his chance to stop this if he could possibly get away with it.

He gave the pilot's wrists one more hellacious yank and the warship dodged wildly out of control. The pilot scrambled to correct and then backhanded English hard across the face.

English tasted blood, but he couldn't fall. He had to keep fighting. The pilot tried one more time to steady his ship and English pounced on him.

English threw all his weight against the pilot's arms, and when that failed to unseat the pilot, English grabbed for the controls, too. He pushed random buttons, twisted every dial in sight, and attacked the controls the pilot had just been using.

The pilot tried to fight English off, but the pilot had to work fast to fix whatever problems English was causing.

The warship wobbled dangerously to one side. English jumped on the controls and went into another frantic scramble to interfere with the pilot's work as much as possible.

He must have pushed the wrong button because the ship lurched away from the battle. The destroyers vanished off the screen and the warship tilted all the way backward. English lost track of what he was doing or which controls he was pushing.

The next time he looked at the screen, the ship was rocketing straight up into orbit and the atmosphere evaporated in front of his eyes.

The pilot attacked him at the same moment and the two got into another wrestling match over the controls.

Adrenaline wiped out every other consideration. English saw himself stopping this alien from attacking USF vessels. English didn't care about anything else.

He stabbed his fingers at the controls and grabbed whatever the pilot wasn't touching. The pilot sprang back and forth between fighting English off, readjusting the controls, and trying to tear his hands out of English's grip.

Without warning, the pilot gave one great bellow of frustration and alarm and threw his arms in front of his face. He stopped fighting entirely.

English glanced up and time stopped when he saw the ship flying straight into the moon. The Strategic Lunar Base soared past his eyes and then the ship smashed into something very big and very solid.

The impact ripped English and the pilot away from the control panel and hurled them both into the back wall. English passed out again.

He woke up in darkness again. The section of the wall that had been acting as a screen wasn't there anymore. A breach in the ship's hull showed him the towering structure of the Lunar Detention Center outside.

He dragged himself into a sitting position again. Everything hurt. He really asked for it by attacking that alien pilot, but at least he stopped the pilot from going after those destroyers.

None of the controls were working anymore. The breach in the wall let the Detention Center's artificial oxygen atmosphere flood the flight compartment. He didn't see the pilot anywhere. English was alone.

He was just thinking about getting up and going to look around when he noticed that the breach wasn't really a breach. The edges ran in smooth curves from one point at the top to a matching point at the bottom.

They made a pointed lozenge shape that couldn't be an accident. It must be some kind of door in the wall.

The minute he made that connection, the pilot stepped into the gap from outside. He stopped there and studied English through the mask. English froze. He couldn't read this alien's expression.

The creature walked over to him, stopped to study him again, and then kicked English hard across the head again.

English flipped back onto the floor fighting to stay conscious. His head pounded and he felt something shatter in the middle of his face.

He rolled onto his side groaning in agony only for the alien to kick him hard in the body this time.

English grunted in pain and then collapsed clutching his sides. He couldn't breathe....but he had to.

The alien stood over him staring down at him until English scooted all the way back against the wall. That was as far as English could get from the creature.

All thought of fighting back vanished out of English's head. He couldn't fight this creature. English had to think. He had to come up with some way to get off this base and get back to Earth.

No one knew he was up here. That was the worst of it.

He tried to remember if anyone had been at the Strategic Lunar Base during the civil conflict.

The loyalist force had been so busy fighting the war that he and his fellow captains didn't pay much attention to the moon. It had been too close to Earth with the rebel fleet standing in the way.

If anyone was here, English might be able to get to them—and then what? No one human would be able to help him against these aliens.

The pilot stood in front of English waiting for English to pull himself together. English lay panting on the floor.

He stole a few sidelong peeks at the pilot and then looked away. The creature's mask made it look spooky and inhuman—because it was.

Out of nowhere, the creature asked, "Who are you?"

It used some kind of mechanical device on its mask to make the sounds of monotone words. It sounded like some mechanized translation tool to change the pilot's words into English.

English gasped a few more times. "I'm.....I'm Captain...Sailor....English......of the *USS Lightning Rod.*" He struggled to push himself up and sit against the wall. "But you already knew that. That's why you captured me."

The alien just stood there staring down at him for way too long before it spoke again. "You are the commander...."

"No, I'm not!" English snapped. "I'm just a ship's captain. I'm nobody."

The creature kicked him again in the side, but this time, English stayed sitting up. He doubled over groaning and trying not to sob.

"You answer my questions," the creature ordered in its metallic, monotone voice. "You don't speak."

English gasped and struggled to blink the overwhelming darkness out of his eyes. If this went on much longer, he would pass out again. He might not wake up.

The pilot straightened up and waited for English to settle down. He finally collapsed against the wall fighting to breathe.

"You are the commander," the alien repeated. "You lead the others. We have seen you. You will die."

"If you wanted me dead, you would have killed me already," English fired back. "What do you want from me?"

"You know the defenders' strategy. You will tell us."

"We don't have a strategy." English waved toward where the screen used to be. "Have you seen us putting together any strategy? Do you see us offering any defense? You're messing with me."

The alien studied him for a few more minutes. English took the time to huddle on the floor and stop himself from breaking down completely.

He was never going to get away from this creature. He knew that now. He was already too injured to do anything.

Whatever this creature wanted to know, English wouldn't be able to tell him and then the alien really would kill English. No one would be able to stop the alien from doing exactly what he wanted.

Chapter 21

Racer and her fellow pilots lounged on the couches in the enlisted mess. Laughlin sprawled on his back with one arm draped over the back of the couch, one foot propped on the coffee table, and the other propped on the arm of the couch.

He kept picking up cookies from the table near him, sticking them in his mouth, and chewing them while he looked at the ceiling. "The first problem is even getting close to one of the warships to get the captain out of it."

"The first problem is even finding out which warship the captain is on," Walker countered from an armchair across the room. "Trying to get him off a warship he isn't on would be a waste of time."

"Can't we track which ship he's on using log data from the battle?" Smythe asked from the dining table. "We should be able to see if they move him from one ship to another."

"What's the point of finding out which ship he's on if we can't get near enough to rescue him?" Laughlin pointed out. "We need to find a way to defend ourselves against their weapons, use a weapon of our own to attack them, and then somehow locate the captain, get him off the warship, and bring him back."

"All without getting ourselves killed in the process," Waterman finished.

"Exactly," Laughlin replied. "I was just about to say that."

No one else said anything for a minute. Ezra had scooted all the way down on his couch so that his chest and midsection lay horizontally on the lower cushion. He rested his head against the back cushion where he could see the rest of the group.

"Checking the log data from the battle wouldn't do anything," he muttered. "The aliens could have used their transport beam to send him to any other ship."

"Why him?" Ritchie asked. "Why did they capture him specifically? The aliens could have captured anyone from the *Lightning Rod*. There were hundreds of people standing out there during the battle."

"He was all by himself," Racer pointed out. "No one else was near him."

"Maybe they identified him as the commander of this group of destroyers," Sean suggested. "He's gone into battle against the aliens before. He's fired stolen weapons on their warships and brought them down. He took all the stranded crews on board the *Lightning Rod*. It wouldn't be too much of a stretch for the aliens to notice that he's in a command position in Earth's defense—or this part of it, at least."

"So you're saying they wanted to take him out because he's in command?" Hoskins asked. "That makes no sense. They could have splattered him all over the field with one shot. They didn't have to capture him."

"I didn't say they wanted to kill him," Sean replied. "Racer says they hit next to him and that's what knocked him down. They could have killed him then. They probably want to interrogate him and find out what he knows."

"How can they interrogate him when they don't speak English?" Hughes asked and then grinned. "English? Get it?"

"None of this is getting us closer to finding and rescuing the captain," Walker pointed out.

No one responded. Racer still didn't have the first notion of how to go about rescuing English.

Right then, Captain Church, the younger Captain English, and Charlie Frasier walked into the mess. The pilots scrambled to stand up in time, but it took way too long considering the positions they'd been in until just now.

"At ease, folks," Church told them, but his presence told them the opposite. "I have another mission for you."

"Yes, Sir," Racer replied. "We're ready for anything, especially anything that might include rescuing Captain English."

"We aren't there yet, Gunny. I want you to take your birds, get out of Earth's atmosphere, and take a look around the solar system."

Racer frowned. "Can't you do that from the bridge, Sir?"

"The aliens are going after any USF vessel that shows her face out there," Hughes pointed out.

"That's why I'm sending you," Church replied. "Your birds are the only ships we have that can move fast enough to evade the warships."

Sean snorted. "Hardly, Sir. They can move faster than we can even see."

"I mean in battle, Gunny," Church corrected. "They can move fast to intercept, but they have to stand still to shoot. You can move around better than we can—I mean, you can move around better than a destroyer can. We can scan the planet and the solar system, but I want you to check things out and see if we're missing anything."

"Like what would that be, Sir?" Hoskins asked. "The aliens aren't doing anything you don't already know about."

"You might be right, but I want you to take a tour around the solar system anyway. I also want to see what the aliens do about one wing flying around that isn't involved in any battle."

"They already blocked us from going to South America," Janacek pointed out. "We were one wing flying around then."

"The aliens didn't send a warship after you until the wing from Fort Lauderdale moved to join you," Church corrected. "Every other wing in the air has been involved in hostilities in one location or another. I want to see just how many birds we can put up before they act. We need to know how much we can move around, in what ships, and how far they're willing to let you go."

"Yes, Sir," Racer replied. "Anything will be better than sitting around staring at the wall."

"So when do you want us to go?" Hughes asked.

"Immediately," Church replied. "Lieutenant Frasier will be your Squadron Commander."

Racer frowned. "Not Lieutenant Rickenbach?"

"No, Lieutenant Frasier is the senior squadron commander on board."

Racer opened her mouth to argue and changed her mind. If Frasier was the senior squadron commander on board, why did Captain English assign Rickenbach to command the wing on their last run?

Ritchie asked the question for her. "Is Lieutenant Rickenbach okay, Sir? We haven't seen him since we got back."

"He's fine, Airman," Church replied. "Why do you ask?"

Ritchie frowned. Some of the other pilots exchanged glances, but when no one said anything, Church ordered them all to carry on and left the mess along with the other two officers.

"Something weird is going on," Hoskins murmured.

"You can say that again," Laughlin replied.

"Do you think this has something to do with the conspirators?" Smythe asked.

"How can it?" Ezra asked. "The conspirators don't have anything to do with the aliens."

"Maybe the captain wants to get our birds off the ship," Racer suggested. "Maybe there's been another threat of mutiny and the conspirators want to steal our birds to use against the Force."

"There are only two conspirators left—Sandoval and McKee," Janacek pointed out.

"There are only two conspirators left that we know about," Sean corrected. "There could be others we don't know about."

Just then, Charlie Frasier came back into the room, looked around at them all, and clapped his hands. "Welp! Let's get rocking. What are you waiting for? Get down to the deck and load up."

Racer turned around to look at him. "Is there something going on here that we should know about?"

"Of course not!" Frasier replied. "You just heard him. He wants you to go take a look around.

"So.....is he in charge now?" Sean asked.

"Yep," Frasier replied. "He's the new captain of the *Lightning Rod.*"

"Who promoted him?" Hughes asked. "Is he working for the rebel officers?"

"No!" Frasier countered. "He promoted himself. I mean Captain English—the younger one—and Captain Radcliffe—well, they didn't exactly promote him. They just decided amongst themselves that Church would take over. It was all over in a few minutes."

"I thought the younger Captain English was taking over," Racer remarked. "He was sure acting like it after the battle."

"No, he specifically said he didn't want to."

Racer frowned again. She'd never heard of someone promoting themselves, especially not to a rank as important as captain.

Frasier didn't notice all the furrowed brows in front of him. "Let's go, gasheads." He turned his back on them to leave, so the pilots followed him downstairs.

Chapter 22

"Wing 1 is away, Sir," Lieutenant Rickenbach reported from the logistics station.

"They're heading south toward South America along their previous route," Eismann added. "No enemy interference so far."

"Keep an eye on things," Radcliffe ordered.

"There's no USF activity anywhere else, either," Admiral Simpson reported. "No destroyers or birds in the air anywhere."

Radcliffe pursed his lips. "Then our birds will be the only ones the enemy sees. I guess we could have timed this better."

"Maybe not, Sir," Rickenbach suggested. "If we flew our birds when the USF was attacking, the enemy might assume our birds were doing the same thing. Right now, the enemy could assume our birds are just traveling somewhere."

"I'm not ready to start assuming what the enemy thinks," Radcliffe replied. "If the enemy does make a move on our birds, bring them back on the double and we'll defend their retreat with enemy weapons."

"Yes, Sir," Rickenbach replied. "Squadron Command is standing by to order our birds home at the first sign of enemy contact."

Just then, Captain Ted Church stuck his head out of the ready room door. "Would you please come in here for a minute, Matt?"

Radcliffe looked up from his station. Eismann, Simpson, and Rickenbach all looked up, too.

Radcliffe exchanged glances with them and Church held the ready room door open for him to enter. Andy was already in there.

Church shut the door behind him and returned to his desk where he opened a communications channel. "Go ahead, Admiral."

Three people appeared on the screen. General Wesley Redding and Admiral Carlton Gehring were both older, greying, and gruff, rough types.

They both seemed like they belonged on the flight deck ordering pilots around instead of commanding the whole United Space Force.

Admiral Jacqueline Kennedy was a young woman by comparison. She was only forty and wore her long hair in one braid down her back. She had an easy-going nature that hid a heart of steel underneath.

"Are you absolutely sure about this, Ted?" she asked. "We can't risk any more destroyers."

"We've driven the warships off more than once and destroyed about ten of them using stolen alien weapons," Church replied. "These weapons are the only thing that does any good against these warships."

General Redding frowned and rubbed his chin. "If fighting these things on the ground gets us weapons we can use against them, maybe you better stay where you are."

"What's the good of getting these weapons if we can't use them where they count?" Andy asked. "We need to distribute these weapons through the whole force."

"Not to mention studying them to see how they work," Church added. "We've gone as far as we can with it here. Someone with more expertise needs to take over and figure them out."

"The weapons don't work forever anyway," Radcliffe interjected. "You might be able to use the weapons two or three times in battle before they run out of juice. Then we're back to square one. We might even use them up defending you while the engineers repair the ship."

"All the more reason we need to bring the *Lightning Rod* and the *Greyhound* back into the fold," Admiral Kennedy decided. "We need every destroyer we can get."

"How many destroyers do you plan to send out?" Church asked.

"Four should do the trick," General Redding replied. "We'll create a diversion down here at Adelaide and send them up to you. Have your people standing by to defend us once we get there."

"Yes, Sir," Church replied and signed off. Then he straightened up and faced his two XOs. "You heard him. Get everyone outside, armed up, and ready to defend the ship. Send word to the *Greyhound* to get all their people out on the ground, too. Tell them to come over and arm themselves before the destroyers show up."

The three men left the bridge and gave orders to Eismann and Simpson. They sent out a ship-wide alert to the rest of the crew.

Those few minutes of leeway gave Church, Andy, and Radcliffe the time they needed to get to the cargo hold and arm themselves before the crush of people swarmed the place.

They attacked the pile of alien weapons. The crew had collected too many of them to fit in the weapons locker.

The crew poured outside just as the *Greyhound* crew tumbled out of their ship, hustled over to the *Lightning Rod,* and armed up.

Both crews surrounded the ship and aimed their weapons at the sky. Nothing happened for a minute and then Radcliffe heard engine noise.

Four destroyers streaked out of the eastern sky with the sun behind them. Radcliffe squinted into the glare. He couldn't make out which destroyers they were—not that it mattered.

He didn't watch them for long. He concentrated all his attention on the sky behind and around them. All the rest of the *Lightning Rod* and *Greyhound* crews rotated to the east side of the ship, but no one paid any attention to the new arrivals.

The two crews trained their weapons on the sky and nearly everyone swiveled from one side to the other to cover every possible angle of approach. The crews kept their backs to the destroyers that landed behind the defenders.

The four destroyers set down between the *Lightning Rod* and the *Greyhound*. Dozens of people disembarked and the engineering teams raced to the two damaged destroyers. The rest of the crews went into the *Lightning Rod's* hold.

There weren't many alien weapons left to go around. Those crewmen who didn't get alien weapons joined the ranks with conventional USF plasma rifles.

Morrison went from rank to rank giving orders to everyone, lining them up, and reminding them all again and again to stay alert for the enemy.

Radcliffe's nerves stretched to the breaking point. The silence would have been oppressive enough. Then the engineering teams started grinding, welding, banging, and yelling orders to each other about the repairs they were doing.

The noise grated Radcliffe's nerves more than anything. He really wished they would shut up, but just when he thought he couldn't take it a second longer, a warship zoomed out of nowhere and stopped dead right over the field in front of the crew's guns.

Four more warships materialized just as fast. "Fire!" Morrison bellowed. "Combine your fire to take down each ship one after the other!"

The whole crew unloaded. Radcliffe fired at the first warship, but it took a second for everyone else to make up their minds about which ship to shoot at first.

Energy shots scattered all over the place and the warships retaliated by flattening the *Greyhound* completely. The first overwhelming shot squashed the ship as flat as a pancake along with all the engineers working on her.

The first warship turned its guns on the *Lightning Rod,* but that one moment of hesitation gave the ground crews time to combine their firepower into a reasonable defense.

Dozens of the defending crewmen turned their weapons to join Radcliffe's. Their guns spat together just as the first warship opened fire on the *Lightning Rod.*

The crew's shots smashed in the warship's hull right where the blast had been about to come from. The hull imploded and an explosion went off.

The other three warships changed tack and bombarded the ground crews. Concussions burst all around Radcliffe, but he just had to keep shooting.

He pounded the warship until the explosions escalated into an unstoppable cascade. Then he jerked his weapon sideways and fired at the second warship.

The noise of deafening booms prevented anyone from hearing anything. He didn't take the time to order anyone to join him. They did it automatically and the whole crew turned its firepower on the second warship.

That didn't stop the other two from firing into the ground force again and again. Blasts, screams, and thunderous explosions pounded Radcliffe's ears.

He blocked it all out and focused every particle of his being on the point where his energy beam struck that warship.

The spot dissolved in flames and another eruption of burning gas and debris ejected from the spot. He and his closest comrades kept up the barrage until that ship went up, too. There were two left.

Radcliffe snapped his weapon sideways to target the third warship. He could keep doing this all day long.

He erased the sound of explosions from his ears. He would just keep shooting until one of the enemy shots took him out, too.

He fired at the third warship. Not as many people joined him. He didn't dare to look away from his target. He didn't want to see the mayhem, death, and destruction all around him.

His beam hit the third warship, but as soon as his beam made contact with it, the last two ships blipped away and left the landscape as silent and devastated as it had been before.

Radcliffe kept his weapon up. He didn't want to let his guard down, but in that silence, he heard all the screaming, moaning, and choking behind him.

He turned around and his stomach dropped. A carpet of mangled bodies surrounded him on all sides. The place where he'd been standing was one of the very few the aliens hadn't bombed to a moonscape.

The minute he turned around, Dr. Cassidy and her team hustled out of the *Lightning Rod,* but they couldn't do much with so many dead and dying people around.

Radcliffe's arms wilted to his sides. He couldn't hold his weapon up anymore. He blinked at the destruction and then something happened to him that he didn't understand.

He dropped his gun right there, went over to the medical team, and started helping them out in any way he could.

The doctors from the *Champion* and the *Cobalt* along with most of their medical teams had come on board the *Lightning Rod* in the last few days.

The three doctors split up to cover more ground and Radcliffe wound up working with two medics from the *Cobalt* and two nurses from the *Champion*.

The three doctors went from person to person giving orders to either transport someone inside to Sick Bay, bandage or split their injuries here, or to leave them be.

Radcliffe tried not to look at all the people lying on the ground around him. He didn't know most of them. They belonged to one of the other ship crews—the *Cobalt*, the *Greyhound,* or the *Champion*.

He was just putting a splint on some young female pilot's leg when Dr. Cassidy yelled out, "We need a stretcher over here. Take him inside right away. He needs surgery."

Radcliffe stuck on the last piece of tape and went over to the patient she indicated. He and the rest of his team put the stretcher down next to the patient and Radcliffe froze when he saw that the patient was Ted Church.

He looked like one of the alien blasts might have hit him in the chest. Most of his torso had been torn away with one arm and shoulder hanging off and his pelvis disconnected from the rest of him.

He was still conscious and breathing, though. The undamaged side of his chest still worked. He gasped and panted for air and his eyes darted around in a frenzy.

"Ted...." Radcliffe choked.

Church's eyes snapped over to him. He tried to speak, but his lips quivered so badly that he couldn't form words.

"Don't talk. We're getting you inside." Radcliffe pounced on the stretcher. "Just hold on, Ted. We're taking you to Sick Bay."

Radcliffe and the medics did their best to get Church onto the stretcher. Radcliffe tried not to move Church's mangled limbs too much, but he didn't seem to be in any pain. He was too far gone or maybe just too deep in shock.

He barely blinked when they picked up his shredded arm. Radcliffe scooped his arms under Church's knees. He was so big and muscular that it took both medics and a nurse to hoist his upper body onto the stretcher.

"Matt....." he gasped.

"Don't talk, Ted." Radcliffe heard his own voice shaking. The *Lightning Rod* was in serious trouble without Church. "Just sit tight. Dr. Cassidy is going to take you to surgery."

"Matt...." Church husked. "Take......command......"

"Be quiet," Radcliffe snapped louder than he meant to. "We aren't talking about that right now."

He moved over to the end of the stretcher—the end near Church's feet. Dr. Cassidy followed Radcliffe and one of the medics to Sick Bay. She directed them to put Church in intensive care.

Then Radcliffe had to leave him there and go back outside to tend to the rest of the wounded. There was no shortage of wounded.

Church gave Radcliffe a pleading look before he left, but then Dr. Cassidy gave Church an injection of something that knocked him out.

Radcliffe waited a split second and looked down at Church's unconscious face. He really had been the best of the three captains to take over the *Lightning Rod*. No one ever questioned Church's authority to command this ship.

Radcliffe didn't question his own authority to command the *Lightning Rod,* either. He'd been Captain Ogden's XO for years. He could step into the role with no problem.

Maybe serving with all these other captains did something to him .....or maybe he just admired the other three captains too much.

Maybe all four of them serving together had somehow eroded the chain of command so that he had difficulty reestablishing it.

He didn't have time to think about that right now. He went back outside and spent the next five hours treating injuries, carrying people on board, and carrying dead bodies to the ship's morgue where they could be cremated. No one had time to conduct funerals for all the dead.

The engineering crews kept working through the whole gruesome ordeal. The whole senior staff of the *Greyhound* had been killed in that one devastating shot that destroyed the ship forever.

Now nearly two hundred people from the *Greyhound* crew stood around with nowhere else to go.

"You can all come on board the *Lightning Rod,*" Radcliffe told a young lieutenant who approached him about the crew's problem. Radcliffe studied the guy a little closer. His name was Pendleton and he couldn't have been more than twenty-four. "Are you the most senior officer left from the crew?"

Pendleton averted his gaze and nodded. "Yes, Sir. We have a few gunnery sergeants who are older than me and five other lieutenants. Everyone else was on board the ship when she got hit."

Radcliffe gripped the man's shoulder. "Never mind about that, Lieutenant. Bring your people on board and I'll transfer you onto the *Lightning Rod's* crew roster."

"Thank you, Sir," Pendleton muttered and took himself off to give the word to the rest of the *Greyhound* crew.

The survivors stood off to one side talking with their heads together. Two dozen had joined the medical team in helping the wounded. The others didn't know what to do with themselves.

Radcliffe watched them all go on board. He would need to transfer the crew roster from the *Greyhound* to the *Lightning Rod* so he would be able to tally up who was still alive, who had been wounded and was now in the *Lightning Rod's* Sick Bay, and who was dead.

He didn't want to abandon the medical team when they still had so much to do, but he hadn't seen Andy since before the battle started. Someone needed to keep running the ship.

He went up to the bridge and got a surprise when he found Andy there working at the XO's station. "Where the hell have you been?" Radcliffe demanded. "Ted Church is in intensive care undergoing surgery for life-threatening injuries."

"I know," Andy replied. "I've been supervising the repair crews. We're almost ready to take the *Lightning Rod* back to the Strategic Supply Base at San Juan Island. We were just waiting for you to show up so you could sign off on the repairs and the diagnostic results."

"You could have done that yourself," Radcliffe countered. "You didn't need to wait for me."

"No, you have to do it." Andy pulled a portable computer device out of the port it had been docked in under the XO's station. Andy handed it to Radcliffe. "You're in command of the *Lightning Rod* now."

"Why me? You've been up here all this time. You should take command."

"No, it has to be you. I heard Church tell you to take command. He wants you to take over."

"How do you know that if you've been up here supervising the repair crews?"

"I was outside supervising them when you were working on him. I heard him clear as day."

Radcliffe narrowed his eyes at Andy. "Do you have a problem with being in command because your dad isn't here? Is that it?"

"Of course not. You're the best man for the job. That's the only reason. You know the *Lightning Rod* and her crew better than I do...."

"Don't give me that shit," Radcliffe countered. "Is it because you were a rebel? Are you worried the crew won't accept you?"

"Will you knock it off?" Andy snapped. "Just take command of the damn ship, already. What's the problem?"

He turned back to the XO's station like he had so many other more important things to do. Radcliffe glared at the side of Andy's head. Now Radcliffe really was certain that Andy had a problem with taking command.

Maybe he didn't want to fill his father's shoes or maybe Andy had some other reason not to want to take command of the *Lightning Rod*.

Radcliffe could think of a thousand arguments to insist that Andy take over as captain of the *Lightning Rod*.

Then Radcliffe's brain switched gears again and the whole issue evaporated. He crossed the bridge to the captain's chair and sat down in it for the first time.

He'd only served as captain of the *Infinity* for a few hours. He didn't believe before he took command of the ship or even while he flew her in battle that he even was a captain.

All of that disappeared off the map now. He was a captain and he was in command of his ship. The *Lightning Rod* was his ship if he had any ship at all. Maybe that's what Andy meant.

It didn't matter because she needed a captain and he was it. He checked the repair reports and the diagnostic results.

"The reports look good....and the diagnostics are all within normal ranges. We're clear to launch as soon as the crews get on board and the medical teams finish with the casualties."

"We're receiving a hail from San Juan, Sir," Eismann called from Logistics. "It's General Redding."

"Put it through," Radcliffe ordered.

General Redding's rugged, lined face appeared on the screen. He frowned when he saw Radcliffe. "Captain.....we've been monitoring the situation on our scanners. The battle didn't go so well." He hesitated. "Where's Church?"

"He's in Sick Bay, Sir," Radcliffe replied. "I'm taking command of the *Lighting Rod*. We're finalizing repairs now and I'm taking the rest of the *Greyhound* crew on board. We should be arriving in San Juan in a few hours as soon as we finish taking our casualties on board."

"So.....some of the Greyhound crew survived?"

"They were outside fighting the aliens with us when the ship got hit. We have a few lieutenants and gunnery sergeants and everyone below them in rank—no senior staff."

Redding winced and looked away. "I'm sorry to hear that."

"It can't be helped now, Sir. We'll get the *Lightning Rod* underway and I can give you a full report when I get to San Juan."

Chapter 23

Racer pushed her throttle a little farther forward. She scanned the horizon on her way across the Texas panhandle. "Still no sign of the enemy," she remarked.

"We're approaching the spot where we encountered the warship last time," Hughes reported.

Racer glanced to her left. "No activity out of Fort Lauderdale."

"How far south do you want to go?" Sean asked. "We don't even know what our original destination was supposed to be."

"Let's peel it back around to the Pacific and then we'll climb up into orbit and see what we can see." Racer pulled her helm to starboard. "Hold formation and stay alert."

She banked sideways over Mexico and headed out toward Hawaii. She was just pulling north when seven USF destroyers launched from Adelaide heading for Karachi.

"What are they doing?" Hoskins muttered. "They're asking for trouble launching that many destroyers. What do they really think they're going to accomplish?"

Racer almost answered when five warships hurtled across her bird's nose. "Whoa!!" she hollered and yanked her controls away just in time.

They rocketed past her so fast that they were already gone. They intercepted the destroyers from Adelaide and plowed into a punishing battle.

"What did I tell you?" Hoskins growled. "What a waste of a bunch of perfectly good destroyers."

"When you become an admiral, you can run the war your own way," Hughes told him. "What are we doing, Racer?"

She checked on the state of battle. "None of the warships are coming after us. Let's get into orbit and see what the planet looks like from upstairs."

She climbed up into orbit. "Holy guacamole!" Janacek breathed. "Take a look at all these warships! There must be forty or fifty of them up here."

"They aren't taking part in subduing the planet," Walker observed. "They're just sitting here doing nothing."

"Heads up!" Laughlin called. "Four destroyers moving in on the *Lightning Rod!* It looks like....."

The crew fell silent when the *Lightning Rod* and *Greyhound* crews flooded out of both ships, armed themselves with alien weapons, and surrounded the two destroyers to defend the ships.

The four newly-arrived destroyers landed on the ground behind the defensive line. "Now I know why the USF launched those destroyers from Adelaide," Hoskins remarked. "It was a....."

He broke off when four warships blasted out of the west. Racer didn't see where they came from.

In a fraction of a second, they halted over the *Lightning Rod* and a battle broke out between the warships and the crews on the ground.

"We gotta get down there!" Hughes barked. "Come on! We gotta draw the enemy's fire."

"We can't go down there!" Racer countered. "Our weapons are no good against the warships. We have to stay out of it like Captain Church told us to."

"So we're just gonna sit here and leave our people to die?" Sean interjected. "I don't think so."

Racer cast a hopeless glance around. She could see the devastation the enemy was wreaking on the *Greyhound* and the ground crews.

A fighter wing going down there and getting involved in the battle would only put the *Lightning Rod* crew in more danger.

She hesitated to give the order one way or the other, and in that moment, she spotted something. "No damn way!"

"What?" Hoskins asked.

"Take a look at your scanners." Racer's heart started pounding. "There's a downed warship at the Lunar Detention Center with two life signs—one alien and one human. I bet you anything it's Captain English. Come on. We're going to get him."

She yanked her bird away. "Wait, Racer!" Ezra yelled. "You don't know it's him!"

"Who the hell else would it be? Come on!"

She didn't wait for anyone to answer. She ripped her bird into reverse, skidded around, and slammed her throttle to the wall punching out of orbit.

She blasted through space, but she was far enough away from the warships that they didn't come after her.

She gunned her engines for the moon and the rest of Wing 1 caught up a minute later. "This could be a big mistake, Racer," Sean told her.

"We've been racking our brains trying to find a way to get to him. If he's down there with one alien and a wrecked warship, this could be our only chance to get him before the aliens move him somewhere else."

She didn't wait around to hear any more. She plunged for the Lunar Detention Center and dodged between buildings getting closer to the human life sign in the distance.

It was the only human life sign on the whole moon. It had to be English. It just had to be.

She veered around another building and spotted the crashed warship ahead. It lay on its side with one part of its hull embedded in the Detention Center's exhaust stack. The stack had crumpled on top of the hull, but she could see that the warship wasn't functioning at all.

The alien life sign showed up outside the ship. The alien pilot walked around on the exhaust stack's upper repair scaffold.

A ladder extended from the scaffold to the Detention Center's south concourse, but the alien pilot apparently didn't want to explore the Lunar Detention Center.

He paced to one side, examined something on the side of his ship, and then went off and did something else.

He stopped working when Wing 1 blasted over his head and kept going to the other side of the Detention Center.

"I don't see the human," Waterman remarked.

"He's showing up on the scans as being inside the ship," Laughlin replied.

"That will just mean he's protected when we start shooting at the cocksucker who captured him." Racer pulled around for another pass. "Let's go, Wing 1."

She plunged downward between the buildings again, burned up on the exhaust stack, and opened fire on the scaffold. The alien dove sideways, grabbed a weapon, and turned it on the fighter craft.

Racer dodged, rocketed past the warship, and throttled in for the killing strike.

She planned to unload and plaster the alien to the hull of his own ship, but when she got within shooting range, he wasn't there anymore.

"Where is he?" Waterman asked. "I don't see him."

Racer looked everywhere and then glanced at her scanners. "He's inside his ship, too."

"We could go down there and confront him," Ritchie suggested.

"We're unarmed, you dipshit!" Sean countered.

Racer opened her mouth to answer when a brutal eruption of energy fire blasted out of the fallen warship's hull. It might have been aimed at Wing 1, but it sailed wide.

"He's shooting at us!" Hughes hollered. "We gotta pull out!"

The whole wing peeled hard to port, but the warship kept unloading in random directions. It fired dozens of shots, but they all sprayed wide and scattered into space. None of them came close to threatening Wing 1.

Racer and her comrades hovered off to one side where they'd be out of danger. The warship spat a few more shots into the air and then they died away.

"The alien and the human are right on top of each other!" Janacek pointed out. "They must be fighting for control of the ship."

"The person's vital signs are fluctuating," Stoval pointed out. "He must be injured."

"We're going in to get him," Racer decided. "Come on. We'll just have to take our chances."

She tilted downward to make another run to the scaffold, but right then, three warships skidded out of position. They'd been holding still near Mars with no regard to the conflict raging on Earth.

Now they soared over to the Lunar Detention Center. Two of them stood guard while the third descended right down onto the scaffold.

"Aw, hell no!" Ritchie growled. "They are not taking him right in front of us! You bastards!"

He punched his throttle and blasted down to the Detention Center. He zoomed right up to the warship and opened fire across its hull to drive it away from the stricken ship.

The warship opened fire, but he evaded, swooped around the other two warships, and charged away without taking a single hit.

Racer gunned it to follow him. She might not be able to stop the aliens from stealing English, but she could damn well give it her best shot.

The warship hovering closest to the scaffold swiveled to follow Ritchie with its guns. Racer took the opportunity to open fire on the same ship.

It veered to shoot at her, but the rest of the pilots dove in and bombarded the same ship before they all sprinted out of danger.

The warship turned one way and then the other trying to keep up with them. "It's working!" Sean called. "Keep them distracted. We gotta keep them busy so they don't land."

The wing burst into a wild tangled mishmash of flight patterns buzzing all around the three warships. Racer bombarded any ship within range, but most of her attention went toward avoiding the warships' shots.

She peeled around the other side of the grouping when a blast of gunfire exploded from Earth. The Ufa Long-Range Alert Station unloaded its battery and punishing shots ejected as far as the Lunar Detention Center.

The station had never opened fire on a USF target before except during the civil conflict. The big guns were designed to drive off alien invaders, but this was the first time they'd fired since the invasion started.

Racer and her fellow pilots barely got out of the way in time before the shots pounded the warships away from the scaffold. All three took off for Earth and left Wing 1 alone on the moon with the downed warship.

Racer waited for something else to happen. The alien and human life signs on board the ship had separated. The human life signs were fluctuating again. They were getting worse. Captain English was in trouble.

Just then, Charlie Frasier called into her ear, "Squadron Command to Wing Leader 1. Report, Wing Leader 1."

"We got a lead on Captain English's location, Sir," Racer replied. "He's at the Lunar Detention Center."

"We *think* he's at the Lunar Detention Center," Hughes corrected. "We don't know for sure if it's him."

"Well, someone is down there injured and an alien prisoner," Racer countered. "If it isn't him, then someone else needs to be rescued."

"The *Lightning Rod* is shipping out to San Juan Island," Frasier informed them. "If you don't have a clear shot to get him out, then come on back and we'll work it out another way."

Racer pushed her throttle forward, but right then, the downed warship spurted another three shots into the sky. These came much closer to hitting the crew and she had to pull away.

"Come on, Racer," Ezra murmured. "We'll have to come back for him."

She didn't want to leave. She couldn't have come this close to finding English, only to turn away at the last second.

She would never find a better time to save him than now when only one alien was guarding him. Coming back later would only make it harder to find him and to get near him.

The aliens wouldn't go to such lengths to capture him if they didn't plan to keep him. They would guard him much more closely after this.

That warship must have crashed on the moon when the pilot was trying to take English back into space.

The other pilots pulled away. She stayed where she was and watched the life sign readings on her controls.

He was down there. She knew it now.

He was injured and he fought that pilot to stop the alien from shooting at Wing 1. Who besides English would do that?

She hated to leave, but when Stoval said, "Come on, Racer," one more time, she had to pull away.

She switched her scanners away from the moon so she wouldn't see anything more. She didn't want to see just how badly English's vital signs kept fluctuating.

Was he dying? How much longer did he have? He could be dead by the time Wing 1 came back to get him.

She was supposed to be in command of this wing, but she followed the others back to the *Lightning Rod*. The ship was already in the air and on her way to the Strategic Supply Base at San Juan Island.

Hughes led the wing. Racer wasn't looking forward to getting back to the ship and informing everyone about what she and the wing found out.

Chapter 24

E nglish dragged his battered body off the floor—again. He couldn't do more than push himself up into a sitting position and lean against the wall.

He couldn't see very well. Everything in his head felt wrong, but at least he stopped the alien pilot from shooting at the fighter wing.

He didn't know which ship those fighters came from, but they never would have survived a direct hit from an alien warship.

The alien pilot didn't have any trouble knocking English away from the controls. English had hit the wall again. He didn't want to think about how long he'd been unconscious this time.

For some reason he couldn't figure out, the alien wasn't working the controls anymore. He wasn't walking around the scaffold outside, either.

He squatted in the middle of the flight compartment doing something on the floor. English couldn't figure out what that was, either.

The alien placed some kind of geometric chips in certain patterns. English didn't see anything like writing or symbols on the chips. They were just shapes.

English took a chance, cleared his throat, and asked, "Who are you?"

"Be quiet," the alien replied through his mask. His mechanized voice expressed no emotion.

English fell silent for a while, but pretty soon, his curiosity got the better of him.

To hell with it. If he was going to die on this base, he might as well ask. "What's your name? You know mine."

"My name is none of your concern," the alien countered without looking up.

"What sector of space do you come from? What species are you?" English asked. "We don't know anything about your kind."

"You do not need to know anything about my kind. We will alter this planet for our own use. You and your kind will disappear and none of you will find out anything about us."

"My kind won't find out anything about you because I won't get a chance to tell them. I'll be dead long before that happens, so you might as well tell me who you are. Those warships tried to come and get us, didn't they? Were they trying to rescue you or were they trying to stop my people from rescuing me?"

"Will you ever be quiet?" the alien muttered under his breath.

English had to laugh and stopped himself when a stab of pain lanced into his chest. He wound up coughing, which hurt even worse.

"Probably not," he choked. "One of two things happens when I get injured. Either I get surly and hostile or I talk a lot. I guess this is one of the times when I talk a lot."

The alien looked up, stared straight in front of him for a second, and then turned his masked face to stare at English. English still couldn't read anything about him.

Without warning, the alien raised his hand and did something to his mask. The black tint hiding his features vanished and the mask became transparent.

He had reptilian eyes with a nictitating membrane that took a split second longer to move across the eye. His skin had the same leathery quality as his arms and hands. It didn't have scales like a reptile.

"My name is Omai," the alien replied through his mask. "Will you be quiet now?"

English grinned at him. "Omai. I like that. It's a pleasure to meet you."

The alien stared at him even more intensely if that was possible. Then he went back to what he was doing.

English sighed. He should probably be satisfied with that, but the silence only made him want to fill it.

He'd been so curious about these aliens since the beginning. Now he was isolated with one for who knew how long.

English might not get another chance to find out if they had any vulnerabilities. He probably wouldn't get a chance to tell anyone what he found out, but it was worth a shot.

"So what species are you?" English asked.

Omai didn't respond.

English decided to throw caution to the wind and go for broke. "How many of your people usually fly one of these warships? Were you alone when you picked me up? We searched one of the warships we shot down with your troops' weapons. There were twelve people in here and they'd obviously been working the controls right up until the ship crashed. Why were you flying me around by yourself?"

Omai did the same thing. He looked up, stared at the wall like he had to work hard to contain his annoyance, and turned around to stare at English again. "Why do you talk so much?"

"Because I'm curious about your kind. Just tell me what species you are."

"Will you be quiet if I do?"

English wound up laughing again, grimaced in pain, and crammed his arm against his ribs to try to steady himself.

"I would kill you to keep you quiet if I could," Omai muttered.

"Why can't you?" English asked. "Are you under orders to bring me in alive? Why did you even capture me in the first place?"

Omai bent over his chips and pretended not to be answering. "I captured you to answer questions about your military. I would not have taken this job if I had known you would talk so much."

"You captured me to talk. Now I'm talking. Maybe you could keep me quiet by answering my questions. Then I wouldn't have to ask so many of them."

Omai turned around for the third time. He didn't even try to keep the rage out of his eyes. English could read his expression so clearly now.

"I belong to the Vikak people. Are you satisfied now?"

"And you plan to terraform Earth, is that right? What happened to your home planet? Why would you travel this far? There must have been other closer planets than this."

"Nothing happened to our home planet," Omai replied under his breath. "It is still there. We are colonizers in search of new planets to colonize."

English frowned to himself. "Where's your nearest colony? It can't be in this galaxy."

"You have asked enough questions for one night. Be quiet now."

"No way. I'm just getting started."

Omai glared at him even more ferociously. "What will it take to silence you?"

"You want to ask me questions about our military. If there's one thing you have to learn about my kind, it's that we're insatiably curious."

"Apparently," Omai muttered.

"So your military sent you out alone to capture one of our kind?" English thought it over. "You were flying with those other warships that attacked the *Lightning Rod.....* "

"Lightning Rod," the alien repeated. "What is that?"

"That's the name of my ship—the ship that crashed on the coastline where you captured me. My crewmen were the ones who took your weapons from your ground troops and used the weapons against the warships."

Omai glared at him even more dangerously. "You were the one who did that?"

"Well....me and my crew."

Omai blinked extra slowly. He stared at English for so long that English didn't ask anything else. Something in the creature's intense stare silenced English more than anything else could.

Omai turned away suddenly, scooped up all his chips, and put them into some kind of pocket-like compartment of his armor. Then he stood up and paced around the compartment.

"Have you tried to contact your people to tell them where you are?" English finally asked.

"I have already tried," Omai muttered. "It is no good."

"I know something about ships," English offered. "If you told me how this one works, I might be able to do something about it."

Omai didn't answer. He stopped at the opening leading out onto the scaffold. He stood there staring up at the stars.

A few warships hovered close enough for him and English to see them. The warships didn't come down to pick up either of the two men. The warships just stayed there in one place without moving.

English could think of a lot of things to ask this alien—like how their technology worked, what energy source they used to power their ships, whether they'd been watching Earth or just suddenly appeared in this solar system, and why they decided to terraform Earth of all planets and not some other uninhabited world like Venus, say.

The aliens obviously couldn't breathe an oxygen atmosphere since they always wore these masks. There must have been some other planet somewhere that would be better suited to building a Vikak colony.

Omai didn't strike English as one of the commanders of this colonization mission. He wouldn't be going out alone to capture an enemy hostage if he was one of the commanders.

He also wouldn't have to wait for someone else's authorization to kill English if he wanted to.

Omai eventually turned around, came back, and squatted down facing the other wall so he wouldn't have to see English.

Omai surprised English by speaking first. "You are not talking anymore. You are becoming surly and hostile."

"Naw," English replied. "I'm just thinking."

"Your people tried to rescue you," Omai remarked. "That was exceptionally foolish. Their small craft could not withstand one of our warships."

English sighed. "Yeah, we can get exceptionally foolish when one of our own is in danger."

"One of your own," Omai repeated. He still wouldn't look at English. "Did you know the men on those ships?"

English looked away. "I don't know. I didn't see them."

"They tried to rescue you. They must have known you."

"What about you?" English countered. "That warship that came here to pick us up—did you know someone on it?"

"I doubt that. The commander wanted you."

English didn't say anything. That must really suck—not to have people who cared enough to come and get you when your ship crashed. English would have hated that.

Now he understood why Omai was being surly and hostile. He was stuck here with the prize from his supposedly important mission and no one would come and pick him up to deliver it. The other Vikak just left him here.

English could think of a lot of people on the *Lightning Rod* who would care enough to come and rescue him—if they hadn't been in the middle of fighting a war, that is.

Knowing they wanted to and couldn't meant just as much as if they did come and get him. It was one of the few things keeping him going right now.

He actually felt sorry for Omai all of a sudden. These Vikak couldn't be very good people if they did that to one of their own.

Chapter 25

Radcliffe strode into the Strategic Supply Base at San Juan Island. Andy went with him, but Andy occupied the place behind Radcliffe's shoulder where the XO should stand.

Radcliffe didn't mention this. He didn't mention Andy taking command at all—ever. Radcliffe just assumed the role of captain. Life was easier for everyone this way.

He checked in with the Logistics Desk and found the conference room where General Redding, Admiral Kennedy, and Admiral Gehring were waiting for him.

They shook hands with him and then with Andy. "So good to have you gentlemen back," Admiral Gehring exclaimed. "You and your crew sure have been giving the aliens hell up there in Alaska. You were practically a whole army all on your own."

"Captain English did most of it," Radcliffe replied.

General Redding and Admiral Gehring exchanged glances and frowned. "Yeah, it's a shame we lost Sailor. He was a good one."

"You talk about him like he's dead or something," Andy cut in. "He's alive and he's the aliens' prisoner. Our fighter wing spotted them on the moon and the captain is injured. We should be mounting a rescue mission to go get him. There's only one alien up there with him.

We could get down on the Detention Center, kill this alien, and lift off the captain before the warships attack."

"We can't do that, son," Admiral Gehring replied. "The warships are right there within spitting distance of the Lunar Detention Center."

"So you're just going to abandon him up there?!" Andy snapped. "He's the one who has mounted the most effective defense against these aliens so far. He was running the whole loyalist effort until just a few days ago. He's too valuable for you to just write him off like he's already dead."

"Whether we mount a rescue mission to get Sailor back is secondary to defending the planet against these aliens," General Redding interjected. "We brought the *Lightning Rod* back here to help us do that."

"How are you going to do that without any weapons?" Radcliffe asked. "So far, the USF doesn't have a single weapon that can counteract these warships."

"That's what we need you two for," Admiral Kennedy replied. "We want both of you to join the new USF Command Staff. So far, it's just the three of us. We want you two to join us in coming up with a strategy—including what weapons to use against these aliens."

"We'll be inviting Ted Church to join us as soon as he recovers," General Redding added. "For now, it will just have to be the five of us."

Radcliffe and Andy exchanged glances. Radcliffe cleared his throat with difficulty. "Um....excuse me for contradicting, Sir. I'm sure Andy and I are both humbled and grateful that you would consider us to join the Command Staff, but we would both be more effective commanding ships. I can stay on the *Lightning Rod* and you can assign Ted and Andy to whichever other ships you need captains for."

"We don't have enough ships for all our captains," Admiral Kennedy replied. "We don't have a ship we can assign Captain English to. That's one of the reasons we need you here and not out there."

"What about the *Lightning Rod?*" Andy asked. "She can still fly. She'll need a captain."

"Not until we have a strategy that will work against these aliens," Admiral Gehring replied. "For now, you're both grounded until we know we can actually do something about this."

"I don't know what good we'll be to you," Radcliffe pointed out. "There is no strategy we can use against these invaders until we get some weapons that work."

"Then you can help us prosecute the rebel commanders," General Redding replied. "I understand you have some of them on board the *Lightning Rod.*"

Radcliffe's jaw dropped. "You want to prosecute the rebel comm anders.....now? Are you out of your minds? Bringing up the rebellion now would undermine what little unity we have left. Captain English has been adamant all this time that we put the rebellion behind us and work together to fight the invasion. That's why these officers are on board the *Lightning Rod* to begin with. He was hoping they would forget about the rebellion and we could all combine our resources the way we should have been combining them when the rebellion broke out."

"How did that work out?" Admiral Kennedy asked. *"Did* they put it behind them and pull together?"

Radcliffe and Andy exchanged another glance. Radcliffe didn't want to tell her about all the times the rebel officers tried to interfere with English's command.

"Executing the rebel commanders will send a message to any other rebel elements still active in the Force," General Redding went on.

"We'll turn over some of your alien weapons to the scientists to study. Until we get their results, this is the best way to ensure the kind of military discipline we need to unify the Force."

"You plan....to execute them?" Radcliffe gasped. "All of them?"

"Of course—everyone who rebelled against the Force and instigated the civil conflict," Admiral Gehring replied.

"We'll leave it to you two to take them into custody since they're still rostered on your ship," Admiral Kennedy went on. "You can incarcerate them in the brig here at the base until we convene our tribunal. You're both dismissed."

Radcliffe and Andy looked at each other for the third time. Was Radcliffe hearing this right?

He had to take the rebel officers into custody, including Admiral Simpson. He'd cooperated with English and supported Church, Radcliffe, and Andy every step of the way. Radcliffe would never let anyone execute Simpson.

The others had experienced their ups and downs, but they didn't deserve execution. That was just outrageous.

He struggled through saying, "Yes, Ma'am," to Admiral Kennedy, saluting all three senior officers, and he and Andy left the conference room the way they entered it. Neither of them spoke until they got out into the hall.

"Are they flippin' serious?" Andy muttered under his breath.

"They're out of their gourds," Radcliffe hissed back. "Your dad was right. This is the last thing we need right now."

"So what are we gonna do about it?" Andy asked. "We can't disobey a direct order. That would be insubordination. It would be mutiny and treason."

"So we're just gonna hand the officers over, throw them in jail, and stand aside while they get executed? I'm sorry, but I could never do that to Admiral Simpson. Your dad would never let me live it down."

Andy didn't reply right away. He stared straight in front of him while they walked down the corridor.

"Well?" Radcliffe murmured. "Are you gonna help me come up with a way to save them?"

"I was just thinking.....maybe there's a way to do both."

"Both what?"

"Rescue my dad and save the rebel officers. Maybe there's a way we can do both."

"What way would that be? You just heard them give us a direct order to throw the officers in the brig pending execution. How do we get around that?"

"We need to come up with a rescue mission plan to get my dad off the Lunar Detention Center—a plan that we can't execute without the rebel officers. Then those three goons would have no choice but to keep the officers on the *Lightning Rod* so we could carry out the plan."

Radcliffe blinked at the side of his face. "Um...okay. I'm listening. So what's the plan?"

Andy jerked his head around and cracked a grin. "I haven't come up with it yet."

"Well, you better hurry up. We're almost back at the ship."

"I can see that," Andy replied and they pushed the base doors open to walk outside.

They started to cross the tarmac on their way back to the *Lightning Rod* when the fighter craft from Wing 1 set down next to the ship. The pilots powered down, climbed out of their cockpits, and swarmed Radcliffe and Andy talking fast.

"We have to go back up there and get Captain English!" Racer insisted.

"He was all alone with only one alien," Ezra pointed out.

"We could have gotten down there after the Ufa Station started shooting," Hughes suggested. "We could have gotten him if we'd only stayed a little longer, but Lieutenant Frasier ordered us to come back here."

"If we're going back up there, we have to go right now," Ritchie added. "We have to go back before they bring in any kind of reinforcements or try to lift him off again."

Radcliffe raised his hands. "Settle down, all of you. We're going to get him. We just need to figure out how."

"So how do we do it?" Sean demanded.

"I'll tell you how we do it," Hoskins countered. "We load up in our birds—with weapons, this time—alien weapons. We fly back out to the Detention Center, land on the damn scaffold, shoot the alien cocksucker that took Captain English, and bring him back. What's so complicated about that?"

"You might need a little more firepower than that to counter any warships that happened to stop by," Radcliffe pointed out.

"That's easy," Janacek told him. "We just get the Ufa Station to bombard the bastards if they decide to come near us."

"Who are you gonna get to order the Ufa Station to fire on the moon, genius?" Hughes retorted back. "None of us has the rank to give an order like that."

Radcliffe and Andy both spun around fast and stared at each other. Radcliffe saw the same idea going through Andy's mind.

Redding, Kennedy, and Gehring didn't technically have the authority to assign themselves to the new and improved USF Command Staff.

The USF being in disarray due to the civil conflict and now the alien invasion didn't mean just anyone with any old rank could install themselves in charge of the whole United Space Force.

By rights, Halstead, Simpson, Levitt, Chambers, Schroder, Roderick, and Thorburn had as much authority to command the USF as Redding, Kennedy, and Gehring.

In peacetime, the Command Staff had voted to induct new members into its ranks.

This wasn't peacetime and the whole chain of command had been thrown out the window. Going strictly by the letter of the law, Redding, Kennedy, and Gehring had no authority to order Radcliffe and Andy to do anything.

Radcliffe pulled himself together with an effort. He waved the pilots toward the *Lightning Rod*. "All of you go to the flight deck and check in with Lieutenant Frasier."

"What about Captain English, Sir?" Racer asked. "Tell me we aren't gonna leave him up there."

"Or let the aliens take him somewhere else," Hoskins added.

"The longer you stand around here talking about it, the longer it will take before we can mount some kind of rescue," Radcliffe told them. "Now go inside and don't leave the flight deck. Understand? Stay there and be ready to deploy as soon as I send word through Squadron Command."

None of the pilots moved for a second. Radcliffe realized the need to move quickly, but he couldn't begrudge that they needed to take in what he just said.

Racer finally squared her shoulders, growled, "Yes, Sir," and turned away. She and the other pilots hurried back to the *Lightning Rod,* but not without plenty of backward glances in his direction.

Radcliffe had to work hard to control his excitement. He set off for the ship trying his best to stay calm.

"Have you ever done anything like this before?" Andy whispered on their way through the cargo hold.

"Are you serious?" Radcliffe whispered back. "I've never done anything like this before and I sure as hell hope I never do anything like this again."

"If it doesn't work, you and I will be locked up in the brig awaiting execution, too," Andy pointed out.

"Thanks for reminding me," Radcliffe muttered. "Tell me again why we're doing this."

"To save my dad's life," Andy replied.

"Oh, yeah."

"And Simpson's life and the lives of all the rebel officers....and possibly our own."

Radcliffe nodded. He knew all that. He didn't need to be reminded.

They took the elevator up to the medical deck and found Admiral Chambers, Admiral Simpson, Admiral Schroder, and General Halstead helping Dr. Cassidy treat the dozens of wounded in Sick Bay.

Radcliffe made a decision not to even look into the intensive care unit to see how Ted Church was doing. Now was not the time and finding out how Church was doing wouldn't help Radcliffe one bit. It would only distract him from what he knew he had to do.

Dr. Cassidy looked up from her work when Radcliffe and Andy walked in. Radcliffe ignored her, too, and waved at Chambers, Simpson, Schroder, and Halstead. "The four of you stop what you're doing and come with me—now. It's urgent."

They exchanged glances and then looked at Dr. Cassidy. Simpson saved the day by saying, "Yes, Sir," putting down the roll of gauze he was wrapping around someone's leg, and walking out of Sick Bay without another word of explanation.

The other three followed him and Radcliffe pulled up in front of them in the hall.

"What's going on?" Halstead asked. "Are we back at San Juan?"

"Yes, but we're leaving in a few minutes. I need all of you to come up to the bridge. I've just sent word to Colonel Levitt and Captain Thorburn to meet us there."

Chambers raised his eyebrows. "The bridge? You haven't let us set foot on the bridge since Sailor first took us into custody."

"Actually, if you remember, Captain English would have let you on the bridge if you'd been more cooperative with his command," Andy interjected. "He didn't have a problem letting Admiral Simpson onto the bridge."

"You're going to the bridge now," Radcliffe went on. "You're going to use your command authority to order the *Lightning Rod* and what's left of her fighter squadron to assault the Lunar Detention Center to retrieve Captain English. If any warships come around to stop us, you're going to use your command authority to order the Ufa Long-Range Defense Station to bombard the warships to drive them away from the station so we can lift off Captain English. Is that understood?"

Halstead opened his mouth, but Simpson jumped right in and said, "Yes, Sir. We can do that no problem."

Radcliffe found himself beaming at the man. "Thank you, Sir. I won't forget this."

"But..." Chambers stammered. "Aren't we supposed to be under arrest or something? That's what Sailor said. He said when the war was over...."

"The war isn't over," Radcliffe interrupted. "If you don't come to the bridge with us right now and help us rescue Captain English, Andy and I have to take you into custody and lock you in the base brig pending execution. Are you getting the message by now? This is as much a rescue operation for you as it is for Captain English. Can we go now?"

They stared at him opening and closing their mouths for a second. He waited maybe just two or three more openings and closings before he waved to the elevator. "Come on," he told them. "Let's go."

Everything went much quicker after that. They all piled into the elevator and went up to the bridge where they found Eismann and Rickenbach still working.

Radcliffe went to the captain's chair. Andy went to the XO's station. The senior officers scattered to the other stations, and a second later, Thorburn and Levitt showed up.

"What are we doing?" Levitt asked.

"We're going to the moon to rescue Captain English," Radcliffe replied over his shoulder. "Order Wing 1 to arm up with alien weapons and deploy in their birds. As soon as they leave the ship, lift off and set course for the Lunar Detention Center."

"Yes, Sir," Andy replied. "Wing 1 on their way down to the cargo hold now."

"Power up," Radcliffe ordered. "Are there any other destroyers that aren't tied up elsewhere?"

"The *Nightside* is still logged in at the Oaxaca Repair Yard," Rickenbach reported, "but she's listed as fully operational and ready for duty. The *Seagull* and the *Jetstream* are both on the ground outside Trondheim, Norway. They're both listed as active duty, too."

"Send word to launch both ships on course for the Lunar Detention Center," Radcliffe ordered. "Tell all three ships to launch by order of the USF Command Staff."

Some of the senior officers exchanged glances, but Radcliffe pretended not to see.

"Wing 1 is off the ship and powering up," Andy reported.

"Lift off and break orbit," Radcliffe ordered. "Ready all cannon batteries and stand by to engage the enemy."

"Yes, Sir," Andy replied.

Silence fell over the bridge. Andy powered up the engines to launch, but at that moment, a punishing assault erupted out of the clear blue sky. It smashed into the Strategic Supply Base just a few dozen yards from the *Lightning Rod.*

That one shot flattened the building with everything in it, including the three officers who'd ordered Radcliffe to arrest these people. The whole building disintegrated in a steaming pile of rubble.

The next instant, more shots hammered the tarmac all over. "Get us the hell off the ground, Andy!" Radcliffe roared. "Punch it!"

Andy hit the throttle and the *Lightning Rod* erupted off the tarmac. More bone-crushing strikes plastered the base as three warships appeared directly overhead.

They demolished buildings, hangars, ships, vehicles, roads, and everything else in sight. The *Lightning Rod* sprinted for the atmosphere, but Andy had to dodge more than once to get out of the line of fire.

The warships were so busy bombarding the base to smithereens that they didn't pay any attention to the one ship making its escape. Every other ship on the tarmac met its end in seconds.

"Is the wing still away?!" Radcliffe yelled over the noise.

"They're long gone!" Andy hollered back. "They're breaking orbit now!"

"*Nightside* and *Seagull* moving to intercept!" Rickenbach called. "*Jetstream* is just catching up!"

"Tell them to converge on the Detention Center," Radcliffe ordered.

"*Nightside* and *Seagull* falling in formation," Andy reported. "Wing 1 on approach to the exhaust stack scaffold."

"Scan the warship," Radcliffe ordered. "See if Captain English's life signs are still showing up."

"One alien and one human life sign," Eismann replied. "The human life sign is holding steady. It isn't outstanding, but it's stable."

"Order Wing 1 to land and engage with the pilot," Radcliffe ordered.

"We got incoming warships!" Rickenbach called. "Four coming from space and another four coming from somewhere in the Indian Ocean. I swear they weren't there before."

"Belay my previous order and tell Wing 1 to stand off," Radcliffe ordered. "Keep the pilots clear of the Detention Center until it's safe to land."

"*If* it's safe to land," Andy corrected.

"Bring the *Nightside* and the *Seagull* about to confront the enemy," Radcliffe ordered. "Transmit orders to readiness to Ufa Station."

"Ufa Station signaling readiness to open fire," Simpson replied.

"Warships pulling into position over the Detention Center," Rickenbach added.

"Engage and open fire!" Radcliffe ordered. "Signal Ufa Station to fire at will!"

The *Lightning Rod* battery opened fire and the *Nightside* and the *Seagull* joined in. The three destroyers bombarded the enemy warships to drive them away from the Detention Center, but nothing would budge them.

The *Jetstream* raced into the battle a few seconds later and laid into the warships from the side, but all four of the destroyers working together couldn't dent even one warship, let alone eight.

The Ufa Station guns boomed into space and nailed three warships from far out of range. The warships staggered under the barrage and then zoomed back into position.

Seven warships swiveled to the front. One ship dropped back and descended to the exhaust stack scaffold.

"They're making a move on English!" Eismann reported. "The warship is backing up the scaffold!"

"Get Wing 1 down there to strafe the scaffold!" Radcliffe ordered. "Stop anyone from going back and forth between the....."

He didn't get the words out before all hell broke loose. Wing 1 didn't wait for the order. They saw the aliens about to steal English.

Wing 1 dive-bombed the scaffold and smashed the entrance to the flight compartment. The masked alien pilot made a dive to get on board the warship and had to duck for cover under Wing 1's assault.

The fighter craft zoomed past the scaffold again and again hitting the entrance one after the other. They pelted back into space, but it took them a few seconds to wheel around for the next pass.

The pilot took that instant to leap across the gap. His life signs vanished inside the warship.

"The human life sign is still on board," Rickenbach reported. "He isn't moving."

Radcliffe opened his mouth to give the order for Wing 1 to make another pass, but at that moment, the incoming warship fired its transport beam through the flight compartment entrance into the hollow inside.

"He's gone, Sir," Eismann murmured. "The human life sign isn't there anymore."

"He can't be dead," Chambers remarked. "He was just there a second ago."

"He's on board the other warship," Andy countered. "The pilot's life sign vanished the minute he got inside."

"Pull Wing 1 out," Radcliffe ordered. "Tell them to get clear of the moon....and tell the *Nightside, Jetstream,* and *Seagull* to fall back to Earth. Tell Ufa Station to break off."

No one answered when Andy reversed away from the moon. The warships let the destroyers retreat. None of the warships fired a single shot through the whole maneuver.

Radcliffe didn't take his eyes off the scaffold. English wasn't there anymore. He was on board the other warship.

Now the crew would never get him back—not until they found a way to defeat these aliens—and maybe not even then.

Chapter 26

E nglish jerked right and left, but he couldn't free himself. He looked and looked, but he still couldn't be sure where exactly he was.

One minute, he'd been lying on the flight compartment floor watching USF ships in battle over the Lunar Detention Center. He should have gotten up and done.....something.

He just couldn't move anymore. His whole body had locked up with pain, swelling, and something else that felt like death creeping up on him.

He'd seen Omai jump across the scaffold to board another warship. It opened its flight compartment to let him in.

Then English found himself here. His body still wouldn't move, but not because of his injuries. He could move his head from side to side. Some other, outside force immobilized his limbs.

A smooth surface of what looked like water separated him from another compartment. It looked like the oblong flight compartment with masked aliens working on panels of lighted symbols. The symbols flashed across the panels the same way they did on Omai's ship.

English sensed that this wasn't the flight compartment. It didn't have a giant screen on one wall to show him where the aliens were taking him.

Even if this had been the flight compartment, he wouldn't have been able to do anything about it. His window for doing something about anything in this war had closed.

He made one last effort to struggle and failed. He just had to stand here and watch.

He wasn't standing, though. He stood upright, but his feet didn't touch any surface. Gravity didn't weigh him down. He felt like he was suspended in something, but he couldn't see or feel what it might be. It just felt like air.

His body didn't hurt as much as it did before. In fact, it didn't hurt at all when he struggled. He could push against whatever this was. He could push against it hard and yank his body in any direction without causing himself any pain.

His chest didn't hurt when he breathed and whatever had been wrong with his head didn't feel broken anymore. Was this tank some kind of medical device?

Wherever the aliens were taking him took a long time to get there. He used the time to study this chamber holding him. It wasn't mechanical or electronic. Two sheets of the watery substance sandwiched him in front and behind. He couldn't see anything else about it.

He didn't see how the chamber healed him. He was too grateful to ask any questions.

He was also still in an oxygen environment. He could breathe normally and the aliens still had to wear their masks.

In the end, the trip took so long that he just stood there and waited for them to get wherever they were going.

He didn't see them land. This tank or whatever it was cushioned any feeling of movement and blocked out all sound.

The aliens just stopped what they were doing and left the compartment. They left him suspended in his tank. Yes, he was definitely going to start thinking of it as a tank.

He had to smirk to himself. The aliens must be keeping him in some kind of terrarium like a goldfish or a captive lizard. That was the best analogy he could come up with for his situation.

He waited another fifteen minutes before a blast of blinding energy hit the compartment outside his tank. It gleamed brilliant white like the aliens' transport beam and then the compartment blinked out when the aliens transported him somewhere else.

They transported him into another identical tank. The compartment with all the symbols on the walls vanished.

He found himself somewhere completely different, but he understood now that that's what they were doing. They were using their transport beam to move him from place to place.

It was the perfect setup. They didn't have to worry about him potentially escaping this confinement chamber or whatever the hell it was. He wound up just as confined and immobile in the second tank as he'd been in the first.

The second chamber wasn't a flight compartment or anywhere with lighted symbols on its walls and panels nor was it oblong.

It was a large room in a flowing, organic shape without any straight walls or right-angle corners. The walls undulated in waves like they'd been hollowed out by the wind.

The place glowed with a soft, pale, bluish-pink color that radiated from the walls. The walls' flowing surfaces rose from the floor to form counters and workbenches all over the room.

The room was empty except for a single masked alien standing right in front of English's tank. The black surface of the creature's mask prevented English from seeing who it was, but he already had a pretty good idea who it was. It could only be one person.

The alien did something to his mask to make it transparent. English wasn't even surprised when he saw that it was Omai.

Then, in front of English's eyes, Omai did something else to his mask and it unlocked from his head. He pulled it off over his head and revealed his true appearance.

He had an elongated head attached to his body by a short, thin neck. The head also had a flat, disc-like shape as if it had been compressed front to back. It wasn't round in the back like a human head.

His leathery skin extended down over his mouth with an extra long upper lip and a retracted lower jaw that seemed to vanish into his neck.

Two wide, flat nostrils took up most of the front part of his face where the cheekbones would be on a human being.

He didn't have any nose that stuck out from his face and his flat head stretched out farther to the sides than a human face. English didn't see if Omai had any ears.

"Where am I?" English glanced around at his tank. "I don't even know if you can hear me or understand me."

"I can hear you and understand you, English," Omai replied, and this time, his voice didn't sound metallic or mechanized. All the inflection came through whatever translation device he was using.

"You are on our warship—our flagship," Omai told him. "You are our prisoner and now you will answer our questions."

"*Our* questions?" English searched the lab. "You're the only one here."

As if his words made it happen, four more Vikak entered the room at that moment. None of them wore a mask.

They walked around one of the undulating walls from somewhere else. Omai left English's tank, went over to them, and stopped in front of one of them while the other three spread out around the room.

They all got busy doing something, but English couldn't tell what it was because the room appeared to be completely empty.

Omai and the other Vikak faced each other talking for a second. English couldn't hear what they were saying. Then the two of them embraced and held each other at arm's length for a second.

They looked at each other with such obvious affection that English could hardly believe what he was seeing.

Omai had been so hostile and standoffish. English struggled even to recognize him around this other individual.

English couldn't tell if any of these Vikak were male or female. They all looked the same to him and they all wore the same armor over their bodies as the alien ground troops.

Omai and his companion talked for a minute and then Omai accompanied the other Vikak over to English's tank.

"Well, well," the second Vikak remarked. "What have we here?"

"His name is English," Omai told him. "He is the captain of the ship that used our weapons against us."

"Is that so?" The other Vikak made some facial expression that English didn't recognize. Their faces were so much more expressive, now that English saw them with their masks off.

The second Vikak had a slightly higher register to his voice. He didn't growl and mutter as much as Omai. This individual actually sounded like he was trying to be friendly in a false, manipulative way.

"You have caused us all a great deal of trouble," the second alien told English.

"I hope so," English replied.

The alien didn't react. "You have killed our people and destroyed our ships."

"You've killed our people and destroyed our ships, too," English pointed out. "We didn't travel to your homeworld and do it there, though. We defended ourselves and we'll do it again until we drive you out of our solar system."

"I doubt that," the second Vikak countered. "We plan to colonize this planet and remove your species."

"I know that," English replied. "Omai told me."

The second Vikak barely glanced at Omai. Omai glared at English through the whole conversation.

"You are lucky he did not kill you before he brought you in," the second Vikak went on. "I am surprised he did not. He could have dumped you out into space and gone back to Earth for some other captive for us to question."

"He told me that, too," English replied.

"Do you know why he hates you so much, Captain?" the alien asked.

English spun around and raised his eyebrows. "He hates me? Why? I never did anything to him."

"You and your people shot down a warship of which his brother was an officer. His other brother was an officer in command of the ground troops your people killed when your people turned our weapons against us. If you fail to cooperate with us, I will have no choice but to turn you over to Omai and he can do what he wants with you."

English glanced over at Omai. He kept glaring at English in murderous fury. English didn't realize before now that Omai's expression *was* murderous fury. English thought Omai was just intense—or maybe that all the Vikak were like that.

Apparently not. He didn't move through English's conversation with the other alien. Omai never took his eyes off English once. Omai actually looked like was waiting for the word when he could kill English in revenge for his dead brothers.

"My name is Urai," the second Vikak went on. "I am the supreme commander of the Vikak colonization mission to this planet. I oversee all our operations, including the operation to modify this planet for our own use.....which is why you are here, Captain. You are going to help us change the environment, climate, and atmosphere of this planet. All your kind will die and our people will inhabit this planet from now on."

English's eyes snapped back to the second alien as a hundred puzzle pieces slotted into place. This creature—this alien standing in front of English right now—he was the man in charge of all this.

English's resolve hardened. "I won't help you do anything—especially not anything that threatens my people or my planet. I don't care what you do. I won't cooperate. You can do what you want to me."

"Oh, we will do what we want to you," Urai replied. "And you will help us whether you want to or not. Just you being here will help us. We need a human sample to test our processes on. I won't turn you over to Omai just yet. Taking another human captive would cost time and effort we have already spent capturing you. You are here and you are human, so we will test our processes on you."

English didn't like the sound of this, but he couldn't exactly stop them from inside this tank.

Urai turned away to one of the tables. He bumped his hand against Omai and Omai turned away to follow him.

The two of them stopped near one of the other Vikak who was taking a bunch of lab equipment out from under the table. Omai and Urai stood there talking for a few more minutes.

English marveled at the obvious connection between these two. They knew each other much better and talked much more intimately than they would have if they'd only been commander and subordinate.

Something in the way they stood near each other made English wonder if Urai was Omai's brother, too—or maybe they were just friends.

They stayed over there for a long time. English studied his tank again. No matter how much he moved or how much muscle power he put into struggling, he couldn't even raise his arms or kick out his foot. There was no way to escape.

If the aliens kept him confined in here, he might not be able to do anything. They would run their tests on him and he wouldn't be able to do a thing to stop them from terraforming Earth and wiping out everyone on it.

Just when he started to give up all hope, another four Vikak entered the room outside his tank. They didn't exchange words with anyone else in the room. They approached the tank, did something to it, and the walls evaporated.

English instantly started to choke on some other poisonous gas in the room outside. It buckled his knees, but the aliens grabbed him and yanked one of their masks over his head.

It had a hard, glassy feeling like a helmet that encased his whole head, but at least he could breathe.

They marched him out of the room, left Omai and Urai behind, and escorted him down some more hallways made of the same curved undulating walls. They wound in all directions for miles.

English considered struggling and trying to break free from the aliens' grip, but he decided against it. He already knew how strong the Vikak were and there were four of them and only one of him.

He decided to save his strength until he found a way to get off this ship. At least he wouldn't stay locked in that tank forever. That would have been terrible.

They stopped in front of what looked like a plain wall somewhere. English couldn't see any difference in any of these walls nor could he see any other rooms or compartments.

Another lozenge-shaped opening parted in the wall and the Vikak pushed him into a small, bare room with the same curved walls. The Vikak took off his mask and he started to suffocate again until the opening closed.

The Vikak must have pumped oxygen into this room because English could breathe just fine as long as the door stayed shut.

Other than that, there was nothing in this room to give him any comfort. The walls were all perfectly smooth and the door didn't open for him. He would never have been able to get out of this room if he searched a hundred years.

The room had no other furniture or even a blanket to lie down on. He finally stretched out on the floor, shut his eyes, and fell asleep. Staying conscious for even one more second was more than he could stand.

Chapter 27

Radcliffe bent over the scanner station and watched a raging battle going on down on Earth.

The Ufa Station battery in central Russia, the Tripoli and Gibraltar batteries in northern Africa, and the Seychelles battery bombarded ten warships hovering over Damascus.

The warships had been pounding the USF Fleet Shipyard there and the four batteries hammered the warships with punishing fire. The USF had finally found the one weapon on the whole planet that actually worked against the warships.

The batteries didn't do as much damage as they might have. They still couldn't destroy the warships the way the *Lightning Rod* crew destroyed them with alien weapons.

The batteries definitely stopped the bombardment, though. The warships turned their fire away from the shipyard to blast the batteries instead, but the batteries kept the warships on the ropes.

The warships tried to open fire, but each battery plastered the warships with such intense concussions that the warships staggered backward under the assault.

"How may other destroyers are listed as ready for action?" Radcliffe asked.

"Fourteen at Adelaide, seventeen at Karachi, six at Oaxaca, and twenty at Fort Lauderdale," Eismann reported.

"Get them all off the planet now while the warships are tied up with the batteries," Radcliffe ordered.

Eismann looked up. "Uh.....all of them?"

"Yes, all of them. None of them are safe on the ground anyway. Get them in the air and outside Earth's orbit. We can mount a more effective defense from out here."

Eismann bent over his controls. "What are you going to do, Matt?" Admiral Chambers asked from the back of the bridge.

"I already told you. I'm going to get Captain English and find a way to defeat these aliens."

"You can't go after the warships," Admiral Schroder countered. "You would get all our ships destroyed to rescue one man. We need those destroyers to defend Earth."

"Whatever the aliens want English for can't be good and he's the one person on the whole planet that's actually made contact with these people," Radcliffe pointed out. "He can tell us what they want and maybe give us some useful information about them. If he can't, at least we'll stop them from doing whatever they plan to do to him—which I'm quite certain affects all of us. They risked a lot to capture him and take him back to their warships. They want him for something that works in their favor and against us."

"Incoming destroyers," Andy reported. "The *Gryphon* and the *Afrikaans* are both hailing you."

"Tell them to fall in formation and transmit to them the identification coordinates for the warship that took English on board."

"Ten more destroyers coming in from Karachi," Rickenbach added. "The others are preparing to launch."

Radcliffe took one more look at the battle going on down on Earth. The batteries were giving the warships hell, but the aliens didn't send out additional warships.

He checked the warships out in space. They didn't move to intervene. They left those ten warships to handle the USF resistance alone.

English was on one of those hovering warships. Radcliffe didn't see anything special about it. He didn't see anything special about any of these ships. They all looked the same to him.

Another twenty destroyers launched from Earth. At that moment, the warships that had been attacking Damascus rocketed into the atmosphere and started climbing for orbit.

"Now!" Radcliffe ordered. "All destroyers—target that warship and fire at will!"

The *Lightning Rod* plunged in and blasted the warship in question. The other destroyers joined her. The fleet ships surrounded that one warship just as the ten enemy vessels broke orbit on their return from Damascus.

They dove into the mix shooting at the destroyers, but enough destroyers combined their firepower that the incoming warships couldn't stop them.

The alien craft that had been hovering so quietly near Mars also had to open fire to drive the destroyers off. The battle turned to mayhem with destroyers buzzing all over the place.

None of them released their fighter wings, though. That would only put the pilots in danger when the fighter craft couldn't damage the warships.

The *Lightning Rod* darted inward, blasted the warship holding English, and skimmed clear before the warship could hit the ship. So many destroyers whizzed all around the warships that they couldn't hit everyone.

"The warships are adjusting their formation!" Andy yelled over the noise. "They're moving to surround the target ship! They're turning their fire outward to drive us off!"

"Signal all the other destroyers to close ranks and blockade Earth!" Radcliffe replied.

"Destroyers in position!" Eismann called. "They're combing their assault!"

"Engage our feint maneuver!" Radcliffe ordered.

The *Lightning Rod's* battery unleashed an equally punishing barrage and the other destroyers opened fire at the same time.

They hammered the warships until the enemy vessels advanced from their position to finish off the USF fleet.

At Radcliffe's order, the destroyers fell back toward the planet's atmosphere. The continuous bombardment lured the warships a little farther forward to push the destroyers back to Earth. Then the ground batteries opened fire.

The destroyers fell back into battery range and the batteries plastered the warships in the face. The impact slapped the warships back into their former position. They couldn't advance any deeper toward Earth's orbit.

Eismann chuckled low. "Ha ha! Eat it, you cocksuckers!"

"Alert all batteries to hold the enemy here," Radcliffe ordered. "Signal all destroyers to fall back to the Mars Repair Shop. Order all the captains to meet me in the main Command Concourse to discuss our next move."

"So.....we're just going to abandon Earth?" Admiral Schroder asked. "You've cleared every active-duty destroyer off the planet."

"The destroyers weren't defending Earth anyway," Radcliffe replied. "They were sitting ducks down there. We got the warships off the planet. Now we have to find a way to defeat them." He stood up and turned around.

Simpson and Halstead had taken stations around the bridge to help Radcliffe pull this maneuver. All the other senior rebel officers stood behind him watching and listening to him coordinate the USF defense effort.

He would have walked away from them, but he couldn't just take over the whole Force like this. He didn't have the authority to do that.

He'd used these people's rank to order captains all over the Force to do his bidding. He wouldn't be able to do anything more without these senior officers behind him.

He took a deep breath. "You should all come with me to confer with the other captains. We should elect a new USF Command Staff. We need to reestablish the chain of command. There is no one left on Earth that's doing it or can do it. It has to be us."

Admiral Chambers cleared his throat with difficulty. "You've been doing an outstanding job on your own, Matt."

"I'm not electing myself in charge of this thing. We're doing this by the book or not at all." He waved toward the door. "Let's go. We'll meet the other captains and see what they have to say."

He headed for the exit and Andy stepped out of line to come with him. Radcliffe nodded to Eismann on his way out the door. "Contact every active ship, base, station, and yard in the whole Force. Take a tally of which officers are still on duty from captains up. I want to know who's still out there, who's in command of what forces, and where everyone is."

Eismann said, "Yes, Sir," and Radcliffe left the bridge.

He paused at the elevator and turned to the rebel officers. He really needed to stop thinking of them as rebels. "Go onto the station and meet all the other captains on the concourse."

"Where are *you* going?" Admiral Simpson asked.

"I'm going to see Ted Church. I want to see how close he is to getting back on duty."

Radcliffe waited while the officers got into the elevator.

"It probably wouldn't be a bad thing if they *did* elect you to command the whole Force," Andy remarked after the doors closed with the officers inside.

Radcliffe snorted. "Yes, it would be a bad thing."

"Why? You're kicking ass out there."

"No one except the enemy is kicking ass anywhere in this war," Radcliffe countered. "We're still nowhere."

"Don't be like that," Andy told him. "You got the aliens off the planet. You're holding them at bay with the batteries. That's more than all these so-called Command Staff people could do."

"Someone was bound to figure out about the batteries sooner or later."

"Maybe, but you were the one who stepped up and did it. Now we know the batteries can hold the enemy off. We're here meeting as a combined force because of you." Andy turned to face him. "Do you have a problem being in command because my dad isn't here? Is that it?"

Radcliffe made a face and turned away. "Of course not."

"Then what's the problem? If you're the most qualified man for the job, why would you hesitate to take it? If you're the one who's the best suited to defeating this enemy and saving the planet, you should be ready, willing, and able to do that for the sake of all Earth."

Radcliffe didn't reply. Becoming a captain was one thing. Becoming the commander of the entire USF defense effort was a completely different story.

He wasn't the most qualified man to lead the USF defense effort. He didn't need anyone to tell him that.

He and Andy took the stairs to Sick Bay. It was still packed with people, and when Radcliffe and Andy went into the intensive care unit, they found that packed with people, too. Radcliffe had never seen it so crowded.

Twenty beds sat one against the other with barely enough space to walk between them. None of the patients was Ted Church.

Radcliffe spun around and stormed over to Dr. Cassidy. "Where's Captain Church? He isn't in ICU. Did something happen to him? Did he make it through surgery?"

Radcliffe kicked himself for not checking on Church before now, but Dr. Cassidy only smiled and jerked her thumb over her shoulder. "He's over there."

Radcliffe followed the gesture. She motioned across the hall to a crew lounge on the other side of the corridor. The medical staff had removed all the furniture to make room for more beds.

Ted Church sat on the edge of one of the beds. He was wearing a pair of Sick Bay-issued pajama pants and nothing else.

Stitches dotted a huge red scab running across his chest, over his shoulder, and down his back. Both the front and back ends of the incision vanished under his waistband running under his pajamas.

He sat on the edge of his bed dangling his legs over the side. His legs were so long that his bare feet touched the floor. He was reading something on a portable computer device.

"Are you sure you should be up?" Radcliffe asked when he and Andy walked in. "Your incision looks terrible."

"I'm fine. Thanks for asking." Church put his device aside. "I'm glad you're here. You can tell me what's going on with my ship."

"So now she's your ship!" Radcliffe countered. "Since when?"

Church cracked a grin. "I hear you've been doing great things with her."

Radcliffe looked away. "I've just been doing my job."

"So we're at the repair shop. What are we doing here?'

"Maybe I shouldn't tell you if you're still a patient."

"I'm not that much of a patient," Church told him. "If there's anything interesting going on, I want to be a part of it."

Radcliffe surveyed Church's mangled body. It didn't look so mangled apart from that incision. "Can you walk?"

"Of course." Church stood up, turned to face Radcliffe, and spread his arms just in case Radcliffe hadn't been able to see him earlier. "What do you want me to do?"

Radcliffe hesitated for another second. Andy elbowed him from behind. "Just tell him. You need him too much."

Church's expression hardened. "What do you need me for?"

"He needs you to get your uniform on and come onto the station concourse to meet the other captains," Andy informed him. "We'll be voting in a new USF Command Staff and he needs everyone there that he can count on to make sure the former rebel officers or anyone else doesn't swing this against us."

"Oh, is that all? Why didn't you just say so?" Church pushed past them both. "Just let me get my uniform on and I'll meet you downstairs."

Just then, Dr. Cassidy came in and saw Church about to walk out of what was supposed to be part of Sick Bay. "What's going on?" she asked.

"We're taking Ted to a Command Staff meeting," Andy told her. "Don't worry. He won't be doing anything more strenuous than walking over there, standing around, and talking a lot."

She arched her eyebrow at him, then at Church, and finally at Radcliffe. She waited, but when he didn't contradict, she said, "Okay. See you later."

"Just like that?" Radcliffe asked. "Is he released for duty, then?"

She shrugged. "Let's call it light duty."

Church walked out of Sick Bay without another word. Radcliffe had nothing else to do here, so he took the elevator to the cargo hold to wait for Church to catch up with them.

Radcliffe opened the hold and watched all the loyalist captains disembark on the repair shop concourse.

The place didn't look right without hundreds of crewmen milling around, shopping, relaxing, and enjoying themselves. The place was utterly deserted except for the captains.

Radcliffe tried not to check which captains had been fighting on the rebel side until just a few days ago. He had to follow English's instructions and put that out of his mind. Everyone on both sides of the civil conflict was in the same boat now.

Church showed up wearing his normal uniform. He looked exactly the same as he always did. The uniform hid that he'd ever been injured and he moved normally, too.

The three captains walked out onto the concourse. Radcliffe sensed Church and Andy dropping back to walk behind his shoulders the way they would have if he had been their captain and they had been his subordinates.

He didn't want them as his subordinates. He'd really started to like working with them as equals, but that couldn't last. No ship could function without one man in charge. The only question was which one of them it would be.

Chapter 28

R adcliffe, Church, and Andy walked into the conference hall at the Mars Repair Shop. Nearly fifty captains crowded inside all talking at once.

They all fell silent and turned around to stare when Radcliffe, Church, and Andy walked in.

The rebel officers who'd been on the *Lightning Rod* stood off to one side hobnobbing with a few other senior officers.

They all stopped talking, too, as soon as Radcliffe, Andy, and Church showed up. The senior officers turned around to face the three captains and dead silence fell over the room.

Radcliffe advanced the rest of the way into the room and approached the big center table to take his place there. No one moved or spoke. They all just stood there watching him.

He glanced toward the senior officers again. None of them moved or spoke, either.

He was just coming to the realization that they were all waiting for him to address them when Lieutenant Eismann hustled into the room. He skidded to a halt next to Radcliffe and handed him a portable computer device.

Radcliffe glanced down at it. The screen displayed the names, ranks, and current posts of every officer holding the rank of captain and above—all the officers not currently in this room right now. There were only six of them. Everyone else was dead.

Radcliffe glanced around the room again and made up his mind. If these people needed him to save Earth, he had to do it.

He stepped away from the table, walked to its far end, and took his place there at its head. "As you all probably know by now, the USF command structure has been irrevocably shattered, first by the civil conflict, and now by this alien invasion that has killed so many of our senior officers. We need to vote in a new Command Staff that can take charge of Earth's defense to drive the invaders out of our solar system."

"Why can't you do that, Matt?" someone called from the back of the crowd. "You've been directing us just fine."

"I can't do that because not everyone agrees that I should. Whoever takes command needs to have the sanction of the whole force—and whoever takes command can't be one man. We need an elected body the way we had before—a body that everyone approves." He raised his device. "Apart from the people in this room right now, we have Colonel Clyde Tibbs, who is currently in command of the Ufa Long-Range Alert Station in place of Captain Daniel Caleb English, Admiral Joanne O'Dell currently stationed at the Adelaide Strategic Supply Base, Major General Connor Schmidt at Karachi, Captain Yusuf Ferrero in command of the Oaxaca Repair Yard, and General Dorian Coswell in command of the Fleet Naval Yard at Fort Lauderdale. We'll include their names in the roster of potential officers up for election."

No one said anything for a minute. They all waited for him to say something else.

"So the first order of business is to take nominations for Command Staff," he went on. "Does anyone want to offer any officer for nomination?"

"I nominate you, Matt," Admiral Simpson piped up. "I nominate Captain Matthew Radcliffe to the Command staff."

"I nominate all three of them," General Halstead added. "Captain Matthew Radcliffe, Captain Ted Church, and Captain Andrew Carter English."

Murmurs of approval went around the room and a bunch of people nodded. Radcliffe raised both hands. "I think the three of us would be better served staying posted on fleet ships to fight the enemy. If you really want my opinion, we should nominate these senior officers here along with the senior officers I just mentioned: Tibbs, O'Dell, Schmidt, and Coswell. That's twelve names. We can vote on them. They all have more experience running the USF than we do."

"They don't have more experience than you do at fighting these aliens," one of the captains pointed out.

"We should nominate Sailor English," someone else added. "He's an alien prisoner, but he won't be forever. We'll get him back. He's the most qualified to lead us."

"We would need a full Command Staff to direct our efforts in his absence," Church pointed out. "It's like Matt said. One man can't do it alone."

"We can't vote in O'Dell," a captain on the other side of the room argued. "She fought with the rebels."

"All of these senior officers did," someone else added. "They should be hanged right now."

"We aren't going there," Radcliffe snapped. "We're here to fight the aliens, not each other. These officers have as much right to do that as we do. I'm sure there are captains in this room who fought with the rebels."

A tense silence fell over the room. A few people looked around at the captains nearest them, but most avoided making eye contact with each other.

"I still say you should take command, Matt," someone went on. "You can do that from the *Lightning Rod's* bridge the way you've been doing it the last few days. Ted and Andy can do the same thing."

A bunch of people said, "Yeah!" and "Good idea."

Radcliffe glanced at Church and then at Andy.

Halstead spoke up. "We'll put the first three names to a vote. All in favor of Radcliffe, Church, and English being voted to the new USF Command Staff say, 'aye'."

A deafening chorus of voices called out, "Aye!"

"All opposed?" Halstead asked.

No one said anything. Then a few people snickered.

Radcliffe sighed. "All right. Have it your way. So who are the rest of our staff going to be? I nominate Admiral Christopher Simpson and General Caleb Halstead. All in favor, say, 'aye'."

Another resounding tide of voices voted in favor, and again, no one voted against. That made five.

"We need at least two more," Radcliffe announced. "Who would like to nominate someone?"

"I nominate Colonel Tibbs of Ufa Station," Andy suggested. "He's been on the ball for us against the aliens."

"And General Coswell," someone else added. "He's been coordinating the whole North American Force since the invasion started—and before."

"All right," Radcliffe replied. "Let's shorten the process. Does anyone object to Tibbs and Coswell joining the new Command staff?"

No one objected. Radcliffe looked around at everyone. It couldn't be this easy.

The rest of the assembly looked around at each other, too. Church finally nudged him and Radcliffe cleared his throat. "In that case, you're all dismissed back to your ships to await orders on our next campaign."

It took a while for everyone to get out of the room. The other senior officers gave Radcliffe and his friends backward glances before the senior officers left, too.

Halstead and Simpson stayed behind and approached the three captains. "Don't think this changes anything," Halstead told Radcliffe. "You're still basically in charge."

"We all are," Radcliffe insisted. "At least I won't have anyone ordering me to arrest you and imprison you for execution."

He was just about to turn away when Simpson said, "Could I have a word with you in private, Matt?"

"Uh...okay. Just give me a second." He turned to Church and Andy and consulted his device again. "You two will need to take command of two different destroyers. You shouldn't stay on the *Lightning Rod* anymore. We need senior staff too badly."

"Admiral Kennedy said we didn't have enough destroyers for all the extra captains," Andy reminded him. "Where are you going to get two more destroyers? All our ships already have captains."

"Actually, at least five of the destroyers currently at the repair shop have lost their captains since the civil conflict started." Radcliffe consulted his device again. "Three of them are being commanded by their XOs and two are being commanded by lieutenants. The Force hasn't had anyone in any position of authority to assign them new captains."

Church frowned. "Which ships did you have in mind?"

"You could take the *Thunderclap* and Andy can take the *Saratoga,*" Radcliffe suggested. "Both of them are being commanded by lieutenants."

Andy burst out laughing. "We used to joke about the *Thunderclap* at the Academy. Getting assigned to that ship would give you one hell of an itch."

He slammed his hand on Church's shoulder. Church glared at him. "You better shut the hell up."

Radcliffe bit back a grin. "I could switch your assignments if you really want me to."

Andy's smile evaporated. "You wouldn't dare."

"Fine." Radcliffe scrolled down his list. "You can take the *Solar Flare*, Ted."

"If the *Thunderclap* is being commanded by a lieutenant, then I have to take her," Church replied. "We couldn't send a ship into battle being commanded by a lieutenant."

"I can find another commander or other officer to assign to the *Thunderclap*," Radcliffe replied and had to stifle laughter.

Andy didn't bother to stifle his. He laughed in Church's face. Church glared at both of them. "I'm gonna make you regret this."

Andy pressed his wrist to his mouth, but nothing would stop the laughter from boiling out of him. "I already do, pal. Believe me."

"If you don't shut up, I will reverse the postings and put you on the *Thunderclap*," Radcliffe told him.

Andy pulled himself together with an effort, but he wouldn't stop smirking when he said, "Yes, Sir."

Radcliffe turned to Church. "Are you okay with this?"

"Of course I am. She's a good ship. Some idiot with a schoolboy sense of humor can't change that." Church shot Andy another death glare.

"Fine," Radcliffe decided. "You two take your posts. I'll send orders to both ships to expect you. We'll just...."

A deep boom shook the repair shop followed by another, louder concussion that rocked the station.

"Get on board!" Radcliffe pushed his two friends away. He secretly thanked the stars he didn't have to say a long, painful farewell to them.

The three of them rushed to the door, but Admiral Simpson raced over to Radcliffe before he got out of the room. "I need to talk to you!"

"Not now!" Radcliffe countered.

"It has to be now!" Simpson yelled back. "It's important!"

"More important than the aliens attacking?"

"Yes!" Simpson fired back. "More important than that!"

Radcliffe looked around. Church and Andy were already charging away. The rest of the captains raced back to the concourse to get on board their ships.

Another deafening boom rocked the repair shop. "All right!" Radcliffe yelled. "You can come with me to the *Lightning Rod* and tell me on the way."

He took off running for the ship. He wanted to get there quickly so he wouldn't have to deal with whatever Simpson thought was so important.

Simpson kept pace with Radcliffe all the way. Another blow jostled the station and made them stagger every few feet.

"The rebels are conspiring again!" Simpson told him on the way. "Sandoval and McKee have been talking to Levitt and Thorburn about retaking control of the Command Staff. They want to restart the rebellion—which means they'll start looking for a way to replace everyone on this new Command Staff with their own people."

Radcliffe paused just long enough to let that sink in. "Did they approach you in person about restarting the rebellion?"

"No, but I heard them talking in the officers' mess."

"What were Sandoval and McKee doing in the officers' mess?" Radcliffe countered.

"That's what I'm telling you. They shouldn't have been in there. Levitt and Thorburn must have brought them in so they could discuss it."

"Then how did you overhear them?" Radcliffe asked. "They wouldn't have been talking about it anywhere they thought you might be listening."

"They didn't. They were hiding in the showers where they thought no one would find them. I walked into the latrine and heard them talking. I listened just long enough to make sure I didn't make a mistake about what they were saying. Then I left."

Radcliffe didn't reply. He didn't have to worry about the senior officers getting onto the new Command Staff now. He, Church, Andy, Halstead, and Simpson would handle things from now on.

Radcliffe couldn't tolerate anyone conspiring to overthrow the USF—not right now. Simpson was right about one thing. This was important. Radcliffe would have to do something about it quickly. He needed to stamp out this contagion before it spread.

Just then, he and Simpson rounded a corner of the concourse. Punishing smashes of alien weaponry struck the destroyers docked there.

Radcliffe pulled to a halt and turned to face Simpson. "Thank you for telling me. I'll deal with it. Stay here and try to keep everyone calm. We'll use the repair shop as a base from now on. We'll be able to mount a more effective...."

At that moment, a blast of enemy fire smashed into the dock, struck the *Thunderclap,* and the ship went up in a massive explosion that took out the *Jetstream* and the *Raphael.*

Church and Andy came running down the concourse at the same moment. "Get to the Solar Flare, Ted!" Radcliffe ordered. "Let's go!" He turned back to Simpson one last time. "Stay here and keep an eye on things for me."

Radcliffe turned away for the last time and charged on board the *Lightning Rod*. The ship decoupled from the dock and glided out of the repair shop on her way to join the battle.

Chapter 29

E nglish didn't have time to fully wake up before some more Vikak pulled a mask over his face and hauled him to his feet. He stumbled back down the corridor.

By the time he blinked the sleep out of his eyes, he was back in the tank facing Urai in the same curved room as before.

This room must be some kind of lab. The Vikak wanted to test their terraforming process on English to find out the effects it would have on humans and the wider environment.

The armed Vikak that brought English here parked him in one section of the floor and the tank materialized around him. He didn't see that they did anything to make it appear and disappear. They could just create it out of thin air.

It confined him the same way it did before. He couldn't move, but he could see everything going on in the lab.

Urai supervised his subordinates while they arranged their equipment on the counters and worktables. These people must be scientists or technicians, but they didn't wear lab coats or any other markings to show their rank or duty.

Urai went from one station to the next telling everyone what to do, but they were too far away for English to hear what they were saying.

He could pick out one or two words here and there. His tank translated them into English, but he couldn't make out what Urai was actually telling these people to do.

Urai finally approached the tank and looked up at English with that fake friendly expression that Urai used last time.

"It's time to get started, Captain. If you have any objections or resistance to make, you can do so now. Once we start, we won't stop until we complete our task."

English didn't respond. What did this fool really think English was going to do—break down and cry because he couldn't get away?

English was starting to understand what kind of person Urai was. He enjoyed this way too much.

How much of this did the Vikak really need to do and how much of it was just Urai having fun with a helpless captive?

English made up his mind not to let Urai bait him into anything. English would take what Urai dished out and that was all. English wouldn't give Urai the satisfaction of seeing English beg or plead for mercy.

This could only end one way and that was with English getting killed. He only wished he could get some of what he learned back to the Force. Someone on Earth would be able to put it to good use.

That thought solidified in his mind that he had to find a way to escape. This had nothing to do with saving his own life. Earth needed to know who the Vikak were, what they planned to do, and how.

Urai crossed the room to one of the tables and came back with a piece of flat metal.

All the symbols English had seen in the warship's flight compartment covered this metal sheet.

Urai tapped on it and the symbols flashed in different patterns. It must be the Vikak equivalent of a computer device.

"Prepare to inject the Tasalt plasma," he ordered over his shoulder to the people behind him.

Anther Vikak came over to English's tank and stuck his arms straight through the watery field holding English confined. The technician or whatever he was stuck a needle into English's arm and took a blood sample.

The blood filled a glass vial and the technician took it and his hands out of the field with no problem.

English frowned at the guy and at the vial. If the Vikak could move in and out of this field, maybe there was a way for English to do it.

He didn't get a chance even to think about it before Urai gave the order, "Inject the plasma."

A hiss sounded above English's head and a spray of yellowish gas clouded into the tank.

It drifted down over English's head and suffocating, choking fumes filtered into his nose and mouth.

They changed the breathable air into the same toxic substance that stopped him from breathing when the Vikak soldiers took him out of this tank.

He thrashed against the field holding him, but he couldn't get away from it. It flooded his lungs and stopped his ribs from expanding. He couldn't even inhale the fumes.

He started to black out when, without warning, the fumes vanished and sweet, clean, breathable air flooded the tank again. He gasped and panted trying desperately to breathe in every precious particle of that air.

His mind took longer to clear. He heard Urai talking to him, but English couldn't understand him. English's whole body felt limp. He would have collapsed if the tank didn't hold him upright.

He felt another prick in his arm. His brain swam into focus just long enough to see someone take another blood sample from him.

The technician moved away and left Urai standing there in front of English's tank. Urai had plastered an equally fake look of benign concern on his face. He waited for English to come back to his senses.

"That was excellent, Captain. You make an excellent subject." Urai consulted his device again. "I estimate it will take approximately three minutes for the plasma to convert your atmospheric gas concentration from its current mixture to a mixture more favorable to our species. That is much better than I hoped. We can expedite the process by deploying the plasma in multiple places around the planet. The cascade will occur faster that way."

English didn't answer. He hung limp in the field and glared out at Urai while English caught his breath. These bastards planned to wipe out not just humans, but every other living thing on Earth. They were going to completely alter the atmospheric gas concentration of the whole planet.

English had to get out of here. He just had to figure out how.

Urai went over to the technician who took English's blood. The technician had set up some kind of large machine on the table, dripped a single drop of English's blood onto a microscope slide, and slotted it into the machine.

Urai and the technician bent over the machine reading the results on a screen. The two of them talked it over for a long time.

The delay gave English all the time he needed to regain his strength and focus. His head eventually cleared and he could hold himself up again.

After at least half an hour's wait, Urai came over and scrutinized English again. "Are you back to feeling somewhat normal? We want you in a state of mental equilibrium for our next test. Would you say you're feeling as normal as you can be under the circumstances?"

English shrugged. "I guess so."

"That's excellent," Urai exclaimed. "I can't tell you how pleased I am with the selection Omai made. I couldn't have asked for a better subject."

English would have liked to argue back. He sure as hell didn't want to be this asshole's perfect subject, but English couldn't do anything to stop him.

Urai crossed the room again and came back with one of the full-head masks the Vikak wore on the surface.

English didn't see Urai do anything to the field, but when he got near it, it disappeared just down to English's neck.

He instantly started to choke on the Vikak's air until Urai pulled the mask over his face.

"That's fine, Captain," Urai mused for no particular reason. "You can breathe and hear me just fine through the mask, can't you?"

English nodded. He really didn't want to find out what the next test would be.

Urai told the technicians to prepare to inject the Tasalt plasma again. Urai and his team had to go through several more minutes of fiddling with their stuff before they got ready to actually inject it.

English could move his head much more easily, now that he had it out of the field. He took the time to study the lab.

There must be some other control that allowed the Vikak to decide when to erect the field, when to take it down to release him, and when to only remove part of it so they could access his body when they wanted to.

While he waited for them to get ready, Omai returned. He exchanged a few words with Urai and the technicians. Then Omai crossed the lab and stood next to one of the tables nearer to English's tank.

Omai glared at English so ferociously that English didn't want to ask why Omai was here. English didn't have to guess.

He found out a second later when Urai ordered, "Inject the plasma."

The same yellow gas drifted into the tank, but this time, it surrounded English from the neck down. It didn't do anything at first. It couldn't choke him since he wasn't breathing it.

After a few minutes of contact with his skin, it definitely started to do something. It didn't burn or harm him in any way.

It started as a tingling on his skin and escalated slowly over a few minutes. It became an itch and then a maddening clawing, crawling, gnawing sensation all over him.

He gritted his teeth and willed himself to hold it together, but after another five minutes, it became intolerable and eventually excruciating.

He roared out under the mask and fought with every ounce of his strength to break the field, but he couldn't get out. Nothing stopped the plasma from eating its way into his skin. The sensation got worse and more infuriating with every passing second.

He bellowed himself hoarse inside the mask, but he absolutely refused to ask Urai to make it stop. If this was the way they planned to kill him, then English was ready.

He yelled so loudly that he didn't hear Urai give the order to remove the plasma. It just evaporated and left him weak and gasping for air again. He collapsed in the tank and let his chin hang on his chest.

The sensation didn't go away immediately. It took at least ten minutes before his skin returned to normal. He had to drag his eyelids open to check that the stuff didn't really dissolve his flesh off his bones.

He let his mind swim. He didn't even care that Urai and Omai were watching him. They probably enjoyed watching him writhe in agony. In fact, he was certain they were. That must be why Omai was here—to watch English suffer.

Urai came over to his tank long before English fully recovered. Urai removed English's mask and then reestablished the field so English could breathe normally without it.

"You did splendidly well, Captain," Urai told him. "You held out for ten full minutes. That is much better than I expected. I estimate it would take your species approximately that long or possibly as long as fifteen minutes before tactile contact with the plasma would cause you to turn on each other and annihilate each other down to the smallest individual—not that your kind will get that chance. Releasing the plasma into the atmosphere is the quickest delivery method. You would all suffocate long before it affected your skin."

Omai strolled over to his friend's side and surveyed English with those hate-filled eyes. "Have you determined how to decompose the bodies?"

"I will not be able to do that while he is alive," Urai replied.

"It would be better if you could deploy the decomposition agent along with the plasma," Omai suggested. "Then we could clear the planet and begin our colonization efforts immediately without worrying about decomposing the bodies."

"One thing at a time," Urai replied. "I need to finish experimenting with the subject before we get to that."

"What more do you need to experiment on?" Omai asked. "You already know the plasma works to change the atmosphere. What else is there to decide?"

"Not yet," Urai replied. "There may be something else in their physiology we do not know about—something that could cause us unforeseen complications."

Omai made a disgusted facial expression. "The sooner we clear this planet and get rid of these vermin, the better."

"We do not have enough Tasalt to expose the whole planet," Urai told him, "not in the concentrations we would need to convert the entire atmosphere. The inhabitants are putting up a much stiffer defense than we expected. We need our Tasalt supply to refuel our ships and weapons. The war is draining our supply more quickly than we planned."

"What are you going to do about that?" Omai asked.

"I have another shipment of Tasalt on its way here. We must keep the population under control until the new supply arrives. Then we can convert the atmosphere."

"If you converted the atmosphere now, we would not need additional Tasalt to fight the war," Omai pointed out.

"As I said, we no longer have a sufficient supply to convert the atmosphere. We must wait."

"We should have converted the atmosphere the moment we entered orbit," Omai muttered. "We never should have fought this stupid war in the first place."

Urai changed his tone to a threatening snarl of exaggerated patience. "As I just said, we could not convert the atmosphere immediately. We would have run the risk of unforeseen consequences—such as an explosive cascade that could have wiped out our entire colonization fleet. I have conducted my experiment on this subject. I know now that deploying the plasma will convert the atmosphere. We only have to hold the population at a stalemate until the new shipment arrives. That is the end of the discussion. I allowed you to come and watch the experiment for your own satisfaction, not so we could debate my military decisions."

Omai fell silent. He kept glaring at English as though English was the one responsible for all this.

English took in their conversation with interest. Omai drilled English to the core and English saw that Omai understood that English understood.

The Vikak didn't have enough Tasalt plasma to change the atmosphere. They had to wait for another shipment to arrive. English had to get this information back to Earth at all costs.

He also found out that the Vikak used the same plasma to fuel their ships and weapons. They couldn't fight the war without it. This was the crucial vulnerability he and his crew had been racking their brains all this time to find out.

If he could somehow alert the Force that this shipment was coming—if the USF could somehow destroy this new supply of Tasalt—the whole war would come to a halt. The warships would stop attacking. The Vikak would all die in space and Earth would be free.

The only question was how to get the information to Earth. English didn't even really need to escape. He just needed a way to communicate with one person from the Force—someone he could trust to take the information to the right people.

This warship English was on right now—it was in space somewhere between Mars and Earth. USF destroyers would be flying around him right now. They were all so close and yet so far away.

He hadn't seen any communications equipment since the Vikak took him as a prisoner.

Or, to put it more accurately, he'd seen plenty of communications equipment on board Omai's warship.

English just didn't know how to use any of it, much less how to use it to contact someone from the USF. The two systems would be incompatible, to put it mildly.

English got so consumed with planning how to get his hands on some communications equipment that he didn't pay attention to what Omai and Urai were doing.

Urai seemed to be obsessively interested in the results of his experiments. He went back and forth between the technicians checking everything. Omai stayed in one place glaring at English in bloodthirsty resentment.

English understood the man better every time English saw him. When this was all over and Urai finished experimenting on English, Urai would hand English over to Omai so Omai could take his revenge. English never doubted that for an instant.

Urai would hand English over no matter if English cooperated or not. Urai's bond with Omai would make it inevitable that Urai would give Omai the one thing he wanted more than anything else.

English didn't really care about that, either. He really didn't care if Omai cut him into tiny little pieces so long as English sent a warning to Earth first.

English startled back to his senses when the armed Vikak returned to take him out of his tank. Omai moved back out of the way when they approached the tank.

The field vanished. This time, he saw them coming for him and he held his breath while they put the mask on him.

They took hold of his arms to lead him back to his own containment room. They turned toward the hallway leading out of the lab.

At that moment, Omai darted forward, pulled a curved, pointed blade from under his armor, and stabbed English right in the neck.

Blood spurted from the wound and sprayed all over Omai's face. He screamed as smoke sizzled up from every tiny fallen droplet. The blood burned into his hand where the blood gushed over his skin and droplets fizzed in smoke on his arms where the spurt landed.

English grasped at his neck trying to stem the tide. He choked on his own blood and his vision went blurry.

He heard Urai yelling in the background, "Put him back in the tank! Hurry up! Put him back in there immediately!"

"Look at this!" Omai roared. "Do you see this? You do not care about me! You only care about your stupid experiments!"

"I should demote you for that!" Urai spat. "I should throw you out of the army for trying to kill him when I still need to experiment on him. Put him back in the tank, I said!"

English floundered to see or even think straight. Cold gripped him all over and he felt himself shaking as blood poured down his neck and chest.

A second later, the armed Vikak tore off his mask, put him back in the tank, and it closed around his head. He instantly felt better as a blissful sensation of warm relief flooded him.

He groped at his neck trying to close the wound, but it had already sealed itself up. He couldn't figure out how, but he was okay. That was close.

"I never should have let you come in here!" Urai snapped. "Do not ever come in here again."

"Do not act like that," Omai told him. "I went to a lot of trouble to get him for you. Is it asking too much that I want to take my revenge while I can?"

"One of these days, you will push our relationship too far," Urai growled back.

Omai crossed to the nearest table, took something out from underneath it, and started wiping the blood off his face. He winced and snarled in pain every time he touched one of the burns. Then he put some kind of liquid on his hand and wrapped it in a bandage.

"His blood burns," he hissed. "All the more reason to get rid of his kind."

"There must be something in their blood." Urai went to the technician who'd been studying English's blood. "I do not see anything here, but there must be something. All the more reason to continue to study him. You could have cost me dearly today, my friend. If you were anyone else, I would eject you out into space without a moment's hesitation."

Omai made another facial expression. English had seen it before. Maybe it was the Vikak equivalent of a smile. "You would not do that to me."

"Of course I would not," Urai muttered. "You are an annoyance to me."

Omai finished wrapping his hand and left the lab. Urai waited until Omai left and then Urai turned his back to the room with a grimace.

English wilted in relief. He couldn't take any more of this today. He really hoped Urai was finished so English could go back to his solitary room and collapse on the floor.

He prayed to God Almighty that Urai would enforce his threat not to let Omai come back to the lab, but English didn't hold out much hope for that.

Omai obviously meant a lot to Urai. Urai would give Omai what he wanted. If Omai wanted to come to the lab, he would.

Chapter 30

Radcliffe charged on board the *Lightning Rod* and raced upstairs to the bridge. He had to check himself when he saw Eismann at the XO's station.

Andy wasn't here and neither was Simpson. Eismann and Rickenbach were the only men on the bridge besides Radcliffe himself.

He jumped into his chair. "Get us out of here, Brock!"

"Yes, Sir!" Eismann hit the throttle. The *Lightning Rod* was one of the last ships still docked at the repair shop. He must have been keeping her running waiting for Radcliffe to come on board.

He fired the engines, but before he could uncouple, another blast of alien gunfire struck the *Continental Drift*. She flew in front of the *Solar Flare* which flew in front of the *Saratoga*. Radcliffe, Church, and Andy were the last captains to leave the repair shop.

The shot smashed the *Continental Drift* to smithereens and the ship detonated right there in the dock entrance. The shockwave struck the *Solar Flare* and hurled the ship backward to slam into the *Saratoga*.

"The other destroyers are setting up their barricade to draw the warships down into battery range!" Rickenbach hollered.

Radcliffe checked the scans. Seven warships sat right outside the dock entrance. They hammered any ship that showed her face outside the repair shop. If this kept up, the enemy would destroy the repair shop with every ship still inside it.

"Come about and aim our batteries at the back wall!" Radcliffe ordered.

Eismann looked up. "Sir?"

"I said come about and open fire on the back wall! Blast our way through the repair shop itself! We can't get out any other way! Signal Church and Andy to follow us. As soon as the debris cloud disperses, the enemy will destroy the *Solar Flare* next. Open fire, Brock!"

Eismann fired into the back wall. The impact snapped back and pummeled the *Lightning Rod* just as hard, but Eismann gritted his teeth and fired again four times in rapid succession.

The wall weakened and then punched through into open space. "Gun it!" Radcliffe ordered. "Get away from the repair shop double time—and make sure the *Solar Flare* and the *Saratoga* make it out, too. Tell them to beat it out of the area before the warships come after us."

Eismann dropped the throttle to the wall. He kept unloading the battery into the station wall, but he still had to ram his way through an opening that wasn't big enough for the ship to fit.

The breach's torn metal edges screeched along the *Lightning Rod's* hull....and then she burst outside into the open stars. "Go, Brock!" Radcliffe ordered.

Eismann already had the engines wound up as high as they would go. The wrecked dock held the ship back, and the next minute, she broke through and soared away into space.

"*Saratoga* and *Solar Flare* right on our tail!" Rickenbach reported. "*Saratoga* is hailing and requesting orders!"

Radcliffe opened Andy's hail. "Good shooting, Matt! We're clear! Where do you want us to go?"

Radcliffe checked the solar system. "The rest of the fleet is falling back behind battery range. Join up with the rest of the fleet."

"Yes, Sir," Andy replied and signed off.

The *Solar Flare* and the *Saratoga* stayed with the *Lightning Rod* as all three destroyers fell in formation with their sister ships. The aliens tried to descend and engage the destroyers, but the batteries held the aliens at bay.

Radcliffe stayed on the bridge for a few more minutes just to make sure the situation wasn't about to change any time soon. He really needed to come up with a strategy to fight these aliens. He couldn't let the war grind to a halt like this.

Holding the aliens in space wasn't enough. They sat out there blocking anyone from going out into the rest of the solar system. He needed to get rid of them, and for that, he needed something to tip the scales in Earth's favor.

He went into his ready room for a while and signaled Charlie Frasier to come up to the bridge from Squadron Command.

Radcliffe worked on the ship's roster for a while. The crew looked a whole lot different now than it did when English first came on board.

Radcliffe considered the *Lightning Rod* his own ship now. He was her captain. He didn't question that anymore. She was his to do with what he chose.

He left his ready room and found Frasier on the bridge with Eismann and Rickenbach. "Consider yourself promoted to XO, Brock," Radcliffe told Eismann.

Eismann turned white as a sheet, gulped, and barely rasped, "Yes, Sir."

"Charlie, I'm promoting you to Master Chief."

Frasier lowered his eyes and growled. "Yes, Sir. Thank you, Sir."

"Maverick, you're permanently assigned to the bridge from now on."

"Yes, Sir," Rickenbach replied.

"You men carry on with your duties. You have the bridge, Brock."

Radcliffe left them to think about it, but he didn't worry too much about their new assignments. They'd already been performing so admirably up until now.

Eismann might not think he was ready to become XO of a USF destroyer, but he sure handled it well when Radcliffe told him to bust out the back of the repair shop.

Eismann could step up when he needed to. He'd assumed the role of XO more than once since the ship crashed at Point Hope.

Radcliffe went down to the flight deck. Every other department on the ship was packed to bursting with extra personnel since the *Buckingham Palace, Apache, Cobalt,* and *Champion* crews all came on board.

The flight squadron was the only department lacking sufficient personnel. Radcliffe needed to do something about that. The squadron would be crucial to fighting this war. He needed pilots.

He would probably need to transfer some new recruits from other departments. He could assign them to Racer and Ezra Duran the way English assigned Wing 5 and Wing 10.

Racer and Ezra could train up the new pilots. They just wouldn't be able to use the Cyllene training arena to do it.

Radcliffe would have to come up with some other solution, but he got a surprise when he left the elevator and found the flight deck full of fighter craft and pilots.

Every wing had parked their birds in their usual places. All the pilots from Wing 8 occupied their side of the deck along with Hughes and Hoskins.

They surrounded their former crewmates, hugged and clapped each other on their backs, and fired questions, stories, and exclamations back and forth.

Racer stood apart on the righthand side of the deck. In addition to Smythe, Walker, Laughlin, and Waterman, Amber Briscoe, Joe Payton, and Diego Reyes had all found their way back on board the *Lightning Rod*.

Wing 10 talked rapidly about what they'd all been doing since they got separated. Racer's cheeks glowed with pride and pleasure. She talked just as fast and just as animatedly as the others. She was in her element.

Radcliffe stood in front of the elevator watching them. He hated to disturb this reunion, but he had to.

It took a long time before any of the pilots noticed him standing there.

Hoskins noticed Radcliffe first, lowered his voice, and whispered something to his crewmates.

The others glanced over and their talk died to whispers and murmurs when they realized the captain was on the deck.

Rosa Smythe noticed Radcliffe first from Wing 10. She went through the same process of whispering to everyone and they fell silent, too.

Radcliffe took a step forward. Racer, Sean Duran, and Sam Hughes all exchanged glances across the deck and then both wings advanced to meet up with Radcliffe.

Racer saluted him. "Sir! Please excuse our lapse in protocol. We didn't see you there."

"At ease, Gunny." Radcliffe glanced back and forth between both wings. "What are you people doing back on board the *Lightning Rod?* Are you assigned to other destroyers?"

"We're still logged onto the Lightning Rod, Sir," Thorpe informed him. "I'm pretty sure, Sir. I checked."

"In that case, we'll need to reshuffle a few things," Radcliffe replied. "Ezra doesn't have a wing anymore."

"That's okay, Sir," Ezra replied. "I don't mind going back on Wing 8."

"You're senior to Racer," Radcliffe pointed out. "By rights, you should take command of Wing 10."

"No!" Smythe blurted out. "You can't take her away from us! She's our gunny! We don't want anyone else."

"We came back to the *Lightning Rod* to serve under her," Reyes added. "If I wanted to serve under a total stranger, I could have stayed on the *Cryptid* where I was."

Radcliffe raised his eyebrows. "Do you all feel that way?"

The other Wing 10 pilots nodded. "We voted Racer in command," Sean chimed in. "Of Wing 1, I mean."

"There is no Wing 1 anymore," Janacek grumbled. "That was one kickass wing, too."

"In that case, we'll keep these wings the way they are," Radcliffe decided. "Ezra, you're back on Wing 8....."

"Yes!" Ezra threw himself into his crewmates, chest-bumped them, high-fived them, and they all hugged him.

Radcliffe waited for them to finish. He couldn't begrudge them this. War took enough from all of them. They didn't need to lose this, too.

"Racer, you can stay in command of Wing 10....which means you'll all need a new squadron commander," Radcliffe finished.

"What about Lieutenant Frasier....and Rickenbach?" Hoskins asked. "We already have two squadron commanders."

"Not anymore," Radcliffe told him. "Frasier and Rickenbach are both permanently assigned to the bridge. I just promoted Frasier to Master Chief and Eismann is XO. So you don't have any squadron commander at all now."

"Lieutenant....Eismann.....is XO?" Racer gasped. "No flippin' way!"

"He's Commander Eismann now," Radcliffe replied. "Which means you're the most senior gunnery sergeant on the deck, Sam. Consider yourself promoted to lieutenant and Squadron Commander."

All eyes turned to stare at Hughes. He didn't notice his crewmates' reaction. He blinked up at Radcliffe in stunned disbelief.

Babbitt whispered one more time, "No way!"

"Congratulations, Sam." Radcliffe jerked his thumb over his shoulder toward the squadron commander's desk. "You might want to go over there and familiarize yourself with the computers. If you need help with anything, you can contact the bridge. I'm sure Eismann, Frasier, and Rickenbach will be more than happy to answer any of your questions." Radcliffe turned to Wing 10. "Gunny Franz, do you mind if I have a word with you in private?"

Chapter 31

C aptain Radcliffe turned away and the flight deck exploded as the pilots mobbed Sam Hughes. They grabbed him, jostled him, messed up his hair, picked him up, yelled at him, laughed at him, and generally made a fuss over him.

Racer followed Captain Radcliffe to the stairwell, but she paused there to look back.

She would have liked to get right in there with her fellow pilots and congratulate Sam on his promotion. This would probably be the last time his friends would be able to treat him with this kind of comradely affection.

He would be their commanding officer after this. They would have to treat him with the proper courtesy and respect. They wouldn't be able to mess up his hair or laugh at him or tell him rude jokes.

Racer would have liked to share that moment. She experienced a flashback of her first meeting with him when she threatened to tear him apart for shooting at her in battle.

She would never be able to jump around or pick someone up or rumple their hair or any of that anymore. Something was dying right now right in front of her eyes. Maybe it was the old Wing 8 that was dying.

In fact, she was the one who was dying. Her old self was slipping through her fingers. It would never come back. She'd changed too much.

She was an officer now in charge of her own wing. Her pilots had refused to serve under any other gunny because they wanted her instead. She could remember feeling that way about English. Now she was the one taking that role with someone else.

All the miles and time she'd put into Wing 1 didn't change her position with these people. She was too high ranked to be a gashead pilot anymore. She would never go back to the days where she could be one of them the way she used to be.

She couldn't even be that for her old wingmates. They would serve on another wing under a different gunnery sergeant. They would never serve under her and she would never fly with them as their equal again. Something had broken—something that could never be repaired.

Her throat constricted watching them laugh, talk, and shove each other around. Their cheeks shone and their eyes sparkled with so much pleasure and warmth for each other. Even Hughes looked like that. Did he know? Did he realize that this was the last time?

She tore herself away with a pang of regret, but in a way, this was what she wanted. This was what she made up her mind to become that day when she and the crew came back from their mission on the *Infinity* to rescue the younger Captain English.

She made up her mind then to put her past behind her and she succeeded. She became someone who could step up and be the officer that Earth and the USF needed her to be.

She'd become the person Sailor English had been guiding her to be. It just hurt to say goodbye to her old self and all the connections that made her what she used to be.

She turned around to find Radcliffe watching her. He didn't reprimand her for not coming immediately. He just waited until she was ready.

He led her to a different deck and stopped outside the enlisted mess. "Gunny..." he began. "I want you to know I'm extremely pleased with your conduct on this mission—all of it—from start to finish. You really distinguished yourself in every possible way."

She couldn't look at him, so she lowered her eyes to the floor and mumbled, "Yes, Sir. Thank you, Sir."

"Your crew is obviously dedicated to you," he went on. "That says a lot, but even apart from that, I need a pilot—a very special pilot to go on a very special mission for me."

Her head shot up. "Sir?"

"I want you to take your bird and run a sortie around the warship where the aliens are holding Captain English. I want you to check it out and see if you can bring back any useful information we can use against the aliens."

Racer frowned. "Won't that be....you know....really dangerous? I mean....of course I'll go, Sir.....I was just wondering......"

"That's why I'm sending you alone—and I don't want you to tell your crewmates what you're doing. I want you to keep this under your hat, and in a few hours after they leave the deck, I want you to take your bird and go out alone. The aliens don't usually attack any craft they don't see as threatening. They won't see a single bird as threatening and you don't have to fly anywhere near the warships. You can go off in a completely different direction and come back toward them from Ganymede or Cyllene or somewhere like that—somewhere so far out in the solar system that they couldn't possibly see you as a threat. Do I make myself understood, Gunny? We need information about these aliens and we can't gather that information while we're in battle against them."

She gulped and squared her shoulders to face him and look him in the eye. "I understand, Sir. Consider it done."

"Excellent," he told her. "Take yourself off duty for now and don't tell anyone when you go back on it. Don't inform your squadron commander or even the bridge. Just wait until the flight deck is clear, load up in your bird, and go."

She dipped her chin once. "Yes, Sir. I understand perfectly."

"Carry on, then, Gunny." He walked away and left her standing there.

She had to marvel at the irony that he'd brought her to the enlisted mess—the one place on the ship she would never go again.

She no longer belonged there. She wouldn't fraternize with her fellow pilots. She wouldn't lounge around with her subordinates. All of that was in her past now.

She went to the officer's mess instead. She had the place to herself, so she curled up in a corner of the couch, got out her device, and studied destroyer layouts for a while. Then she turned to scans of the solar system.

Captain Radcliffe was right about one thing. No one would be able to figure out what these aliens were doing by watching them from Earth. Everyone in the whole USF had been watching the aliens and no one had come up with anything useful yet.

She didn't know what she would be able to come up with, but she had to try. If there was even the remotest chance of finding out something the Force could use against these aliens, she had to risk it.

She wouldn't be risking anything if she did it Radcliffe's way. He was right about that, too. The smaller a craft or group of craft, the less likely the warships were to attack.

She checked the scans again, but a few hours later, Rickenbach entered the mess. He raised his eyebrows when he saw her alone. "Gunny?" he asked. "Is everything all right?"

"Everything's fine. Congratulations on your promotion to the bridge, Lieutenant."

He frowned. "Um....thanks."

She stood up and waved her device at him. "I'm gonna go crash. Have a good night, Sir."

"You, too, Gunny." She saw him frowning more deeply at her, so she made herself scarce and went to her quarters.

She didn't have to wonder why he found her presence in the officers' mess so unusual. She'd always stayed close to her crew even after she got promoted to gunnery sergeant.

She'd never set foot in the officers' mess before except for the time she, Hughes, and Stoval came to see Rickenbach about investigating the saboteur. She couldn't remember even once eating alone since she first joined the Force.

She went to her quarters, but she was too wound up to even sit down, much less lie down or get any sleep. She paced the floor for an hour, and when that failed to calm her down, she went down to the flight deck.

She didn't expect it to be deserted and it wasn't. Reyes, Smythe, Ritchie, and Manheim were all down there. Hughes stood behind his new desk furrowing his brow at the computers.

Racer had to grin when she saw him. He bent his head and squinted at the screen so closely that he didn't see her come in.

She went over to Wing 10 and started working on her bird. She went through every system one after the other, fine-tuned everything, adjusted everything, and then dug around in the engine compartment just to keep herself occupied.

The others laughed and joked the way they usually did. Ritchie and Manheim came over to talk to her for a while, but eventually, all the others took themselves off duty to eat their dinner and go to sleep.

Hughes stayed behind his desk long after the others left. He was so deep up to his eyeballs in his new job that he didn't realize she was still there when he left.

She pounced on her bird as soon as the door shut. She darted over to his desk, used his computer to open the launch bay doors, scrambled into the cockpit, fired up the engines, and floated out into the night.

She hit the throttle, steered far away from the destroyer ranks standing guard in orbit, and sprinted for the part of the asteroid belt farthest away from the alien blockade.

She had to cut a wide circle and fly far out into space before she could double back toward Jupiter. She swooped through the Acheron Colony and ran a few laps through the Cyllene training arena before she dared to stick her head up and take a look toward Earth.

Chapter 32

Racer surveyed the alien blockade in the distance. A flank of twenty warships faced off against the USF just outside Earth's orbit.

The warships held their line between Earth and Mars. The destroyers wouldn't be able to get back to the Mars Repair Shop with all those warships in the way.

The destroyers kept to their own side of the line just inside the defensive batteries' firing range. The warships couldn't descend any lower without flying into the batteries' guns.

Another twenty warships hovered behind the front line. They stayed closer to the asteroid belt. These ships hardly ever moved out of position. They just sat in one place not doing anything other than watching the conflict play out below them.

Racer turned her bird around, ran the opposite way through the training arena, and hopped from Cyllene to Europa. The moon gave her better cover where she could observe the battle line inside the asteroid belt.

She hid behind the moon where she could see what the aliens were doing—or what they weren't doing. They just sat there. Did they ever even change their position?

The instant she thought that, one of them glided toward the ship right next to it. It happened so subtly that no one would ever have noticed. No one did notice.

The whole Force, from the captains all the way down to the pilots—they'd all been studying these aliens for weeks trying to see what they were doing.

These warships never did anything. They never engaged USF destroyers. They never fought anyone. They just stayed there. Either no one noticed any random warship changing its position or else everyone assumed that such a subtle change in position couldn't be important.

The warship drifted slowly and casually behind the warship next to it. Racer expected the first warship to pass and take up a position farther down the line. She expected them to just reverse their positions for some reason she couldn't figure out.

They didn't reverse their positions. The first warship stopped behind the second warship and stayed there. She had to strain her eyes. Was she imagining things or did the first warship move closer and actually lock onto the second warship?

She couldn't be sure, so she kept watching. The first warship remained attached to the second warship for at least an hour.

They stayed together in a synchronized orbit, but she couldn't think of any reason why they would stay so close together if they weren't locked together.

She needed to make sure. A little while later, the first warship moved back into its former position where it had been before.

Nothing happened for another hour and then the first warship changed places with the ship on its other side. They didn't lock together nor did they stay one behind the other.

She studied them trying for the life of her to figure out what the hell they were doing. Then, just when she was about to give up and go back to the *Lightning Rod,* a third warship moved behind the second warship and docked with it, too.

Adrenaline started pumping through her veins when she saw that. These warships were all docking with that one ship. Why?

This meant something. It meant something big. That one ship must be strategically important—possibly the most strategically important ship in the whole alien fleet.

The other warships wouldn't dock with it to transfer personnel. They must be transferring something else—something all the other warships needed—like maybe a power source or fuel or something.

Commander Lowery said the alien weapons needed to recharge. They had a port that looked like each weapon needed to plug into something to refuel with whatever power source made it work.

What if the aliens' ships worked the same way? The ground troops' guns, the warships, and the transport beam—they all used the same power source.

She stayed hidden behind Europa and watched four more warships dock with that one vessel. None of the others docked with each other.

The alien fleet went through several complicated maneuvers to ensure that every single warship docked with that one craft.

The aliens just made sure to do it very slowly. They constantly reshuffled their positions either to the front line or to the rear line to allow every ship to dock.

She flagged that one ship on her scanners. That must be the aliens' mothership. It looked like any other warship, but it must be important. Did anyone else in the Force figure this out? She couldn't be the only one.

She wanted to double-check her conclusion, so after the fourth ship docked, she flew far around the other side of the solar system and drifted into the asteroid belt. She didn't think she could hide from the aliens seeing her, but she stayed so far away that they wouldn't see her as a threat.

She floated there and observed three more ships approach the mothership from behind.

She was right. They did dock. They locked onto the mothership from behind and rode with it for about twenty minutes each time. Then they unlocked and floated back into position so another ship could take its turn.

She would have liked to watch the alien line from behind while the forward ranks went into battle. She wanted to see how frequently the warships had to dock with the mothership. How long could they go before they had to refuel?

She'd already been out here nearly all night and she needed to get this information back to the *Lightning Rod*.

Racer landed her bird on her launch pad and spotted Sam Hughes glaring at her from the squadron commander's desk. The new Lieutenant Hughes didn't take long at all to get over the adjustment. Now he was really starting to act like the squadron commander.

She also saw her fellow pilots give her sidelong looks through her cockpit cover. None of them would hold eye contact for more than a few seconds before they looked away and pretended to go back to work.

She blew out a deep breath, popped the cover, and climbed down. She better get this over with.

She set off across the deck toward the stairs. No one came near her or said a word to her, not even to ask where she'd been all night.

Hughes narrowed his eyes even more dangerously. She had to walk past his desk to get off the deck.

She got halfway there before he stormed out to confront her. "Where the hell have you been? Do you realize you could get bumped off the Force entirely for leaving the ship without authorization?"

"Leave me alone," she muttered out the side of her mouth, dodged around him, and picked up her pace heading for the stairs. She had better things to do than explain herself to him.

"I'm talking to you, Gunny!" he snapped in her ear. "You don't just get to fly your bird into a war zone whenever you want to. You aren't setting a very good example to your crew with this behavior, especially not after the faith the captain put in you yesterday. Now I have no choice but to write you up on disciplinary charges for insubordination, conduct unbecoming...."

"Go right ahead," she fired back and vaulted up the stairs. He stayed behind, no doubt to go report her to the bridge. It didn't matter because she was on her way there right now.

She walked onto the bridge and saw right away that Eismann, Frasier, and Rickenbach all already knew about her absence.

"Gunny," Eismann greeted her. "What can we do for you?"

"I need to see the captain," she blurted out. "It's an emergency."

He jerked his thumb over his shoulder. "He's in his ready room."

She tried her best not to tremble on her way to the ready room door, but her hands shook when she rang the doorbell. Captain Radcliffe called from inside, "Come in!"

She took a deep breath and walked in. His head shot up when he saw her. "Where have you been? You've been out all night. I thought something must have happened to you."

She drew in another shaky breath. "It did, Sir. I found out what you wanted to know."

He stiffened. "What is it?"

"One of the warships out there.....I think it must be their mother-ship. The other warships are drifting in and out of position to dock with that one ship. They've been doing it for hours—taking turns, locking up with it, staying locked with it, and then disconnecting so someone else can take a turn. They do it slowly so I guess that explains why no one has noticed. They're either refueling....or some-thing. That's the only thing I can figure."

His eyes blazed brighter than she'd ever seen before. "Are you sure?" he half-whispered. "You're absolutely sure? There's no mistake?"

"No, Sir. That's why I was out so long. I was watching them...and they're definitely docking up with that one ship. It's the only ship in the whole fleet that they do dock up with and they *all* dock up with it. There's no mistake about that—and it's the same ship where they're holding Captain English. The aliens go to incredible lengths to hide that they're docking up with it. They move the docking ship behind the mothership where the mothership will block anyone on Earth from seeing what they're doing."

Radcliffe bowed his head, sighed, and ran his fingers through his hair. "Damn it! I knew we were missing something." He got up and paced back and forth behind his desk. "This is exactly what we needed, Gunny. Thank you. This is exactly why I asked you to go out."

"Yes, Sir.....I guess you've already heard from Lieutenant Hughes that he's gonna write me up for....well, everything."

Radcliffe spun around and laughed. "Yeah, I heard. Don't worry about it. I'll take care of it."

"Are you gonna tell him I was out on your orders?"

"You can tell him yourself. You can tell anyone who questions you about last night. In a few hours, the whole damn Force is gonna know about this anyway."

She looked away. "Yes, Sir."

He stopped in front of her. "You did outstanding work tonight, Gunny. Thank you. One behalf of the whole Force—thank you."

She squirmed. Now he was making her uncomfortable. "Am I dismissed, Sir? I really need to go get some sleep."

"Yes, you're dismissed. Stay off duty for as long as you need to. You've earned it."

"Thank you, Sir."

She left as quickly as she could, but on her way to her quarters, she stumbled upon Ash Walker, Rosa Smythe, and Bobby Laughlin. "Lieutenant Hughes says you're gonna get bumped off the squadron, Gunny," Smythe began.

"Don't worry about it," Racer told her. "He'll cool down in a few hours."

"He says he's never seen conduct more unbecoming," Laughlin added. "He says you're a disgrace to the squadron."

"Yeah, he told me the same thing. He said I was setting a bad example to all of you."

"What are you gonna do about it?" Walker asked.

"I'm going to my quarters to get some sleep. I didn't sleep at all last night."

"What if he's right and we wind up with some other gunny?" Smythe asked. "None of us wants to lose you."

Racer turned around and faced the three of them. "You won't lose me. I promise. Just go back to your duties. Everything will be fine. You have my word on that. In a few hours, this whole thing will blow over. Trust me."

They exchanged glances and she saw that they didn't believe her. She couldn't worry about that.

She got herself something to eat from the officers' mess, ate it alone, and crashed in her quarters.

When she woke up and went back to the flight deck, she walked in on a very different scene entirely. Hughes jolted away from her like he'd been slapped when she stepped out of the stairwell.

He cleared his throat and squared his shoulders. "I owe you an apology, Gunny."

"Don't worry about it," she told him. "The captain asked me to keep it a secret."

Hughes opened his mouth, but no sound came out. His eyes went through a dozen shades of emotion.

She had to smile at him, but she didn't have to explain. She squeezed his arm, went over to her wing's side of the deck, and went back to work like nothing ever happened.

Her crew gave her some significant looks, but she ignored them, and in a few minutes, they all went on as before.

Chapter 33

E nglish groaned when the Vikak soldiers dragged him off the floor and yanked the mask over his head.

He made absolutely no attempt to help them by standing up on his own. He made them do everything.

He refused even to walk back to the lab. Why should he cooperate with anything these aliens did to him?

They were only going to kill him in the end anyway. Why should he kid himself about that or pretend to cooperate? He only hoped Omai wouldn't be in the lab again today.

The soldiers parked him in the same place and reestablished the talk around him so they could take his mask off.

English didn't see Urai in the lab, either. All the same technicians and scientists were in there, but Urai didn't show up for at least an hour.

When he did, he worked with his people and paid no attention to English. Urai kept him encased in the tank all day—or however long it lasted.

In the end, the soldiers took him out, put the mask back on, and led him back to his cell. The whole process infuriated English so much that he made up his mind to escape right then and there.

Why wait around for these bastards to kill him? He could force the issue by trying to escape. If Urai needed him so badly, English's best chance to subvert the Vikak's plan would be to get himself killed. He kicked himself for not thinking of this to begin with.

This time, he made sure to walk on his own feet back to the cell. He stood still while the soldiers fitted on his mask. English scrambled in his mind for any way to fight these aliens.

They were much stronger than he was. He wouldn't be able to defeat them in a flat-out battle of strength. He needed to come up with a different strategy.

He'd been so cooperative before now that Urai had reduced the number of guards who escorted English back and forth to his cell. They started out with five. Now Urai only assigned two of them, one for each of English's arms.

They didn't hold onto him unless they needed to drag him somewhere. His behavior up until now had lulled them into a false sense of his own submission.

He measured the odds on his way back to the cell. He'd have one chance at this.

The good news was that he was wearing his mask. He would be able to breathe anywhere on this warship. He just had to find his way around it and then off it—somehow.

The soldiers turned one of the passageway's many corners. English had walked up and down this corridor so many times that he recognized it now. He knew where he was. He was only a few dozen yards from his cell. He couldn't let them put him back inside it.

He waited for the next turn and the soldiers stopped in front of the cell. The entrance opened for them. They pulled him to a stop and turned him toward the soldier on the right so the guy could remove English's mask.

He lunged for the soldier and snatched the alien's weapon. The Vikak overcame English's strength in seconds and yanked the weapon back to tear it out of English's hands. He had to act now.

The soldier on English's left spun around and raised his weapon to shoot. English took that moment to give the gun in his hands one almighty yank, aimed the weapon's muzzle over his own shoulder, and the gun went off in his hands.

The blast exploded the second soldier's head and the body hit the floor, but that left English with one more Vikak to deal with.

The soldier in front of him reacted in a heartbeat, threw his weight against English, and tackled English flat on his back with both of them still struggling for control of the weapon.

The soldier's weight fell on top of English with the weapon trapped between their bodies. They both struggled to turn it on the other, but neither of them could overcome the obstacle of the soldier's weight lying across the weapon.

The soldier gave the weapon another almighty jerk. English lost his grip. He couldn't fight an alien this strong.

In his last moment of desperation, English glanced around and saw the dead soldier lying right next to him.

The soldier's weapon lay across the floor within English's reach. He just had to somehow get his hands on it and turn it on the second soldier without the soldier shooting him first.

English took a chance, shot out his hand, and stabbed his fingers into the alien's over-large nostrils. It was the most available handle he could use to bring the alien's head into weapons range.

The alien bellowed in pain and rage and tried to yank himself out of English's grip. English gritted his teeth and commanded himself to hold on or die trying. He hooked his fingers deeper inside the alien's face.

The alien's nostrils must have been sensitive because English's grip overcame the alien's strength. The soldier didn't fight back as hard as he could have if English had been holding onto any other body part.

English felt the soldier give just a little and English doubled down. He vented all his frustration, pain, and humiliation on this one soldier, gave a brutal yank, and used the alien's nostrils to slam the guy's head down onto the floor.

English dove for the weapon. He didn't have time to lift it. He just plastered the alien's head in front of the muzzle, grabbed the firing mechanism, and pulled the trigger.

The gun went off and the alien's head dissolved in English's hand. He had to struggle out from under the dead soldier's weight to get to his feet.

He had to work fast before anyone caught him. He snatched both weapons, shoved both bodies inside the cell, and bolted down the corridor.

He realized a second too late that he was running into a part of the ship he didn't know. He didn't know any of the ship except the corridor between his cell and the lab.

His instincts told him to move as far away from the lab as he could—not that he knew for sure that Urai was down there.

English dodged from one corner to another keeping one of the weapons trained in front of him at all times.

He traveled a long way before he encountered any resistance. He needed to find a place to hide—somewhere he could find out more about this ship and how to move around it.

He turned another corner and ran straight into a squad of ten soldiers. None of them had their weapons up or they would have killed him for sure.

He opened fire on them and mowed them down in seconds, but that only confirmed what he already knew. He couldn't keep running around on this ship. Someone was bound to find out that he'd escaped and then the jig would be up.

He took more care to turn corners after that, and a few minutes later, he saw what he was looking for.

He hid behind a corner and watched three Vikak working on the ship. One of them knelt on the floor by one of the curved walls. They'd removed a panel in what English had always assumed must be stone.

Now he saw that it was metal fabricated to resemble stone. Maybe the Vikak homeworld had a lot of this kind of curved stone architecture and they wanted to reproduce it on their ships. How should English know?

Another Vikak lay inside what looked like a crawlspace inside the wall. The first Vikak handed his comrade tools while the second one tinkered with something inside the wall.

English watched them. That crawlspace looked like his best option to find out how the warship worked. He also saw some of the lighted panels of symbols on the walls in there.

His chest hurt from holding himself so stiff and tense for so long, but he didn't dare to move or breathe.

He also didn't want to kill these aliens. They were just doing their job. The more Vikak he killed, the more obvious it would be that he had escaped. The trail of bodies would lead Urai straight to English.

He waited for what seemed like ages. The two Vikak finally finished working. The second one crawled out followed by a third and a fourth Vikak who had also been inside the wall. There must be a lot of room in there.

The workers straightened up, dusted off their clothes, and the fourth one fitted the panel back into place. They discussed their next job and their voices sounded like they were speaking English. His mask translated their language for him.

He waited until they left, tiptoed out to the panel, worked his fingernails into it, and popped it out. It wasn't locked in place. Why should it be? The Vikak had no reason to keep escaped prisoners out of their crawlspaces.

English weaseled himself and his weapons into the hole and pulled the panel into place behind him. Now what was he supposed to do?

It would really have been helpful if he understood the Vikak language, but that wasn't likely to happen.

He studied the symbols on the wall, but only for a second before he crawled deeper into the tube. It met up with another crawlspace running sideways in both directions at a T intersection.

He had no idea which way to go. He just wanted to get as far away from the dead soldiers and anywhere else he might have happened to have been recently.

He turned a bunch of random corners, but after a long time of crawling and not getting anywhere, he heard engine noise in the distance.

He headed for it and the noise got louder. He was getting closer to the warship's engines. What would he find there?

He finally maneuvered himself into a crawlspace directly over the source of the noise. The vibration became deafening. It buzzed through his stomach from just below him.

He hunted around and found another panel in the crawlspace's lower edge. It took him a while to figure out how to open it without knocking the panel downward into whatever lay beneath him.

He eventually twisted the panel sideways, pulled it up, and peered through the opening at another large chamber beneath him.

A massive reservoir of some throbbing yellow gel sat a dozen yards away. The Vikak working around it looked tiny by comparison.

The stuff swirled inside the reservoir, and every now and then, a hiss of yellow gas ejected into a transparent tube running off to one side.

It was the same yellow vapor Urai had used to suffocate English. This had to be the Tasalt plasma the Vikak used as a power source.

The Vikak worked around the plasma reservoir and then, in front of English's eyes, a giant sliding hull section of the ship slid back to reveal the stars floating in space outside.

A watery protective field like his tank covered the opening to keep it pressurized. He stared in amazement as another warship drifted up to the opening, locked onto this warship, and a deafening hiss of plasma vapor ejected through the tube.

The gel inside the reservoir swirled faster for a second. It rotated into a vortex that drained through the bottom of the reservoir, and after a while, the other warship unlocked and floated away. The hull section slammed shut and everything went on as before.

Two Vikak went over to the transparent tube with the gas ejecting through it. They adjusted some symbols on their wall panels and then crossed the chamber to another wall panel directly beneath English's crawlspace.

"The atmospheric concentration on the ship is too low," English heard one of them report to the other. "We need to turn up the concentration before the levels start to affect the crew."

"We can't turn it up," the other Vikak replied. "Our orders are to conserve plasma for the other warships and to recharge our weapons. We're already running low on plasma. We can't use it for non-essential systems."

"Do you call life support a non-essential system?" the first Vikak countered. "If we don't turn it up, we could all die. What's the point of bringing a colonization mission to this planet if we have no one left to colonize it after we win the war?"

The second Vikak made a face. "You know what Urai is like. He might cut life support to one of the passenger compartments to conserve plasma. He's done it before."

"We should tell him the level is getting too low," his companion insisted. "He lives on this ship. A concentration that low would affect him, too."

"Are you out of your mind? He already knows about it. He knows everything that goes on in the whole convoy."

His companion muttered something else and the two Vikak left to go check the gas tube again.

English's heart threatened to explode out of his chest. This was better than good. This surpassed his wildest dreams.

So the plasma controlled the warships' life support systems, too. The Force had to interfere with this plasma. It was the key to winning the war.

The Vikak colonization force was already running low on Tasalt. If the USF just waited long enough for them to run out completely....

That wouldn't work, though—not with Urai's new shipment on the way. The USF needed to find a way to destroy that, too.

The USF couldn't do any of that because no one on Earth knew about this plasma. He was the only person who knew. He had to alert....someone—but how?

While he lay there thinking about it, another warship came in to dock and refuel. English found his gaze migrating to the ship. If he could just get on board one of them, he could fly it back to Earth.

He didn't know how to fly one. That was the problem. He needed to figure it out and he needed to figure it out right now. He needed some way to learn the Vikak language and fast.

He backed into the crawlspace, pulled the panel into place, and forced himself to think. He had to find a way to learn their language, learn his way around their controls, and somehow hijack a warship—all without getting himself killed.

He retreated down the crawlspace to the next panel he'd passed on the wall. The symbols on its lighted surface resembled the chips Omai had arranged on the flight compartment floor at the Lunar Detention Center. They must mean something.

He studied the symbols. There appeared to be about twenty different shapes, each one arranged in a different position compared to the others. These shapes must be letters or sound symbols.

They didn't run across the screen like lettering, though. They just flashed on and off. English wasn't getting anywhere staring at them. This was taking too long.

He went back to the engine room, reopened the panel, and studied the workers much more closely. They used different control stations all over the compartment.

English couldn't see what the workers were doing from here, but he did see some other crawl tubes above their control stations.

He crawled over there as quietly as he could and opened another panel directly over the control station. From here, he could look down right onto the workers' hands.

He started to recognize some of their movements. Omai used the same combination of buttons for different operations.

This station didn't have a helm or throttle, though. English thought he recognized which controls he'd seen on the warship that he didn't see here.

He lay in one place for hours and studied everything the worker did. He opened communications channels with each warship coming in to dock.

The worker relayed orders on the incoming warship's speed, trajectory, and gave clearance both to dock up, take plasma on board, and to unlock when the time came for the warship to depart.

English still didn't understand the Vikak language, but he understood now how the Vikak communicated between warships. That was better than nothing.

Now English just had to figure out how to use the same system to contact any USF asset. He didn't care what it was as long as he talked to someone human.

He was just planning to back away and go look somewhere else when a deafening siren went off somewhere down below. A flashing red light strobed through the compartment and all the workers scurried for cover.

The hull section where the warships docked up slammed shut again. All but five Vikak evacuated the chamber and left only those workers standing directly behind the control stations.

English stared as they changed their controls and brought up video footage of a battle going on somewhere on Earth.

Warships and destroyers fired at each other. English tried not to pay too much attention to destroyers getting hit and exploding in the atmosphere.

Then, like something out of a dream, he heard a human voice coming through the Vikak communications channel.

"*Seagull,* come about and hold the line with *Saratoga* and *Cryptid!*" a woman's voice yelled.

A man's voice answered. "*Chimera* is hit! She's going down! I can't...." An explosion cut him off.

"Pass word to Captain English to bring the *Saratoga,* the *Seagull,* and the *Cryptid* around to the south!" another man ordered. "*Saratoga,* do you read? Come about to defend the *Chimera!*"

Another ear-splitting boom echoed down the line. "The *Chimera* is gone!" the same woman called. "Pull back and regroup at Singapore! We can't hold them here!"

English's hair stood on end. He was listening to a USF communications channel, but it was coming through the Vikak controls. The Vikak were listening in on USF communications.

The worker directly beneath English shifted to a different part of his panel, engaged some other controls, and relayed what he'd heard. He didn't get a response from the other end.

English heard human voices all over the chamber talking about what all the USF destroyers were doing, where they were going, and their next maneuvers. So the Vikak had been casing Earth. They'd been monitoring USF communications for God knew how long.

The Vikak must have figured out that Earth was tied up in a civil conflict. No wonder the Vikak chose now to launch their colonization mission.

English went to great lengths to pull the panel back into place to hide himself. He rolled onto his back and stared at the ceiling only a few inches above his face.

He had to get onto that control panel somehow. He had to contact the USF if it was the very last thing he ever did.

It probably would be. As soon as he showed his face down there, the Vikak would recapture him and probably kill him.

None of that mattered. He had to do this. Nothing was more important than getting this information back to Earth, preferably into the hands of someone who could make use of it.

Telling some shepherd in the Himalayas would be better than keeping it to himself. He didn't know how long he had left to live anyway.

He stayed where he was for a long time, but after an hour, the noise beneath him changed. The engine noise died down and he didn't hear any voices coming from the compartment—either human or Vikak voices.

He held his breath to listen, and when he still didn't hear anything, he opened the panel again.

The workers still tapped on their controls, but in a few minutes, they left the compartment. They abandoned their controls and left the whole compartment empty.

English craned his head around to see something—anything. No one came. Was this some kind of trap? He had to take the chance.

He hung his two weapons over his shoulder, lowered himself through the opening, and dropped down right behind the control panel.

His pulse raced when he extended his hands to the controls. Did he dare to hope this would actually work?

He had to act fast. He tapped the controls and navigated back to the USF channels he'd heard before.

His heart nearly exploded when he heard Sam Hughes talking to Wing 10.

"*Chimera* Squadron is requesting emergency assistance," Racer reported. "They're requesting emergency posting to the *Lightning Rod* until the Command Staff can reassign them to different ships."

"Stand by, Wing Leader 10," Hughes replied. "I'll relay their request to the bridge. Take a run around Australia and make sure no more warships are threatening Adelaide."

"It's all clear, Sir," Racer replied. "The warships are moving off into the atmosphere."

"That makes no sense," Hughes countered. "They didn't just up and decide to leave when they were kicking our asses."

"I smell a rat, too, Sir, but they aren't here. They're clearing off Singapore."

"Stand by, Wing Leader 10," Hughes told him. "Hold your position and await further orders."

"Yes, Sir," she replied.

English scrambled to adjust the controls. He'd seen the workers receiving USF broadcasts. He didn't know how to transmit.

He pushed some random buttons and Racer's voice came back through the channel. "Is that you, Lieutenant? You're broadcasting through a different channel. Did you change something?"

"He doesn't answer, Racer," Vinnie Waterman told her. "Something weird is going on with the system."

English gulped to get his throat working. "Racer......can you hear me?"

Dead silence answered him and then her voice cracked down the line. "Captain? Is that you?"

"You have to listen to me, Racer." English fought his voice under control, but he couldn't stop it from shaking. "I don't know how long I have on this channel. Just listen. You have to tell the Force. The aliens have this plasma on their ship...it's called Tasalt and they use it as fuel for their ships and an energy source for their weapons. It also creates the atmospheric gas that they use for life support on board their warships. They plan to release this plasma into Earth's atmosphere to terraform the planet and colonize it. There's one reservoir of the plasma on their mothership. That's all they have and it's already running low. The aliens have another shipment of the plasma coming in. They can't terraform Earth until the shipment gets here. The Force has to stop this shipment from deploying. If you can find a way to destroy this plasma, the invasion will fall. Do you understand? The ship I'm on right now—it's carrying the only source of plasma. If you can destroy this ship, the rest of the invasion will be over......Do you hear me, Racer?"

"I heard you, Sir. I'll tell Captain Radcliffe. We've already seen the warships docking with that ship. We just didn't know the rest. We're trying to rescue you, Sir. Just hold on a little longer. We haven't given up on you. I promise."

English swallowed down the lump in his throat. Thank God he got her of all people. "Thank you, Gunny."

He would have liked to say more, but at that moment, the power to his panel blinked out. He tapped on it, but nothing happened. It didn't respond at all.

A sneering voice startled English out of his skin. "What a touching little interlude."

English spun around and froze when he saw Urai, Omai, and a dozen armed Vikak stride into the compartment. This time, the soldiers all had their weapons up and aiming straight at English.

Chapter 34

Racer collapsed in her seat, shut her eyes, and rested her forehead on the dashboard of her fighter craft. She still felt herself trembling after her conversation with Captain English. God only knew how he managed to contact her.

That didn't matter. He did contact her and now she had the information she needed to finally defeat these rotten aliens.

Those words kept ringing in her ears. *If you can destroy this ship, the rest of the invasion will be over.*

He didn't have to explain what he meant. He wanted her to destroy the mothership even if he was still on it.

He must have risked his life to get her this information. He didn't care if he survived. He only cared about saving Earth.

She couldn't calm down. Her heart wouldn't stop pounding, but she couldn't keep sitting here until it did.

She popped her cockpit cover and climbed down onto the *Lightning Rod's* flight deck. She needed to see Captain Radcliffe on the double. He probably already knew about English's transmission.....or maybe he didn't.

Communication with Squadron Command had cut off right before English made contact with her. Whatever English did to establish that connection must have interfered with Hughes communicating with the wing.

She had to report to the captain either way. This was too important to sit on it. She had to tell as many people as possible.

She made only the most fleeting check on her bird and hustled away toward the stairs. She barely turned around when Diego Reyes, Joe Payton, and Bobby Laughlin stopped her.

"Where are you going, Gunny?" Reyes demanded.

"Get out of my way, Airman," she snarled.

"We all heard Captain English's transmission," Laughlin told her. "We have to assault that mothership."

"We?" she countered. "*We* aren't assaulting any ship, Airman. Now stand down. I have some business to attend to."

"What business do you have to attend to that's more important than saving Earth?" Payton asked. "We heard what Captain English said. We have to destroy that ship."

She opened her mouth to tell him that the Force was in the process of doing exactly that, but Reyes cut her off. "We should go out there right now and just do it. We know where the reservoir is. We can fly in behind the warship group, open fire, and it will be done."

"You better wait for orders from up the chain of command before you do that." She turned away. "I'm on my way there right now."

"We don't have time for that," Laughlin countered. "We can't take the chance that some politician will decide to delay. The whole planet could go up in smoke while we sit around waiting for orders from On High."

Racer started to lose her temper. She'd committed herself not to ever lose her temper again, but the strain of trying to save English and now receiving such a hopeless transmission from him—she couldn't take it anymore.

She rounded on Laughlin. "What the hell is wrong with you, Bobby? How can you be going along with this? You've been rock-solid dedicated to this wing since the beginning. You could have a promising career in front of you and now you want to throw it all away." She turned to the other two. "Do you honestly think the Command Staff is so stupid that they haven't thought of everything you're thinking right now? Did you ever stop to think for two seconds that some of your senior officers might know something you don't—like the fact that fighter craft can't get anywhere near these warships without getting blown straight back to Hell where they belong? Do you honestly think you're God's gift to pilots that you can do what no one else in the whole Force has been able to do?"

"So you're just gonna sit around and wait for someone to come up with a plan when you already know what we should do?" Payton countered. "If Earth gets hit, it will be because people like you are too gutless to act when you have the chance."

She opened her mouth to argue with him….and changed her mind. She didn't have time to argue with him and she really didn't want to.

She drew in one last shuddering breath and lowered her voice to a husky murmur. All her anger died and transformed to icy cold determination.

The rest of the wing had gathered around to listen to their conversation and she addressed her next words to all of them. "I am ordering you, as your commanding officer, to stay on board the *Lightning Rod* no matter what until you receive orders to leave it from me or another superior officer. Any of you that fails to follow this order will be out on your asses before the day is over. Now get back to work and don't ever let me hear you question my orders again."

She turned on her heel and stalked off to the stairs. What a pack of idiots!

Did they really think she didn't want to fly out to the mothership with guns blazing? Didn't they realize that blowing the mothership would kill English along with probably everyone else within range?

It might even destroy Earth in the blast. How the hell should she know? Thank Heaven she wasn't qualified to make these decisions.

She dashed up to the bridge and found Radcliffe standing at the XO's station with Eismann. Radcliffe waved at her the minute she showed her face. "We heard every word, Gunny. You don't have to tell us."

"What are we gonna do, Sir?" she asked. "We have to get Captain English off the ship before we blow the plasma supply."

"We might not have to," Rickenbach chimed in from his station. "We might be able to wait the aliens out. Their plasma will run out and their life support systems will shut down. Problem solved."

"What about the other Tasalt shipment?" Frasier asked.

"At least we know it's coming," Rickenbach replied. "We have Tasalt samples in the stolen weapons. Our scientists can isolate it, study it, and come up with a way to harness it to use against the aliens who bring out the new shipment. If we get lucky, the warships will have shut down before the new shipment comes in. Then there won't be anyone left to use the new shipment."

"That's taking a pretty big risk," Frasier countered. "We might need to take steps to defend ourselves before that happens."

Radcliffe raised his hand. "Cool it, all of you. None of this means a thing if we can't find a way to fight these warships. The only way we're going to....."

An alarm sounded on Rickenbach's station. He spun around and attacked the controls. "Unauthorized fighter craft launch! Three birds launching for orbit! Reyes, Payton, and Laughlin are making a run for the mothership."

"NO!!" Racer screamed and lunged forward, but there was nothing she could do.

Eismann switched his controls to a display of the three ships sprinting for the alien line. Her guts twisted. She told them not to. She tried to stop them and they went anyway.

They didn't even follow their own suggestion by skirting the alien line and approaching the mothership from behind.

None of the warships reacted to the fighter craft's approach. The warships didn't even move out of the way to let the three ships through.

Racer tried again and again to look away, but the sheer stupid audacity of what they were doing made her watch until the very end.

They got near the mothership and zoomed wide to circle behind it. The three pilots didn't try even the slightest attempt at subtly or subterfuge. What in the world were they thinking throwing three pint-sized fighter craft at a whole flank of alien warships?

She couldn't even be happy that they were about to taste the ultimate consequences of their recklessness. They were going to die and she couldn't do a thing to stop it.

They skimmed to the mothership's side and angled in to fly behind it. Almost as if someone on board the mothership wanted to toy with the three pilots, the ship waited until the last possible second. The three fighter craft whizzed in behind the mothership and the ship opened fire. Crack! Crack! Crack!

It was all over in a split second and nothing remained of the three pilots or their birds. What a useless waste and all because they couldn't keep their egos in their pockets and wait for orders.

She staggered away from the XO's station, but she couldn't think where to go. She needed to sit down somewhere private where she could be by herself, but she couldn't stay upright long enough even to leave the bridge.

She stumbled to the chair at the logistics station. It was empty because Frasier was standing at a different station across the bridge.

She collapsed into the seat, her shoulders slumped, and she stared down at the floor. This whole disastrous day was finally catching up with her. This whole disastrous year was finally catching up with her.

She'd finally heard from English, but she couldn't even be happy about that. Destroying the mothership meant killing English.

She wanted more than anything to fly out there and rescue him. She would almost have rather traded all of Earth just to get him back. Now that would never happen.

Radcliffe came over to her and rested his hand on her shoulder. "You did all you could."

She shook her head fast. She couldn't look up even as she felt the other three bridge officers watching her. "This is my fault. I should have trained them better. I should have taught them the chain of command. I should have....done something."

"You would never have done something like this—not even when you first came on the squadron as a lawless little punk," Frasier murmured. "This had nothing to do with you. This was just plain stupid."

Racer swallowed hard. She should believe him, but some part of her still wanted to blame herself. "I'm no good to command a wing. I'm no good to command anybody."

"You commanded them just fine when we were at Point Hope," Rickenbach pointed out. "You pulled your wing together better than anyone else could have. Why do you think the other three gunnies followed you? Your whole wing voted for you to take charge of them. That says it all in my book."

"I was responsible for them," she choked. "I shouldn't have let them stay on the deck. I should have bumped them off for even suggesting that we disobey orders. Then they would be alive right now."

"The fact that you feel so bad about this is proof that you belong in command." Radcliffe took hold of her arm, pulled her out of her chair, and turned her around to face him. When she still wouldn't look at him, he cupped her chin and lifted her face so she had no choice but to make eye contact with him. "You still believe in the chain of command, don't you, Racer?"

"Of course, Sir."

"Then I'm ordering you to return to duty and to carry on as you were. You still have four good pilots who need you. I'll be taking new recruits from the rest of the crew and they're going to need a good, solid gunny who cares about them to train them and bring them up to speed. Now go off duty. We have some work to do to get ready for our next campaign."

She gulped again. "Sir.....you won't blow up the ship with Captain English on board, will you?"

She wanted more than anything for Radcliffe to assure her that he wouldn't, but no one could tell her that.

She couldn't even be sure *she* wouldn't blow up the ship with Captain English on board. If she had to blow up the ship to save Earth, she would do it. One man wouldn't stop her no matter who he was.

Radcliffe confirmed her worst fears by looking away. "I'm going to do my absolute best not to, Gunny. You're dismissed."

Chapter 35

Radcliffe went into his ready room, collapsed into his chair, and buried his face in his hands. He hated to lose those three pilots, but right now, he had to concentrate on a much more serious job.

He rubbed his face extra hard before he put his hands down, took a deep breath, and opened a line of communication to the *Saratoga*. He went through the bridge officers and got Andy on the other end.

"What's the word?" Andy asked. "Did you get Chris Simpson's damage report on the Mars Repair Shop? That place is gonna need some serious work before we can use it again."

Radcliffe hesitated only a second before he blurted out. "We just heard from your father, man."

Andy did a double-take. "You what?"

"He somehow found a way to use the aliens' technology to contact Racer while she was flying around in the battle zone."

Radcliffe gave Andy a rundown on English's message. Radcliffe didn't have to paint Andy a picture of what it meant.

Andy's features hardened. "We should blow the ship right now," he growled. "That's what he wants us to do. It's the right thing to do and it will only get harder if we delay. We need to hit it now while we still have the firepower to do it."

"Use your head, man," Radcliffe countered. "We don't have the firepower even to damage one of their warships, let alone blow a hole in their most heavily defended ship. We would have to fight our way through the whole fleet just to get near the thing and then we wouldn't be able to damage it enough to blow the plasma reservoir. It's a no-go."

"We have to. If you won't give the order, I'll get Ted Church to come with me. We'll blow the ship and save all the rest of you cowards."

Radcliffe didn't answer. He didn't blame Andy for getting testy about this. Radcliffe had to concentrate hard not to let his own emotions run away with him.

"Listen to me, man," Radcliffe finally replied. "Your dad is still on board that ship. If he's able to get access to communications equipment to send us that message, he's still active enough to do something to help us. Just cool your jets and give him a chance. Going in there guns blazing and blowing the ship with him on it might be the worst thing we could do."

Andy clenched his jaw. He wouldn't look at the camera.

"I'm gonna sign off now, man," Radcliffe told him. "Don't do anything stupid that could get you and Ted and possibly your dad killed. Wait until you hear from me." Radcliffe hesitated. "Promise me you won't do anything until I tell you to."

"I promise," Andy snarled through gritted teeth. "I'm not that stupid."

Radcliffe hung up and immediately left his ready room. He couldn't sit around dwelling on this or he might lose his mind.

He went back out to the bridge and crossed to Rickenbach's station. "Any luck?"

"Nothing," Rickenbach replied. "The aliens are scrambling all their own communications, and the few snippets I can pick up are in their language. Our database hasn't been able to translate it yet."

"Keep working on it." Radcliffe turned away to return to his ready room. "I have to go work out a battle plan for a fight we can't win."

He walked across the bridge, but when he passed the XO's station, a spurt of noise came out of Rickenbach's controls. He heard explosions and then a burst of words in some foreign language.

Radcliffe didn't pay any attention until the signal changed and a spat of English came through on the same line. *"Fiji* and *Shadrack* in position,"* a man's voice announced. "Awaiting...."

The signal cut out. Everyone on the bridge spun around. "What was that?" Radcliffe asked.

Rickenbach went into a frenzy. "It's English, Sir! It's coming through the aliens' communications channels."

"How is that possible?" Eismann asked. "They were talking about USF destroyers."

Frasier rushed the logistics station and ran through the controls. "The *Fiji* and the *Shadrack* are both in battle against the aliens over Singapore."

"See if you can get them back." Radcliffe bent over Rickenbach's station to see what he was doing."

"That's what I'm saying, Sir. It came through the alien channels we've been monitoring."

Rickenbach did something else on his controls and another fountain of alien dialogue came through.

"Keep trying," Radcliffe told him. "If the aliens are...."

Another burst of English cut him off. *"Shadrack*—fall back! Get behind the line before they....."* An explosion garbled the transmission and then Rickenbach picked up another torrent of alien conversation firing back and forth between multiple individuals.

"That confirms it, Sir!" Rickenbach called over his shoulder. "The aliens are monitoring our communications."

"Are you saying they have some way to understand our language?" Radcliffe asked.

"They would have to," Rickenbach asked. "They wouldn't listen in on our communications if they didn't understand what they were hearing."

"Or maybe they're trying to understand us the same way we're trying to understand them," Frasier pointed out.

"It makes more sense that they already do understand it," Rickenbach replied. "We've been speculating all along about how the aliens knew to attack us when we were in the middle of a civil war. If they understand our language and they've been monitoring USF communications channels, that would explain how they knew to hit us when we were least able to defend ourselves."

"That settles it." Radcliffe turned away again. "We're hitting that mothership. Send word to every destroyer we still have left. Order them to disengage with the aliens and withdraw. Land them on the ground if you have to. Just get them out of battle. We need every destroyer we have to break through the line."

All three bridge officers turned around to stare at him. "What about Captain English?" Eismann asked.

Radcliffe waved that away. "This is more important. We need to end this war as soon as possible. We can't risk the fate of Earth for one man."

Chapter 36

The Vikak soldiers shoved English down on his knees and aimed their weapons at his head. Urai strode past English, scrutinized the control panel English had just been using, and came strolling back like he had all the time in the world.

"I see now that your kind are too underdeveloped to utilize this planet the way it should be utilized," Urai mused. "You fell right into my trap by coming down here and using our communications system to contact your people. It doesn't matter. Now we know that they know. We will be able to maneuver around them and they still aren't able to penetrate our warships. They will not be able to destroy the plasma....so your efforts were fruitless in the end."

English glared at him through the mask. "You won't get away with this. We'll find a way to stop you. You can kill me, but my people will find a way in the end."

"No, you see, our second shipment of Tasalt will arrive and then your kind will cease to exist on this planet. There will not be any of your kind to stop me."

English clamped his mouth shut and didn't answer. He'd done what he could to help Earth.

If Urai killed him right now, at least the Force knew about the plasma. They knew where it was, which ship it was on, and how important it was to destroy that one ship. English could die knowing that he got them the information in time.

Urai turned to Omai and clapped him on the shoulder before he faced English again. "I think my friend here will conduct our future experiments, Captain. He seems particularly suited to negotiating with you. Would you agree?"

English's gaze snapped to Omai and English's brain flipped. If he was going to face Omai, then English had nothing left to lose.

He had nothing left to lose even if he wasn't going to face Omai. English had nothing left to lose regardless of what happened next.

Urai waved to the soldiers standing around. "Take him back to the lab. We will keep him in the tank from now on to stop him from escaping."

Those words triggered English to react on pure adrenaline. The soldiers extended their arms to pull him to his feet.

He rocketed up way too fast and charged the soldier standing nearest to Urai. The other soldiers surrounded English on all sides.

English lunged for the soldier's gun, but the guy was ready for him, brought the gun up in a flash, and aimed it at English's head.

English didn't stop. He dove for that one soldier. Urai yelled out, "No! Do not shoot!" but it was too late.

English clapped his hand over the gun barrel just as it went off. He dodged his head out of the way in time and the blast went through his hand.

The shot disintegrated his fingers and half his palm. Blood, torn flesh, and bone fragments sprayed across the room and hit the soldiers standing behind him. His blood burned into their faces and they dropped their weapons to grab at their eyes and cheeks.

The shock of having his hand shot off switched off all the pain. English was too far gone even to care about his hand.

He snatched the gun barrel with his other hand and jerked it out of the way. He couldn't counter the Vikak's strength, so he didn't try. He just moved the gun sideways enough to get past it and jammed his bloody stump into the soldier's eyes.

The soldier buckled screaming and English spun around still holding onto the soldier's weapon. English tugged it to get it out of the soldier's hands, but the man held on too tightly.

The gun went off and English directed a burst of energy to mow down the soldiers standing behind him. They toppled, but at that moment Urai and Omai tackled English to the floor.

They overpowered him in seconds. Omai slammed English down flat, mounted on top of him, and punched English hard in the face three times before English could defend himself.

Omai seized English by the shirt front, pinned him to the floor, and Omai grimaced down at him in snarling blood fury.

English raised his right arm in front of his face to protect himself, but when that didn't work, he used the only weapon he had.

He used his good hand to grab Omai, pull him down, and English jammed his torn hand into Omai's eyes, too.

English held Omai there and pressed his bloody stump into Omai's eyes as hard as he could. English let loose all his rage and hostility for these people. He wanted to hurt Omai.

Omai screamed and reared away to break English's grip. In that moment, Urai stepped in and kicked English hard across the side of the head.

English couldn't break free with Omai's weight on top of him. English lashed out and whipped his bloody hand in Urai's direction. Blood sprayed across the Vikak commander's face and he staggered backward.

English attacked Omai even more furiously and crammed his hand into Omai's nostrils. The nostrils seemed to be the most sensitive part of the Vikak's face.

It worked and Omai screamed even more. He thrashed to get away from English, but English held on and Omai wound up pulling English off the floor with him.

English sat up and let go of Omai so the alien could stagger away. English sprang for one of the fallen weapons, and without getting to his feet, he fired it into Omai's head.

The body hit the floor. That left one Vikak alive in this place—Urai.

English dragged himself up slowly and turned around to confront his tormentor. Urai stood a few yards away covering his eyes with one hand.

He staggered from one direction to another, held his other arm in front of him, and turned right and left trying to find the control panel.

English could think of a lot of things to say to this man right now, but none of them seemed as fitting as just ending the bastard once and for all.

English walked over to Urai and positioned himself in front of the Vikak commander where Urai would walk into him. Urai's arm bumped English and the Urai patted him down to find out who it was.

Urai froze when he touched English's mask. "Captain....we can discuss this.....we can repair your hand and....."

English glanced down at his mangled hand. It didn't seem real. It still didn't hurt.

It felt like it belonged to someone else or maybe that it was some kind of make-believe special effect. His brain didn't accept that he no longer had a hand.

Urai patted him down a few more times. He kept saying, "We can discuss this," again and again and nodding like they'd already agreed on it.

Then Urai turned away and held out his hand into thin air. "Show me where the control panel is and I will call my people to repair both our injuries...."

English fired his weapon into Urai's face and the Vikak commander's head exploded. Even the body thumping on the floor didn't seem real. None of this seemed real.

English woke up from his trance when he turned around and saw the throbbing reservoir of plasma. He had to destroy it even if it meant dying in the process.

He walked over it and aimed his weapon at it. This gun in his hands would blast the reservoir to kingdom come if anything did.

He hesitated just to give himself a minute to think about his life. He did his duty to the Force and to Earth. He didn't regret anything and he sure as hell didn't regret the way he was about to die.

He shouldered the weapon. He had to rest it on his left wrist to hold it up. Even that seemed fitting.

He fired into the reservoir, but one of those watery protective fields cascaded down the glass and the shot bounced off. English let his arms drop. Of course the Vikak must have put a protective field around the reservoir to keep it safe.

He couldn't destroy it—not with this weapon. He needed something bigger.

He glanced around, and right at that moment, a noise on the control panel drew him over to it. A stream of dialogue came through the Vikak communications channel.

"Fall in formation, *Afrikaans,*" a man's voice ordered. *"Saratoga, Lightning Rod,* and *Solar Flare* flanking to starboard. Get around them from the Mars side. *Seagull*, *Isaac Newton*, and *Octopus*, draw the enemy away so the forward flank can swing around to the rear."

He pounced on the controls and found the scanners the Vikak workers used to monitor incoming warships.

The USF had launched all its available destroyers. They soared into orbit and then burned farther outward to engage with the Vikak front line.

A squadron of four destroyers angled toward Mars trying to cut behind the warships and come at the mothership from the rear. They didn't know how well protected the mothership and the reservoir were. The Force wouldn't be able to destroy it even if they made it this far.

English attacked the controls, but he couldn't figure out how he contacted Racer last time. It had been an accident. He didn't have time to figure it out right now.

At that moment, another voice came through on a different channel. English had watched the workers long enough to know that this was the channel coming from the other warships. English's mask translated their words for him.

"Warship Oliri in position and ready to dock," a Vikak voice reported. It was the signal the workers used to communicate with each other during the refueling sequence.

English's heart pounded when he hit the control to slide back the hull section. The warship glided closer into position to dock with the mothership.

English did his best to steady his voice when he opened the channel on his end. His hand leaked blood on the controls, so he had to wrap it in the end of his shirt while he worked. "Come on board," he told the Vikak pilot. "Commander Urai wants to speak with you. It's urgent."

The Vikak pilot changed his tone. "That's unusual."

"Orders from the top," English replied and held his breath to see if it would work.

"I guess we have no choice." The pilot cut the signal and the warship started to turn around.

English got busy tearing the edge off his shirt to wrap his hand. Then he inched forward to the opening where the warship was backing up to the mothership.

If English was right about this, the warship would have a maximum of twelve or fifteen Vikak in its flight compartment.

English planted himself in front of the opening and counted down the seconds before the warship docked.

The watery field keeping the compartment pressurized connected with the warship's hull. The diamond-shaped opening parted to let the pilots out of the flight compartment and enter the mothership.

The field created the same diamond-shaped opening. English caught an instant's glimpse into the flight compartment and he opened fire. He did his best not to hit the controls.

The pilots inside all stood right behind the opening waiting to disembark. They were all unarmed.

English sliced his weapon back and forth to cut them all down. He didn't care anymore how many Vikak he had to kill to get the hell off this ship.

One thought kept repeating in his mind. He was about to get his hands on a Vikak warship. He could use the ship's weapons to blow up the plasma reservoir. If a Vikak warship couldn't blow it up, nothing would.

He tossed the bodies back inside the mothership and dove on board. He had to work fast and he still didn't even understand all these controls.

He only vaguely remembered which buttons Omai used to fire on the fighter squadron. English didn't know how to fly this ship at all.

The instant he got on board, the diamond opening closed behind him and the big screen reappeared. It showed him more than he wanted to know about the battle going on.

The *Saratoga*, the *Lightning Rod*, the *Omen*, and the *Solar Flare* worked together to flank the Vikak rear line. All the other destroyers engaged the Vikak warships to the front to draw the enemy away from those four ships.

The four destroyers rushed the Vikak rear line again and again trying to break through. It only took three warships of the whole invasion fleet to hold the destroyers at bay.

They couldn't get anywhere near the mothership and they still didn't know about the protective field. They would never be able to hit the reservoir—not like this.

He had to act now before the destroyers took any more damage.

English finally found the controls to decouple the warship from the mothership. The two vessels unlocked and the warship drifted away, but then he went through another flurry of confusion trying to find the ship's propulsion.

He couldn't find it. His frustration escalated. He didn't have time for this, so he turned to the weapons controls. This was his last best chance to finish this for good.

He targeted the mothership right at the open hull section. He could see straight inside it to the reservoir pulsing with yellow light. Vikak bodies covered the compartment floor.

The field still protected the compartment, though. Would this actually work?

He fired, but nothing happened. A red triangle appeared on the screen over the spot where he was trying to shoot. It kept flashing a warning every time he hit the weapons controls. The warship wouldn't fire on one of its own.

He wilted behind his station. Now what was he supposed to do? He was adrift in the middle of space in an alien warship with no weapons, no propulsion, and no left hand.

He couldn't fire on any enemy target, now that he'd finally gotten his hands on a weapon that could actually damage them.

The pain, shock, and blood loss were all starting to catch up with him, now that he was finally free. Urai and Omai were both dead.

He felt himself starting to shake and his knees sagged. He needed to contact someone before he passed out.

He switched over to the communications system, but it took him a while before he found the right channel. He didn't want to interfere with any destroyer's communications.

He studied the Vikak controls while he waited. He tried a few things, and when he pushed a few more buttons, the ship lurched forward and soared out of position. That must be the throttle.

He almost flew straight into the battle, but he adjusted his angle and flew off to one side. Now he just needed to alert one of his own people and tell them where he was.

He finally got the communications channel for Squadron Command on the *Lightning Rod.*

"Peel around to starboard, Wing 8!" Hughes ordered. "See if you can wheel the mothership away from our destroyers!"

"Four more warships moving in to defend the mothership!" Thorpe called. "These assholes definitely know what we're up to."

"Coordinate with the *Seagull* squadron," Hughes ordered. "Draw the warships' fire away so the *Seagull* squadron can skirt to the asteroid belt. Come about to starboard, Wing 10. *Fiji* squadron is cutting wide to Jupiter and coming back into the battle from behind."

English chose that moment to open the signal. "Hughes......it's me.....It's Captain English."

Hughes gasped out loud. "Captain! Where are you?"

"I'm on board one of the warships. You can see me. I'm off to one side by myself. I stole the ship.....I escaped."

"Hold on, Captain!" Hughes voice shook. "I'm sending Wing 10 out to get you. Just hold your position."

"Wait, Sam....." English interrupted, but Hughes was already calling out to Wing 10.

"Racer! Walker! Captain English has escaped! He's on board that isolated warship on the Jupiter side of the battle! He needs a pickup on the double!"

"We're on it!" Racer called.

"Sam....." English choked. "Listen to me....."

"They're coming for you, Sir. Just tell us where you want them to go to get you." Hughes hesitated. "How do they get you off the ship?"

"Listen to me, Sam. We need this warship. I have to fly it back to Earth. Tell Wing 10 to escort me down to the planet. Tell the other destroyers not to fire on me....okay? We need this warship to destroy the plasma reservoir."

"Uh....oh. Okay, Sir," Hughes stammered. "Um....let me think.... .Just give me a second, Sir. Hold your position.....please."

He switched back to his other channel and transmitted the information to Wing 10. English tried not to let his own emotions run away with him when he heard how excited the pilots were.

"Wing 10 and Wing 8 moving into a guarding posture, Sir," Hughes told him. "Go on back to Earth. The two wings will escort you and make sure no one......" He broke off and had to change to a completely different channel. "Fall back, all squadrons! Orders coming down from USF Command! Fall back and return to Earth! Sorry, Sir. Where do you want to set down?"

"No problem," English replied. "Where does USF Command want me to set down? It will need to be somewhere our people can work on the warship.....somewhere secure."

"Stand by, Sir," Hughes told him. "Lemme just get word from Captain Radcliffe."

"Standing by, Lieutenant."

English sagged against the control panel while he waited. Cold sweat broke out all over his body. He must have lost more blood than he realized, but what did he expect from getting his hand shot off?

He shut his eyes and rested his forehead against the control panel. He had to stay conscious just a little longer—just long enough to get the warship on the ground. It was the Force's best tool to fight the Vikak.

Hughes voice startled English into waking up. He must have passed out without realizing it. "Captain Radcliffe says for you to set down at Adelaide, Sir. The techs there will work on the ship. He's giving orders for Wing 10 to lift you off and bring you home to the *Lightning Rod*, Sir. Just put the warship on the ground and we'll take care of the rest."

"Thank you, Sam," English husked and cut the signal. He felt himself starting to fall apart in every possible way.

He concentrated hard to steer the ship in a straight line. He still hadn't mastered the controls and the warship wobbled. His eyes were starting to lose focus.

He had to make multiple passes before he banged the warship down on the tarmac at the Strategic Supply Base at Adelaide.

He collapsed as soon as he got the ship on the ground. He only barely had the strength to open the diamond-shaped door so the *Lightning Rod* crew could find him and get him the hell out of here.

Chapter 37

Radcliffe had to take several deep breaths in the elevator on his way down to Sick Bay. The *Lightning Rod* crew had barely been able to function well enough to fly the ship to Adelaide when they heard that Captain English was back on Earth.

Radcliffe stepped out into the corridor to find all the Wing 8 and Wing 10 pilots crowded in the hall outside Sick Bay.

Radcliffe glanced around at all the faces staring up at him. He just barely got his voice working to ask, "How is he?"

"He lost a hand," Racer husked. "He lost a lot of blood and he looks like he's been beaten up pretty bad. He was out cold when we found him and he's been unconscious ever since. He's with Dr. Cassidy right now."

Radcliffe would have liked to question her further about English's condition, but Radcliffe just had to see this for himself.

He walked into Sick Bay and spotted English lying on a bed in the corner by himself. Nearly everyone who got wounded at Point Hope had already been released. English was the only patient in here now.

He had his eyes closed and a white sheet covered him up to his neck. Some kind of heavenly glow seemed to shine all around him as though nothing bad could ever happen to him.

It could, though. Radcliffe could see what Racer meant about English getting beaten up.

Swollen purple bruises covered half of his face. The medical staff had shaved off part of his hair where a line of stitches crossed his scalp.

None of that spoiled the effect, though. The same light hovered around him like he might be some kind of saint or martyr.

English was no saint, but Radcliffe still hesitated to approach him. Radcliffe ached to talk to him, but English somehow seemed too good even for that.

Dr. Cassidy came out of her office just then. "How is he?" Radcliffe asked.

"I've seen him a lot worse. He lost all four fingers on his left hand and it's been amputated mid-palm. He'll need to go into the Command Center Hospital to have the hand reconstructed, but since the Command Center Hospital no longer exists, I'm not sure there is a medical facility still operational on the planet that will be able to reconstruct his hand. We also don't know if the weapon that did it somehow altered the tissue. He might not be able to get his hand back."

Radcliffe turned back to stare at English. "At least he's alive and free. We got him back."

"Other than that, he's mostly just exhausted. He's going to make a full recovery. It could have been a lot worse."

"What about those stitches in the side of his head?" Radcliffe asked.

"He had three skull fractures. It's a miracle he stayed on his feet as long as he did."

She walked off back toward her office and left Radcliffe there alone. He stared down at English not knowing what to do. Radcliffe wouldn't disturb English—not now.

Standing here staring at the man didn't accomplish anything. Radcliffe really needed to go back to work, but just then, English stirred, sighed in his sleep, and rolled his head across the pillow.

He turned to face the room....and his eyes opened. He frowned when he saw Radcliffe. "Matt?"

Radcliffe gulped down the lump in his throat. "Welcome back, Sir."

English shut his eyes, sighed again, and shifted his position in bed. "It's real. I got out."

"Yeah," Radcliffe croaked. "You got out."

"I wasn't sure if it was real or if I dreamed it." English's eyes suddenly snapped open and he jerked his head toward Radcliffe. "Listen, Matt. The reservoir....the aliens have some kind of protective field around it. You won't be able to destroy it—not with any conventional weapon."

"Are you sure?" Radcliffe asked.

"I tried. I fired one of the aliens' rifles into the reservoir and then I used the warship to try to shoot it, too. The field around the reservoir protected it from rifle fire and the warship....." English swallowed to clear his voice. "The aliens' weapons systems won't target one of their own assets. The system has some kind of lock that prevents the ships from firing on their own."

"That makes sense." Radcliffe frowned. "You shouldn't be talking about this. You should rest. Your hand....." Radcliffe glanced down at the sheet covering English's body.

English raised his hand. The sheet fell away to expose English's arm up to his shoulder. He wasn't wearing a shirt.

His hand didn't look real with the fingers missing. A bandage surrounded the stump where it had been severed at the thumb joint. His thumb stuck out at a strange angle. It almost looked like some kind of alien hand in the wrong shape.

It looked awful, but to Radcliffe's surprise, English burst out laughing, collapsed back on his pillows, and grinned up at Radcliffe. English's cheeks glowed with happiness and his eyes shone with relief.

"It's wonderful!" He sank onto the bed still laughing. "It was downright glorious!"

"How can you say that?" Radcliffe countered. "Dr. Cassidy says you might not be able to get it reconstructed. You might have only one hand for the rest of your career."

"Good!" English exclaimed. "This is a good thing. Trust me, Matt. I'm happy about it. I couldn't be happier. It's the best thing that has ever happened to me."

Radcliffe frowned at him. "Maybe I should call her in here to make sure you didn't injure your brain more than she realizes."

English laughed even harder. He tried to stifle it when he saw the pilots peeking through the door at him.

Just then, Maverick Rickenbach walked into Sick Bay and stopped next to Radcliffe. "The *Saratoga* just landed, Sir. Captain English is on his way over now."

"How are you doing, Lieutenant?" English asked him.

Rickenbach nodded. "I'm pretty good, Sir. It's great to have you back on board."

"Rickenbach has been trying to hack the aliens' communications channels," Radcliffe told English.

English's eyes flew open. "Really?! I need your help then, Lieutenant."

"With what, Sir?" Rickenbach asked. "We can't understand their language."

"I need you to help me figure out how to work the controls on that warship I brought in," English told him.

"Don't you already know how to use it?" Rickenbach asked. "You flew it in, didn't you?"

"Barely. I need you to help me understand all the controls I can't read."

Rickenbach shrugged. "Yes, Sir. I'll do my best, but we probably need a linguist for that."

English fell back against his pillow. "Right. We need to get onto that right away."

Rickenbach glanced at Radcliffe. "Aren't you supposed to be recovering, Sir?"

"I'm fine," English replied. "The sooner we destroy that plasma, the sooner we can all go home."

"You might want to check with Dr. Cassidy about that," Radcliffe told him.

"Why did you tell me he was working on their language if you didn't want me to get involved in fighting the enemy?" English countered. "What did you think was going to happen?"

"I didn't think you would get involved in trying to translate their language," Radcliffe replied. "That isn't exactly your wheelhouse, is it?"

"Well, we need to. We need the warship to destroy the plasm."

"What good will that do?" Radcliffe asked. "You just told me we can't use the warship to target any alien asset."

"It's complicated." English turned to Rickenbach. "How soon can we get started on translating the warship's controls?"

Rickenbach glanced at Radcliffe again. "Um.....well, we would probably need Command Staff approval for that......"

"Consider it approved," Radcliffe interrupted.

English's eyes flew wide open. "You....*you're* on the Command Staff now?"

Radcliffe squirmed, but Rickenbach interrupted. "He *is* the Command Staff. He's the man in charge since you've been gone."

English's eyes fell out of their sockets. "Seriously?"

Radcliffe waved that away. "That doesn't concern you. You're a casualty of war. Now lie down. You're supposed to be unconscious."

English laughed again. He really looked incredibly happy—much happier than he had a right to be considering his condition. "In that case, I need to see the Command Staff in an official capacity. I need to see the Command Staff immediately."

"Get yourself released from Sick Bay first," Radcliffe replied. "Then you can see them whenever you want."

"You're really taking this command thing too far," English told him.

Just then, Dr. Cassidy came out of her office again. Radcliffe expected her to tell him and Rickenbach to leave English alone, but at the same moment, Andy appeared in the Sick Bay entrance.

He looked across the room at English and English looked back.

Radcliffe bumped Rickenbach's elbow. "Let's get out of here, Lieutenant. We'll see you when you get out of Sick Bay, Sir—not before."

Radcliffe left with Rickenbach. Andy didn't even see them. His gaze remained riveted on his father in the bed across the room.

Andy passed Radcliffe without acknowledging him. Radcliffe pulled Rickenbach out of the room and steered the other pilots where they wouldn't see English and Andy, either. They needed privacy right now.

"How is he, Sir?" Racer asked. "Just give us the word if we can do anything."

"He's gonna be fine. He's awake now and he's talking to his son. You can all go back to work. He's going to make a full recovery and he'll be back on his feet pretty soon. You don't need to keep hanging around."

"What are we doing about the plasma and the mothership and the aliens and everything?" Walker asked. "We can't just sit around and do nothing."

"Captain English is working out a plan for us," Radcliffe told them. "He's working out a plan that will actually allow us to destroy this plasma. The aliens have defenses around it that only he knows about. Until he tells us what will actually work against the aliens' defenses, there's no sense in us throwing lives and ships away from nothing. All of you stand down and wait for the word. It will come soon and then we'll be able to kick some alien ass the way we all want to. Until then, you all need to go back on duty where you belong. You aren't accomplishing anything up here."

Chapter 38

Racer tugged her dress uniform jacket down, smoothed her hair with her hand, and took a deep breath to try to steady herself.

"Stop fidgeting," Sean Duran told her. "You look fine."

"You're fidgeting as much as I am," she countered. "You must have straightened your shirt cuffs ten times since we got into the elevator."

He grinned at her, but it came out more as a grimace. "Okay, so I might be a little nervous."

"There won't be anyone in there we don't already know," she told him. "There will be Radcliffe, Andy, Church, Hughes, Eismann, Frasier, and Rickenbach.....and English. This is no big deal. It's nothing we haven't done a hundred times before."

"Then why am I so nervous?" Sean adjusted his shoulders inside his jacket again.

"This is just a briefing," she told him. "Nothing more."

"It's a little more than a briefing," he countered. "This is THE briefing—the briefing on the battle plan to end all battle plans. We wouldn't be meeting with Church, Radcliffe, Andy, and English if it was just a briefing."

Now it was her turn to twist inside her jacket. "You might be right."

Just then, the elevator doors opened and the two gunnery sergeants stepped into the corridor outside the Lightning Rod's conference room. Lieutenant Sam Hughes stood there waiting for them.

Racer saw right away that he was just as nervous as she and Sean were. Hughes pretended not to be and furrowed his brow at their uniforms. "Are you both ready for this?"

Racer nodded. "Yes, Sir. Let's get it over with."

"All right." He squared his shoulders. "Come on."

The three of them walked into the conference room. Church, Radcliffe, and Andy stood at one end of the long table talking to each other. Frasier, Rickenbach, and Eismann stood by their chairs farther down the table.

Radcliffe broke away, came over to the three new arrivals, and saluted. "Welcome. Why don't you three take your seats? We're just waiting for Captain English."

Racer had to restrain herself from asking if he was all right. No one on the flight squadron had been allowed to visit English while he'd been in Sick Bay.

No one had seen him *since* he got out of Sick Bay. Racer had to remind herself that he was even still on board.

Radcliffe continued to fulfill the functions of the *Lightning Rod's* captain—because he was her captain. English was nothing but a passenger if he was anything at all. He definitely didn't fulfill any command functions.

Hughes, Sean, and Racer took three seats together on one side of the table opposite Frasier, Eismann, and Rickenbach. None of the three bridge officers gave anything away. If any of them had laid eyes on English since his escape, they didn't mention it.

Racer didn't dare to sit down—not while the other six senior officers remained standing. She was just starting to wonder for the hundredth time if English was all right when he walked into the conference room.

The swelling in his face had eased slightly in the last week, but the colors had only faded a little bit. He still looked like he just got run over by a truck.

He still had his hand wrapped in bandages, but he acted like he'd never lost his hand at all.

Everyone stiffened to attention and saluted him. He saluted back. "At ease, folks," he began. "We're all friends here. Take your seats and let's get this briefing underway."

Racer sat down along with everyone else. She became acutely aware that she was the most junior officer in the room. She really shouldn't be involved in this briefing at all. She only came because Captain Radcliffe ordered her, Sean, and Hughes to attend.

English crossed to the other end of the table and plugged his computer device into the conference room's systems. "As you know, Rickenbach and I have been working on translating my stolen warship's controls. We can't use the warship's weapons systems against the mothership, so we have to use the next best thing."

"Which is what?" Church asked. "Alien weapons are the only things that work on those warships."

"It's true that the aliens' weapons are the only things that damage the warships' exterior, but we aren't shooting at the warships' exterior. We only care about shooting at the plasma reservoir and that isn't armored the way the warships' exterior is."

He switched on the conference room's controls and brought up a schematic of a Vikak warship. "The Logistics, Security, and Engineering teams have gone over the warship with a fine-toothed comb and drawn up this layout for us to study. As you can see, the flight compartment is here. The warships don't really have a forward and aft sections, so we're only calling this section the forward end because the flight compartment is there."

"Excuse me, Sir," Racer interjected, "but the warships docked up with the mothership in the aft end. The plasma reservoir must be there."

"It is in the aft end, Gunny," he told her and pointed to the section all the way opposite the flight compartment. "The warships dock up here at this coupling slightly beneath the reservoir. Shooting at that part of the hull wouldn't damage anything, much less the reservoir."

"So how do we hit it?" Hughes asked.

"That's what I'm here to tell you. When the warships dock up, a hull plate slides back up here just above the docking port. The reservoir is behind that hull plate, but the reservoir and the opening are both protected by plasma energy fields—one that keeps the compartment pressurized and one around the reservoir itself. I fired one of the aliens' weapons directly into the reservoir and the shot only bounced off. We won't be able to destroy it without lowering both fields."

"How do we do that?" Sean asked. "Please Dear God in Heaven tell me you don't plan to go back on board that ship."

English smiled at him. "You couldn't pay me to go back on board that ship. Fortunately, none of us has to. We're going to use the warship's controls to remotely open the hull section and deactivate both fields. One decent shot from one of our birds should send the plasma up and then it's all over. Then we can do the same thing with the second shipment when it arrives."

Eismann frowned. "How will you use the controls to open the hull section and deactivate both fields? You wouldn't be able to do that from the ground and you wouldn't be able to fly the warship against the enemy if you can't use the warship's weapons to target enemy assets."

"The controls won't be on the ground. They'll be mounted on one of our birds. That's the only way to get the controls close enough to the warship."

"Whoa! That makes no sense!" Church threw up his hands. "The enemy would see the signal coming from a USF fighter craft! That would never work."

"I don't think so," English pointed out. "I watched the Vikak communicating with their warships before, during, and after the docking and refueling process. We know from Racer's intelligence that the battles are the times when the Vikak are the most active in refueling ships. They want the battle to give them cover so fewer people notice what they're doing. From what I can tell, the Vikak rely entirely on communication to allow a ship to get close enough access to dock. The warship's communications system has translation technology so the Vikak can eavesdrop on USF transmissions. As long as the Vikak hear their ship requesting permission to dock in their own language, the workers will open the panel. Then we'll use the controls to remotely take down the fields and we're done."

"So....you want to mount these controls on a bird and fly that bird up to the mothership, use the communications system to trick the aliens into opening their hull section, and then use the same bird to shoot the plasma reservoir?" Racer asked. "Who did you have in mind to fly this bird? The pilot would have to have some cast-iron balls to pull a maneuver like that."

"I'm going to fly the bird, Gunny—so thank you for the compliment," English told her and immediately turned back to his diagram like he really didn't just say that. "The Vikak are already touchy about us going anywhere near their mothership, so we'll have to launch another massive assault. We'll deploy all our fighter squadrons in the area to hide the bird in question in the swarm. That's the only way I'll be able to get near enough to deploy the communications."

Racer blinked up at him. He was not doing this—not after just escaping from those aliens.

How did anyone know if he would survive the blast? The blast radius could wipe out the entire squadron and every other ship in the fleet. The blast might scorch the whole half of Earth that was facing the mothership when it detonated.

English read her mind. "As soon as I give the word that I'm going in, every ship on the field will need to break away and flee to the other side of the planet. We'll alert everyone on that side of Earth to take shelter beforehand. Early-warning and emergency management teams will need to stand by for tsunamis, wildfires, and any other disasters a blast of that magnitude might cause."

No one answered for a second. The other three captains stared up at him. Frasier scowled at the table. Eisman blinked up at English like someone just slapped Eismann with a fresh mackerel.

Only Rickenbach sat in his seat as calm and composed as ever. English must have explained all of this while the two of them were working to crack the aliens' language. None of this surprised Rickenbach because he'd already heard it.

English waited for someone to say something. When they didn't, he shifted his weight to his other foot. "Any questions?"

The three captains exchanged glances. Racer didn't have any questions. She still found it difficult to believe that he actually came up with this plan—with himself executing the most dangerous part of it.

Why should that surprise her? He sure as hell wouldn't float this plan by suggesting that someone else fly the bird that would strike the killing blow.

She might have been inclined to think he wanted revenge against the aliens who hurt him, but she knew him better than that. He wouldn't send a pilot to do a job he wasn't willing to do himself. He wanted to make sure the job got done right.

He was the only one who could reproduce the aliens' communications process. He was the only one who could convince the alien workers to open the hull section. He was the only one who had heard their dialogue.

No one else at the table spoke. In the end, it was English who squirmed. "Come on, people. One of you must have some question or objection to make."

"Apart from you putting yourself in danger again?" Andy countered. "I don't have any objections beyond that."

"I have to go," English insisted. "I'm the only one...."

"I know that," Andy snapped. "You don't have to explain it to me. I didn't say we should send anyone else. I just don't want you putting yourself in danger again. I know you have to, but I don't have to like it."

Radcliffe stood up, pushed back his chair, and squared his shoulders to confront English. "Thank you for your presentation and your proposal, Captain. On behalf of Captain Church and Captain English here and myself—and on behalf of our fellow Command Staff officers who couldn't be here today—we accept your proposal to be carried out immediately. Proceed with all preparations and coordinate with the bridge to communicate the day and time to the rest of the fleet." He turned to Hughes, Duran, and Racer. "You three will be responsible for informing and preparing the squadron. Captain English will be assigned to the *Lightning Rod* squadron as a pilot on Wing 10 for the duration of this mission."

Racer's head shot up. She stared at Radcliffe and then her head snapped around to stare at English. He was coming back to the flight deck, but not as her gunnery sergeant.

Their positions had completely reversed. She was the gunnery sergeant now and he would be one of her pilots—except that he was a captain. He wouldn't exactly be her subordinate.

He smiled down at her with so much warmth that her stomach flipped. This was really happening.

She didn't know if she had it in her to order one of her own pilots to undertake this mission. She would rather go herself.

She wouldn't be ordering him to do anything. She couldn't. Captain Radcliffe just ordered her to take Captain English onto her wing. What else was she supposed to do?

Everyone in the room saluted each other and left the room. Sean collapsed against the elevator wall as soon as the doors closed with him, Hughes, and Racer inside. "Jesus Christ!" Sean croaked. "That guy is inhuman!"

"The blast could kill him," Hughes murmured.

"He knows," Racer husked. "That's why he's doing it himself. He doesn't want to risk anyone else."

"Thank God he's on your wing, Racer," Sean exclaimed. "I couldn't take him on my wing. Can you imagine having a captain as a subordinate?"

"He isn't my subordinate," Racer countered. "He's.....well, I don't know what he is."

They exited on the flight deck and all their pilots crowded around asking a million questions. Sean and Racer took turns explaining the mission.

As soon as the pilots got it through their heads exactly what was supposed to happen, another tense silence fell over both wings.

"You are NOT serious," Ritchie muttered at last. "Captain English just got his hand shot off by those aliens and they're sending him back out there to probably blow himself up on top of it all? Hell no!"

"No one is sending Captain English anywhere," Sean explained. "He's sending himself. You know what he's like."

"Our only job is to attack the enemy so he can hide his bird inside our swarm," Racer explained. "We're just supposed to treat him like a normal pilot...."

"A normal pilot!" Walker snapped. "We're just supposed to treat Sailor English like a normal pilot?! That's the stupidest thing I've ever heard!"

"There will be hundreds of other birds in the air," Sean explained. "We'll all be so busy fighting the enemy we probably won't see what the captain is doing."

"We better not!" Thorpe countered. "I don't trust myself not to stop him if I see him going near that ship."

"You can't," Racer told him. "We need to pretend he isn't there. We need to act like we don't know he's trying to get anywhere near the mothership."

"Until he signals us that he's on approach," Hughes corrected. "Then we cut bait and clear off so he can light up the plasma."

"Shit!" Waterman growled. "That is one hell of a plan."

"It's exactly the kind of plan he would come up with," Janacek remarked. "It's got his name written all over it."

"It doesn't matter because it's already underway by order of Captain Radcliffe," Racer finished. "Now it's up to us to execute it and make it happen. Earth is counting on us and we won't let the Force down."

Another silence fell over the group, and in that much more oppressive silence, the stairwell door opened and English stepped out onto the deck.

Everyone present turned around to stare at him. He still wore his dress uniform from the briefing. He didn't look like a pilot at all. He never would have passed the physical to fly a squadron fighter craft with only one hand.

Hughes recovered first and saluted him. "Sir! Welcome to the flight deck."

English saluted him back. "Thank you, Lieutenant." English stepped forward. His eyes flicked from one face to the other.

This was the first time any of the Wing 8 pilots had seen him since they retrieved him from Adelaide and brought him back unconscious to the *Lightning Rod*.

Ritchie finally stepped forward and stuck out his hand. "Welcome back, Sir. It's great to see you again."

English burst into a grin when he shook Ritchie's hand. "Thank you, Ben. It's great to be back."

"It's gonna be just like old times, right, Sir?" Janacek exclaimed. "Old Wing 17 together again!"

English laughed. "Yeah. It will be great."

"You better dust out the cobwebs if you want to keep up with me and Racer, Sir," Ezra told him. "You've been sitting behind a desk for too long."

English beamed at him and then at everyone else. "You two can school me like you used to."

Then everyone surrounded him talking at once. Laughter broke out in the ranks and they all started talking about the mission.

Walker, Smythe, Waterman, and Briscoe stood off to one side and stared at English in awed silence, but Wing 8 bombarded him with questions about the aliens, the mothership, and everything they'd all been doing since they saw him last.

Racer found herself on the outside again. She somehow had gotten too close to him even to take part in this.

She didn't want to take him on a suicide mission. At the same time, she considered it the greatest privilege of her career to be with him when he did this—his last most selfless act to save Earth. She wouldn't want to be anywhere else.

He caught her watching him and smiled at her across the deck. Of course he understood why she couldn't get involved in all this talk and comradely exuberance. She wasn't part of all that anymore.

It had nothing to do with her rank. Hughes and Sean got just as involved in the conversation as the other Wing 8 pilots.

She shared something with him these others would never understand. She didn't understand it herself, but that silent communication between them was enough. She would do this for him and for Earth. If he could do it, supporting him was the least she could do.

Chapter 39

E nglish stepped out onto the flight deck in his pilot's jumpsuit and immediately got laughed at by the rowdy pilots from Wing 8. "Not so fancy now, are you, Sir?" Babbitt crowed.

"He actually looks like a real person dressed like this," Ritchie agreed and the two young men high-fived each other.

English spotted Sean and Ezra grinning both at him and each other. English made a command decision not to engage with them, went over to Wing 10, and saluted Racer. "Ellis English reporting for duty, Gunny. Which bird do you want me in?"

She laughed at him, too, and her cheeks colored. "Why don't you take that one over there?" She pointed to one of the old birds from Wing 5. "No one else is using it."

"Yes, Ma'am." He grinned at her and went over to move the bird closer to the rest of the wing.

The other four pilots gaped at him like he had three heads—and maybe he did. Bruises still darkened his face and he had to be careful when he combed his hair to cover up his stitches, but at least he was back on duty.

He started working on his bird with the other pilots, but he had to adjust how he did everything. He only had one hand and an extra thumb. It made every job astronomically more difficult.

Never mind. He just had to get through this one battle. Then he would never fly again. He wouldn't be qualified to fly without two hands. He'd be lucky if the Force didn't retire him after this.

He fumbled one of his tools and it hit the ground with a deafening clang that echoed across the whole deck. He heard Babbitt and Ritchie laughing in the background, but English ignored that, too. Let them have their fun while it lasted.

A few minutes later, Rickenbach showed up with three engineers from the Adelaide mechanical team. They carried in a huge section of components scavenged from English's stolen warship.

Racer came over to watch them hook it up to English's bird. "Will your bird be able to fly with that thing on board?"

"They aren't connecting all of it," Rickenbach told her. "Just certain pieces from the communications system."

"How did you figure out so much about it so quickly?" she asked. "I would never have been able to understand it."

"I didn't," Rickenbach replied. "These guys did it. I don't understand this stuff at all—and it was the linguists who cracked the controls. All those shapes are supposed to be like letters or something."

The other pilots gathered around for a few minutes, but there was nothing to see but a lot of wrenching, tightening, wiring, and adjusting.

One of the engineers finally waved at English. "Why don't you go on board and see if it's working?"

He climbed into the cockpit and switched on the channel that was supposed to connect to the Vikak communications channels. A torrent of gibberish came out of it, and when he switched on the translation technology, it changed to English.

"It's working!" he called down.

The same engineer called up from under the fighter craft's fuselage. "Try the remote deactivation controls!"

English tapped out the controls they'd agreed to during the research phase of this mission.

"It's working!" the engineer called up. "You're ready to go."

English glanced toward Hughes's desk and Hughes gave him a thumbs up. The whole Force had been counting down the hours until the technicians, linguists, and engineers would give the word for the fleet to carry out this mission.

Hughes relayed the order to both wings and the other pilots scrambled on board their birds. English's blood started pumping when he shut his cockpit cover and slipped on his helmet.

Hughes's voice came through the headset. "Squadron Command to Wing Leader 10, stand by to launch."

"Wing Leader 10, standing by," Racer replied.

English went through the familiar routine of adjusting all his controls. He automatically checked the other pilots' settings and adjustments, but they were all running at optimum. Wing 8 was all squared away, too.

"Now we gotta wait for word to come down from the rest of the Force," Sean announced. "This could take a while."

"Destroyers are launching all over the planet," Hughes told him. "Check your scanners, brainless."

English switched on his scanners. The *Lightning Rod, Saratoga,* and *Solar Flare* had been parked on the ground at Adelaide ever since English's escape.

Now they and all the other USF destroyers took wing and blasted into the atmosphere on their way out to the Vikak front line.

The warships never moved from their positions—not that English could see. Those in the front line stood their ground. Those in the back line hovered in place. Anyone looking from the outside would think they stayed like that all the time.

The *Lightning Rod* and her sister ships broke orbit. "Squadron Command to Wing Leader 10!" Hughes called. "You are clear to launch! Squadron Command to Wing Leader 8, you are clear to launch! Fly safe, brothers and sisters! Let's get this done!"

"Wing 10—launch!" Racer ordered.

English hit the throttle, but he had to wait for the other pilots to clear the launch bay before he could get outside.

He flew into a massive cloud of fighter craft all gunning for the Vikak front line. Dozens of destroyers converged from all over Earth and the fighter wings plunged into the battle shooting everything in sight.

They surrounded the Vikak warships and the enemy opened fire. The fighter craft dodged, weaved, and zoomed around, behind, and on all sides of the Vikak front line.

In seconds, the combined USF squadrons got all mixed up with the warships in both lines. Fighter craft from every squadron buzzed around the mothership to distract it, dodged hits coming from neighboring warships, and pelted back into the battle to harass the Vikak front line.

English lost track of who belonged to which squadron. He couldn't see his wingmates anymore. He heard their voices, but they got lost in the mayhem—just like he was supposed to.

He hit the throttle and plunged into the chaos. He twirled around the frontline warships and opened fire. He hammered them all over their outer hulls and paid special attention to where he thought their flight compartments might be.

He didn't stay in one place long enough to see if he did any damage. He already knew he wouldn't. That didn't matter.

He worked himself deeper into the swarm behind the front line and made a dive for the back line, but he didn't go near the mothership—not yet. Who was in charge over there, now that Urai was gone?

English ran a few maneuvers through the back line and helped his fellow pilots bombard every ship they came across. The warships gave back just as hard and a handful of fighter craft exploded on both sides. Was one of them a *Lightning Rod* pilot?

English needed to stop screwing around and execute this mission before anyone else got killed. He flew to the warship nearest the mothership and opened the communications line.

Another outburst of Vikak exploded through the line and he switched on the translator. "Stand off until the battle cools down!" someone ordered. "It isn't safe to dock! I repeat, stand off!"

That didn't sound good. English didn't anticipate this.

He backed off and took refuge in the swarm of fighter craft. He was just about to contact Hughes about changing their plans when a different warship fired at one of the fighter craft from a different squadron.

English didn't see who it was or which squadron the pilot was from. The shot struck the craft's wing and the bird twirled out of the battle in a wild corkscrew. The ship slammed into English's bird and the starboard engine exploded.

The impact hurled him sideways and his port side ricocheted into the nearest warship. His port engine detonated and the shockwave flung him clear. He barely had time to realize he was adrift in the middle of the battlefield when Racer plunged out of the mix and circled him.

"Captain!" she hollered. "Are you hurt?"

"No, Gunny." He fumbled with the controls. "I can't say the same thing for my bird, though. I'm dead in the water. I'm not going anywhere—and the aliens have locked down their docking port until the battle cools off. We need to change our strategy."

She glanced around the battlefield. "I have an idea. Stay put."

He didn't tell her he didn't have a choice about that. Fighter craft whizzed all around him, but he couldn't move. He tried more than once to fire up the engines that weren't there, but of course nothing happened.

She came pelting back from somewhere. "Hold on, Sir! This could get choppy."

"What are you going to do?" He shouldn't have asked.

"We're going in!" she hollered. "Contact the aliens and get them to open that hull section. Now's our only chance!"

He didn't want to do that, but once again, he had nothing to lose. The Force had bet its last chip on this battle.

He bent over the controls and opened the communications line to the mothership. He started the translator and the voices changed to English.

"Request permission to dock and refuel," English interrupted. "We're nearly out of plasma. We have to refuel now!"

"The enemy is occupying every ship in the fleet!" someone yelled back. "It's too dangerous to come near the mothership now!"

"We have to come in to dock and refuel!" English insisted. "If we don't refuel now, we'll be defenseless! The enemy will destroy our warship! We have to dock now!"

His gamble paid off. "All right," his counterpart agreed. "You can dock and refuel, but make it quick."

"Approaching now," English replied and switched off the communications line.

He glanced around searching for Racer. "Gunny—where are you?"

"Coming up on your tail, Sir!" she called. "Brace for impact!"

"What?!" he hollered and tried to turn around to see.

He got half an instant's glimpse of a fighter craft bombing out of the swarm. She hurtled toward him from behind and he braced both arms a split second before she collided with his bird.

The ship shot forward, passed the nearest warship, and skidded into position right outside the hull section. It slammed open and he looked straight inside at the plasma reservoir.

"Do you still have weapons?" she asked.

"Yeah, but...."

"Deactivate the field," she ordered.

He opened his mouth to argue back. This wasn't what they planned.

The plasma reservoir throbbed right in front of his eyes. As soon as he took down both fields, he could shoot the reservoir and blow the whole Vikak fleet—and himself along with it.

"Fall back with the squadron, Gunny," he told her. "It's time to go home."

"Not without you!" she hollered. "Take down those fields, Sir, and call the retreat, but don't shoot yet. Do it, Captain!"

He shut his mouth and bent over his controls. "All squadrons—fall back! Retreat to Earth! I repeat—all squadrons and destroyers—break off and retreat!"

He waited until they broke away from the enemy and then he took down both fields.

The compartment depressurized. The workers inside scrambled to save themselves. They raced to the back wall and tried both to get out their emergency equipment and escape the compartment at the same time.

"Stay here, Sir!" Racer roared one last time and throttled her ship toward the opening.

She made it as far as the reservoir and opened fire. She twirled her bird from right to left gunning down all the workers, but she made sure to point her tail toward the reservoir so she wouldn't hit it.

"What are you doing, Gunny?" English whispered, but he already knew.

She didn't answer. She killed everyone inside and then skidded back out to where his bird sat. She wheeled in behind him, jammed her bird's nose against his tail, and shoved his bird into the compartment.

"Transfer to my cockpit on the double, Sir! We gotta get out of here!"

He opened his mouth to argue, but he was too grateful to say a word. She was doing this for one reason—to save his life.

It would have been so easy for her to fly away and leave him to shoot that reservoir by himself, but she didn't leave.

He couldn't let her efforts go to waste. She went to all this trouble to save him. They were only a few seconds away from freedom and victory.

She landed on the deck so close to his bird that their cockpit covers touched. She cracked her cover and he cracked his. The tearing sensation of depressurization nearly tore him apart before he toppled into her cockpit.

She didn't wait for him to straighten himself out before she slammed the cover closed with both of them inside. She punched the throttle and blasted out of the compartment. Theirs was the only bird left in the air.

She soared clear and turned back to shoot the reservoir. At that moment, the neighboring warship fired at her bird and smashed off the port wing. It exploded and the impact flung the craft wide.

Racer pulled the trigger and a single blast of her gunfire exploded inside the compartment with her fighter just a thousand kilometers from the mothership.

The shot struck the back wall, bounced off, hit English's bird, and the crippled fighter hurtled straight into the reservoir. Another explosion went off inside the compartment and then an almighty boom ruptured the back of the mothership.

That ejection of burning plasma swatted Racer's bird away. The craft tumbled head over heel and all the controls shorted out.

By the time the craft stopped spinning, it floated in space beyond the Oort cloud at the solar system's outer rim. The ship revolved slowly in space and then a blinding flash erupted in space beyond the asteroid belt.

Racer and English sat in their seats and watched the explosion envelop the mothership and another dozen warships nearest it.

"Do you think Earth will be okay, Sir?" she half-whispered.

"I sure hope so." English checked the controls. "We still have partial propulsion. Let's head back and check the damage."

She took the helm, but she kept her speed slow on the way back to the inner planets. She had to constantly adjust to compensate for her missing engine and the damage to her hull.

She paused just inside the asteroid belt. Part of the Vikak fleet hovered in orbit over Earth, but the mothership was gone.

"That was one hell of a shot, young lady," English remarked.

She shot him a grin over her shoulder. "Not too bad for such a useless punk, huh?"

He had to laugh. "You definitely earned your bars today."

She squinted toward Earth. "I don't see any damage. I expected half the planet to get burned."

"We can't see enough from here. I'm sure there will be some tsunami damage, but maybe Tasalt doesn't burn the way we think it does."

"We still have to deal with the second shipment," she remarked.

"Then we better get down there and start making our plans. Take us home, Gunny."

She started forward, but when she crossed the asteroid belt, a dozen fighter craft launched out of the atmosphere and surrounded their bird. "Gunny!" Smythe exclaimed. "You made it! You did it! You destroyed the enemy mothership!"

"Don't sound so surprised," Racer replied. "That's what we set out to do."

"Was there ever any doubt?" Walker asked.

"Where's the *Lightning Rod?*" Racer asked.

"Follow us," Thorpe told her. "Captain Radcliffe sent us out to escort you home."

Epilogue

E nglish stepped into the gathering hall at the new USF Command Center in Paris. The place buzzed with hundreds of voices of captains, colonels, admirals, generals, and dozens of lower ranked officers and service personnel.

Everywhere he looked, English saw people he knew. People came forward to shake his hand and congratulate him, but he kept pushing his way through the crowd before he found the people he most wanted to see.

Radcliffe, Church, Eismann, Frasier, Rickenbach, Hughes, the Duran brothers, and Dr. Cassidy stood together in one big group.

He spotted Racer twenty feet away. She was talking to her parents.

Her dark hair had grown out since English first met her. Now she wore it twisted up into a tight bun on the back of her head. She really looked like the USF officer she was in her immaculate dress uniform.

She said something else to her parents, separated from them, and met up with the group just as English got there. Radcliffe and Church split apart to let English join them.

"It sure is nice to be back in Paris," Church remarked. "I never thought we'd make it back here."

"Where's Andy?" English asked. "I thought he was with you."

"He should be here." Radcliffe looked all around him. "He said he would meet us here. He said he had something important to do on the *Saratoga*."

"What's more important than tonight?" English asked. "The war is over."

"Not quite," Rickenbach replied. "We picked up another Vikak warship entering the galaxy. We have six months before it gets here. We have to be ready to destroy it when it comes."

"The good news is that the Science Academy finally isolated an independent sample of Tasalt," Dr. Cassidy added. "They'll start working on some weapons that run on the stuff. We'll be ready."

English furrowed his brow at the surrounding crowd. The Science Academy isolating a sample of Tasalt didn't interest him nearly as much as why Andy wasn't here tonight. He belonged here....so where was he?

Just then, someone stepped onto the stage at the end of the hall and spoke into a microphone. "If you would all take your seats please..... the Command Staff is ready to call this convocation to order."

The crowd started to drift to their seats. English half-considered leaving and going to find out where the *Saratoga* was, but when he turned toward the doors, the crowd parted and he saw Andy coming down the aisle.

He burst into a grin when he saw his father. English strode over to him. "Where have you been? I thought you were going to miss this."

Andy didn't answer. He waved at the person next to him. English had been so focused on Andy that he didn't recognize his own daughter walking into the room at Andy's side.

English grabbed her in a huge hug. He couldn't even speak to ask if she was all right or how she got here or what she'd been going through since he last saw her.

He pushed her back and held her at arm's length to beam at her, but her beautiful face blurred in his tears. She was back. She was alive. He could forgive everything else, now that he had her.

Just then, Admiral Chambers spoke through the microphone, "This convocation will come to order."

English had to separate from Melanie. He and Andy rushed to their seats at the front of the room just as the Command Staff took its place on the stage.

Admiral Grace Schroder, Colonel Landon Roderick, Colonel Mackenzie Levitt, Captain Nathan Thorburn, Admiral Christopher Simpson, General Caleb Halstead, Colonel Clyde Tibbs, Admiral Joanne O'Dell, Major General Connor Schmidt, and General Dorian Coswell sat in rows on the stage while Admiral Chambers read the announcements through the microphone.

"This convocation is convened to recognize those outstanding service personnel who distinguished themselves in exceptional feats of bravery, selflessness, and dedication to Earth and the human race both during the civil conflict and the recent alien war. The following service personnel are awarded the United Space Force Medal of Honor along with commendation to rank and compensatory elevation in dispensation packages."

He started reading down a list of dozens of names. Officers and service personnel filed onto the stage to receive their decorations. There were so many of them that they had to walk on, take their decorations from General Halstead, shake his hand, and then return to their seats.

Cheers broke out at every name. The *Lightning Rod* squadron jumped out of their seats, cheered, and whistled when Admiral Chambers called, "Lieutenant Samuel Hughes, Squadron Commander of the *Saratoga,* Lieutenant Sean Duran, Squadron Commander of the *Cryptid,* Lieutenant Natalie Franz, Squadron Commander of the *Lightning Rod,* Gunnery Sergeant Ezra Duran of the *Lightning Rod,* Gunnery Sergeant August Stoval of the *Lightning Rod,* and Gunnery Sergeant Richard Hoskins of the *Jetstream....*"

English clapped and whistled with the rest. Racer beamed from ear to ear and her cheeks turned bright red when she accepted her Medal of Honor. She deserved it.

Plenty of other captains cheered just as loudly for all their people who worked so hard to win the war.

Admiral Chambers granted the Medal of Honor to over three hundred people. It took a long time for all of them to come up and get their decorations and the Command Staff's congratulations.

Then Admiral Chambers said, "Our next award goes to those outstanding captains who defended Earth from every enemy and ensured that we could all sit here in peace tonight. These captains are awarded the United Space Force Silver Eagle for Merit and Service along with commendation to rank and compensatory elevation in dispensation packages."

He read out another fifty names, including, "Captain Matthew Radcliffe of the *Infinity,* Captain Andrew Carter English of the *Saratoga,* and Captain Theodore Church of the *Solar Flare.*"

The captains filed onto the stage, and this time, they stayed there until all fifty of them gathered where everyone could see them.

English's heart turned a somersault when he saw Radcliffe, Andy, and Church all beaming out at the crowd. English had never served with any finer captains. He only regretted that they were all splitting up to command their own ships.

The USF was in good hands with them in command. Another generation would rise under their guidance. He didn't have to worry about the future with men like that defending the planet.

The crews and officers in the audience cheered, hollered, and whistled just as loudly for the captains as they did for their crewmates.

English clapped his one good hand against his thigh and whistled through his fingers. His face hurt from laughing and smiling so much. He never thought he'd live to see this night.

The captains filed back to their seats and then Admiral Chambers read out a bunch of special decorations for people who'd distinguished themselves even more exceptionally than the previous crewmen.

Chambers went through several where he read out the stories English hadn't heard about before. So much had been going on in different theaters of the war. He'd only seen a small part of it.

Chambers finally got to English. "My next award is for outstanding bravery, dedication, and sacrifice in the defeat of Earth's enemies. The United Earth Confederation bestows its highest honor, the Gold Medal of Heroism, on Captain Ellis English of the *Lightning Rod* and Lieutenant Natalie Franz, Squadron Commander of the *Lightning Rod.*"

English expected more cheers to follow him up to the stage. Instead, a hush fell over the crowd. Everyone turned around to stare when he and Racer stood up from their seats.

They sat across the hall from each other—English with the other captains and Racer with her fellow crewmen.

They met in the aisle and her face burst into such a beaming flood of light that English suffered another heart palpitation when he saw her. She was the one who should be accepting this award by herself. She was the one who really earned it.

He shot her one beaming smile. Then they both turned to the stage, climbed up, and received the honors from Admiral Chambers and General Halstead.

The silence persisted right up until English and Racer turned outward to face the crowd. One or two people started clapping and then the noise built to a deafening tide of applause. The whole crowd stood up and applauded.

The applause just went on and on as though it would never stop. English glanced over at Racer just as she glanced up at him.

The look in her eyes tore down the last barrier and he turned around and hugged her. He wouldn't be here now if not for her.

He heard General Halstead reciting the story of English's capture and escape, his plan to blow up the plasma reservoir, his bird getting damaged in the battle, and Racer helping him carry out the mission.

Halstead didn't tell the audience that English wouldn't have been able to carry out the plan at all if not for her. Halstead didn't tell the audience that the aliens would have won if not for her. She was the one who won the war for all of Earth. English just paved the way.

He knew now that she would rise in rank. She would probably become a captain. She might even become captain of the *Lightning Rod.* He wouldn't be the least bit surprised.

The End.

Keep Reading

Battalion 1 Series

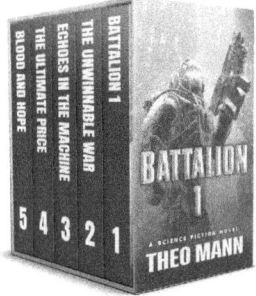

When a lab experiment goes disastrously wrong, the fate of the free world will depend on a band of broken soldiers just trying to keep what's left of their sanity in a landscape of destruction.

Captain Corban Rhodes should have died on the battlefield when a spaceship crashed on top of him. When he wakes up in the hospital fitted with robotic cybernetic implants, the consequences will leave him and those like him struggling just to survive against cataclysmic forces.

Now the fate of the galaxy rests on Battalion 1 averting a devastating alien invasion that will tap these wounded soldiers' worst fears and decide once and for all if they're still human.

You can find it at your favorite book retailer.

Sign Up Once--Get all Theo Mann's free books including brand new releases

Humanity on the brink of annihilation.

A mysterious package, a corrupt officer, and a conspiracy that goes all the way to the top? What could possibly go wrong?

When a routine mission goes horribly wrong, Warrant Officer Ewing Archer and a handful of faithful friends get trapped in a battle to save the last survivors of Earth.

The human race has abandoned the ecological disaster of Earth. Now all that remains is a network of interconnected ships, stations, and satellites surrounding the planet.

But when war breaks out, Archer becomes a firebrand that could destroy it all....or save it.

Sign up at www.theomann.com to read it for free

About Theo Mann

I write 70 books per year—and yes, before you ask, all these books are my original creative work. Nothing written under my name is AI-generated or ghostwritten because I write better than AI and any ghostwriter out there.

People don't read fiction for entertainment or to escape from reality. People read fiction to see their humanity reflected in another person's character and story.

This is my promise to you. When you read my books, you'll see your own humanity reflected in the characters and stories. I take this commitment to my readers very seriously. My books are an intimate form of communication between us. I would never disrespect my readers by turning that over to a machine or another writer. This is my bond between me and you as my reader.

I write 20,000 words per day as my daily work output. If anyone with a public platform would like to challenge me to prove this in a controlled environment, feel free to contact me on this website's contact page. How do I do write so much? Find out more on my blog, *Crimes Against Fiction* at www.theomann.com.

I worked as a professional ghostwriter for fifteen years. Now I'm on a mission to set a Guinness World Record by writing 700 books over the next ten years and 1400 books over the next twenty years, all originally written by me.

See my website for the full book list. I'm also the author of *Proof for the Existence of God* and the *Crimes Against Fiction* blog.

If you have a story idea, or if you would like me to explore a series in more depth, or if you'd like me to explore a character by writing a spinoff series about that character or world, leave me a message on my website's contact page. I answer all reader emails, so ask me anything, tell me what you liked and didn't like, and let me know where you'd like your favorite series to go. I would love to hear your ideas and find out what you'd like to read next.

Find out more at www.theomann.com.

Also by Theo Mann (so far)

* 9 7 8 1 9 9 1 4 2 7 1 7 5 *